It's too late. I know it, but I try anyway. I have the same feeling as when you already know you've overslept without even checking your alarm. Except this is so much worse, the comparison seems almost laughable. This isn't like the days we stayed up too late at sleepovers, fuelled by sugar and the thrill of doing something forbidden, where we'd have to rush to brush our teeth and still be late for double chemistry.

I let the water pool around my ankles, then my knees, then my thighs as I wade in deeper and deeper. I know her body so well and I look for any sign of it but I find none. There were footprints on the beach that looked about a size six, but – if I'm honest with myself – I know they could have been anyone's.

I know she came here, because she always did. And I know that this time I didn't go with her and now she hasn't come back. Other than me, the sea was her closest friend, just like it's always been for me too. The backdrop to a million selfies and videos, her in front of the camera and me behind it. She would have trusted it, would have been happy to play the kind of games with it that we did in drama class, like where you fall backwards into someone's arms because you know they'll catch you.

There's no sign of her. A mum and her child play with a bucket and spade further back towards the town, making clumsy castles and studding them with fragments of shell.

An oystercatcher leaves its pointed prints in the sand. A dog scuffs its feet, rolling over itself, so that its afterlife is an abstract painting on the ground. For a moment, I close my eyes and listen to the sea, willing it to give up whatever it knows. When I was little, Grandma used to drag me away from the beach where I would cling on to the whispers of the waves, believing they were just for me. I dredge up that connection again, that feeling that the water has something to say to me.

But today it tells me nothing of her. I'm too late; it's all my fault. I wanted other friends, another world outside of the one I'd grown up in. I wanted newness and novelty, to push at the boundaries of my life and stretch it a little, and if I hadn't wanted that, if I'd just stuck close to what I knew, then I wouldn't be forcing myself further into the water, sharp rocks jagging into me. The icy numbness feels like a punishment. A punishment for not valuing what I had.

I search for her hair, the hard-to-contain frizz that I've plaited a million times. I search for her fingertips, reaching for me like they do whenever we dance. I search for her arms so that I can pull her to me, hug her, promise that we'll never be apart again. That I'll make every choice based around her, that I won't go away next academic year. But there's nothing. The waves come and they go, crashing against my legs, but give me no clues.

After a while – maybe ten minutes, maybe an hour – I'm so cold that my body walks me back to the shore before my brain can do anything about it. I rip off my soaking underwear and change back into my skirt and top, the fabric

THESE MORTAL BODIES

THESE MORTAL BODIES

ELSPETH WILSON

SIMON &
SCHUSTER

London · New York · Amsterdam/Antwerp · Sydney/Melbourne · Toronto · New Delhi

First published in Great Britain by Simon & Schuster UK Ltd, 2025

Copyright © Elspeth Wilson, 2025

The right of Elspeth Wilson to be identified as author of this work has been asserted in accordance with the Copyright, Designs and Patents Act, 1988.

1 3 5 7 9 10 8 6 4 2

Simon & Schuster UK Ltd, 1st Floor
222 Gray's Inn Road, London WC1X 8HB

Simon & Schuster Australia, Sydney
Simon & Schuster India, New Delhi

www.simonandschuster.co.uk
www.simonandschuster.com.au
www.simonandschuster.co.in

The authorised representative in the EEA is Simon & Schuster Netherlands BV, Herculesplein 96, 3584 AA Utrecht, Netherlands. info@simonandschuster.nl

Simon & Schuster strongly believes in freedom of expression and stands against censorship in all its forms. For more information, visit BooksBelong.com

A CIP catalogue record for this book is available from the British Library

Hardback ISBN: 978-1-3985-3510-7
Trade Paperback ISBN: 978-1-3985-3511-4
eBook ISBN: 978-1-3985-3512-1
Audio ISBN: 978-1-3985-3565-7

Typeset in the UK by M Rules
Printed and Bound in the UK using 100% Renewable Electricity
at CPI Group (UK) Ltd

MIX
Paper | Supporting
responsible forestry
FSC® C013604

SUMMER

clinging to my damp skin. They're far too thin and flimsy for the beach, even in the week after school finished – what should be the height of summer. But I wanted to wear something pretty when I went to the pub with Jenny and Erin, and maybe even some of the boys too. I thought Cara would compliment me on my carefully selected outfit, rather than laugh at my desire to be liked by the people who at best ignored us – that want, desperate, pouring off of me like sweat. I should have followed her as she laughed and walked away. That scorn a kind of invitation too – I just didn't realize it at the time as I cursed her retreating body to feel the same kind of bodily hurt as I did at her rejection.

I'm pulling my beat-up trainers back on when I hear a shriek. In that second, I know. It seemed like there was almost no one on the beach, apart from me, the mum and the toddler, but now people are coming from all corners to congregate at the shoreline. Someone's pointing out to sea. Someone's on their phone. Another is holding me back as I'm hurling myself forward without even thinking about it. A man pulls his shirt off and runs into the water, wading then swimming, his arms strong and powerful. I envy the muscles that propel him, interlaced with his confidence, the sinew and attitude that make him so certain of rescue.

I want to move forward but I can't. I feel nothing until I see her, seaweed sticking to her hair like a grotesque crown, and then I feel everything, too much, every feeling that exists under this thin, watery sun all at once and then nothing again, the only option against a flood so big I'm drowning—

TERM 1

Week 1

We cannot sign our names. Not because we are incapable of doing so – we have ensured that we all are able to write, passing our learning among one another – but because we know the consequences of committing ourselves to the page with our earthly monikers. Instead, we sign using a symbol that defines us – you may see that together we make a pattern. A sisterhood is never extricable – once entwined together, our bond lasts for life.

My first afternoon in college I didn't know what to do with myself. My parents dropped me off at the prescribed time. Mum cried a few shuddering tears and Dad held my hand a little tighter than usual. 'You're going to have some great times here, I can tell,' he said, untucking my ponytail from the back of my rollneck where it had got stuck.

We'd stayed in a B&B in some nondescript town the night before, all in one very pink room. It was a long journey across the border and Dad was the world's most cautious driver, adding an extra hour or two at least. He was slow to the point of being a menace, and I found myself leaning forward so much the seatbelt dug into my hips, willing him to go faster. When I got out of the car, there were dark red grooves imprinted on my skin like nails had been dragged across my flesh.

I slept on the sofa bed as my parents' snoring harmonized together, Dad's long, thunderous rolls accompanying Mum's gentle snuffles. The sounds lulled me into some kind of state, but it wasn't sleep. I flicked my tongue back and forth across my teeth, unable to get used to their nakedness. I'd rushed the braces off at the end, desperate during the last days of school – one of my canines was still slightly crooked.

Next morning, they had muesli with full-fat milk while I nibbled on the edge of a slice of toast. Some smoothie cartons sat in the mini fridge, reminding me of the packed lunches of the kids in primary school – the ones with glossy hair and names with too many syllables. Mum gave me lumpy, homemade bread before it was cool and bougie. When it was kind of weird and icky and a little bit sad and only Cara would share it with me.

'Jesus fucking Christ. Ivy, where the hell are we?' Dad's volume increased the closer we got to college.

'Just follow the instructions that I'm giving you.'

'If we all just keep calm—' Mum's forehead was pressed to the passenger seat window.

'I am calm. I just don't like these southern roads.'

'There's the turn off,' I said.

We stopped a half mile outside the city centre. A million miles away from my old life. Exactly where I wanted to be. Needed to be. The camera in my mind was whirring already. The yellow bricks glowed as the sun showed off its last gasp of summer. I laid my palm against them while Dad manoeuvred in the car park, and found they held no warmth. He'd stopped swearing now there were dads of other girls about, him and Mum nodding clipped hellos at parents standing next to shiny cars. It almost looked as if we had belonged there the whole time. If you ignored the rust on the bonnet.

After they left, I missed the presence of something known, even though my skin had itched for their departure. It only took me half an hour to unpack my things. They didn't make the small room feel properly full, even when I spent another fifteen minutes rearranging them. I put the doily Grandma Olive had made on the sill and smoothed it out, its yellowed edges making it look somewhat diseased. The replica Cara had made for me when Grandma went into the home sat next to it, shocking in its comparative newness. I'd travelled so far and yet the cold, sick feeling still bloomed in my stomach whenever I looked at it.

Leafy fingertips tapped on my windowpane, beckoning me outside. We'd walked through neat internal courtyards to get to my new room, but its view looked out onto the wilder, less manicured back of the grounds. They were lit by the ebbing sunshine of the year, leaves getting ready to fall and add to the russet blanket on the ground. I'd never had A View before, just the sounds of the sea – a promise that never delivered. Secrets rustled through the trees, begged me to go out.

The arched corridors were mostly empty with only a few parents and new students popping in and out of heavy wooden doors. Men were the intruders in that space, the dads and occasional older brothers heaving cases and struggling to find bathrooms. The walls of the college were covered in paintings of women who'd gone on to do illustrious things after graduation, which slowly turned to photographs, as the lined faces processed towards the present day.

Down the stone steps, out into the hinterland of college, the thrum of the motorway I'd arrived on was almost entirely muffled by the dying foliage. My interview had been a clammy whirlwind of nerves and a desperate hope I'd tried to focus the power of my mind on, so I'd barely taken in the physicality of the place, hadn't realized how the trees embraced and hid the buildings. Something about the branches and the way the welcome committee had looked at each other when I followed the handwritten signs to collect my room key, smiles playing games on the corner of their eyes, spoke of a pulling together, a tight-knittedness.

Wandering into the woods in only my thin cardigan, the crisp cold hit me like a slap with the back of a hand. I stumbled into a clearing, hidden from the college's glinting eyes, where larger trees parted around land that seemingly no one wanted to touch. There'd been a boy with the girls who formed the welcome committee, his distracting, unexpected presence making everyone laugh and toss their hair. His face was knocking around in my mind, making me pace up and down to get rid of my goose pimples. His curls had fallen over his left eye at such a precise angle that it elevated his smile, made it reach up even further towards his earth-brown eyes.

Thinking I was alone, I leaned against the jagged bark of one of the swaying trees and let out a sigh. It was exactly the kind of place Cara would have loved. If she'd made it to the top university for film studies like she'd wanted, it would have taken her a few hours to reach me on the train. Before, that had felt like a lifetime away. Above the thick, gnarled trunk, the tree's branches were covered with flaming leaves, extended out as if for an embrace. The pull of the place was almost strong enough to take my mind off him, off her – off everything other than being somewhere new and letting that newness soak into me.

And that's when I saw her. Before I even knew her name was Martha, she struck the image of the unnamed boy clean out of my mind. Standing there under the tree, its branches splayed around her as if they were fighting to get away from the trunk. I captured an image of her in my brain, tried to breathe in the exact way her body was positioned so that it would be in my muscle memory and could be replicated at any time. Her red hair and yellow coat made her seem like a naturally occurring phenomenon, as if she had grown right there among the leaves. She gave me a grin, so wide that it split open the heavens, rain spilling in big, fat drops onto my skin. I stood there and let myself become sodden with the view of her, until her voice cracked open the silence.

'Well, are you coming?'

At her invitation, I was able to move again.

'The theme of the bop last year was Around the World but some of the Dragons came in pith helmets. So, this year the senior tutor decided that the occult was a safer theme.' I stared back at Amina Bilel, the second-year who'd been assigned to keep an eye on me and who was rather begrudgingly wearing a name badge that declared her 'happy to help', as we ended our whistle-stop tour full of long corridors and spiral staircases. 'You know, like witches and wizards?'

'Will there be boys there tonight?' I didn't know who the Dragons were but I settled on a safer query so as not to betray my ignorance.

'Something you'll learn about this place is that there's always boys everywhere, even when you don't want them to be. This is Martha's room. I'll drop you off here so you have someone to head down to the bar with. Hopefully, you'll be able to find it on your own next time.' Martha answered Amina's terse knock, all smoky eyes and big hair. Amina squinted at her. 'What are you supposed to be?'

'I'm a cat, obviously,' Martha replied.

'If you say so. I'll see you soon, freshers. Don't be late.'

Martha enveloped me in a hug, careful to avoid smudging her purple eyeshadow whiskers against my cheek. Inside, the room was bigger than mine with a small iron fireplace, a blocked-off chimney and several brocade armchairs that she'd covered in patterned blankets. It reeked of incense and the surfaces were strewn with crystals. Two blonde girls sprawled on the chairs, legs everywhere.

'This is Agatha and Natasha. They're practically part of the furniture.'

Natasha's smile was warm and easy, a cup of tea made exactly how you like it. Agatha went to light a cigarette, tapping the ash off the windowsill. I couldn't understand how they all seemed so close already, wearing each other's clothes, lolling about in their underwear like it was nothing to have that level of ease with another human body.

'We all went to the same school. Me and Nat were there from nursery and then our queen bee here joined in secondary,' Agatha said, answering my unspoken question in a hoarse voice. I'd later find out from a girl at a party who pointed at Martha and said that she'd sat next to her in maths, that Agatha Love, Natasha Smith and Martha Gleeson-Brewer had been collectively nicknamed the 'wayward sisters'. 'So you're the unknown quantity here. Tell us something about you.'

'We need to watch this one, she was away with the fairies when I found her in the woods earlier,' Martha said, winking at me, and I flushed the colour of her wine, clashing with my pale pink dress whose label I had only just cut off. I had brought all my best dresses with me to university but the other girls were wearing clothes that looked like they were from a charity shop, clothes I wouldn't have been seen dead in in my previous life. Even Martha's dress was a little big on her, clinging to her brittle frame like a cub to its mother. I felt overdressed in comparison, too new but somehow not as shiny as the rest of them.

'What was she doing?' Natasha asked, not looking up from her phone. 'Oh my gosh, I found him.' And just like that the conversation was pulled away from me onto something altogether more interesting.

'Who did you find?' I asked but I already knew – there'd only been one person other than Martha that I'd seen so far who could garner that much interest.

'Show me,' Agatha commanded.

Natasha turned the screen towards us, a curly-haired, latte-eyed, smiling face meeting our gaze. A face I'd only seen once for a moment but wouldn't forget in a hurry.

George Svenson, the screen said. Martha waggled her fingers against her mouth, her prints coming away red with lipstick. 'Svenson. Now where do I know that name from?'

'You know him already?' I asked.

'I can't quite place him yet. But I never forget a name or a face. By the end of the night, we'll know exactly who he is, promise.' She turned around to face the others, raising her half-empty glass to the room. 'I always keep my promises, don't I, girls?'

'Every time,' Natasha nodded, patting Agatha's back as she choked on her cigarette smoke.

The cramped underground bar where bops were held must have been literally soil once, but it was hard to see how it could have been much darker and more shadowy than in its present form. A picture of the college Mistress smiled down at us, her grey-flecked hair and regal smile at odds with the kind of chaos that only unencumbered youth can create. My feet stuck to the floor each time I took a step, like the ground was trying to suck me in. The drink of the week, the Red Dragon, lived up to its name, the bright colour giving us an affinity with the other freshers whose teeth it had stained over the decades.

'I'm so glad there's boys here,' Natasha sighed at my shoulder, before disappearing into the crowd. It was true, there were boys everywhere – far more than I'd seen so far in this famed seat of women's learning. Boys with floppy hair, boys with short hair, boys with wisps of beards, boys with booming laughs, boys downing pints, boys laughing as girls told stories.

Boys weren't my forte. I'd never got used to speaking to them in school, never got used to speaking to anyone other than Cara.

A boy with a broad, wasteland face was standing to my left, also at a slight remove from the crowd, although he looked eager to join; my body a straight exclamation mark to his bracket, curving towards the mass of limbs and flesh.

'Have you tried one of these?' I grasped at the drink as a conversation starter.

'Of course.' His smile was genuine and open, transforming his face. 'It's not Freshers without one.'

'I wonder where it gets its name from. The dragon part, I mean.'

'I see you haven't got any family that went here then.'

'How can you tell?' The words spun out quicker than I intended.

'Just a guess. It's named after the drinking society. I mean, the men's one. Well, not *the* as in the only, but the only important one. There's a girls' one too, don't worry – likely the oldest in the university, if not the country. But you didn't hear any of that from me.' The unnamed boy smiled conspiratorially.

'You probably think it's weird this still being a women's college, right?' I asked. To me, the idea of a women's college had seemed comforting – I'd had a female friend in the past, so I could surely have some again – but I imagined the boys hated being separated from girls like Martha.

'Not at all. Everyone here always seems like a family, for better or worse.'

Before I could ask him what he meant, two older guys were upon us, slapping the boy's back and doing the kind of brief but firm hug that I'd sometimes seen my dad do with other men. 'Peter Grosvenor, how the hell are you? We haven't seen you since school.' In the following weeks, I'd learn that, like lots of other students at the university, Peter had been to an ostensibly famous single-gender public school that I'd never heard of. It would become apparent that although he was a legacy student, his family had lost a lot of their generational wealth and he'd attended on a scholarship, a fact that, mixed with his slightly desperate aura, meant he was often the butt of jokes.

Before I could get roped into a conversation I wasn't ready for, I circled the packed room trying to look for

Martha, Natasha or even Agatha. The crush of bodies would have made a great crowd scene, the throb rendering visible the way the loud music was penetrating my brain with every note as I squeezed past strangers. Girls and boys (even after only a few days, my brain had tightened around this binary) moved as one to an old pop song that I thought I recognized but wasn't sure about – I only ever got snippets of the radio if I got a lift to school with Cara's mum. Dad liked news and facts alone and Mum loved radio dramas – the more melodramatic the better – and occasionally classical.

I felt George Svenson before I saw him. Red liquid spilled down my chest as I made contact with his back, unspooling over the pale material so I looked like an extra in a horror movie. 'Woah, there.' He laughed, relaxed, as my body stood taut as a wire crackling with electricity. Reaching his hand into his pocket, he pulled out a handkerchief and gave it to me so I could dry myself off. The pack of girls that were gaggled around him followed his every move.

'So anyway,' said a third-year girl who I'd seen talking to Amina. She tightened her pink silk scrunchie and glared at me as I tried to rub away the crimson marks. I'd later hear from Natasha – who loved to be the bearer of gossipy titbits – that her name was Sophia Herod and she was a medical student. She too had gone to their school and she was known for being a star lacrosse player, the hostess of amazing parties and an oil heiress, although not necessarily in that order. 'Is it true that you moved to the Middle East because your dad's a spy?'

'That's classified, I'm afraid.'

George turned round in time to catch me rolling my eyes. The grin he shot me in return took me by surprise, making my own smile widen involuntarily.

'I'm just going to grab another drink, do you want one?' he asked me. The rational part of my brain knew it was just a coincidence that we'd bumped into each other, and that him offering to get me a drink was surely a product of good manners. But the romantic, storytelling part of me felt like it was fate that he'd been on my mind – as well as everyone else's – and then we'd literally collided.

'I'm okay, thank you.' I wanted an excuse to keep talking to him but my head was already spinning. 'Don't you want this back?' The stains weren't coming out of my dress – I'd only succeeded in making the white material of his handkerchief red too – and I held the stained cloth out to him.

'Keep it – as a memento.' I slipped the splattered hanky into my pocket, on the edge of saying something more to him. Something witty or charming that I was certain would arrive fully formed in my brain as soon as I opened my mouth – until I saw Martha and my attention was stolen away, like a moth to her flame-coloured hair.

'I remembered where I recognized the name from.' Martha caught up with me as I was adjusting the straps on my helmet, her voice even breathier than usual. The bike tour of the city was due to leave in ten minutes and I had left plenty of time to unlock my bike, sort my helmet out and check my hi-vis was safely stowed in my rucksack. Martha wasn't part of my plan. She was never part of my plan. But she was there regardless, slowing me down as I got ready for what Amina had told me was an essential part of Freshers Week – orienting myself before term properly started.

'I remembered,' she said, 'because when I was in international school before – well, before we moved to the countryside – when I would have been in the equivalent of prep school, he had just moved from Bangkok to London, and we were all obsessed because him and his brothers were so cute with their curly hair. They were like little cherubs. In fact, I'm pretty sure he was my first kiss in a stupid game of kissing tag when we were like eight years old. He's only got better with age, hasn't he?' She wasn't part of my plan, and yet when she bumped her hip gently against mine and smiled, I let out a breath I didn't know I was holding. As she spoke, the image of her red hair in the glade flashed against my vision like I'd looked at the sun too long.

'Anyway, did you have fun last night?' She poked me in the ribs, giggling, making me shiver. There was a chill wind that day, I'm sure of it. It was always windy by the bike sheds.

'I don't know what you're talking about.'

'Oh, come on, don't be coy. You and George looked cosy.'

'The only reason we spoke is because he spilled his drink on me. Though it was my fault, really.' Any thoughts that me and George had been fated to bump into each other had shrivelled and died with the cold, bright light of the morning.

'I don't believe for a second that one of you didn't orchestrate that. You only had eyes for each other last night.'

'That's not true. It definitely wasn't me who orchestrated it,' I protested but Martha was having none of it.

'It is, and I'm even going to come on this boring old bike tour with you so I can hear more about it.' I smiled in spite of myself, as we joined a group of girls, ready to swoop into the city.

It turned out I could ride a bike, which was a relief. I hadn't learned until I was twelve because the only physical activity I'd ever really been interested in was swimming. When Dad finally convinced me to have a go, my shaky, skinny body perched on a rusty frame like a cherry on a cake, Dad's hands clasped in a mixture of joy and exasperation as Mum looked out on the green from her bedroom window, having defied her migraine to watch me triumph.

Having long outgrown that one, I bought a cheap new bike at the Freshers' Fair, drawn to its cool turquoise colour and the fake flowers attached to its wicker basket. These probably weren't the things I should have been looking for because it turned out to be heavy, making me even slower when I cycled up the small hillocks of the city. Still, I was made somewhere hilly. It wasn't the slopes that unnerved me so much as the flat countryside where there was nowhere to hide.

Martha's hair was a coppery, slippery river in the wind as our bodies flooded towards the spires and stained glass of the town, the cobbles juddering our bones as we dodged tourists with a death wish. In the marketplace with its colourful striped awnings and overpriced loose-leaf tea, Martha bought ten packets of Lady Grey while I smelled the different herbal concoctions, taking comfort in their earthy scents.

'Let's have tea and cake in my room, shall we?' Martha's easy smile bit into me as I thought of the afternoon of study I'd had planned.

'I'd love to but I was thinking of going to the anthropology library. You know, get a feel for it before I have to do an actual essay.'

'The library? I don't even know where the art history library is yet.'

'I should really be studying. I've already been sent reading for this term and I only just finished the pre-reading we were meant to do over the summer.'

'You can't study, Iv, it's Freshers Week,' Martha laughed. 'Besides, no one does the pre-reading. Even the supervisors know that.'

'They don't?'

'I promise you, they don't.'

'Okay, if you say so.'

'So, tea?'

'You're a bad influence but tea it is then. Can we try some of that smoky stuff you gave Natasha the other day?' I asked.

'The lapsang souchong? For sure.'

Back in her room, Martha lit incense and plumped

cushions before I sat down. Being with her felt like slipping into the warm baths Grandma Olive had run for me when I was little. Apart from Cara, I'd never felt like I connected with someone so seamlessly before.

'What's with all the crystals?' I asked.

'They're for protection,' she shrugged. I picked up a pink quartz, feeling its ridges underneath my fingertips.

'Usually, I don't like people touching them but with you – something about your energy feels different.'

'Oh, sorry.' I let it go too fast, and it clattered back onto the side table.

'No, don't be sorry. I always mean what I say. Here, why don't you have that one.'

'Are you sure? You don't have to,' I said but I'd already picked it up again, captivated by its blush colour which reminded me of cherry blossom and the way Cara's cheeks flushed when she giggled.

'I know I don't have to, silly. Come on, take it – you can see I have loads. Besides, my mum gave me that one.'

'Thank you.' Whatever I might have said next to Martha – about the crystal, about what it meant to me, about how it was the first gift I'd received in the longest time – was stopped by two sharp raps on the door. Agatha walked in, followed by Natasha, without waiting for an answer. I slipped the crystal into my pocket, my fingers unable to stop playing with its smooth surface.

'Gosh, I'm knackered. We've been all over town buying stationery and bits and bobs before term starts properly. Here, Martha, we got you this.' Natasha handed her an orange leather notebook with an embossed leaf pattern on the front.

'Cute. My signature colour and all.'

'Enough with the stationery, Nat. I can't bear to hear you talk about gel pens anymore. Just because you're a fine art student doesn't mean you get to bore me half to death with the merits of various underrated writing tools. Let's discuss our plans for tonight instead.' Agatha grabbed a tangerine-coloured nail varnish off Martha's shelf and started expertly applying it as we talked through various parties happening that night, and which boys might be at which event. I tried to make my smile meet my eyes but I couldn't shake the sense that something had slipped out of the room the moment the others arrived. The energy had shifted.

'I hope George is at one of them,' Natasha sighed, and I choked on the smoky tea, the taste of fire suddenly violent in my mouth. The hot water filled my throat, made it impossible to breathe, until Martha was behind me, patting me firmly on the back.

'You okay?' she asked as Natasha tittered nervously.

'I'll live,' I croaked. She stood with her arms cradled around my shoulders, and I let the heat from her body sink into me.

The next morning, I woke up sweating and alone. The night before, I'd emptied my pockets and placed Martha's crystal and George's handkerchief side by side on the windowsill, a few inches away from Grandma Olive and

Cara's embroidery. I'd dreamt of a white sheet covering my body, red splodges appearing on the material as I twisted and turned. In the dream, the sweat had come from someone else's body too, but awake, I realized it was only mine festering in the bed. I didn't trust dreams – not since two summers ago, when Dad had shaken me awake from a nightmare about Grandma Olive falling off the edge of the pier, to tell me she'd had a stroke. Since then, I'd willed my nights to be deep and dreamless – almost as if they hadn't even happened.

There was commotion in the corridor, shouts outside. Some of the scientists and mathematicians had supervisions already. You could see them leaving from the main tower, cycling towards their faculties, doddery on their bikes. Anthropologists didn't have any lectures yet. I didn't even know properly what anthropology was and I thought I'd be excited to find out, but I was already forgetting the reason I'd worked so hard to come here in a haze of prosecco bubbles and expensive perfume. Last year, it had seemed so important to have my own goals, my own passion – important enough to diverge from the plan Cara and I had made that we'd both go to the same uni, maybe even do the same course. That first week, hours sloshed around days without shape or outline. How had it got to be Sunday?

Sunday 3 October
  Rise and shine, freshers! We heard some of you had
  a little bit too much of a good time this week (though of
  course naming no names).

10am – Yoga and cake. Come and meet your welfare
team! No experience necessary! Worth getting out of bed
for, we promise – even if you have to kick someone out
to make it.
    10am – Five-a-side football. Meet at the cricket
pavilion for a friendly kickaround.
    11am – Choir auditions. Now that you've had four
days to settle in, come along to find out more about the
college choir and potentially audition; we are looking for
talented, committed individuals to join. The talent can be
raw but it must be there.
    11am – Community choir. If you love singing but
don't love commitment then community choir is here for
YOU! We meet every Sunday afternoon (not too early so
you have plenty of time for that famous college brunch!).
All welcome!!
    3pm – Nature walk. If you need a bit of R and R or
have found the experience of Freshers Week overwhelming
or isolating, come along for a chat and a chance to explore
the abundant nature we are lucky to have right here in
the college grounds.

I had slept through the yoga. I didn't sing. There was no lunch on Sundays, I'd been told, only brunch. I didn't like eggs or the way they congealed across the plate like there was something still living about them. Movies and filming had been my escape before but here there wasn't even a film night – and anyway, anything through that lens ran the risk of making me homesick. If it's possible to feel that way about a place that doesn't really exist anymore. Which left the nature walk. The sun was spilling through the unopened curtains, attention-seeking, flirting with the shadows on the floor. I didn't feel I had much choice but to go.

A girl with an unravelling purple braid in her hair was waiting at the imposing arch at the front of the college. A few other first years stood nearby, too small and unacquainted a crowd to be comfortable together.

'Hey there. You just made it, we're about to head off,' said the girl with the braid, who looked to be in charge and was holding a seemingly unnecessary clipboard.

Our small group straggled by the trees, the last leaves getting ready to hit the ground as we walked further away from the twisting turrets of the college. A couple of squirrels scurried in front of us, and the leader clapped her hands excitedly. 'Oh, look, guys, there's another fungus over here.'

The only other person on the walk willing to make eye contact was a girl with long blue and black twists and a dress that was too summery for the chill of the day, her bare legs peeking through slits that ran up to her thighs. Goosebumps adorned her flesh like sequins, each one adding texture to her shivering skin. 'I just wanted to get some fresh air, wake myself up a bit. Kind of just wishing I'd done some mindfulness on my phone,' she said.

'I slept in so late, I really needed to get outside,' I admitted. I recognized her high cheekbones and the soft angles of her face from the bar the night before, where she'd rested her body lightly against the exposed stone wall rather than join in the dancing.

'I'm Primrose. Primrose Manu.' Her smile was like a cup of tea with sugar – good for a shock. 'It's nice to get out though. This week is a little intense, isn't it? I went to boarding school for a bit when I was younger so I thought I was used to being away from what I know but this is a funny mix of the new and the familiar.'

'I feel like I've travelled thousands of miles, not hundreds,' I said. My voice was scratchy with the possible beginnings of a cold, echoing the rasp of the wind that rattled the leaves.

'I know what you mean. My parents are lawyers who travel a lot for work and they used to take me with them sometimes, so I'm used to a bit of culture shock. But this feels really close to home but different at the same time.'

The others were a way in front now, looking at rotten tree stumps and a plaque commemorating some historical event. A heron flew overhead. I'd seen one – maybe the same one – on the day of my interview, before I ascended a turret to be bombarded with questions by three elderly women. A charm bracelet jangled at Primrose's narrow wrist, tiny silver pencils and miniature books knocking at her bones. Maybe this bird could be my good omen.

'I feel like I've talked to so many people but barely got to know anyone. Apart from people I already knew from school and I'm not particularly interested in knowing them better. Still, it's early days.' Her nose ring glinted against the lowering sun. 'Or is that just me?'

I nodded but didn't elaborate on how, actually, I was getting to know Martha better than I knew anyone – maybe even myself. I'd been hollowed out when I came here, but she was starting to make me feel like I could be whole again. I thought the world had run out of gifts for me but then she turned up when I needed her most – though there was no way for her to know just how much she meant to me. 'I'm Ivy, by the way.'

She smiled, glancing upwards, squinting into the sun. 'Maybe your namesake can make you feel at home.' And sure enough it was there, snaking over the thick trunks of the trees to turn them a shade darker, the glade which sprouted Martha visible through the branches.

Week 2

Leaves fall around us. We dance as they fall, knowing that we will see them in bud again soon enough. They die and then they return, their life is a repetition, not a full stop. Although we were in church but this morning, the woods are where our real worship lies.

Dear students,

I hope you have enjoyed your first few days at the college and have settled in somewhat during Freshers Week (although a week isn't quite the right unit of time to delineate the few days you have before work kicks in, is it? But alas my fiancée tells me I need to stop being such a pedant!).

I will be supervising you for Introduction to Political Thought this term and look forward to hearing your thoughts (hah!) on Marx, Weber, Durkheim (strictly speaking a sociologist but I don't make the rules) and Arendt among others. I am a third-year doctoral student writing my thesis on all things dialectic – although don't tell my supervisor, she'd like it to be a bit more specific than that!

For our first session, I don't want to prescribe
anything too heavy but it would be great if you could
read The Communist Manifesto *and take a look at at*
least one or two of Marx's other works (although even I
will admit to never having read Grundisse, *from cover*
to cover!). The CM *is at least pretty light and I suspect*
that most of you may well have read it already, even
if only in your spare time. You'll need to get used to
reading fast over the coming years!
Looking forward to meeting you all next week.
Best wishes,
Harold Bakewell
D Phil.

Anthropology was the study of humans – that much I
knew. After a summer of being alone, university and the
hope of being able to understand other people became the
focus of my survival. The only way forward was to study
the patterns of behaviour and societies – to know as much
as possible, to leave nothing to fate, to make it so that I
could never misunderstand someone else – or myself –
again. But since I'd arrived at college, the idea of learning
had floated to the back of my mind and I'd done hardly
any reading. The hours had spent themselves in Martha's
room, as I sprawled across her bed, my legs stretching out
across the quilt her grandmother had bought her in the college colours of navy and pink. I felt certain that if Grandma
Olive was still alive, she'd have made me a better one with
her own two hands, not purchased one from a shop.

Like every girl in the building, Martha had decorated her room with fairy lights, but somehow hers looked different, classier. In the subdued lighting, her white skin glowed in the dimness and I found it impossible to drag myself away from the warmth and the chatter, the people coming and going, orbiting around her. Martha's room was always busy, no matter what time it was. Everybody wanted to be her best friend, and I was no exception. I sometimes caught myself as I washed my face at night making the kind of silly wishes that I'd made as a child about being bound to someone for ever. Then I'd snap myself out of it by splashing my cheeks with cold water. Still, you could just feel how she was the focal point of everything. Her dinky alarm clock would strike midnight, then one, and I'd still be in her bedroom discovering you could learn from a different altar.

I had never read *The Communist Manifesto* and never really thought or knew anything about Marx in any meaningful sense. I had applied for anthropology and politics because it was – to my mind – the perfect combination to help me become a documentary maker, the only job my imagination stretched to. From the moment I met Cara by the craft cupboard, where she was complaining that the glue wasn't sticky enough, I'd loved listening to her talk about everything that was wrong with the world, followed by how she was going to fix it. As we got older, the topics grew more serious than Pritt Sticks and I learned to catch her best angles and thoughts with the camera. And it wasn't just her – other people's stories came naturally to me. At school, I'd been quiet but I'd listened carefully. Whenever I did speak to someone other than Cara, I had to pretend that I hadn't already picked up on so many details in their life. I'd learned to act like I was hearing new information if someone in my French class mentioned they had a brother or a pet dog.

At the interview, the questions I was asked by those three professors high up in a round tower revolved around what my thoughts would be if I found a Roman coin in the college grounds and what a brightly coloured herbal teabag would tell someone from the future about this century. They clearly liked my answers about status and conspicuous consumption because three weeks later my acceptance letter landed on the doormat, the thick paper making an audible thud as my own future was spelled out on a wet Friday morning just before Christmas. I'd hidden that letter from Cara until January, when I couldn't bear keeping it from her any longer, even if I knew she would see me choosing a different university as something close to betrayal. We'd long ago vowed to stick together and she wasn't the kind of person who broke her word, being a firm believer in the sanctity of promises.

So that night I stayed up until three, reading the Wikipedia page on Marxism. At three thirty, as the black eyeliner Martha had applied for me was starting to itch, there was a creaking noise in the hallway coming from somewhere near the tiny shared kitchen. It wasn't loud enough to wake me if I'd been asleep – there could have been a murderer right outside and I'd never have known.

I'd slept through a fire drill the day before, only realizing when Agatha complained about it at lunch. Sleep weighed heavily on me, unwanted dreams of my old life following me into my new one.

'You put it through. You're the one who insisted on her being invited.' There was no mistaking that it was a masculine voice. Boys. Boys where they shouldn't be, in the middle of the night. I'd only ever seen them in the college at sanctioned events, apart from the one time George had infiltrated the welcoming committee; maybe they had a secret way in? There were the muted sounds of a minor tussle in the corridor, flesh struggling with flesh, laughter badly hidden under hands.

'Just get on with it, George.'

An envelope slid underneath the door. My desk was so close to the door that a body was now only inches away from mine. His body. I didn't dare move in case the floor creaked and betrayed me.

'Who's next on the list?' I heard one of them say as the footsteps and stifled giggles faded away. My chest rose quickly under my old sleepy T-shirt that used to be Dad's gym gear. The envelope read *Ivy Graveson,* the ink lying thick with a heavily indented full stop after my name. My breath was shallow as I ripped open the thick, expensive-feeling paper.

> *The Red Dragons request the pleasure of your company at an exchange at 8pm on the 13th of October. Pre drinks held before dinner in Freddie and Eddy's joint suite.*

(When you arrive at the college, please come up the back
stairs to circumnavigate the porter's lodge and avoid
raising any suspicions!) We'll end the night in Cave if
you make it that far. Carriages at dawn. No plus ones as
this is a select gathering.

Exchanging. That was the name for when equal numbers of
boys and girls went to dinner together. I'd learned that much
from Martha, who was desperate to get started yet patient
in teaching me all the terminology that everyone else just
seemed to know. But my only information was what she had
passed on to me; I hadn't heard of the Red Dragons beyond
the bar's speciality drink and Amina and Peter's allusions.

My heart beat fast in my chest and I took in a big drink
of air to calm my overstimulated brain, like the guidance
counsellor at school had taught me. This agitation felt different though. It felt kind of good. No one had ever invited
me to something exclusive before, something selective. The
only secrets I'd had were sad and a little bit dirty. Even
the pub trip with Erin and Jenny was a general invitation
to pretty much all of the sixth form. *I'm ready to be part of*
something bigger, I told myself, whispering the words over
and over, visualizing myself at the centre of things, never
alone again.

My noticeboard was bare, save for a couple of family
photos taken on holiday in the countryside, one of
Grandma Olive in the home on her eightieth birthday and
one of me by myself, looking relieved on my last day of
school. My braces had only just come off and I still had

my teeth sucked into the seams of my smile. I'd packed more, dozens of selfies of me and Cara, but I hadn't been able to put any of them up. Pictures of us looking arty on the beach with matching beige berets we'd bought as a joke. Pictures she'd taken of my side profile in black and white where I looked almost pretty, my nose and boobs forming little black hills against the white of an autumn sky. Pictures she'd taken of me as I filmed her, my mouth open to tell her off for disrupting the footage even though I knew she'd tell me it just made it more natural. All turned to rubbish. Mum had left some pins shaped like ladybirds as a room-warming gift for me, crawling garish and red over the cork. I stabbed one through the invite and placed it in the middle of the board.

There was no going back to Marx, his candyfloss beard staring out at me, knowing that I was thinking of only one kind of labour. Sleep wasn't forthcoming either, so I reached my hands into my pants, and tried to think of only the right sort of forbidden things.

Harold was more handsome than I imagined. Or maybe I was more sexually frustrated than I'd thought. His room was halfway up a spiral staircase in a different college, a five-minute cycle away – I knew I'd have to get fitter to keep up with all the tucked-away offices. Faces of wizened old men stared down at me from portraits, instead of faces of wizened old women.

The space was full of books with the kind of musty smell that made me feel at home but put me to sleep nearly as fast. Agatha was there already, legs and arms folded around her tall body. She glanced at me, like me and Marx should be close just because I hadn't brought my laptop to the supervision in a designer bag like she had. I struggled to open my mouth, afraid that I would yawn if I did.

'What do you think?' Harold asked, turning to me after a whistle-stop tour of Marx's works. Dust motes fell in what was to be one of the last true sunbeams of the year. Here it was; the moment I had waited for after Cara stopped wanting to hang out with me as much, knowing I was leaving, when I spent endless hours on the beach with no one but the screeching gulls and my camera for company. The moment that had caused me to scream when I opened my acceptance letter. The moment that divided my life into a before and after, like some crappy makeover show – even if I hadn't understood the irreversibility of that division at the time.

'Um. I think that you can really see the differences between the audiences he is writing for in each of the texts. *The Communist Manifesto* feels like something that could go viral. I mean, it speaks to the masses. If I was a worker fed up with my life this would appeal to me,' I said. Harold pressed his pen against his lips and, seeming satisfied enough, moved on. I didn't speak again for the rest of the supervision.

'So there we have it. Ivy and Agatha, you're going to be supervision partners for all of this term seeing as you're the only two taking both anthropology and politics from your college. Two is the ideal number for intellectual enquiry and I never have supervision groups bigger than three at an absolute maximum. I might swap you around after Christmas, but let's see how that goes, shall we?' He jabbed the lid of his pen down. That was that. First supervision over and it hadn't been so bad. I started to pack up, only to see that ink had leaked onto my hand, leaving blue marks like some kind of fungal infection. I was glad that Agatha had already left the room as soon as we'd finished so that she didn't witness my clumsy mess. Harold handed me a tissue from a box resting on a shelf stacked with tomes on medieval witchcraft and persecution. I couldn't help pausing to look at them, gold leaf peeling from the spines.

'Ah, yes. Those are some of my favourite books. I keep getting distracted by gruesome tales of sixteenth-century executions, much to my supervisor's chagrin. But seriously, there's some absolutely fascinating stuff in there. Pertinent to modern scholarship too.'

'I know, I wrote my dissertation in school about witches.'

'Did you really?'

'Yes.' My cheeks flushed, worried I was saying too much. 'There were some witch trials in my home town. I started to write a documentary script about it actually.'

'How interesting. You could carry that on here if you wanted, I'm sure – there's all kinds of myth and magic weaved through this place. I believe there was even a rather grisly case to do with witches linked to your college.'

'Maybe. I haven't filmed anything since I got here though, or written anything other than essays. It's hard to find the time, especially when I'm trying to make friends and do the reading and the work.' My hand fell from the book I'd been stroking absent-mindedly.

'Oh, I remember that feeling like it was yesterday. In many ways, an undergraduate degree is the most stressful of them all. But you made some good points in there, you know? If you continue like that without getting distracted you might just be in danger of nabbing yourself a first.' A picture on the desk glinted in the light, the only thing in the room that was free from dust. A woman with gappy teeth and a discreet cross around her neck smiled back at me.

Harold held the door open for me and smiled. 'It's worth remembering, Ivy, that those who speak the loudest don't necessarily have the most to say.'

'I knew I recognized your face from somewhere.'

'Right? Me too. It must have been Harry's New Year party back in sixth form. You came with those twins with the big hair,' Prim said.

'Oh, gosh, I remember. Helena and Mattie. I never speak to them now. Aggie and Nat are the only two girls I still hang out with from school.' Martha lit the candles on her mantelpiece with a lighter, the line of flames casting a soft glow over Primrose's face.

'How come?' Prim asked.

'Oh, we just fell out over something silly. I can hardly remember now. Something boy-related, I think. Helena thought I was flirting with her boyfriend or something stupid when I totally wasn't.'

'Did you guys actually speak before or were you just in

the same place at the same time?' I chipped in, wanting to be a part of the conversation.

'No, Prim and I didn't get a chance to chitchat before. So thank you for introducing us formally,' Martha said. Primrose turned to Martha to do a silly bow before topping up our wine glasses. Even though I was acutely aware of how I was the newest member of their social circle, I couldn't help but feel a slight thrill run through my body at the thought they might not have become friends without me. I noticed that Martha's hair was a little static – everything around us seemed to crackle with energy, like this was the start of something special.

'Is there anyone else from your school or town here, Ivy?' Prim sipped her wine. I wasn't exactly an expert, but even I could tell that everything I'd drunk so far in college was a cut above the £5 bottles Cara and I used to neck.

'Oh, not that I know of,' I said, trying to hide that this wasn't the first time I'd been asked that question.

'Well, that's okay. You've got us now.' Martha slung her arms around my shoulders, pulling me in for a hug.

'I do. And now you've properly met each other, I'm happy,' I said. 'The nature walk was really nice though, Martha, you should have come.'

'I prefer walking in the grounds on my own, to be honest, for the peace and quiet. And I was still sleeping off a hangover.'

'We're so lucky to have so much green space around us, aren't we?' Prim opened the window to let a gust of fresh air into the room. 'Except – did you notice that plaque in the woods, Ivy? About remembering women who suffered there or something?'

The hairs on my arms stood on end as the cold blew in from outside. 'No, I was looking at the light and the squirrels. I didn't stop to read it.'

'Oh, that plaque.' Martha moved her hands away from my body. 'I wasn't listening properly but Mum told me about that when we were here for the open day and said we have a family connection to the women or something. I think it's highly unlikely but she's a real sucker for pouring money into that kind of thing. They must give her some juicy stuff to keep her coming back.'

'Your mum came to pick you up from that party, remember?' Prim said. 'She looked very glam, wouldn't have guessed she'd be interested in all the ancestry stuff.'

'God, did she?' Martha scrunched up her face. 'How embarrassing. But yeah, it's been an obsession of hers since – well, for the past couple of years.'

Martha had started picking the orange varnish off her nails and I wanted to give her an out. 'So, are we all going on this exchange?' I didn't even ask whether they'd been invited. I just assumed.

'Wouldn't miss it for the world, darling.' Up on her feet, Martha was already rifling through her wardrobe, full of silks and velvets in a whole rainbow of colours.

'I'm not sure how I feel about it,' Primrose said.

'Really? I thought it would be fun for us all to go together.' I tried not to let a wobble enter my voice as I turned to face Primrose.

'I just don't know if it's massively my thing. I'm a bit of a homebody. It's got to be something really good to tempt me out these days.'

'What about the party you two met at?' I demanded.

'Ah, my misspent youth,' Prim chuckled. 'I've already clocked a lot of hours at parties with men who like the sound of their own voice.'

'Not everyone gets invited to this exchange,' Martha said. 'It's select. The Dragons operate on a semi-secret basis. Loads of people could do their whole degree here and never even hear of them, let alone become friends with them. How else will we get to know the boys?' Martha had moved onto shoes now, looking through row upon row of heels and trainers.

'Please come?' I reached out to grip Primrose's hand and bit down the 'for me' that I'd almost added. 'I don't know the other girls going like I know you both.'

'I promise I'll consider it.' Prim placed her hand on top of mine.

'Okay, I can take that,' I said, not wanting to push her any further than I thought she might bend.

'I'll take it for now.' Martha grinned. She had selected a blood-red dress and was holding it up to her body as she stared into the mirror.

'What do you mean, the Dragons are semi-secret?' I asked, trying to keep the disbelief that I could be invited to something so selective out of my voice.

'Well, you know, those who know know and those who don't don't,' Martha replied. 'Some of the senior tutors and professors from the mixed colleges used to be Dragons so they have their tacit support but they keep their activities select, on a need-to-know basis. We shouldn't talk about it beyond our group. I only know because my older cousin was a Dragon and his lips get loose after a few drinks at Christmas.'

The words 'our group' made my heart beat faster. I loved my new friends already, but to realize that they were part of an exclusive group, and that I was too, made me almost breathless. For so long, I'd spent my nights wishing that I would find my person – or my people – again and now I was where I was supposed to be, I was certain of it. Growing up on the outside of things gives you a sixth sense for the feeling of belonging.

'What else are we up to this week?' I asked, keeping my tone casual, trying to hide my giddiness at the thought that this town might be ours for the taking. 'There's that formal hall in a few days.' The phrase tripped out of my mouth like I'd been saying it for years and not like I'd only recently learned the term for the later dinner service that happened twice a week where formalwear was required.

'Yep, can't wait,' Martha nodded. 'And I was thinking that at some point we should do lunch or brunch or something.' My breath caught, willing it to be just the three of us, waiting for her to mention inviting Natasha and Agatha, but she didn't add anything else.

'Sounds fun,' Prim agreed and I felt a flood of relief. 'It's so nice to have two people to do things with already. You're beginning to make me feel at home.'

'Same here.' I grinned at Prim, my cheeks flushed from the warm room and the feeling of finding a cosy nook in the fabric of the city and slotting right into it.

'Maybe you'll even convince me to come on the exchange.'

'I hope so,' Martha said. 'What's the worst that could happen?'

Once a week, at the only formal hall where they were permitted, boys could come to dinner in our college and sit under the dark portraits of old Mistresses and the intricate stained glass depicting miracles committed by female saints. The hall was always noisy with the chatter of hundreds of students, but on those days it had a particular buzz and energy that only young men can bring. Even the smell was different. If you breathed in, you could tell that there were boys underneath the vaulted ceilings – the usual scents of cooking, incense and perfume were tinged with sweat and excitement.

Primrose, Martha and I tried to arrive for the start of the dinner service, when the heavy oak doors swung open to reveal the long wooden tables and low benches. Those two girls were becoming my routine. I almost resented Harold and cycling to lectures in the morning drizzle because it meant less time sprawling on Martha's bed. But dinners were gems to look forward to at the end of the day. At those tables, we had no past and no future. Freshers live in the eternal, glorious present. It was too early for talk of spring weeks, internships, vac schemes – even exams. Too heady and new for discussion of parents, siblings, previous lives, boring hometown boyfriends. We were helium balloons with no pasts to pull us down.

Two weeks to the day since I had arrived in my new life, George Svenson sat next to me at formal hall, his thigh brushing against mine. Even that brief contact between our bodies felt like a spark of something, reminding me with a jolt that he'd chosen to sit next to me out of all the possible options. I opened my mouth to talk to him but Martha's voice was crystal clear above the din, cutting through all other conversation.

'We can't possibly go to a chain pub for pre-drinks before the exchange,' she declared.

'What's wrong with that?' It was meant to be a question but somehow it came out defiant as I spoke. The smile froze on Martha's face. Her impeccable lipstick was the colour of ketchup – even when there was nowhere to go, there was someone to impress.

'It's just a bit grimy, don't you think?' Martha said.

'If it's the one I think you mean, I like it there,' I shrugged, thinking of nights back home with sticky floors and cheap, garish drinks, Cara dancing next to me.

'I like it there too.' George turned the full force of his attention towards me. I felt like a cat, basking in a warm pool of sunshine.

'I just want to be able to get chips on my night out, I don't think that's too much to ask,' I muttered, surprised but pleased that me and George could connect over carbs and cloying carpets.

'Me too. I'll be there. At the exchange, I mean,' he said.

'So you're a part of the society?' My voice didn't falter as I acted as if I hadn't heard him outside my room in the middle of the night.

'Yes. Well, I haven't been initiated fully yet but I'm invited to all their events. They know how to put on a good show. You'll enjoy it. Though we probably shouldn't talk about it so loudly.' He scanned the room. 'I know everyone here is invited, but you never know who might be listening. Sometimes I think even the walls have ears in this place.'

'I'm excited,' I whispered. It wasn't a lie. I wanted to dance. I wanted to drink fancy cocktails. I wanted to exist in the same room as Martha and George, their easy confidence filling the space with warmth and golden light.

'I'm pleased you'll be there.' He smiled and it had all the quiet force of a sunrise on a clear summer's morning.

'What do the initiations involve?' I tried to keep the conversation going to cover my blushes, my voice still low.

'I'm not entirely sure yet. But any awful stories you've heard are definitely exaggerations.'

'I haven't heard any awful stories,' I said, hoping he'd expand but he didn't offer any new information. 'I keep thinking that it would be so interesting to make some kind of film about the drinking societies. It's fascinating – there seem to be so many rules and layers.'

'Don't let Freddie hear you say that. Freddie Alexander,' he added, seeing the lack of recognition on my face. His voice turned serious, the easiness vanishing from his face. 'He's the president. Well, the co-president with Eddy Smithson, but really, we all think Freddie's the one in charge. And the presidents are entrusted with preserving the society – and its secrecy – for future generations of Dragons.'

I had the urge to laugh and I squirmed on the bench to try and subdue it. It was a sentence that could only make sense within those hallowed walls.

'It's important to us, you know. These boys – they're more than friends, they're family.' A grin broke through the clouds on his face.

'It's sweet that you're all so close.' I couldn't help smiling back at the way his features leapt back to life.

'That's what this place does to you. There's no other bond quite like it.'

'I'm starting to think you're right.'

He glanced behind my head at a portrait of a group of women with the same grey eyes staring out of the frame. 'Do you ever feel like they're watching us? All the people who used to sit in these seats?'

The gong sounded before I could reply, its echoing reverberations a signal to vacate the hall now that the meal was over. The bar was closed on a Thursday night – rumour had it this was done on purpose to stop any mixed gender drinking after dinner – and boys began to drift away in dribs and drabs. Our moment had passed.

'Until next time then, George.'

'Oh yes, I'll be waiting.'

George Svenson was stuck in my head, in my mouth. He was on the tip of my tongue. His brown eyes were seared into my mind. He was all I wanted to talk about. He was precisely the kind of person I'd thought I'd meet if only I managed to make it to this university – sophisticated, beautiful, confident. The kind of person who forged their own path and didn't let anything destabilize it. Fortunately for me, everyone else wanted to talk about him too.

'It was so cute the way you guys chatted all through dinner,' Martha said. We were in the study room with the open fire crackling away behind us, a more relaxed option than the library where stern women hushed our whispers. Martha was rearranging her pens into colour order, reds fading to pinks and then to purples.

'You could do better, seriously.' Prim was still trying half-heartedly to work, biting the end of her biro, the clear plastic turning white.

'Better than him? He's like the pinnacle of what this place is all about.' I couldn't keep the indignation out of my voice, putting down my book on Durkheim along with any pretence of study.

'Yeah, exactly.' Primrose went back to writing in her notebook in her neat cursive.

'You know, he looks really like my ex. He's just a bit taller.' The picture Martha brought up on her phone showed a boy in a plaid shirt with tousled hair, his arm encircling her waist. He did look a lot like George, though to my eyes there was something less charming about him. Her smile in the photo was brittle, like it could snap at any moment.

'How did that end?' I asked.

'Oh, same old. He broke my heart or I broke his or some mixture of the two. Anyway, we don't talk now. But I'm sure you'll have better luck, Iv. George actually seems quite nice.'

'I'm not sure I'll have any luck at all,' I sighed. Even early on in the term, I knew how wanted George was. I didn't see any particular reason he'd pick me with how much choice he had.

'Stop with all that "woe is me" stuff. George would be lucky to have you.'

'Far luckier than he deserves,' Prim chipped in, unable to ignore us completely. 'We've only known each other a matter of days, Ivy, and I can already promise you that.'

'I'm really not expecting anything, I literally just think he's handsome, that's all.' But the words felt wrong as they came out of my mouth. Rain began to spatter against the window disapprovingly, like the water could sense I was lying. That it knew I felt a kind of electricity in proximity to George, which seemed almost dangerous.

'Don't we all. We should see him next Thursday and we can assess then. I can't wait. I mean, our first exchange ever. Aren't you guys excited?' Martha squealed.

'Not really.' Prim put her pen down with a sigh, defeated. 'You will both have to come to stay in my parents' flat in the city one weekend and I can show you there's more to life than these four walls.'

'I would love that, if it wouldn't be too much trouble.' My hands squeezed each other under the desk, my nails digging into flesh.

'Because they're human rights lawyers, they're always travelling. In fact, they'd be delighted to think that I've made some new friends. Everyone else in my family is so social, it freaks them out that I like my own company so much.'

'Doesn't your sister live there? She's a few years older than us, right?' Martha asked and something hard and unsightly within me tightened. I hadn't even known that Primrose had a sister. I had been so enamoured with the present that I'd forgotten to ask about her past – forgotten that they both had a head start on me when it came to the background details of each other's lives.

'Lola is in Accra at the moment with family, and then she's moving to Paris for an internship with an environmental organization. London's far too provincial for her now.'

'So chic,' Martha said and I nodded, gathering up all the little details of Prim and tucking them away in my mind.

'We can visit over the holidays sometime,' Primrose promised. 'For now though, I really must finish this essay. I want to make a good impression with the first one.'

'Fine. Get your work done, and then there'll be no stopping us.' Martha squeezed my shoulder. 'This is going to be the best year, I can feel it. Tomorrow's only the start. Just wait and see.'

Week 3

Today there was a man in the woods. We were running hand in hand – as sisters, of course – and we saw him by the pond. A man in the woods makes the trees unhappy, makes the leaves wilt, makes the birds stop singing. We all felt it – the slithering, creeping feeling of something where it shouldn't be. Except one of our sisters did not feel our feeling. She claimed the man was harmless and even wanted to talk to him. We shall watch her. We shall watch her, with all the care of a mother nursing a sick child back to its previous health.

It rained on the day of the exchange. Fat droplets spilled their seed on our heads, every splash producing another. We covered our hair with books and laptop cases as we took the short cut across the lawn to the dining hall. On Thursdays, there was an earlier dinner service where we didn't have to wear our loose-fitting black gowns, which reminded me of childhood Halloween costumes. We grabbed the bare minimum of food to get us through the evening. Looking back, I wonder what we lived on at that time – if it was anything more than air and sex and hope.

We were forever hankering for some greater excitement, some greater pleasure, even as we were living our headiest days without knowing it.

Martha's room was dimly lit after the cheerful lights of the dining hall, her face glowing out of the smog of scented candles and fairy lights. 'Perfect lighting for taking nudes in,' she'd told me.

'Apparently, the boys are going to take care of everything tonight,' Natasha said as she dabbed a spot of pink lipstick from her Cupid's bow with the bell sleeve of her dress. 'And I've been asking around the tennis girls and I heard that our drinking society admits you or not based on your aura. But that's all they'll tell me. Either they didn't know or they're not saying.'

'What does that even mean?' Primrose demanded.

'You know, like an aura, an energy,' Natasha explained in earnest. 'I hope mine is good.'

'I've heard the initiations for girls are in the woods at night. But I haven't been able to find out anything more, annoyingly, not even the society's name. I will though – Prim and Ivy, if there's one thing you should know about me, it's that I always track down the truth in the end,' Agatha said. She fiddled with the tassels of her earring, pressing the threads between her long fingers.

'True that. Do you remember when that girl from another school was texting James when I was dating him and you found out her name and socials for me in, like, five minutes? Anyway, in the woods at night? Sounds spooky. But also fun. I like being scared.' Martha was looking at herself in the mirror wearing only a black thong. She slipped on a pair of heels to match from the dozens of shoes that she kept in a line against the wall, and pulled a silky black dress over her head. My heart hammered in my chest, nervous at the night ahead.

'What are you wearing, Iv?' My eyes betrayed me before I could answer. I glanced down at my camisole and my jeans with artful rips at the knees.

'Oh no, babe, you can't go wearing that. Not for our first ever exchange. Making a good impression tonight will determine the whole year.' Martha's laughter was thunder, low and deep. 'Here, try this instead.' She pulled out a red top from the pile on her standard-issue college armchair, then reached into her cupboard to find the matching skirt. Four sets of eyes were fixed on me as I got changed.

'Ta-dah!' I spun round in a silly twirl to shake the weight of their gaze, hoping that I looked good enough to earn my coveted place on the exchange. Being part of things was where I wanted to be, and I was prepared to wear anything – do anything – to stay there.

'Oh yes, that's much better,' cooed Natasha, compliments forever teetering on the edge of her lips. 'Let's just put your hair up. I've got three little sisters and I always do theirs so I can do it for you if you'd like.' I nodded and she stroked tendrils back from my shoulder, like she was soothing a small animal, and finished it with two velvet scrunchies.

Primrose smiled, half-encouraging. 'Don't even think about it with me, Marth. I will wear boots and floral skirts to my grave.' She wiggled her feet, resplendent in purple faux leather. 'Prise these off my cold dead body.'

Martha leaned down and kissed the top of her head. 'Of course, you don't need fixing.'

I peered over their writhing, giggling bodies in the mirror. Someone who looked like she only went to cheap and cheerful pubs ironically stared back at me. Someone who knew exactly what to wear to be alluring but not desperate. I looked like I'd been in that town three years, not three weeks.

The Red Dragons all lived together on the same staircase in the university's oldest college, a twenty-minute walk or five-minute cycle from ours. We climbed up three flights of stairs to get to the presidents' set – two bedrooms either side of a living room and a bathroom – in a haze of giggles and nerves. As girls filed in like a small army, the room stayed spacious enough for everyone to comfortably manoeuvre around the huge punch bowl placed in the middle of the dining table. The light was dying as the nearly leafless trees waved at me through the window, and I passed my hand over the complicated braids Natasha had made with my hair.

'Do you ladies want some special punch?' asked a boy wearing a silver signet ring and a pale blue shirt, who was dipping a ladle into the bowl already.

'Freddie, what part of that sentence doesn't sound rapey?' Martha's teeth shone as she laughed. 'So, are you going to tell us yet what the plan is for this evening?'

'Ah, if I told you that I'm afraid I'd have to kill you,'
Freddie replied.

'Not even for me?'

'Some of us have more immunity to your charms than
others, Martha dear. Not many but some.'

I turned away from Martha's huffing, not wanting to see
her fail to get what she wanted. The people in the room
were like echoes of each other, some better looking, some
less so, but all crafted from the same note. The Dragons
could have been brothers, with their varying shades of pale
skin and caramel hair. Everyone's clothes were variations
on a theme, although I wouldn't have been able to emulate
it on my own if I tried. Maybe that's what they taught you
at their schools. How to look like one giant family photo.

'At least the alcohol's free.' Primrose slid down onto the
cream sofa I'd sunk into, holding two crimson cocktails
complete with tiny umbrellas. 'I can't believe you two
convinced me to come. I'm going to file this as study for
my elective on ritual and kinship.'

'You get to take anthropology modules even as a historian?' I asked.

'Yes, there's loads of choice actually. I mean, in many
ways it makes sense. I found it really hard to choose
between anthropology and history actually as my main
degree. What's so different about the past and the present? Especially somewhere like this where you can almost
feel the connection between them. But in the end I picked
history because I'm a sucker for all the concrete stuff like
dates but also how much is up to our interpretation. In fact,

I should really be finishing my essay on the limitations of secondary sources right about now.'

'Aren't you having fun?' I gestured at the room full of bodies and noise. There was a current to the evening, like we were all holding our breath collectively, waiting to see what happened next – I couldn't imagine not wanting to find out what that might be.

'Okay, I sort of am. But don't tell anyone, it would ruin my image.'

Girls were touching boys' shoulders and hair was being tossed as more and more bottles were poured into the depleting punch. My eyes searched for George but found Peter instead, and I couldn't see Martha either.

'I've been thinking that I should make some kind of film or documentary-style thing about the societies. I used to like doing that back home,' I said, as two boys scooted past us, one holding the other in a loose headlock. 'There's some great visuals.'

'You should. It would be cool to have an outsider's perspective on all this.' Primrose turned away too quickly to see my frown, her neck flexible from the stretching she stood up to do every half an hour when we were studying. 'Oh, god, here we go.'

The guy with the signet ring was trying to get the attention of the room. 'That's Freddie Alexander. He was the year below Lola at school, so three years above me. I'm pretty sure he took a gap year,' Prim explained in a low voice. 'I should have known there'd be Old Boys here. I managed to learn that he's the president somehow from

Martha despite trying not to know anything about him at all. The other president's called Eddy, I think.'

'Do all their names have to rhyme?' I asked, not explaining that I already knew this information from George.

'It's part of their cult I suppose.'

'And do you all know each other?' The words came out more biting than I'd intended.

Prim put her arm around my shoulder and grinned. 'No. Just the suspect ones.'

Eddy, I'd later learn, was the top cricketer at the famous public school he'd attended. I knew less than nothing about cricket but boys who were into it always nodded when Eddy's name was mentioned. The really keen ones alliterated his family name admiringly so that he became Smithson Safe Hands, leaning into that particular way boys have of calling each other by their surnames. He handed me a black silk scarf before I stepped into the taxi. His fingers were steady as he tied it around my head, making sure my hair didn't get tugged. 'To prevent any peeking,' he said with a hint of a smile in his voice. 'You know we exist but we don't know you well enough just yet to let us show you all our secrets.'

In the cab, we were all titters and jostling limbs, going along with the game even as the blindfold pressed against the eye makeup Martha had painted on my face. Through the material, there were glimpses of cobbled streets and crooked old houses until we pulled up at a dark lump of a building.

As the car drew to a halt, the door swung open and soft, warm hands reached inside to help me out. Then they spun me around and untied the blindfold quickly, like they'd had practice. George was standing in front of me, his hair catching all the light of the moon. My hand twitched by my side, wanting to reach out and stroke his curls. His full lips parted like he was on the verge of speaking until Freddie called his name and he was gone with an apologetic glance backwards, disappearing into an entranceway surrounded by looming neoclassical columns.

The inside was a picture of cold marble floors, plush red carpets and glinting chandeliers. Portraits of severe-looking men in heavy gilt frames stared down at us from amid alcoves full of vases of blooming flowers, their pollen making me sneeze.

'We're off to powder our noses,' Martha called to me as she rushed past, her voice light as air. I was naïve enough back then that I had no idea what they meant. I stood alone, beneath the high ceiling, capturing all the details in my mind and closing my eyes to make sure that I could recreate the scene for myself any time I wanted.

'A lot of the members of this members' club used to be Dragons and they don't mind doing us current students a favour now and again so long as we keep things relatively hush-hush.' George was by my side once more, holding out a glass of champagne. I tried to speak but the noise and the lights and the bubbles were making it difficult to control my lips.

I turned to a waiter to get a glass of water and by the

time I had it in my hands, George was gone again. For someone so tall and eye-catching, he had a good vanishing act. Martha, Agatha and Natasha emerged from the toilets with big eyes and grabbing hands that hauled me down a corridor into a dark blue dining room where silver knives sparkled on a white tablecloth. The presidents, Freddie and Eddy, were standing on chairs directing everyone else to their seats.

I'd never been in a room that big before that wasn't a PE hall. The other girls' brains appeared to just compute what was going on, unsurprised that we'd ended up in this palatial space. They carried on their easy chatter as I committed every aspect to memory, until Eddy interrupted my thoughts to show me where I would be sitting on the end of a long table.

Freddie slid into the seat next to me. Agatha was positioned to his left. I was outnumbered. Prim was nowhere to be seen and I searched for Martha's beacon of red but she was over the other side of the room, Eddy feeding olives into her wine-stained mouth and Peter unable to tear his eyes from her. My body ached to be next to her but she looked happy where she was, her laugh erupting again and again, carrying across the room. Besides, seating on exchanges was strictly boy/girl. There were rules I didn't know and I needed to learn them. A gong, heavier and louder than the one in college, sounded as food began to be served.

'What an honour to be sat next to the president,' Agatha said.

'Ah yes, we invite the most interesting girls to sit next to the presidents. The pleasure's really mine.'

'Ever the flatterer, Freddie. What's the society's plan for this term, then?'

'That's top secret intel, I'm afraid.'

'Oh, come on, we're here, aren't we?' Agatha pushed. 'I just want to have something to look forward to when I'm in the middle of an essay on communism.'

He made an expression halfway between a grimace and a smirk. 'I'm sorry but my lips are sealed.'

'What about our college's society? Peter mentioned them to me,' I chipped in.

'The Coven? Even we don't really know what they get up to.'

'The Coven. So that's their name.' Agatha wiped her mouth with her napkin, giving me no thanks for uncovering this new bit of information. Even in her drawl, the name sounded alluring, so that I repeated it in my mind like an incantation.

After the soup course, Agatha went to reapply her lipstick and Freddie angled his body so that he was facing me head on. 'So, tell me truthfully, Ivy Graveson – how are you settling in?'

'All right, I think. I've made friends.' I surprised myself a little by realizing the words were true – despite everything, I was finally doing okay again. Once the numbness had faded after Cara died, I'd held on to a desperate hope that I could come back to myself at university and things were going pretty much exactly as I'd wished for.

'Certainly seems like it. I've seen you in town a few times with Martha.'

'And supervisions are fine, I'm getting used to them,' I continued, wanting to keep the topic of Martha all to myself for reasons I couldn't quite explain.

'Who's your supervisor?'

'Harold Bakewell.'

'Ah, I had him in first year too. I think he's not so into the modern stuff, his real love is medieval. He's not working you too hard?'

'No, he's nice actually. Encouraging. I might even be able to continue this project I started with a— with someone else in school for my long essay.'

'Interesting. Well, if there's anything we – I – can do to help show you the ropes let me know. I remember when I first arrived, I spent so much time speaking to my mother. I felt like I had to pick up each time she called, what with her rattling around in that house in Canonbury all by herself.'

'You're an only child too?' I asked, surprised. Freddie was always surrounded by people whenever I saw him – mostly boys, some girls – and I'd assumed he'd come from a large family and was used to being at the centre of a group.

'Yes, it was just Mum and me in London. Plus, it's tough leaving a big city for a much smaller one like this. But I suppose we all have issues leaving the places we're familiar with.'

'I couldn't wait to get away to be honest.' I pulled a

face without really meaning to and then reeled my features back in.

'That's what we all think at first. But there will be moments when you miss it or something or someone, trust me.'

'I would miss my grandma but she died about a year ago. I was much closer to her than to my parents.' A grandparent dying was the acceptable face of grief, one that didn't make other people uncomfortable but rather compassionate in a way that made them feel good about themselves. Just the right amount of sad. And although I missed her desperately, a part of me always knew the grief around Grandma Olive was coming sooner or later. It was a more containable kind of tragedy, that didn't make me feel like all my sorrows might spiral out of my body. Unlike with Cara.

'I'm sorry. Really, I am. For me it's my dog, Barney. He's this gorgeous fox-red lab. He greeted me every time I came home with his toy pheasant.' He stopped speaking as Agatha came back from the bathroom, turning away from me to hit her with a pearly smile.

'Was Ivy telling you all about herself?' she asked.

'We're just getting to know each other.' Freddie grinned at me as Agatha tossed her wavy blonde hair.

'Yes, you're still a bit of a dark horse, you know, Iv.'

'Am I? Maybe you just need to listen more carefully,' I suggested.

'You've not spoken much about where you're from at all. What school did you go to again?' Agatha asked.

'You'll never have heard of it.'

'I was only asking – not every question is an attack,' she replied. It wasn't the first time that evening I'd been asked about school, and I obviously hadn't been able to filter out all the impatience from my voice. Everyone else I'd met had been to a school with a reputation that preceded it. I just went to the school in my town.

'Even when it's coming from you?' I thought I hadn't been bothered by Agatha's snark and the way she obviously felt territorial around Martha but as I spoke I realized that her jibes had got to me despite my best efforts to remain calm and collected.

Agatha's mouth formed a perfect circle as Freddie leaned back in his chair, arms folded as he watched the show. She was so pretty, so polished even in her surprise. Her hair looked like it had just come out of plaits, the kind Grandma Olive used to do for me when I was little. Then Aggie's shock turned to laughter and my annoyance crumbled too, any discomfort obscured by alcohol and the easy shapes our three bodies made sitting side by side.

The rest of the dinner passed in a haze of champagne bubbles, elaborate toasts and increasingly slurred speeches. From starter to dessert, Freddie passed me the best dishes and made sure my glass was never empty while my gaze played ping-pong between Martha and George.

When the meal was over, the eventual escape onto the street was a relief and a regret, the night a cold towel pressed against my forehead. The tall shapes of the colleges were a darker black against the almost midnight sky and the low moos of the city cows rolled across the fields where they grazed near the meandering river. I put my hands against my eyes and rubbed until I couldn't tell if the fireworks floating in front of them were internal or external to my mind. A noise sounded from my pocket, making me jump even though freshers were routinely told by senior tutors that this was one of the safest cities in the country, that nothing bad ever happened here.

Martha messaged me to say that she'd made it to Cave, a nightclub that was popular for its cheap drinks and free entry. The street lights were bright but the moon was brighter. I was alone and my skin was dimpling into tiny peaks against my arms, as if my body couldn't agree with itself. It was late and I should have been tired but my skin fizzed with the kind of energy that needs to find an outlet somewhere. So, like an arrow finding its target, I followed her there.

Martha was dancing with her hands above her head, spinning round and round in slow circles. I'd found her against the odds, homing in on her tall body, its pulsating silhouette a flashpoint on the dance floor.

'George keeps looking at you.' She swayed with her eyes half-open, her body languid and loose. I'd seen him when I walked in, standing with some of the prettiest girls in second and third year, girls who were rumoured to be a part of the society I now knew was called the Coven. For a second, I thought I made eye contact with him until he looked away.

'No, he doesn't.' My retort surprised me with its quickness. 'Why would he look at me when I'm standing next to you?'

'Ivy, have you seen yourself tonight?'

I turned to look in the mirrors against the wall, and took a step back. Someone who had notions of confidence I didn't possess stared back at me. Someone who looked almost happy. It felt like seeing a ghost, but instead of there being hollow emptiness there was fullness and a hint of contentment. I ran my tongue across my teeth where my braces used to stand as a barrier between me and the out-side world and felt nothing but an absence. The girl who didn't fit in anywhere was blurring. Maybe there was an Ivy-shaped hole in the puzzle of this city that existed just for me to fill it.

When I spun round, Martha was nowhere to be seen. The smoke machines had been turned on, orange and red searchlights flashing in the fog. I couldn't spot anyone else I knew – I'd never been able to find Prim again after pre-drinks.

Before I could miss her, he appeared on the dance floor like shafts of light sometimes appear from the sky. Angels, Grandma used to tell me when I was little. There's no ele-gant way to dance up to someone through a heaving mass of bodies, but if anyone could do it, it was George. King of blasé. Prince of abandon.

'Do you want to get out of here?' Girls usually hung around him like flies, thick wads of eyelashes tracking his every move. But that night he'd somehow shed the usual hangers-on and he moved more easily for it. His eyes were glazed but they still had a glint to them, like a vein of quartz in stone. That glint drew me in and for a moment I couldn't look away – it was like our energy was matched, like we were on the same frequency.

What else could I have said but yes?

I don't remember the journey back to my college together – those few precious moments when we were alone in each other's company for the first time. Maybe if I did, I'd be able to divine a moment where the course of history could have been changed, where we misread something as dangerous that should have been viewed as farcical. Maybe we could all be together now, looking back at how high-spirited we were as freshers with the urgency of the never-ending present forever on our tongues.

When I lurched out of the taxi door, the distant branches of the college's trees whipped across my vision as the wind picked up. Since meeting Martha and Primrose in the woods, they had all become mixed up together in my mind; the first things to have made me feel at home in this new place. Bringing George there was a departure. It wasn't like there weren't signs of men in the college – muffled laughter behind doors, a misplaced tie lying starkly on wooden floorboards – but after dark, they were kept hidden in the shadows.

Inside, we stumbled through the warren of corridors that I had memorized at some point without noticing. What had been strange a few weeks ago had become familiar already. My floor was deserted and I pulled him inside the door into my narrow room with its arched window. His arm was under my back, slipping up to rest in the middle of my shoulder blades. I couldn't help but shiver at his touch, and George let out a moan as he sensed my reaction.

'Shh.' I pressed my finger to his mouth, finding wetness and heat. My skin crackled, my breath catching in my throat. The only man I'd had sex with had been a bleary thirtysomething who I'd met in the pub on the day I got my braces taken off. Cara had been ghosting my messages so I hadn't been able to share with her my plan of making sure I had sex for the first time before leaving for uni. I'd wanted practice and to get it over with, and instead I got clumsy hands and breath that smelled of beer. I woke up in his one-bed flat, pictures of kids pinned to the freezer, the heating not on, a withered block of cheese in the fridge. Outside the man's front door, I'd wished on a dandelion head that the next guy I kissed would be someone who would make me feel something beautiful and easy, the spores carrying my desires out to the distant sea.

As George unbuttoned his shirt, I could see he was everything I could have hoped for, like he was made with the sole purpose of being unassailable, unattainable and perfect. Except he wasn't unattainable, because he was right there with me in that moment. Just like I'd desired, even before I'd known George existed.

His lips met mine like they were filling a gap, his tongue feathering my bare teeth. His mouth was soft but he drove his hardness into me, hitting me every time I relaxed into a kiss. I forgot my body for a moment, forgot the picture of it in my head as his hands swept every part of me. I was floating, existing in the pure pleasure of the moment, with no intrusions from the past or worries about the future. The darkness helped. Just one dim desk lamp lit up our entanglement as the pile of crumpled clothes on the floor grew.

His tongue was working its way down my body when he stopped. I was so caught up in feelings I didn't know I was capable of feeling that it took me a second to register its absence. As he pulled away from me, I could feel the ghost of heat on the flesh that he'd just touched.

'My head,' he said.

'Are you okay?'

'Just these headaches that come on sometimes. I'm sorry.'

'It's fine.' I ran my hands through his hair, hesitant at first, but also obsessed with the softness of his curls.

'It affects my sinuses too. I feel underwater, like I'm drowning.' He sat up and leaned forward, head between his knees. 'Would you mind fetching me some water?'

'Of course, no problem.' I walked the short distance to the sink in the corner and returned with a full 'World's Best Granddaughter' mug.

'Do you mind if we just talk instead?'

'Talk?'

'Yeah. You know, that other thing we do with our mouths?' His smile was twisted into a grimace by the pain, but somehow he still looked cute.

'Oh, yeah, sure.' My fingers crept up to my lips and I fought the urge to bite my nails, the confidence I'd felt when I'd thought I only had to engage my body flooding out of me.

'Tell me a story.'

'Like a bedtime story?'

'Anything you want. I find it hard to sleep on nights like this. Especially now that I'm distracted by you as well as the pain.'

'I'm not sure I can think of anything.'

'That can't be true. Everyone's got at least one story to tell.'

'If you say so.'

'I do. In fact, I insist. And since I'm sick, you basically can't refuse me.'

'Can it be a spooky story?' I checked. 'Those were always my favourite when I was little and couldn't sleep.'

'Even better.'

'Well, in my home town we have this place called the witching stone. It's kind of a memorial to people – mostly women I guess – who were killed during the witch trials. People leave flowers there sometimes. A friend and I were making a documentary about it when we were in sixth year. But we'd been there a lot when we were wee, usually in the daytime, but one time we dared each other to sneak out and go at night. It was a full moon and my imagination was running wild, even though I kept telling myself everything would be fine. There were fresh roses by the stone and I bent to pick one up and as I did there was suddenly someone else there.' The words felt out of place in my mouth, like no part of my old home belonged in my new one. A branch scraped against my window, a sharp scratching sound making me jump. But George kept his eyes closed the whole time I spoke, helping me to continue to tell a story that had started somewhere else entirely.

'Go on,' he encouraged me.

'They turned around and it was like they were dripping wet and had no face in the dark. A lot of the women were drowned and if you squinted it looked like this person had just been dredged up from the depths.'

'"Dredged up from the depths". Nice touch. What happened next?'

'We ran away screaming. We were just scaring ourselves, we'd egged each other on so much with ghost stories. There was obviously no one there.'

'That you know of.'

'True, that I know of. But if there was someone there, they were probably just leaving flowers out of respect, and it just happened to be too dark to see them. We ran all the way to the sea, so fast that we almost fell off the end of the pier.'

'So, the real danger was the fear itself?'

'Wow, deep even when you have a migraine,' I joked, diverting the conversation away from any questions about what happened next or who my friend was. Although it had felt kind of cathartic to relive a memory of Cara, I wanted George to see the exterior I chose to present, not the messiness of my past. I was leaving that behind;

I wanted George to be a clear-cut and orderly part of my future.

'I have a story about witches too. I'll have to tell you some other time.' His breathing grew heavier and less ragged, and he rested his hand on top of mine. 'Yours was a good one though.'

The first imprint of light was pressing itself into the darkness by the time George fell asleep, his hair a halo on the pillow. I closed my eyes for a moment and woke up hours later with a cold, empty space next to me on the bed. My hair was tangled and the makeup Martha had applied so carefully the night before was smudged around my eyes. Looking in the mirror, I saw I looked good in the way that you only can when you don't try. I flashed myself my liberated canines and they looked like fangs. Though he was gone, George's jacket was still slung over my chair, smelling of sweetness and eau de cologne. My bare back leaned against it as I scribbled down all the details I could remember from the night before, giving them a life outside my brain so that nothing could escape me.

Week 4

Our eyes were red and our mouths yawning as we sat on the hard pews this morning. If our brothers and fathers could have seen us under last night's midnight sky, with the stolen wine from our cellars, frolicking among the trees, they would surely have said we were dancing with the devil. But we know better than that. Many of us have seen the devil, perhaps even felt his hand. And of all the things that our earthly bodies know, the most certain is that the devil does not reside among the leaves, or the grasses, or next to the pond with its waterfowl. Nor does he exist in the sway of the branches or the tangles of thorns at the end of the clearing. No, that is not where he lives at all.

'Oh, my god, he must be kind of embarrassed.' Martha stared up at the ceiling, her limbs spread out across the bedsheets that I hadn't changed after George had been there the night before.

'Don't tell Natasha, will you? And please definitely not Agatha?' I pleaded. I'd never done well with second-hand embarrassment – I absorbed other people's emotions too readily – and I hated to think of George bothered by something as prosaic as college gossip.

She flipped herself onto her front and looked at me until I looked down. Her chin rested on one hand, fingers tapping against her cheek. 'They're not that bad, you know. When I first moved to that school, I'd been having a pretty rubbish time and they both really took me under their wing. For Agatha, boarding school was a kind of escape from her parents who are always on the brink of divorce, so she got it.'

'Please,' I begged.

'Okay, I won't.' She threw her hands up in the air, although I sensed no hint of surrender in her voice. 'But I'm hurt that you felt you had to ask. I'll always keep your secrets, Iv.'

'It's not really a secret. It's just I don't want to … you know.'

'No, I don't know.' She wound a piece of hair around her finger, tributaries branching out from the slash of red that was her mouth.

'I don't want to hurt his feelings.'

'That's okay, Iv. It's okay to not want to hurt someone's feelings.'

'It's not because I actually like him or anything,' I said, not able to stop myself grinning.

Martha hit me with the pillow, its flimsy weight barely registering. 'Of course you like him!' Her eyes disappeared up towards her forehead for a moment. 'You'd be an idiot not to. I mean, we all fancy him a bit.'

We rarely hung out in my room. I was more of a natural guest than a host. Martha made the room feel cosier, lifting some of the chill as the days wended their way into November. I'd listened through brunch, the cacophony of laughs and shrieks, the tales of others' exploits, and sat on my own story. Squashing it, trimming it down to size just for her.

Getting her alone wasn't easy. Boys loved Martha, but girls loved her more. She was like a beacon of aliveness with her red hair and her volcano of a laugh, which erupted every couple of minutes. Everyone wanted a piece of her time, energy or approval. With both of us sat on my duvet, I spilled the story of how I had to put George to bed and not in a sexy way. But when it was out in the open, it festered a little. I wanted to reel certain parts of it back in, stuff them down my throat, keep them as mine.

'That sounds sweet,' Martha said when I'd finished.

'Does it? I didn't actually expect to get to know him. Not like that. Or not so soon anyway.'

'What did you expect? You've been fawning over him for days.'

'I wouldn't use that word. And only from afar,' I frowned. 'I didn't think we'd properly talk.'

'He's not an object. He's going to have a personality beyond those looks.'

'I know, I'm just not sure if I was weird or whether I said too much. I was nervous.' I almost added that I hadn't had much previous experience but I knew from Natasha and Agatha that Martha had been fighting off boys since the age of fourteen, and I didn't want her to think I didn't know what I was doing – or, worse, pity me.

'Said too much – that sounds very dramatic. It was a drunken chat, not anything life or death.'

'You're probably right. I just got to see a little more of him than I was expecting.'

'I'm definitely right. You're getting to know him. It's adorable, plus who knows where it might lead?'

I sighed, letting Martha's reassurance wash over me while the image of a strong, silent, gorgeous George snaked back into my mind. Until three precise raps sounded at the door. I opened it to reveal Primrose balancing a flask of tea on top of a thick pile of books.

'Where have you been? We missed you so much last night.' Martha stood, her pink laptop held close to her chest.

'I kept looking for you,' I agreed. 'It wasn't the same without you there.'

Prim scrunched her lips. 'Drank too much at pre-drinks. Sorry.'

'Well, I think we all know that feeling,' Martha said. 'Anyway, I actually have to go to the library, got to finish this essay on the history of the gaze and the nude.'

'Do you have to go?' I asked, trying to keep my voice even so that it didn't sound wheedling or desperate. 'I thought maybe we could hang out, just us three.'

'Don't tempt me to stay, Iv, or I'll never get anything done. Anyway, we'll be together again before you know it.' She touched her fingers to my shoulder and kissed the top of Primrose's head on the way out. Her hair stood up where Martha's lips had left it.

'So? How was your night?' Prim asked.

'It was good. I mean fine. Not as good without you. Obviously.' My words were awkward, my sentences segmented, as I struggled to keep my cheeks from flushing, remembering George's kisses and the force of the connection between our bodies until it was snapped by his headache.

She threw herself down on the duvet, the one with the elephants that I'd had since primary school, taking the spot that Martha had kept warm for her. 'What is it you're not telling me?'

I didn't say anything. Her eyes cast over the borrowed outfit still on the floor.

'Please tell me you're not sleeping with the enemy?'

When I thought about university, it was the learning that had enticed me. Yes, that's what every applicant says in their interview. But it was the chance to get out of my own head, to be somewhere else, to do something else. I'd loved Cara from the day we'd first met, but in the last few years I'd also had a sense that there were bigger things out there, things that we could both be a part of, together, even if that meant we had to loosen our bond just a little. Perhaps I could even become someone else, transforming myself one fact at a time, so that I gained so much knowledge that my past self became unrecognisable. Yet every time I opened a book, George, Martha or Primrose seemed to get in between the pages, and I'd have to force myself to read the same paragraph over and over again.

Harold's supervisions provided a prick of interest in the otherwise monotonous routine of reading dead men who used words that were too long in books that were too dusty with print that was too small. He was younger than any of my other supervisors and he read our work properly and wrote thoughtful comments in squiggly, spidery ink in the margins. He had no big name to trade off, only a couple of research papers where he was relegated to the dreaded *et al*, and a stack of notes for his thesis on his desk that dropped like confetti when disturbed.

'So, the Nuer, eh? What do we make of them?' Silence fell on top of the film of dust that coated the mismatched furniture.

'Evans. Pritchard.' Harold said the name like it was two words, no hyphen. 'Anyone? Any ideas what can hold a stateless society together?' Aggie had been up late in the college bar the night before, laughing at Freddie's jokes until last orders were called and boys were expected to vacate the college. Her blonde hair framed a look of boredom.

'Well, for example, we could conceive of a drinking society as what comes to fill the gap in an acephalous society,' Harold went on and Agatha's head snapped up. 'In this fine establishment, we see that in colleges where the senior tutor or the various college officials don't exercise much control over the student body, there come to be other mechanisms through which order – or disorder – are enacted.

So, instead of the blood feud, we have various drinking societies with their various rituals, like scheduled fights. This could be conceived of as a kind of way of ensuring that there is a degree of organized chaos, an outlet for frustrations, yet one with enough consequences so that no one ever pushes the boundaries too far. Broadly, it works to ensure that the status quo gets maintained without there being too much collateral damage committed in order to maintain it. Except of course for those who do end up being collateral. If someone wrote this kind of example in an exam, I think they might do very well. It's very imaginative, not to mention topical.'

'What do you know about drinking societies?' Agatha eyed Harold, looking him up and down. I tried to see things through her eyes, imagining the way his crumpled collar and odd socks would look to someone as put together as Agatha.

'I'm not as old as all that, now. I can still remember my youth – just about.'

'Were you a part of one?' I asked.

'Perhaps once. That's a story for another time. But I have a different view of them now.'

'What is your view?' I pressed on, keen for any information, especially coming from a different angle.

'All that glitters is not gold, girls.' The ticking of the clock grew louder, the hands snapping together, signalling our time was almost up. Agatha opened her mouth to say something but then closed it and started to pack her laptop into her purple leather satchel. She was out of the door and down the spiral staircase before I even had a chance to arrange my face so it looked like I wanted to chat to her.

'Ivy, don't forget about the witchcraft project you mentioned when it comes to making decisions about topics for long essays. I'd love to read it,' Harold said. 'Agatha's going to be working with a political economist friend of mine on a paper on trade negotiations but if you want to go down this route, I'd be very happy to supervise you for your coursework. There might be some interesting connections to the modern-day university and stateless societies in there, too. Witchcraft is all about ritual and community, after all. Who's in and who's out. What kind of knowledge is forbidden and what is permissible. That kind of thing. I'm just thinking out loud, you'd have to do the research, obviously.'

'I've been making some notes about the drinking societies, actually. It helps me understand them, and it's interesting.' I'd been starting to think that maybe researching and writing were the things I truly loved about telling stories. Being in front of the camera had always been Cara's thing and, in a new place, I finally had a bit of space to explore mine – even if that came with the odd stab of guilt.

'Have you really? Well, I look forward to hearing more as the terms wear on.' He shuffled papers on his desk, trying to make some order out of the mountains of books, notes and stationery. I'd turned to go when he spoke again, startling me enough that I spilled my pens across the rug.

'You're not part of a drinking society, are you?'

'No, sir.' My hands scrambled to pick up my things as I cursed myself for adding the 'sir' like I was still in school.

'That's good to hear. Take care, Ivy.' I wanted to ask why that was good to hear but he'd already bundled me out of the door with a cheerful smile.

Out in the grey, cold air, the smell of warm pastries from a nearby café was enough to tempt me from going straight home. In the queue, tourists with big smiles and even bigger cameras mingled alongside other fresh-faced students and a pair of elderly male professors in tweed suits. I waited ten minutes, all the while shivering and trying to decipher whether Harold – who might not have been old exactly, but who'd told us he was engaged and owned a semi-detached house in the city – could know something worth knowing about the societies.

'What do you want?' The waitress who was about the same age as me gave me a bored look when I eventually got to the front.

'A raspberry Danish,' I said, without thinking about it. As she handed it over, I began to lose my appetite – if I hadn't felt rushed I would have chosen something else – but I still forced the pastry into my mouth as I sat outside the café. It felt like eating a memory. They'd been Cara's favourite and we used to grab them on the way to school sometimes. I'd started to get friendly with the girl who worked in the café we went to, chatting and laughing each time we went in, until Cara told me that she'd called me a weirdo behind my back.

As the sugar washed over me, Harold's words wouldn't

let me go. He'd been critical of the drinking societies, but it sounded like he'd also got to be a part of one. Perhaps craving being part of a whole lessens once you know it's achievable. But if there were secrets to belonging and community that the societies knew, then I wanted to know them too.

The sweetness got too much after I'd eaten about half the Danish and I shoved the rest in my bag. After I'd licked my fingers clean, I went to unlock my bike from the bridge where I'd left it. The thoughts that were still whirring in my mind made me clumsy, and I managed to scrape my thumb. My obscenities startled a serene family of swans on the river and as I tried to shake the pain away, droplets of blood fell, spattering one of last spring's cygnets with red.

It was just a small nick really, but any kind of injury – however tiny – made me squeamish. When I was small, Mum had always told me to look away when she bandaged my cuts, back in the before-times where I thought that all wounds were visible. The ones I could see made me feel sick, but at least they were obvious. By the time I got to college, I was feeling faint enough to almost miss the note in my pigeonhole as I rushed to go and write down all my thoughts sparked by the supervision.

Sorry, Ivy. You were an excellent nurse – but I'd prefer it if you got to be the sexy kind, not the actually useful kind. Let me make it up to you?

P.S. Plus, I think I left my jacket in your room.

A number was scrawled at the end of the note, right where I'd managed to leave a small bloodstain. It wasn't signed but it didn't need to be. I tucked it into the inside pocket of my rucksack, not ready to share it with anyone just yet.

It wasn't really that much of a secret given that half the college had seen me leave the club with George. But he had a way of making you feel special, like you were in on something together. The way we kept colliding, it felt like luck – or perhaps something deeper – was on my side. That day, I walked over the dead grass, the sticky pastry not nearly the sweetest thing in my bag.

The sun was hanging low in the sky, threatening to disappear any minute and take the last vestiges of warmth with it. We'd found a bench in the orchard away from the hustle of college, which had a dedication to the Saint Clair sisters, whoever they were. I always read dedications after Dad got a bench for Grandma near her favourite stretch of beach, imagining people's lives and judging how much effort had been put into the wording.

'Poor boy, he's been left hanging. Bet he's not used to that,' Martha sighed. We were huddled together for warmth, Martha's hands and mine entwined and wrapped inside my scarf to keep the chill off.

'He's the one who left my room without saying goodbye,' I protested.

'He probably wanted to leave you to your beauty sleep. You do look very angelic when you're sleeping,' she added.

'How do you know that?' I asked, glad that my hood was up so it would hide my blushes.

'You're always drifting off when we stay up late.'

'Am I?'

'It might be good for him to wait. He's probably never waited for anything in his life.' Primrose snuggled in closer so that there was hardly a centimetre of space in between our bodies.

'I'm just not sure about it,' I replied. The few days between receiving George's note and dissecting it with Primrose and Martha had been enough to make me start to worry about all the ways any date could go wrong. Like a lot of things in life, boys had always seemed easier – and safer – in theory than in practice. 'On the one hand, obviously he's – well, George. And on the other—'

'Why wouldn't you want to go out with him?' Martha cut across me. 'Anyone would.'

'Not me,' Prim said. Beneath her boot, a rotting apple collapsed in on itself with a squelch as she stamped her feet up and down.

'Yes, but that's because you don't date men,' Martha said.

'Why aren't you interested in him, Marth?' I asked. It was a question that had entered my mind when I'd seen them sit side by side at the exchange, limned by light, looking cherubic and regal at the same time.

'Oh, I don't know. He's like a lot of people I've known in the past. And he seemed really into you so quickly. Plus, I technically have kissed him when we were kids – remember that game of kissing tag I told you about, Iv.'

She shuddered involuntarily. 'I'm getting cold, can we go in soon?'

'Just a little longer. I can hardly feel my toes but I love the light at this time.' Prim gazed out towards the college woods, the dying, dappled sunshine strewn over the tree-tops like glitter.

'Well, if you insist on us sitting out here freezing, I'm going to accept George's proposal on Ivy's behalf.' Martha grabbed my phone without asking but I didn't protest. I liked the way her long nails clacked on my screen and the smudged fingerprints she left behind.

'I honestly do think you're much more special than him.' Prim patted my knee but didn't turn her eyes away from the sunset. I silently disagreed – if I was as special as George I was pretty sure nothing bad would ever have happened in my life – but her words still filled me with a cosy warmth.

'There. It's sent.' Martha jabbed on the screen with triumph. I didn't know what was more exciting; the undis-guisable note of satisfaction in her eyes or the fact that I was going on a date. My first proper date. Even if it didn't go well, I had the best new friends in the world, I was sure of that. What could I possibly lose?

Everything exciting that year happened when I was wear-ing someone else's clothes.

When Martha opened the door, she gave me her look that said that I had been assessed and found wanting in some imperceptible way. She flew clothes around her room, bright pinks and greens and oranges – colours I would never normally wear – before settling on a wine-red dress made of stretchy material. Paired with my trainers, it looked like I'd made an effort but not too much.

'I'm just worried you'll be cold.' Prim fussed at the dress, adjusting the straps so it sat perfectly against my body.

'It's vintage, Prim, before you say anything.' Reaching up to the top shelf of her cupboard, Martha pulled down a fur coat and held it open for me to slip my arms into the sleeves. It was the softest thing I'd ever touched, an over-sized hug. My two new friends helping me get ready for a date felt like something out of a cutesy teen movie – Cara would have laughed at the cheesiness of it but I had no complaints.

'Don't do anything I wouldn't do.' Martha winked at me on my way out.

The moon lit up my walk to the restaurant, so full it seemed like it could burst and coat the whole world in its milky shine. One foot in front of the other, the cows mooing in the gloaming, my pace quick enough to keep any anxiety from flowering in my brain. It only took fifteen minutes to get there but it was a part of the city I hadn't been to before; my life had become confined to a few square miles and a whole different world.

George stood outside a rustic stone building, wearing chinos and a tight-fitting shirt. He was looking in the other direction as I arrived so that, for a moment, I got to stare unobserved at his chiselled face. The sound of the river obscured his greeting, and I was left with the warmth of his embrace in the absence of his voice. Inside, we were ushered towards a table next to a roaring fire, taxidermy heads of animals – mostly deer – looming over us.

'What made you choose this place?' The menu was long but George was already laughing with the waiter and ordering a host of dishes for us to try. Growing up, we'd never eaten out much. I was out of my depth in a fancy restaurant but something about his presence made me feel at ease. Maybe the sheer force of his confidence could rub off on me a little.

'I went here with my mum on the day of my interview,' he explained. On the day of my interview, I'd travelled alone and stayed overnight in one of the rooms usually reserved for conference guests, the heron outside the window my only company. 'My parents actually went on their first date here.'

'Really? Is this your lucky charm then?'

'Well, it certainly turned out all right for them. For a while at least. Now my mum gets sick of how much we have to move around for my dad's job.'

'I would have loved to move around when I was younger. Nothing ever happened where I lived.' As soon as I said it, I realized it was a ridiculous thing to say – something enormous had happened and I would have lived another ten decades of boredom to reverse it.

'But did you get to have friends?' George's question jolted me back into the room.

'I had one.'

'See. You got to make a friend and keep them. That would

have been such a luxury for me. My brothers are both a lot older than I am so I was a pretty solitary kid. At least my mum got the parties and the jet-set lifestyle. You don't really care about that when you're eight.' The flickering candlelight cast his features into darkness for a moment. 'But enough about me. Tell me about where you're from.'

'Oh, there's nothing interesting to say about it. It's just a small town.' I shifted in my seat, the conversation already more penetrating than I was comfortable with.

'Come on. It can't be that boring considering that story you told me about the witching stone. What's it like?'

'It's by the sea. Like, really, the sea rules the place. And that suited me for a long time – maybe it sounds a bit woo-woo but ever since I was a child I felt this connection to water. It's a bit touristy in summer but then everyone leaves around the end of August. That's when I like it best. Liked, I guess.' I placed my hands under my thighs to stop me chewing on my nails.

'I understand. When we lived in Thailand – that's where I was born – I used to hate all the touristy bits that Westerners flocked to. My aunty and my cousins live on this quiet island, and that's always my favourite place to visit. What about your family? Do they get on?'

'Martha says my parents should be the perfect match because of their star signs – she got us to tell her all our parents' birthdays.'

'Oh, god, please tell me you're not into astrology.'

There was no time to reply before Freddie appeared out of nowhere, with a bored-looking blonde girl in tow. His smile towards me was real but fleeting, before he turned his attention towards George, where it remained.

'Is it all right if we join you?' he asked, signalling the waiters to pull over extra chairs.

The rest of the dinner passed in a rush of popping corks, extra-loud laughter and risqué jokes. George's presence next to me was solid – there was nothing flimsy or slippery about him. I knew precisely who he was, his contentment written all over his face. I leaned against his shoulder, feeling his muscles through his checked shirt, the comforting bulk of him against me. We were back on the safe ground of the present. Everything was easy. Nothing required thought.

As the dessert bowls were cleared away, I reached into my bag to pull out my purse before George waved me away.

'Relax. This is on me.' Mum had taught me never to let a man think that he can buy you but she wasn't there and I wasn't going to make a fuss over something I wasn't even sure I believed in. Besides, there was something comforting about the sense of being looked after that I'd missed over the last few years of Mum being Mum, Grandma getting older and then Cara.

Getting out into the moonlight was a balm, the air fresh and scented with soil and leaf mulch. Freddie and the blonde girl left in the opposite direction and George and I walked back in a comfortable, satiated silence, the silhouette of my college growing larger against the starry sky. The silver sucked out the pale yellowness of the bricks, leaving the buildings grey with a few windows providing eyes of light, like the college's skeleton was exposed. We slunk past the night porter who rolled her eyes but gave us a long-suffering smile, snuck past the bar, which still had stragglers in it, and raced up the stone staircase to my room.

'Did you know this place is haunted? The story I was going to tell you was about this coven here.' His voice was breathy, almost girl-like, with a hint of nervousness. I leaned in to kiss him and we sank into the bed, legs tangling together to close the space in between our bodies. 'It's where the girls' drinking society got its name, I think.'

Outside, an owl hooted but otherwise the college was silent like every single being was asleep apart from the two of us. In the quiet, punctuated only by our heavy breathing, thoughts of other bodies threatened to flood my brain. I forced myself to focus on George, on the way he made me feel both comfort and possibility. I wanted ease, I wanted goodness to rush through my body, I wanted him. I kept on driving myself into him, until his words died down and he began to undress me, with fingers at first gentle and then frantic. When he put his arms behind my back, something about the way his skin touched mine made me shiver, igniting memories of cold, crisp mornings hundreds of miles and another lifetime away.

I shut my mind to my past and let myself sink into what was right there in front of me, my nails digging into George's flawless skin. I already had too many ghosts. I wasn't looking for any more.

Week 5

Even in winter, we dance. Our feet are forever raw the next morning but in the snatches of night we don't feel them. In those moments, we are sky and earth, light and moon. There are no words to describe us. We reach for them – oh, how we reach – but even the beauty of our chants cannot capture the way our bodies melt, move, become one. In those moments, we have no pain, even as the ground bites into us. We barely have bodies at all. We trust this place – the one place we can be free. We trust that no serious harm can come to us. It is but a scratch, sister, we tell one another, if we see each other in the daylight, and see marks upon our flesh.

I read once that people only believe in relationships if they get why people are drawn to each other on a deeper level. Apparently, it's not enough for two people to be attractive, available and near each other at the same time. All I can say is that person must not have gone to university.

Things move fast in college. It acts like an oak-panelled pressure cooker. Two days after our first date, I saw George again, this time at his college. The buildings were made of slate-grey stone and there was stained glass everywhere, creating pool after pool of tiny rainbows. Walking on the grass was forbidden, so he led me round the edge of the squares, pointing out statues of famous men and families of swans floating by on the river. There were boys every-where – some of whom I recognized from the exchange, all of whom seemed pleased to see George and by exten-sion gave me friendly greetings as well – but there were girls too. The boys weren't looking at them the way they looked at us, in our space where they would never fully belong. It was like the girls had lost their power, and were just shadows scuttling past, clutching laptops and books, their heads cast downwards among the masculine whoops and shouts.

Up four flights of tightly wound stairs, George's room was bare, clean and tidy. Even though there weren't that many intimate traces of him, my body still felt a little out of place. It was the first time I'd ever been in a boy's room when my courage wasn't fuelled by alcohol. I picked up one of the family photos on the marble mantelpiece to take a closer look at the dark-haired woman with impeccable makeup who had her arm around George but I put it down again quickly – I didn't need to know any of his past or his complications.

'What's the tie for?' Green and yellow, it hung on the back of his chair next to the jacket that he'd remembered to take back from my room.

'Oh, it's the Dragons' tie. We've got another dinner later this week. It's boys only this time I'm afraid, though.'

'That's a shame.' I meant it. Getting George alone felt like winning a prize, but there was a pleasure in being out in public with him too and the way people looked at us together.

'It is. Because it's in a private social club near the history library that I'd like to show you. There's some beautiful art there, I think you'd enjoy it.'

'Next time maybe. I'd love to see more places in the city. The building we were in for the exchange was incredible.'

'Incredible? Did you think so? Good columns, I suppose.'

'Good columns? I love that that's what you noticed.'

'I'm a sucker for ancient history, what can I say?'

'I guess that's a good trait for a historian to have.'

'That it is. That's what I want to specialize in, really. Next year, I should be allowed to drop modern and medieval.' He gestured to me to come sit with him on the bed. My mattress wasn't bad but I could tell immediately that his was definitely comfier. I made a mental note to tell the others later – the older girls were always griping that we were hard done by as a women's college. Maybe they had a point.

'Have you been initiated yet?' I asked.

'No, that's still to come.'

'Are you excited?'

'Like I said, these boys are family to me, so it's just legitimizing what's already there. Kind of like getting married.'

'Cute. Do you know when initiations will happen?'

'Sometime soon but Freddie and Eddy are in charge.' He paused, his brow creasing. 'Why are you asking so many questions about the Dragons anyway? I thought we'd spoken about this already.'

'Just interested, that's all.' I gulped down my discomfort. Asking too many questions had got me into trouble before – I knew it annoyed people, so I'd tried to train myself out of it. Mostly I was successful, but sometimes if I got fixated on something it was hard to dampen myself down. 'Tell me about that story about the witches.'

'Oh, I was just going to tell you about your college's resident ghosts. But then pretty much every square inch of this place has some supernatural being attached to it.'

'It sounded like you were going to say something specific.' I needed a distraction from my faux pas but he had already moved on, slipping his hand inside my jumper to rest on my bare skin. My breath became shallow as he began to run his fingertips in light circles.

'I've got other things on my mind right now,' he said.

'Is that so?' I'd wanted details about the Dragons to add to my notebook but I settled for George's touch, the way his skin smelled like laundry detergent and honey, the gentle weight of his hands against my limbs.

'Yes, like spending time with my girlfriend.'

The word jolted into me, my eyes snapping open. But George was too busy nuzzling into my neck to notice. The mirror on the wall behind us showed our bodies entwined, not a millimetre of space between his golden skin and my pasty whiteness. We looked like the perfect couple, complementing each other. I kept on staring as he worked kisses down my torso, the sensation of his mouth never fully computing. I was a statue and his lips were moulding me. Into what I wasn't quite sure but I knew that we were greater than the sum of our parts.

Week 6

We saw our sister with the man today. She will no longer be allowed to read this book, nor contribute to it. Not until we know her intentions. If we had seen her with a man in society, at church, or on a chaperoned visit to some stifled garden they call nature, we would have understood even if we had not approved. But we saw her in the woods. Perhaps she thought we would not see her in the light of day as we are usually forced to restrict our visits to the witching hours.

But we did.

We see everything.

I never knew the city the way I knew it with George. When I was by Martha's side, I saw the bars where she knew all the staff, the boutiques where the labels had no prices on them, the shortcuts through alleyways as she led me to party after party. With Prim, I saw the libraries – we were trying out the one for each faculty, the tea rooms with comfy chairs and wedges of vegan sponge, the start of walks we promised each other we would do together in the summer each time we passed them on the way back from a study date.

On the best days, these two worlds would meet and the three of us would rush towards some deadline together, our stress and expectation sharpened into swords only to find the enemy was made of paper when we got there, collapsing into heaps of giggles, high off each other's company. Agatha and Natasha pierced our bubble occasionally, but for the most part, we were a triptych. We made promises to each other that I can barely remember now, soft paper chains tying us all together.

With George, day and night were combined – not a binary but a seamless mass of material, waiting to have pleasure wrung out of it. More than any anthropology essay on cognitive universals, he showed me how time was a construct. When he was talking about rugby or his family, five minutes was an hour, but when he was trying to teach me to cycle with no hands, sixty minutes passed in the time it took for him to reach my side whenever I wavered and looked like I was going to topple. The seriousness of exam term seemed like a distant prospect in the way things only can when you've never experienced them before. The days were short and cold, but we snatched every moment from them, breathing our breath into dragon swirls, chasing down the evenings where our bodies intertwined under my single duvet.

Essays were slipped into corners, twisted scraps of time in the morning after sleeping in, or late at night when I wasn't in the company of George, Martha or Primrose. Words came out of my fingertips without me thinking, the excitement of finishing an assignment and getting back to my new friends keeping me going. I got comments from supervisors like *lots of raw potential, needs some polishing!* And *A proper scholar knows how to reference. Please look up Harvard or APA for your next submission. Some good work though.* Harold tried to catch my eye at the end of our tutorial on the concept of anomie but I slipped out ahead of Aggie, taking the uneven steps on the spiral staircase two at a time so that I was dizzy by the time I got out into the chilly fresh air.

Agatha and I didn't talk during supervisions or in lectures but we found an uneasy peace as the days bore on, drilling a tunnel of light towards the Christmas holidays. The highlight of the term was supposedly the Christmas formal before everyone dispersed to their various family homes. Each girl was allowed to bring a plus one, and obviously I was bringing George. The idea of sitting next to Martha, Primrose and him, under twinkling lights with the choir singing carols behind us, kept me awake at night. The image was so perfect that sometimes I couldn't breathe. I couldn't even think beyond that point – couldn't imagine what life waited for me outside the city limits.

Martha passed me the eggnog as we sat in the common room, making decorations for the formal. The boys were there too, wearing Christmas jumpers and generally not helping very much. But we didn't mind. Their presence made the event an occasion, elevating the everyday in a way that only outsiders and unfamiliarity can.

'Be careful not to spill the glitter,' Natasha fussed, in her role as Entertainment Society Decorations Officer.

'We're only doing this as a favour to you, Nat. Don't be bossy.' Agatha was surrounded by silver and gold paper chains, glinting like shackles. 'God, I'm not cut out for arts and crafts. You really should know that after almost fifteen years of friendship.'

'It's fun, don't worry.' I squeezed Natasha's hand. It was true – I liked having work to do with my fingers, something to use them for other than the half-formed ideas I wrote down in snatched pockets of time about witchcraft and drinking societies.

George stoked the fire, its crackles mostly hidden by the sound of the wind whipping against the trees outside. It was a job that a girl would do in the absence of a boy – how else would we have kept it lit? – but whenever there was a boy present they took over the duty without question. Perhaps they thought we were always cold when they weren't there.

Officially, Halloween had been and gone but every holiday had a long shelf life at the university and there were still remnants of a pumpkin lying on a coffee table, alongside some blood-smeared sheets, which had probably once been a costume.

'I didn't get a proper fright this year,' Martha pouted.

'What about that scary story you started telling me the other night?' I squinted up at George's face, his features hard to distinguish in the dim light.

'I'm not sure you were really in the mood for a story that night,' he smirked.

'I'm listening now.' I pushed forward, ignoring the

hidden currents of his words, how he'd wanted to pull us together towards further closeness with the memory of our tangled bodies. That kind of heat wasn't something that felt safe to stir when we were with other people. Anything that had the potential to spiral out of control – even in a good way – was something to be compartmentalized.

'It was about the Saint Clair Sisters,' he obliged.

'Who?' I asked.

'They were a group of three sisters who were executed hundreds of years ago. People say their other sister was the one to report them.'

'Report what? Why were they executed?' Prim perched on the edge of the sofa, her hands twisting round each other.

'For supposedly being part of a coven, I think,' George said. 'They had connections to this college so I thought you might have heard of them already.'

'That's what the plaque in the woods is for. And they're the same women who that bench in the orchard is dedicated to.' The realization slipped out of my mouth before I could stop it. Talking about my academic interests with Harold was one thing, but delving into the details of witch trials out loud felt a little close to home.

'Didn't you say something about possibly being related to the women on that plaque?' Prim frowned at Martha.

'Huh?' Martha looked spaced out and it took her a moment to catch up. 'Oh, yeah. Well, Mum said it. I don't know if it's true. She got really into family history for a bit when she was between boyfriends. I didn't know they'd all been murdered though. The women, not the boyfriends, I mean.'

'Actually, a lot of the older families can trace their lineage back to one or more of the original founding families of the university. The Saint Clairs were an important family back when this place was more of a theological college than what we'd think of as a university.' The light from the flames flickered against George's face, his drawling voice punctuated by the last splutters of once magnificent trees.

'How do you know so much about this?' This version of George who knew a good deal about the history of the university, who could speak in long sentences about tiny details, wasn't one he'd let me see before. He was reading history and he liked to listen to podcasts about ancient Rome when he was working out but his degree usually seemed to come after everything else – rugby, the Dragons, drinking, hanging out with me. Part of me was drawn to George's depths and intricacies, and another part of me was quite happy playing in his shallows where I knew I was safe from any undertow.

'My middle name is Saint Clair. It's a family name on my dad's side.' He shrugged. 'My mum's into genealogy stuff too. She told me there might be a connection but who really knows.'

'George Saint Clair Svenson.' The name rolled around in my mouth. It seemed overly long but pleasant to say. 'Does that mean in some distant way you're related to each other?'

'You guys do have similar energy,' Natasha said as she glanced up from where she was sitting adding red glitter to sprigs of holly. George and Martha both rolled their eyes but I caught the flash of a smile between them, gone before I had the chance to feel jealous that I wasn't included.

As the conversation meandered away from witches, it was a struggle to stay alert in the cosy comfort of the room. My gaze was unfocused and blurry when something slammed against the window, jolting me back into the moment with a sudden violence. Natasha screamed. George gripped my hand so tight that it hurt. My eyes sharpened enough to see a lumpen shape sliding down the glass, all feathers and blood.

My feet slopped around in unlaced shoes as we ran out into the dark to see a bird of prey – a buzzard maybe, I wasn't sure – tangled in an unnatural heap on the frozen ground. Grandma Olive had taught me to identify birds but I was a bit rusty. It was dead but pristine, moonlight catching on its talons. George put his arm around me, squeezing my shoulder, his fear transformed into solid reassurance. The others turned towards the door to escape the cold.

'We can't just leave it there,' I protested. My voice was scratchy and tears were forming in my eyes. The bird had obviously been in its prime. I could taste bitterness in my throat that it had died just because it was in the wrong place at the wrong time. It had made just one fatal error – not noticing a window – but it didn't matter that it was only a momentary lapse. Some mistakes can't be undone.

'Poor thing,' Prim murmured, reaching out to the body to check that it was definitely dead, and giving me a slight nod to confirm it.

'We can. Something else will eat it.' Martha's mouth was set, her face full of facts, not emotions. 'I'm getting tired anyway.' She yawned with effect and whatever spell had descended upon us broke. A haar set in as the others started to shuffle away, leaving the unfortunate body to the mist.

'I'm sorry,' I muttered and followed them inside.

'I still have chills.' Martha hung off the bannister on the way up to her room, her glossy hair a cascade of red. George, Freddie and Eddy had cycled off into the fog and we'd slipped out of the common room to leave Natasha and Agatha to pick up sequins off the floorboards. Saying goodbye to George wasn't so disappointing when I had an evening with Prim and Martha ahead of me.

'It's probably the cold air,' Prim said. 'It's halfway to December and all you're wearing is a crop top and a cardigan which is more hole than anything else.'

'That level of criticism sounds like my mum, Prim.' Martha pulled the cardigan tighter, arms taut around her waist. 'It wasn't just that the story was spooky, it's that I felt something too. I don't know how to describe it.'

Primrose looked at me as Martha unlocked her door, a look which wanted to envelope me and hold me tight. I didn't like it, and fixed my eyes on the floor, which needed cleaning. I wanted us to be a trinity always. I knew how easily things could break apart if you didn't smooth over cracks as soon as they appeared.

'Marth, what the hell is that smell?' My coughs were uncontrollable as an earthy scent hit the back of my throat.

'It's sage.' She waved her elegant hands to waft it around the room. A small plastic bag of supermarket herbs sat on the desk next to some discarded underwear.

'Why sage?' I opened my mouth to speak and started spluttering again. 'Aren't you supposed to burn it dried?'

'I read about it online. It wards off bad spirits or something.' She shrugged but I could see her smile in the mirror, creeping upwards.

'You should have put it out properly. It could have started a fire while you were out.' Prim opened the window an inch and cold air fought its way in.

'You're the one who seemed so interested in witchcraft.' Martha wiped the smile away with her hand as she turned back to face us.

'I was interested in the persecution, the history,' Prim retorted.

'Are you staying with us tonight, Iv?' Martha asked, switching the subject away from herself.

'Of course. Why wouldn't I be?' Prim flopped onto the bed where Martha nuzzled into her body, legs folding around each other at odd angles. Martha patted the space next to her and I joined them, our limbs crisscrossing on the tiny bed. My body combined with George's had made a circle, a closed loop, but as a pile of girls we made an abstract, messy shape.

'So you're not going to abandon us for George, then?' Prim said. I baulked, about to reply that I only really hung out with him when she and Martha weren't free, but as soon as the defence came into my brain I wasn't sure it was true. There'd been times where I'd just wanted the ease of his body, the sheer physical release of him to ground me in that city. Somehow he was always there right when I wanted to see him most. Exactly when I needed my mind taken off things – essays, supervisions, the past – he'd appear.

'Obviously not.' I tried to keep the edge of hurt from my voice. There was fear in there too – I didn't ever want Primrose or Martha to be unaware of how much they meant to me, even if I wasn't prepared to explain the ins and outs of why that was. 'This is for ever.'

'Oh, god, don't be so cheesy,' Primrose said, but she was laughing, pleased with herself, with us.

'Let's drink to that, to us three. I've got some pink fizz chilling on the windowsill – didn't want to put it in the fridge in case it got nicked.' Martha leaned out the window – a little too far for my liking – and pulled the bottle inside, popping its cork easily. The wine was as sugary as cheap pick-and-mix sweets. It tasted like the first sleepover where you manage not to cry for your mum, like going too high on the swings in the park, like the first swim of the year. We giggled over nothing that evening, every word funny after the seriousness of dead sisters and mangled birds.

'It's okay, I don't need sage. I've got you two to keep me

safe.' Before Martha could blow out all her candles, a gust of wind rushed down the chimney and killed each point of light. We fell asleep in each other's arms. Unlike when I was a child and something had frightened me, I had no nightmares. In fact, I had no dreams at all.

There were different bits of college artwork hung in all our rooms, probably because there was nowhere else to store them. My walls were bare apart from a mediocre water-colour – nowhere near as good as the ones Grandma Olive used to paint to brighten up my childhood bedroom – of the front of the college back in the fifties. The painter had used the wrong shade of yellow for the brickwork but I liked that you could see ivy crawling up the building and that the tree where I met Martha was visible in the back-ground. In the library, there were three small portraits of a pale woman with brown hair and a slightly severe expression standing against various countryside scenes, including one of tiny saplings in bud. I'd never examined them closely before but when procrastinating from my essay about hunter-gatherer societies, I saw the gilded frames bore the inscription *Millicent Saint Clair*.

I couldn't let it go and neither could Primrose once I'd shown her. We were both drawn to the dark, twisty bits of history, even if sometimes they scared us. The next time George visited, we snuck him into the library just before closing time. Being a place of study for the girls of the col-lege, boys really had no business being there, and George's heavy footsteps echoed up to the rafters.

'Are you trying to get the head librarian to come over?' I hushed him.

'This is just how I walk. I can't be any quieter.'

'You definitely could.'

'Stop it, you two,' Prim hissed. 'You're making nearly as much noise telling him off, Iv.'

'Why am I here anyway, if you're both so worried about it?' George asked, not without interest.

'Because of this.' I held out my arm to stop him. 'Is this one of the sisters you were talking about?'

'Millicent. Yes. That rings a bell.' He peered at the painting and I got a momentary glimpse of what he might look like as a man in middle age, still full of passion but his edges softened.

'Do you know anything more about her?' Prim stood on her tiptoes to look over George's shoulder.

'She was the only surviving woman in her family. Her younger sisters – they were triplets, I think – were all executed, like I told you the other night. The sisters wanted to study, to learn like men. Even, some say, to go to university. Though as I said, it would have been more like a theological college at that time. Her brother, John – there's a picture of him in the dining hall of my college – was one of the first scholars to really think about university in a more secular way. Millicent informed on her sisters.'

'What were their names?' I whispered, hoping George would emulate me and keep his voice down.

'I don't know. There were three of them, and they were very young. That's all I know.'

'Why aren't there more paintings of Millicent if she's so infamous?' I asked.

'Plenty of terrible people to hang on the walls of this place, I imagine.'

'Maybe in the mixed colleges but not here,' I persisted. 'All the women who went here were worthy do-gooders. Nurses, governesses, people like that.'

'I didn't know you were such a history buff.' Prim looked impressed. I should have been happy that she, George and I had a shared interest but all I could focus on was the squirming feeling in my stomach. 'Kind of annoying though that it has to be a man to tell us all this. Why isn't there more information about this around college? I never made the connection that it actually happened here.'

'But I told you about the plaque in the woods,' I said. Prim wasn't listening to me – her hands made wild gesticulations like they did whenever she was fired up. It was as if I'd never spoken.

'How could she do that to her own sisters? I can't imagine anything worse than Lola being hurt. And if I was the cause of it—' She shuddered. 'How could any woman do that to another woman?'

'They say Millicent had a passion for witch-hunting – she was very religious, very devout,' George said. 'And when she found out that her sisters were practising in a coven, reading and writing spells and such, she reported them and they were all drowned. That's the official version of events, anyway. Some other accounts say it wasn't as clear-cut as that.'

'Drowned?' My voice came out as a squeak, like I was one of the mice that I sometimes heard running along the rafters of the library.

'Yes, I told you that already,' George replied.

'You said executed, not drowned.' It was as though water were pouring over me, making my voice strangled and my breath panicky. Before, water had felt like a friend, like I had an affinity with it, but ever since it had cheated me of Cara, I wasn't sure I could trust it anymore. Or myself near it.

'Does it matter? They kind of serve the same function. Now, shall we go to the bar before the librarian's head explodes?' George was right, her tuts were getting louder. But my mind had latched on, and I couldn't let it go quite yet.

'Drowned where? That little pond near where the plaque is?' I dug my nails into my palms, forcing myself to come back into my body and calm down.

'I don't know for certain,' he said. 'The plaque that you mentioned before in the woods? I'm not sure but it's possible.'

'But I met Martha by the tree there,' I said.

'So?' George's eyebrows were raised, and it annoyed me that he looked a little amused.

'So.' A million different reasons danced on my tongue – all of them obvious, I thought. Because Martha couldn't be sullied. Because I didn't like that she'd even stood on the spot where something terrible had happened. Because the past unnerved me. 'It's just weird, that's all.'

'It's not weird. It's fascinating. There's so much more to this place than I knew. Thanks, George.' Prim patted his arm, the way you would a child who's spelled a complicated word correctly.

'No problem. I wrote an essay last week about women as persecutors in history so I've just brushed up on all this stuff.'

'Do you feel a connection to them?' I asked, not caring about his essay.

'To who?' George said.

'The sisters. Because of your middle name.'

'It's just a name, Ivy. It's a sad story but everyone probably has something tragic in their pasts if you look back far enough.' He put his arm around me and rubbed my shoulder, like he'd just revealed some evident yet upsetting truth and I was in need of comfort.

A bell rang. I jumped, knocking George's hand away.

'The library is closing in five minutes. Please, everybody out.'

As we stepped outside, we were hit by flurries of snowflakes, caressing our skin like frozen kisses. George whooped and stooped to make a snowball. Primrose and I hung back to stare at our college, which had been transformed by the first snow of that winter. Some landed in my gawping mouth, a little drop of cold against my tongue. Everything was magical, picture-postcard perfect. So blindingly white it was like there'd never been any darkness.

Week 7

Tonight, we welcome new sisters. We welcome a sister we saw falling asleep on the unforgiving wood of a church pew. We welcome a sister we saw pinching her brother during a sermon so that she would have to leave to take the crying babe outside. We welcome a sister who tucks a blade into her stockings before she takes long turns in the countryside, alone. They do not yet know what we are about. Just that we are a group of ladies who gather as often as possible. We will show them, under the moon and the stars. We will show them, and once they have seen what can be, they will understand that their true lives will be lived out underneath the trees. Everything else will be a façade.

'Look what I found in our pigeonholes.' Martha burst into my room without knocking and chucked an envelope at me, too fast for me to catch. She loomed over me as I picked it up, her hair a red beacon framed by a low-energy light-bulb. The purple paper was sealed with a lipstick kiss and scented with sugary perfume.

'Our pidges, huh?'

'Yes, when I saw one in mine, I obviously had to check

yours too. I opened them as well just to make sure that they were what I thought they were.'

'And what was that?'

'Invites to initiations.' The triumph in her voice was undeniable. I ripped open the envelope and black glitter tumbled out onto the floor.

> *Dear ladies (and any non-binary friends),*
> *You are cordially invited to the annual initiations of the Coven. Wear your finest clothing and be prepared for the most fun, least PG-13 sleepover of your life (but don't tell the porters – or indeed anyone else! Seriously, we mean it). We hope you feel suitably excited at becoming part of a society that so many of your sisters have rejoiced in before you. Everything will be provided – don't worry about a thing. All will be revealed.*
> *Your presidents,*
> *Amina and Sophia*

Amina had been friendly enough to me since Freshers Week, saying hi to me in corridors and once lending me a pen in the library, but I'd had no idea she was co-president of the Coven. She and Sophia were often together, sitting close to each other in hall, the bar or the library and talking in hushed voices, but I'd never considered what they might be discussing.

'I didn't even know the Coven was definitely a real thing,' I said. 'Like, obviously it's been mentioned but it keeps itself so well hidden.'

'That's the exciting part! We're becoming part of the college's history, its secrets. The Coven really does hide itself, I don't think it has the luxury of operating semi-openly like the Dragons.' Martha was right, it was exciting, and its hidden nature made it even more so, no matter the reason behind it. Both of us couldn't keep the smiles off our faces.

'What about Primrose?' I frowned. She was the one detail I wasn't sure of.

'Don't worry. I chatted to Sophia about it at lacrosse practice and made sure she got one too.'

'That's not what I meant.' I hadn't doubted for a second that she would be invited. Although she was studious and sensible, she was also funny and beautiful – there was no way that any secret society would pass up on the chance of having someone as shiny as Prim as a member. 'Do you think she'll be up for this?'

'Of course. Why wouldn't she be?'

'I don't think she loves organized fun.'

'True. But she does love history. And even if she can't admit it, she hates not being involved in things. Trust me. She'll come.'

'I suppose she is interested in the witches. That must be where they get the name from, right?'

'Who cares? It's a great name. Doesn't matter where it came from.'

'I care,' I whispered but Martha was already showing me photos of dresses she might order for the night of initiations.

I nodded along but really I was focused on the weight of

the invitation resting in my hands. I'd thought I'd only be able to think about the societies from afar, or at best when I was hanging on to George's arm. Someone like Martha was a dead cert for initiation into the Coven but I didn't know if you needed connections or especially beautiful hair to get in. But if I was a part of it too, I had a chance to write in my diary about something that was a little bit forbidden and get closer to whatever it was that Harold had felt was worth warning us about. More than that, I had a chance to dig my fingers even further into the fabric of the town.

I didn't know for sure what I was working towards, squirrelling away memories and information, but it felt like a way of making sure nothing slipped through my fingers. By recording everything, all the tiny shimmering details of the societies and the dinners and of Martha and George and Primrose, I could make sure that it wasn't all a dream. That it wasn't something too good to be true.

The Christmas formal took the magic of that term – the newness, the breathlessness, the gorgeousness of it all – to a new level. When we walked into the dining hall, everyone fell silent for a moment – even the boys. The tree towered above us, freshly imported from Scandinavia, covered in twinkling lights and decorations in the college colours. The choir were singing carols and there were hundreds of candles everywhere, casting the whole room in a golden glow. George grasped my hand and squeezed as Martha leaned her head against my shoulder, her hair tickling my cheeks. Sandwiched between the two of them, I could close my eyes for a moment and breathe in this new world that I was a part of where everything good seemed attainable, and everything bad a distant possibility.

For once, I was wearing my own clothes. After Martha said how much the colour suited me, I'd bought a black dress from a charity shop as I cycled back from a comparative politics supervision where the professor had scrawled *pick a side to get a first* on the margins of my essay. The dress was covered in beads and sounded like rain when I moved. Everyone was even more dressed up than they would be for a usual formal – Agatha and Natasha both wore blue, Martha was wearing a purple velvet gown and Prim looked stunning in a dark green suit. There were distractions whichever way I looked.

The gong sounded and we shuffled over to our seats beneath the high table. Freddie sat to my right, pouring me wine, as the Mistress welcomed us and celebrated the successes of the term. She was a tall woman with silver glasses and a carrying voice who looked somewhat amused even when she was listing the mundanities of the lacrosse team's wins – only Martha and Sophia looked interested, and me by extension.

'And with that, I wish a good night to all, but particularly to our young ladies of the future.' We followed her in raising our glasses as servers started to pour out of the door to the kitchens with all kinds of dishes. A girl about our age, who I recognized from previous meals, placed some glazed carrots on our table. I thanked her but my voice was drowned out by the chatter.

The choir had finished singing, but the room was still loud enough that I could only properly hear the people next to me. Prim and Martha were further down the long table, enjoying each other's conversation without me. George was resting his hand on my knee while listening to Peter talk about water polo in the manner of a kindly uncle, indulging an overly talkative child. As I sat in silence, Freddie, sat on my other side, started to serve vegetables onto my plate with the look of someone who has something they want to say.

'So, the Coven. I hear things are afoot.' It wasn't quite a question but I could tell he was waiting for me to answer.

'How do you know about that?' I reached for the Brussels sprouts, hoping that it would add to my feigned indifference.

'Oh, I have my sources.'

'Can I ask what sources they are?'

'You can but I can't answer.'

'Can't or won't?'

'Doesn't really matter, does it? Dragons take their secrets to their grave and all that.'

'Is that some kind of motto?' I bit into a sprout. I'd thought that my new and sophisticated surroundings might have inspired a newfound love for the vegetable but they were still as disgusting as ever. 'The Dragons aren't all that secret.'

'Well, we get to decide who's in the know. You're one of the lucky ones. Anyway, back to the Coven and my sources.'

'I'm not sure if I believe you have any sources at all. I think you're just trying your luck. Probing me.'

'Huh.' He ran his eyes over me, then broke out into a grin. 'You're smarter than they give you credit for, Ivy Graveson.'

'Who's they?'

'Oh, no one in particular. It's just that I see you – you're like me. Observant.'

I sniffed, wanting to know more but not wanting to give Freddie the satisfaction of my curiosity. 'And what about the Dragons' initiations? When are they happening?'

'That's what I'm talking about, right there. I'll show you mine if you show me yours.'

'Don't let George hear you say that.' I kept my voice low but George was still giving Peter his full attention.

'Oh, come on. I'm only referring to a polite exchange of information.' He held his hands up, as if in surrender. 'I'm just interested is all. This college can be such a closed book.'

'I'm sworn to secrecy I'm afraid.' It felt good that it wasn't even a lie. Freddie was on the verge of speaking more but I was rescued by the arrival of the main course, which was enough to tear Peter away from his monologue and bring George back to me. His attention remained with me for the rest of the meal – physically, at least. Though he'd removed his hand from my knee to use his cutlery, he always found some point of contact between our bodies, even when he was laughing at someone else's joke or facing the other way.

As plates were cleared away and we were allowed to

rise, George beckoned me away from the group, into a shadowy spot where we were mostly hidden by the gigantic tree. He wiped his palms on the side of his suit, even though they'd always been dry whenever I'd held them.

'I got you something.' He reached into his pocket as the Christmas lights blinked away behind him.

'But we never discussed presents.' The note of dismay was hard to keep from my voice. 'I haven't got you anything.'

'Relax. I'm not expecting anything back. I just got this for you because I wanted to.' My lectures on reciprocity sprung to mind, particularly the way the middle-aged professor with curly hair had insisted there was no such thing as a true gift.

But the smile on his face was so genuine, so easy that my breathing slowed a little. The package that he pulled out of his pocket was an instantly recognisable colour. It was the stuff of a thousand manufactured dreams, a thousand adverts, a thousand things I'd never have been able to afford. Inside the box lay a silver chain, too small to be a necklace. It was a bracelet but it looked a bit like a dog collar.

'George, you absolutely shouldn't have.'

'Will it fit?' He picked it up, marking the metal with his fingertips. I knew it would – it had an adjustable clasp – but I held out my wrist and let him fasten it, feeling the chain tighten around the bone.

'You look lovely.' He brushed my hair behind my ear, his hands on my shoulders. There was something a little too serious, a little too sentimental in his gaze. It made me want to run. But he was already reaching for my hand again, and when his skin touched mine my brief panic seemed irrational – ridiculous, even. In the lonely months between school and university, I'd made silly romantic wishes for someone to sweep me off my feet and I was lucky that I'd found someone as coveted as George.

'There's something else too,' he said.

'Something else?' Martha and Primrose and everybody else were making their way out of the hall to the college bar. I wanted to be there too with George by my side, basking in the golden light.

'Yes. This – it's a bit silly, I suppose. Maybe that's not the right word. But I hope you like it. Sorry that it's an awkward shape. It was too floppy.'

He handed me the misshapen package, wrapped in thick paper. As I undid the tape, a small circle of white cloth fell into my palm.

'It's embroidery.' George loved explaining what was already there as if he could speak a thing into existence even more than it could do itself. I turned it over, peering at the garish mess of threads on its underside.

'You did this?'

'Yes. I remember seeing the ones you have in your room – by your grandma, you said?'

I nodded because I was too afraid to speak.

'Well, your room is a bit bare to be honest. I guess we have that in common.' He laughed in a way I hadn't seen before – I realized with shock that he was nervous. 'I thought it would be nice for you to have something to go with it. To make you feel more at home here.'

He could have got me a personalized college hoodie or a leather-bound notebook embossed with curly lettering. He could have had my initials etched onto the back of the bracelet. But he used his own hands to drag out an *I* and a *G* and surround them by wonky nondescript flowers on this piece of cloth. He couldn't have known just how at home his gift made me feel.

There were enough lights in the room – not to mention the crackling fire in the grand fireplace – to make it almost too warm, but it was like I'd been drenched in ice. The doily Cara made me to replicate Grandma Olive's embroidery was one of the last gifts she ever gave me, and even though I was surprised and touched by George's efforts it brought too much of my past into what should have been an evening all about the present. George was standing too close to me – I wanted to get away, out, to somewhere simple like an hour or a lifetime before. But I knew how it would look if I just left. It would lead to questions. To complications. So I let the sobs that were threatening to unleash themselves roll over me, salty water leaking down my cheeks.

'Iv, don't cry, it's meant to be something nice.' But George looked pleased with himself as he encircled me in his arms, nuzzling into my hair. I hid my tears as much as possible by leaning into his tall frame, and bit my lip to give me a tangible pain to focus on.

As soon as my eyes were dry, I straightened up. George

had fastened the bracelet too tight and it was digging into my flesh. But the night had started so sparkly and soft and it could continue that way, if only I could pull myself together and get George to pack his emotions away.

'Shall we join the others? We don't want to miss out on anything,' I reminded him. A blip of disappointment passed across his face, like a cloud momentarily blotting out the sun, but he recovered well, all affable smiles again in a moment.

'Whatever you want. Lead the way.'

My back slammed against the bookcase. A small shower of dust pitter-pattered onto my head but I didn't say anything. *Let him have this one*, I told myself.

It had been George's idea. 'Let's do it somewhere different,' he said, after we'd drunk glass after glass of the most perfectly spiced mulled wine I'd ever tasted. Leaving Martha and Primrose again was a wrench, after I'd spent so much of the evening without them, but Martha was enjoying the attention of pretty much every visiting boy and Prim was lost in conversation with a third-year girl with pastel pink hair.

The library was surely the most forbidden place in college to do anything other than better ourselves, read books and study. The thought would never have crossed my mind without George's encouragement. 'Come on, it'll be fun,' he said. 'Don't you want to get back at that stuffy old librarian?' I knew that it should have been enticing, doing it somewhere out of bounds with George and it was, a little bit, but Cara had always been the one to bend the rules, not me. I actually liked the clarity rules provided. Besides, the librarian might have been strict but she always helped me when I couldn't figure out the referencing system, never losing patience with my slowness.

Rain beat against the glass, making a rhythm in my mind that matched George's thrusts. The seat where Martha liked to work was just visible at the end of the narrow row of bookcases, its brown leather cast in shadow. I pushed back into him, joining our bodies closer and closer, my pleasure growing so that I forgot to worry about what I looked like, whether I was putting my hands in the right place or where we were.

George bit into me a little too hard as if I was one of the rotting apples that still festered in the college orchard. 'Sorry,' he mumbled but I found I liked the undeniable physicality of the fleeting pain. The picture of Millicent Saint Clair glowered above us, staring down at me as he left his mark on my neck. I bit back with enough force for him to gasp, and then he was kissing me, all sweat and quivers and something a bit too close to desperation, as thunder boomed outside.

I could have sworn I saw Millicent's mouth move when a flash of lightning lit up her centuries-old features, her nose made crooked by shadow. The whole scene was too schlocky, too obviously spooky to scare me. And yet. And yet and yet and yet. There was a part of me sitting outside myself, crouched low and watchful, no longer just with Martha or Prim but somewhere else entirely. I closed my eyes to it, scrunched tight enough to see fireworks popping off in my mind, and ran my fingers down George's smooth back, leaving a trail of nearly broken skin.

Week 8

Our sister danced with us tonight. As we circled the trees and leapt by the pond, she came back to us. We have not seen her with the man for several moons now. As we are not only her sisters in bond but in blood, we know her movements. We live with her under one roof and we know where she goes, what she does. There is no escaping us. She laughs tonight, she jumps, she sings and greets new sisters. The devil has gone from her, leaving the water to purify.

We walked arm in arm, an unbreakable chain, across the hockey pitches and through the naked orchard towards the detached house where the Coven lived. I'd known before that the tall, slightly crooked building was where Amina and Sophia's rooms were but it was only since being invited to initiations that I'd understood why they and a gaggle of other second and third-year girls lived together at a slight remove from the rest of us. The lights of the windows sparkled, making the outside of their home into a face. If I squinted it looked like it was smiling, but otherwise the higgledy-piggledy windows made it into a lopsided grimace.

'What's that?' A crunch came from somewhere to our left. Martha's nails dug into my forearm, hard enough to hurt.

'It's probably just a squirrel,' I reassured her. But something didn't feel right even as I said it. The noise had been too loud. Too heavy.

'Shush. I think I heard it again.' Primrose was alert, holding us both back with her arms. Martha gripped me tighter. The trees creaked in the wind and faint laughter escaped from an open window somewhere but there were no other sounds that were unnatural or out of place.

'I'm sure it's nothing.' I forced myself to sound confident, scanning for anything that could hurt us but not wanting to induce panic in the others unnecessarily.

We hadn't walked more than a few paces when hands grabbed us and pulled us into the woods. Martha screamed before everything went quiet.

'Let go of me,' I mumbled but something had been placed over my head that deadened the sound. The material smelled of floral laundry detergent with a hint of smoke. The hands were tying something scratchy around my wrists so that they were bound together. The tie wasn't that tight and I probably could have shaken the hood off if I really tried but the shock of it all and the eerie stillness made me compliant. Because I thought I couldn't move, my limbs made it so.

The wind had died down now that we were among the trees, silence punctuated only by clumsy footsteps as we were pushed along. Wet leaves squelched underfoot as water began to seep through to my toes. I almost fell forward as we came to a sudden stop.

'What's happening?' There was a brittleness to it but even now, I'd recognize that voice anywhere. Martha. I'd barely thought of her in my panic. Shame flushed my cheeks at the thought of losing another friend.

A hand snatched the hood from my head and Amina's heart-shaped face came into focus an inch from mine. 'Boo.'

I stumbled backwards, tripping on a root, and peals of laughter broke out around me. We were surrounded. Clots of older girls in long white dresses stood around the clearing, students with names like Hettie or Victoria who I'd seen a few times on nights out or talking to Martha after lacrosse practice.

'I hope we didn't scare you too much, freshers.' Sophia stepped forward, dressed in a floor-length gown that shone in the moonlight. I'd never spoken to her but with her waist-length blonde hair she was instantly recognisable, even if she now resembled a hyperreal version of herself.

Primrose was to my left, her arms crossed but a half-smile playing across her face. A twig stuck out of her tight curls at an angle. Martha crouched beneath the biggest tree in the woods, the one where I'd first found her, her hair bloody and bright in the chilled darkness. For a moment her eyes looked empty even through the gloom, as though whatever made Martha Martha was gone. Then she shook her shoulders and her smile returned like sun bursting through clouds. I let out a breath once I saw that she was okay.

'So, ladies,' Sophia began. 'We've been watching you. We've been watching you since you got here, and we liked what we saw. We liked it so much in fact that we have chosen you to carry the torch of the Coven, chosen you as the next generation to take forward our legacy and protect our secrets. Each and every one of you has got something we prize – whether that's determination, loyalty, passion or a bit of a wild streak.' Sophia nodded at the gaggle of shivering fresher girls in turn, making us stand a little straighter. 'Now, you might be wondering why you're here in the woods.'

'And it's because you need to know what being part of the Coven is about. What it really means,' Amina said, taking over. Her thick black hair flowed behind her, glitter like war paint glistening on both cheeks in the silvery light. 'Centuries ago, three women were drowned in a pond below that very tree. It's said it shrunk in size after they died.'

Natasha let out a gasp as we turned to face where Martha was perched, a shallow circle of water barely visible in the gloaming. I gulped, my throat constricted at the thought of her being so close to where other girls had drowned even if any danger had passed hundreds of years ago. 'Three sisters died, girls. They died because they wanted freedom, fun, an education. And now we have our very own college to call our own. No one can take that right away from us. Or our right to have a good time, to do whatever we want. So, we are damned well going to use it. Am I right?'

The response was muted, all eyes still fixed on the looming tree. My stomach lurched now that it had been confirmed that this scrap of water was where the Saint Clair sisters had been executed.

'Come on, freshers,' Sophia chimed in. 'Is she right or is she right?' The initiated began to light candles, filling the velvet dark with a soft glow.

'Yes.' Martha spoke first, fully herself again. 'Yes. Yes, yes, yes.' She repeated the word, a little louder each time, until we all started to mimic her. My tongue flickered across my chattering teeth, unable to quite catch the beat as I joined the chant.

'Now form a circle,' Amina instructed. The majesty of the tree's great branches accentuated her beauty and her height, her nose ring glinting under the moon. She held her fist aloft, brandishing an object I couldn't quite make out. A flash of silver, the edge of a blade, a collective intake of breath.

The blade opened to reveal not a knife, but a pair of sharp scissors. Amina and Sophia walked behind us, snipping a lock of hair from each fresher with a slow, deliberate cut. Amina placed my lock into my shivering hand, her brown eyes boring into mine. No one protested. We were bound by the moment, by that peculiar concoction of anticipation, drama and freedom mixed with a dash of fear of the forest and the lurking shadows. A rush of dizziness flooded my brain as if Amina had taken away my balance with my hair, and I looked to the sky to steady myself, stars winking at me through the branches.

'We get to live safely, study safely, party safely, but that demands a price.' Amina raised her voice. 'This offering shows that we don't – we *won't* – forget who came before us.' My body leaned towards her, as the wind licked against my skin. The physical pull towards what she was offering – belonging, friendship, family – was undeniable. I was on the edge of something, something that I'd longed and wished for, and my brain was telling me to dive into it, headfirst.

'And that we don't forget the ties that bind us now, as members of not only this college but also this society. Look out for each other, sisters, because we can only truly count on each other.' Amina fixed each of us with her penetrating gaze in turn. 'And no matter what happens over the next months and years, a little piece of each of us will always remain here.'

One by one, we were instructed to drop our strands into the small pond. Bodies that had been shaking, from shock or cold, now stood proud as they walked forward. The chittering of wild animals and the murmur of the trees became hushed. Birds landed on the surrounding branches, and turned to face us with curious, tilted heads. I even thought I spotted the heron and its great wings through the darkness.

My strands fluttered down on top of Martha's, these dead parts of ourselves mingling together for a brief moment before defying the laws of physics to sink beneath the murky water. I was grateful that I could practically see the bottom of the pond – its lack of unknown depths and

currents didn't make it entirely safe but it did make it manageable. There was even an echo of the previous affinity I'd
felt with water in the friendly way the pondweed caressed
my fingertips as I dragged them through the coolness.

'The Coven is your family now. Don't forget your loyalties lie with each other above anyone else.' Sophia and
Amina spoke in unison, their voices blending into a loud
monotone, hands entwined and held above their heads.
Something cracked as they let go of each other, like the
first rain that comes after a heatwave.

As we traipsed back to the house, the atmosphere
reminded me of Halloween with Cara until we got too
old for dressing up as witches and started to think about
them, make things about them, want to be them instead.
All the details of the evening were too much to remember
so I recited them under my breath, knowing that I'd have
to pour them out of my fingertips before I could sleep,
otherwise I'd lose parts of the night. Bottles were passed
around, arms were draped round waists and shoulders,
and the cold no longer crept into my bones. Agatha and
I slipped through the doorway of the society's – *our*
society's – house at the same time, her olive skin surpris-
ingly warm.

'Let the games commence. These gowns have been
worn by sisters who have gone before you and you are
entrusted with looking after them for your future sisters.'
Amina handed out white dresses to all the new initiates
and we got changed in one great, giggling mass of girl.
When I think back to that term, that's one of the things

I remember most; the easiness of our bodies when there were no men there.

In the sprawling house, we played endless varieties of drinking games and indulged in other rites of passage even though we all knew the main part was over and no one had baulked. Natasha lost her new dress in strip poker almost as soon as she'd got it on. Martha and I were blindfolded and spun faster and faster until we were let go to see who could find various crystals hidden around the cosy living room the fastest. Even the Mistress made a brief appearance, arriving with the hood of her black gown pulled up over her reddish hair, and only pulling it down once she stepped through the front door.

'I heard that she's a sister herself,' Agatha murmured in my ear as we watched Amina hand her a glass of champagne. 'Some of the previous Mistresses didn't even know the Coven existed, apparently, but this Mistress is a graduate of our college.' I wondered if perhaps the Coven had some kind of sway over who became Mistress. The extent of their power was an intentional mystery, and I couldn't wait to find out more.

The games continued and everyone wanted Martha on their team. She was the favourite fresher, after all, who everyone already knew. Even the older girls wanted to speak to her, jostling for a piece of her attention. 'I played against you at that lax match a few years ago,' they would say or 'My sister's best friend dated your cousin, I think.' I was the link at the end of the paper chain, connected to no one but her and Prim. And that was fine because I knew that after the festivities were over, it would always be the three of us, lying and laughing together on a too-small bed.

When we were eventually getting tired and Martha had collapsed onto the sofa next to me, Amina clinked her knife against her glass to get our attention. 'We wanted to do a little something where we can all get to know each other better. Although I'm not sure Sophia has quite mastered the cards yet. So, Soph, you take palm reading – remember like I showed you – whereas I'll use my English student expertise to weave stories from the tarot.'

'Anyone who wants their fortune told, follow me into Madame S's bower.' Sophia was already walking out of the room. Martha looked at me and Prim. Primrose shook her head, and although I gestured at her to come with us, she remained ensconced on the sofa. I shrugged. The two of us followed Sophia up creaky stairs to yet another floor of the house, and into a large bedroom hung with tasselled drapes and lit by half-spent candles.

'Wow, I love your room.' Martha picked up a succulent from the bedside table and gave it a quick kiss. One of the plants was going mouldy if you looked closely enough.

'Why, thank you. Hands out, you two.' Martha's hands rested next to mine, a centimetre of space separating our flesh. Sophia ran her fingers lightly over my palm, then picked up Martha's, turning it upwards. The tip of her tongue stuck out of her mouth as she concentrated.

'Very interesting. Both your lifelines are so similar. Almost the exact same. Like mirror images. But wait. What's this?' She peered at Martha's creamy skin, polished smooth by the almond hand cream she used each night. 'Oh, this is exciting. I think you might have what's called a murderer's thumb. Or maybe that indicates tenacity. I'm not entirely sure.' Sophia picked up a small, dog-eared book from her desk and leafed through it.

'What's a murderer's thumb?' Martha teetered towards the edge of her armchair.

'God knows.' Amina was standing over us, eyebrows raised. Sophia began to giggle and then it infected the rest of us, until we were all full-on belly laughing.

'Aren't you supposed to be doing tarot?' I asked as I wiped my eyes.

'Everyone's too wasted at this point,' she sighed. Her gaze fell on Sophia who was telling Martha the names of the succulents. 'Anyway, that's it. You're part of the pack now. Part of the family.'

And just like that, we were initiated. We were in. My first time being almost at the centre of things. Downstairs, the music played louder, slipping into the spaces left by the earlier anxiety and expectancy. We danced and my body was happy, my body was light, my body was free with love and with sisterhood and with the night and the clamour of jumping up and down and catching a feeling as it slides through a sieve, picking out nuggets to savour each one.

For a moment, I felt a strange sensation before I could place it as the absence of pain. The ghosts that haunted my body were loosening their grip, giving me permission to enjoy this moment, which was fresh and new but also an echo of a rightness I didn't think could come back again.

The only thing missing was Primrose, who I'd lost somewhere in the fray. And – forgive me, Prim – her absence
meant that I could hold both of Martha's hands at the same
time as we rose and fell in tandem, our palms together.
Skin to skin, lifelines touching.

CHRISTMAS

There are rumblings throughout the countryside. Our brothers and fathers tell us what we already know – something isn't right. We have a king, instead of a queen, and he is concerned with the unnatural, the supernatural, the natural he cannot understand. He is concerned with witchcraft. He is concerned with that which he cannot hope to comprehend. Trials are happening, up and down the land. Three towns over, a woman who mother used to take us to when father's medicine man could do nothing for us has been taken away. Some say the king himself will speak to her.

As I waited, I tried to avoid eye contact with the sea. Since last summer, I'd made every effort never to meet its gaze, never to look at the waves snapping at the heels of the beach like a terrier. It was hard when I was there over that dreadful, dead-end summer, the town surrounded by water on three sides. It was even harder when I over-heard whispers of gossip wondering what Cara had been doing in the sea. There'd never been a question in my mind that she had just been enjoying one of her usual swims. Thank God college was a proper train journey away from the nearest beach, marooned in the middle of the country.

The short days of winter meant that the sea was often blanketed in darkness, but I always knew it was there. Mum and Dad invited me for endless walks along the length of the harbour, and in the eight days I'd been back home, I'd started to run out of excuses as to why I couldn't come. Not that I really needed one. They knew what the water had given me but also what it had taken; they just thought that the best way of 'getting back on my feet' was to plough on and accept the twists and turns of life.

On the platform, I turned my back against its salty breath. The station clock counted down the minutes, the seconds, until Prim and Martha's arrival. Martha had pushed for a Christmas visit in the last days of lectures and in the hazy glow of college I'd agreed, already scared of the thought of weeks without them before the term had even ended. In the chilly air with the haar rolling in, my breathing was hard to control. Everything was different outside of university. It was another world entirely. There was too much of past me in this town, and I wasn't sure if I could keep all of it stitched up inside.

But before my hands could grow clammier and my

mind could race away from me, the train was pulling in and they were bundling out of the doors, one big pile of hugs and kisses and floral perfume and girl. Martha's hair was all mixed up with her fur coat, and Prim was difficult to hug because of the heavy rucksack protruding from her back like a shell. They were there and everything was fine, everything was happy, my worries whisked away into nothingness by their chatter and their familiarity, which seemed more solid than this place that I'd lived in – that had lived in me – for nearly my whole life.

Once we'd all extricated ourselves from the embrace, Primrose grinned at me. 'I can't believe we're finally here.'

'Me neither.' My smile back was automatic and involuntary. Real in a way that I hadn't thought was possible again there.

'So, what are you going to show us?' she asked.

'Don't worry, I've got a careful itinerary planned so you won't get bored.' I'd written the plan out in the notebook where I'd scribbled down all the details I'd noticed last term, which I was trying to turn into something coherent that I could show Harold in January. In the last supervision before Christmas, he'd asked me to come back with ideas for my long essay on witchcraft and the role of the scapegoat in the history of political thought.

'Great. I'm excited. You never say anything about home,' Prim replied.

'Neither do either of you.' Although that wasn't entirely true. Freshers didn't talk about home much as a general rule but there were always snippets, from Prim especially – chatter about her sister's new boyfriend or her parents' latest cases or her cousins in Accra.

'I'm an open book,' Prim said and held up her hands, encased in purple mittens. 'You two are the secretive ones.'

'How long a walk is it?' Martha swapped the handle of her suitcase to her other hand, stretching out her ungloved fingers in the cold.

'Only ten minutes from here. I can take your bag.' There was hardly anyone else out in the frozen December evening and Martha's suitcase echoed along the cobbled streets as I dragged it towards the pinprick of light where my parents waited.

As soon as we were in the door, I could tell what kind of mood Mum was in. That day was blessedly safe. Uncontaminated. No silent threats crept through the air. Mum helped the girls with their bags and hugged them with bright eyes as strands of hair stuck to her lipstick smile.

'Your house is so cosy, Mrs Graveson.' Prim's voice was genuine, her eyes roaming the poky living area with its hodgepodge of fabrics without judgement.

'Heather, please.'

'Heather, that's a beautiful name. I'm jealous I don't have a botanical name. It's like I'm not fully part of the gang,' Martha pouted.

'We'll just have to have our own gang, Martha. My name's David but friends call me Dave.' Dad gave her a clumsy wink as he put the kettle on, the kind of embarrassing thing he did that made me start biting my nails, especially as I wasn't used to having new friends visiting. But the smile Martha sent back was open and full to the brim.

'Did Ivy never tell you my name before?' Mum shot me a wounded, wounding look.

'Oh, I'm sure she did. We must have just forgotten,' Prim said, saving me.

Mum's smile unfolded itself again, creaky and out of practice but unmistakable nonetheless. 'Hm, I'll make you girls some hot chocolate to warm up. That was always Ivy's favourite when she had a friend over.'

Prim and Martha stayed for two nights, three days in that period between Christmas and New Year where hours and bodies ooze into nothingness, proving that time is a construct after all. Those days have an intimacy. Sharing them with Primrose and Martha was the most comfortable, mundane thing we'd done together up to that point.

On that first night, the three of us lay in my single bed, our bodies adding heat to the low-ceilinged room, which was warm despite its single glazing and the chill outside. When we finished an unmemorable rom-com, Prim untangled herself from the covers and stooped down to her rucksack to pull something oblong-shaped out.

'Tah-dah!' Martha sat up, her pink satin pyjamas matching the sugar-induced blush on her cheeks.

'What's this?' I asked as Prim offered me a thin black box with gold lettering, her hands flat.

'Guys, you shouldn't have.' It was the second time in

as many weeks that I had been caught out by an unexpected gift.

'Nonsense.' Martha placed her arm around my shoulder, her pointy chin digging into me. 'So go on then, open it.'

'But no one said anything to me about Christmas presents,' I protested, though I was more touched than embarrassed.

'Just let us do something nice for you, Iv. Stop complaining.'

'Yes, you're hosting us now, aren't you?' Prim patted my knee.

'Fine. If you insist.' The wrapping paper was trussed up with excessive amounts of tape, and it took a while for my trembling hands to break through. Inside lay a cherry-red penknife nestled in crimson silk. It had dozens of appendages, including a bottle opener and a toothpick, but it was the blade that drew me in. I tested it against the fleshy part of my thumb and left a tiny indent. My parents' gifts that year had consisted of trainer socks, bed socks, sensible pants and, inexplicably, a feather boa. This was the first beautiful thing – aside from Cara's doily and then George's replica – I'd been given since Grandma Olive used to paint me watercolours when I was younger. I couldn't keep the smile from my lips.

'Turn it over.' Prim's voice was soft and clear.

Engraved on the back, were the initials *IG*. They'd missed out the O for Olive, but I'd never told them my middle name so I couldn't blame them, even if it did feel like a part of me was missing too if Grandma's name wasn't there.

'I wanted to get something prettier but Primrose said it had to be practical too so we settled on a penknife because really you can use it in all sorts of situations, especially in the countryside.' Martha gestured around her, even though we were in the middle of a residential housing estate. A bit of the steak Dad had cooked just for the two of them was stuck in her canines.

'Thank you.' The words came out raspy, almost painful.

'Every self-respecting woman should have one. Very useful if you ever need to peel and core an apple on the go,' Prim said, pulling me in towards her with strong arms. Martha scooted over to us and we hugged as a trio, a tight pack of limbs of different shades. I could hardly breathe but I didn't mind one bit.

Martha was the first to break away, placing a kiss right in the centre of my parting and mussing up my hair. I walked the two steps to my desk and placed the penknife next to the framed photo of me and Cara on the beach, my fingers accidentally brushing the cold metal. It was the first time I had touched it – that I had so much as looked at it – since the summer before.

'It wouldn't be a proper trip to the Graveson household without a fish supper,' Dad said as he washed up our plates from lunch, his thick arms covered in suds, even if he knew Martha was the only one who would eat the fish.

'Make sure you take them to the proper one. Not the one at the end of the high street, the one by the beach.' Dad had strong feelings about which chippie was the best in town.

Everyone did. My plan had been to take them to the high street one but our fate was sealed by his recommendation, and Prim and Martha's subsequent expectant looks of excitement.

The wind struck nails down our backs, hurrying us along the roads like discarded rubbish. Without a hat, Martha's hair whipped across her head like it wanted to be free of her scalp. Through the door, the smell of vinegar bit into us. All that salt – from chips, the air, the sea. The takeaway van we sometimes went to after a night out before heading back to college was incapable of smelling like that, no matter how many white flakes you poured on your food.

'I remember you. Not seen you in a while. Ketchup and salt, is it?' The short woman behind the counter had served me at least once a week for most of my life. She'd seen me grow up and change my order when I became vegetarian, and I'd seen her get wrinkles and a few flecks of grey in her ginger hair, but we'd never known each other's names.

'Yes, please.'

'Did you move away for college? It's been a while since I've seen you.'

'For uni, yeah.'

'My son did that too but he ended up dropping out after a year. He missed home that much. Here you go, hen.' She handed me my chips and mushy peas, remembering that I didn't eat fish and I liked lashings of ketchup.

'It's cute that people know you here, Iv.' Prim popped an onion ring into her mouth once we'd found a clean table. 'You made an impression on this place. I went to boarding school for a year or so when I started secondary school and my parents had to move abroad for a bit for a big case. That was different, but apart from that I always felt like growing up in London, I was just another face in a crowd.'

'I wished I'd had that. There was no one around to know me growing up. I only spoke to about five people before I went to an international school for a bit and then we ended up moving back to the countryside after that until I joined the same school as Nat and Aggie when I was fourteen. I think I went a bit crazy then because of – well, because I hadn't had much practice at socializing before,' Martha added.

'Seriously?' I asked Martha, struggling to imagine her world being so small.

'Seriously. Until I was about fifteen, I was pretty shy. There you go, Primrose, there's something about my childhood to pique your interest.'

'Why, thank you. I do enjoy figuring out the puzzles of both your pasts.'

'Nothing to figure out here.' I tried to smile through my mouthful of food. 'I'll go fetch some more sauces.'

I made my way through the tables of pensioners tucking into their senior meal deals, and children with food smeared across their cheeks. There was a queue for the chippie sauce, and the familiar sounds of hunger and contentment washed over me as I waited, my eyes resting on the glowering sky outside that was forcing people to scurry away from the sea. It was the first time I'd properly looked at the waves in months, their spurts of white foam the lightest thing in the landscape. I wondered if the water was starting to lose its power over me—

And then she was there. She was there, like she'd always been, flicking her frizzy hair over her shoulder and throwing her head back to laugh, just the smallest hint of a ketchup stain at the corner of her mouth. Right there. By the salt shakers.

'Do I know you?' The girl jolted her shoulder away from my hand. As she turned to face me fully, I could see that her nose wasn't as snubby as Cara's was. In fact, her whole face was like a mockery of Cara's. Her features were jokes, similar from a distance but not at all the same up close.

'Hello?' She smiled at me, vaguely but not unkindly, and I backed away in silence. Everything was wrong, wrong, wrong. My old home was mixing with my new one and the seams that I'd carefully sewn up were beginning to gape.

My lips couldn't form an apology. Couldn't form any words at all.

Martha and Primrose were practically finished as I stumbled back to our table, my hands sauceless. My appetite had vanished along with the lookalike. I tripped on my way out of the door, turning left towards the beach where I'd taken photo after photo of Cara and then readjusting my course so I was walking anywhere but there. Anywhere other than where we'd filmed each other, practised our accessible documentary maker voices, taken countless selfies. That part of my life was gone and it wasn't coming back.

'You okay, Iv?' Prim's voice broke through the clouds in my head, reminding me of my new life. She hurried to keep up with me, shoving her hands into her coat sleeves.

'Of course she is, those were the best chips I've ever had and just look at that view. How could she not be?' Martha spun around with her arms outstretched, a big grin on her face. We'd reached an intersection in the streets where the cobbles swooped down to the promenade and beyond that the sea, vast and empty apart from a few brave seabirds clinging on to the breakers.

'I'm just a bit dizzy. Maybe my period's coming.' My heart was dancing in my chest, clumsy and pacy, skipping beat after beat.

'Can we go to the beach?' Martha asked. 'It looks wild.'

'Martha, Ivy's not feeling well. Let's just go home.' Prim's tone was what I imagined a concerned mum might sound like.

One foot in front of the other, I took us the long way home without realizing it. Up through the back roads, past the big mock-Tudor houses with chinks of light escaping from windows, until we were into the hinterland of the town. The light was bleeding out of the sky and my foot felt the stone first before I saw it. Prim grabbed my arm, bringing me back into myself and stopping me from skinning my knees.

The stone was about three feet high and nondescript, grey against grey. A few coins were hidden in the crannies, creating coppery veins in a colour not far off Martha's hair. Someone had left a bunch of scarlet, frost-bitten flowers at its base.

'"This stone commemorates all those from this town and the surrounding area who were persecuted as witches in the sixteenth and seventeenth centuries. May we learn from the intolerances of the past. May their deaths not be in vain."' Prim read the inscription on the stone aloud, her voice cutting into the freezing air. 'Wow, how interesting. Thank you so much for bringing us here, Iv.'

'What? Oh, you're welcome.' My mind was in the past, racing through memories of me and Cara playing on this street, of Grandma Olive telling me the importance of knowing one's history, of Mum telling me scary local bedtime stories that weren't really age-appropriate but that I always begged for.

'Can we keep moving? I'm getting cold.' Martha's lips were turning blue, her stamping feet interrupting Prim's interested mutterings as she crouched down to get a better view of the stone.

'Okay,' Prim acquiesced as she straightened up. 'Though I'm going to have to read up on this later.'

'You guys go ahead.' I pretended to tie my shoelace until they were a few steps in front of me, outlines hazy in the gloaming. Then I pulled the knife out of my pocket and carved an *M*, a *P* and an *I* in scratchy lettering against the side of the rock, adding something of the new me to the place where everything started.

As soon as we were in the door, I knew something wasn't right. Everything looked the same, but there was a change in the electricity of the house, like when you sense incoming rain after a drought. Primrose and Martha were still laughing, rubbing their numb hands together, suggesting a hot chocolate before bed. I knew the drill. Knew I was supposed to run to Mum, to tend to her every need. I'd known that since I was ten years old and her migraines had started getting worse, before they were followed by a whole host of other problems too.

But that version of me was loosening and so I made the drinks as quickly as possible and then bolted upstairs to watch an old horror film about a lonely girl who makes a friend for herself out of a mishmash of body parts. That night, I dreamt that it was Grandma Olive and Cara that surrounded me, instead of bodies that came from a different world, one that I'd only known for a few months.

Their train left the next morning. I walked them to the station then cried when I waved them off but only when their carriage had puffed its way round the bend. The two days until I saw them next stretched out longer and lonelier than the weeks before.

Dad texted me to offer me a lift back but I refused it, preferring the biting realness of the cold to the lazy comfort of the car. My route home took me past the graveyard, where I snuck through the overgrown entrance, hampered by dead foliage, and past the deserted church. Headstones stuck up like broken teeth, the oldest covered in soft mosses and lichens. Towards the back, by the churchyard wall, were the newer, shinier gravestones but I couldn't bear to look.

'I made it,' I said to the graves in general, and to two

ghosts in particular. But I couldn't shake the feeling that I didn't know exactly where I'd made it to.

'What on earth is Hogmanay?'

I explained for a second time but Martha and Primrose just fell about in peals of laughter at the end of the king-sized bed.

'Okay, you guys,' I sighed. 'It's not like Gaelic wasn't also a colonized language or anything.' But I didn't really care about winning the point. What I cared about was looking around Martha's enormous country house.

I'd caught the early train, the chill of the last day of the year reaching its fingers under my skin. The whole way, I leaned forward in my seat, willing the sluggish journey to go faster. I was desperate to be there by lunch-time, to get time with Prim and Martha before the party guests arrived.

'It feels like we've hardly seen you. Be good,' Dad said as he planted a dry kiss on my cheek. The urge to say something in reply to his warning, bolstered by one term of sociology, was smothered by the arrival of my train.

Martha picked me up at the other end in a baby blue car with a personalized number plate that read *MDGB* – the only vehicle in the car park of the tiny station.

'Why the D?' I asked, after the obligatory hugs and kisses.

'Wouldn't you like to know?' She took a left, driving onto a winding road flanked by bare trees. 'No, but seri-ously it's for Deirdre. Martha Deirdre Gleeson-Brewer is a bit of a mouthful but I kind of love it because my dad chose it to remember his Irish side.'

The house itself looked like a Deirdre. There were modern touches – the gates opened automatically – but they were unobtrusive, letting you sink into the chintzy fantasy of another world. Inside the huge entranceway, Prim was waiting by the gold bannisters leading to the upper floors to greet me. She smelled of cold weather, old books and herbal tea.

'I'm just going to check we've got enough wine for later. Primrose, you can show Ivy where she's staying now you know the lie of the land.'

'You stayed last night as well?' I asked as Martha receded down a marble-tiled corridor.

'My parents and Lola had gone to visit family so I was alone in the London flat. Wasn't much point in hanging around by myself so Martha said come up early.'

I tried to hide my twinge of disappointment that I hadn't been there with them as I followed Prim up the wide staircase. She took the steps two at a time then threw open the third door on the left on the second floor.

'Wow.' My bedroom for two nights was done up in every possible shade of orange. Tangerine, bronze, burnt carrot, apricot, fire. The tasselled lampshades, quilted bedspreads, ceiling, carpet, walls and furniture were all some variation on the colour. It was like all Martha's favourite things had exploded to create a universe in her likeness. I'd been excited for the trip partly for the party but partly for the chance to get more insights into

Martha and her life, and it looked like I wasn't going to be disappointed.

'I know, it's cute in here, right. Though a little bit one-tone for my liking. Do you want to go for a walk to stretch your legs? The grounds are really cool,' Prim said, already doing up her fleece and calling for Martha.

'Let's wander past the pet cemetery,' Martha decided once we were outside. I attempted to catch Prim's eye, but she was already striding out into the subtle mist of the late afternoon, unfazed and unbothered.

We walked a circular route, taking in a chattering stream, a semi-frozen pond and puddles that crunched under our feet in conversation. When we passed the miniature graves, tucked away in a clearing, Martha picked up the prettiest leaf she could find and left it on a headstone that read *Isobel*. I wanted to ask who Isobel had been but the other two were already ahead of me, and I didn't want to do anything that might spoil the fluffy, floaty mood.

Our laughter shook the branches as we wandered back to the house, giddy at our reunion and the night ahead of us. Our breath spooled out in puffs, our life force visible in the air, and although it was freezing, I wanted to stay marching round and round those sparse little woods for ever. Stand there in the mist and get lost in it. But there were canapes to prepare. And George was buzzing in my pocket.

'I wish I had someone who was that obsessed with me,' Martha said, peering over my shoulder. 'You guys are too cute. I'm going to get jealous.'

'He's not obsessed.' I slipped the phone away, the messages unread, like most of the others he'd sent me over the holidays. I'd smiled whenever I'd received one, but I'd collected them a bit like I had my other gifts that year. Shiny, enticing things that made me feel if not loved, then at least wanted, but that I didn't quite know how to respond to.

'Modesty doesn't suit you, Iv.' She sped up towards the main door of the house, which was flanked by forbidding columns, so that I couldn't reply.

If he'd been there that night, maybe the romance of our first Hogmanay together with a starry sky above us, free of light pollution, would have been bright enough to burn out some part of myself. Some part of myself that was always hypervigilant, always assessing the safest escape route. But he was away skiing with his parents and brothers, a Svenson family tradition at New Year. And I was making new rituals with Prim and Martha.

There were several hours before Aggie and Nat as well as Martha's other friends who I'd never met before were due to arrive. We were in Martha's room, which looked exactly as I expected, albeit a lot less orange than the guest room I was staying in. Being in the orange room made me feel special to be so surrounded by her favourite colour. Martha grimaced as she tried on a fifth dress in as many minutes, the pile of discarded clothes growing behind her like crumpled tissues.

'I don't have anything to wear.' Her stance reflected the baby photos on the walls, small fists clenched by her sides, jaw set ready for a tantrum. In some of the framed pictures, a man with her same shock of red hair clutched her tiny body tightly. She didn't talk about her family much, and I wasn't sure what to expect. All I knew was that she was a fellow only child. There'd been no signs of life in the house so far other than the ones we'd made ourselves and some circular red wine stains on the kitchen countertops.

'Come on, Marth. What's all this then?' Prim gestured at the dresses, trousers and tops strewn on the red carpet.

'No one ever takes me seriously when I try to talk about my problems. I don't feel happy in any of these outfits.' Martha's top lip stood on the edge of a precipice. I reached towards her, desperate to pull her back, to save her – me, us – from tumbling.

'What about this one?' I picked up a chiffony dress the colour of summer sun and whisky in a glass and held it up so that the material caught the light from the chandelier. 'You'll look stunning in this.'

Martha raised her eyebrows, pausing a moment, but then took the dress from my hands. 'Okay, if you say so. What about you, Iv?'

'Me? I'm not stunning.'

Martha chucked a pillow at me. 'I meant what are you wearing. And don't be ridiculous.'

'Oh. I'll show you in a bit. I think you'll like it.' It was hard to keep my smile down as I thought about the orangey strapless dress that I'd found at the back of Mum's cupboard that I hadn't even known she'd owned. I'd started to get used to being next to George and Martha, to having their glow reflect onto me, but I knew I'd found something that gave me a kernel of that glamour all on my own. When I'd tried it on in my cramped childhood bedroom, it had made me stand up straighter and look myself in the eye without flinching.

'And you, Prim?' Martha asked.

'A purple jumpsuit. And Docs, obviously.'

'We have ages before everyone else gets here. Let's do something fun.' A shiny wetness in Martha's eyes replaced the dullness that had been there minutes before. 'Let's find out what the future holds for us next year, girls.' She produced a set of tarot cards, even more intricately drawn and colourful than the ones she kept in her room in college, and splayed them out across the crimson silk bedsheets.

'They're gorgeous,' I whispered, hovering my fingertips above them, afraid to touch their beauty – a beauty that had chased away any hint of mockery or scepticism. For months, I'd been afraid to think too much about the future, worried that paying too much attention to any one thing meant something bad might happen. But I finally felt in a place where looking forward was kind of possible. Prim peered over my shoulder as the last of the wintery light caught the armour of a knight holding a scythe.

'They were my dad's. They're the most precious thing I have left of him.' And just like that a piece of the puzzle that was Martha slotted into place.

The party itself was like an overdose of all things boy. Sure, there were girls there – girls in sequins, girls in velvet, girls in what I really hoped were fake diamonds – but it was the boys who somehow took over every inch of the house. The darkness of the evening hit hard and early, the drinks harder and earlier still. Guest after guest poured in, bringing gifts of chocolates and brightly coloured bottles to Martha. As she became pre-occupied with other people, I stood near the royal blue Aga, smiling at those I recognized and those I didn't but not quite managing to talk to anyone. Until some-one grabbed my shoulders and turned me to face them. Amina's long, black hair was in French plaits and her hazel eyes sparkled with gold makeup and something else. 'Let's go make some magic.'

We slipped past all the various kinds of boys – boys lounging against the bannisters, boys raising their voices to be heard, boys pulling cards out of their pocket to show girls tricks. Upstairs, the Coven were arranged in a circle in a pale green sitting room, a half-dozen pretty faces greeting me as I walked through the door. The space didn't have the presence of the college woods but they'd lit can-dles and it was cosy and smelled soft and sweet like only a clique of rich girls can. There were paper chains, scissors and drawings of rudimentary figures all over the wooden floorboards. It reminded me of crafts with Grandma Olive and I immediately felt at home.

'We're casting spells for the new year. Make something – or someone – to wish on,' Amina said.

I sat on an armchair and began to cut out white paper bodies with the idea of somehow linking them together.

'Who's that?' Sophia asked me. I shrugged because I

hadn't decided whether to give the figures red or caramel hair yet. Or what I was wishing for.

I just kept cutting and chopping, soothed by the rhythm of manicured hands making the same motions around me.

The room grew hazier and bodies began to come and go and then suddenly I was the last girl in the room, the last member of the Coven, staring out of the window at the twinkling stars as I sat surrounded by discarded paper body parts.

Stumbling out into the high-ceilinged corridor, I hoped that I might find Martha or Primrose after losing them too early in the evening. Freddie's booming voice cracked through the air and I ducked into a door that opened onto yet another sitting room, this time done up in shades of white.

'You look lost.' The room was empty apart from Agatha, who sat on a cream couch so deep that it looked like it was trying to smother her. Tiny clouds of cigarette smoke billowed around her, making me cough.

'Oh, it's you. I was just looking for—'

'Martha.' It wasn't a question.

'Or Primrose actually,' I said.

Agatha sighed – a heavy sound, with more weight to it than her usual sarcasm. 'You know, it's impossible to be like her. I should know. I've known her since pre-prep. We lost touch for years before she came back for secondary, but I still remembered her even though we'd been little kids. Her presence has always been that strong. She pretended she remembered me too but I don't think she did, really. The likes of us can only be near her and hope she notices us from time to time.' She tapped her ash into a flowery saucer. A sprinkling fell to the floor, smouldering on the otherwise spotless rug. 'You and me have more in common than you think.'

'I'm not wearing her clothes tonight. Just her shoes. This is my mum's dress.'

'I didn't mean just the clothes.' She eyed Martha's slingbacks that had pinched my toes since the moment I put them on. 'Orange isn't your colour. It isn't anyone's colour apart from hers.'

'What about Natasha? Why aren't you with her?' I was as unused to seeing them on their own outside our supervisions as I was to having an in-depth conversation with Agatha.

'God knows. Probably getting cosy with one of the boys out there. I love Natasha but Natasha lets you love her. That will always be the difference between her and Martha.'

I disguised a giggle at her seriousness as a sneeze and wandered back into the corridor. Agatha might have known Martha significantly longer than I had but I had a feeling in my chest that if push came to shove she'd choose me and our bond over mere length of acquaintance. I didn't have a particular reason for this conviction other than that often my thoughts seemed to come true – even the terrible ones, which is why I felt I had to be careful about controlling them.

Walking towards the other wing of the house, I slammed

into a solid mass coming out of one of the bedrooms. Gin and tonic spilled down my front, cold hitting my tummy and the tops of my thighs.

'Jesus, watch out,' I called out.

'Sorry, I didn't see you.' Freddie was in front of me, his height blocking out the light. Something in his tone was colder than usual. His gaze was hard but it went right through me, punching into the wall behind. Then it softened like he'd finally recognized me.

'Well, you should have,' I retorted.

'I am sorry, Ivy.' His voice was back to normal, equal parts mocking and friendly. 'I was somewhere else entirely. Let me get something to clean you up. We can't have you looking like that come the bells. George would never allow it.' He patted my arm then left.

I didn't wait for him to come back but fell through different doors again and again until I found the Coven, dancing in a circle, arms reaching out to pull me in. And then – finally – Martha was grabbing my hand and Prim was there too and we spun round and round and sang Auld Lang Syne even though they didn't really know the words, and I kept finding that it was only my mediocre singing voice that remained for the verses. For a brief moment, it was just us in the room until a boy with sandy hair pulled Martha away and Prim wandered off to talk to a girl with blue locks and purple lipstick.

The grandfather clock in the corner told me it was almost twelve. Primrose and Martha were nowhere to be seen but George was calling me, greeting me, telling me *happy New Year* as fireworks popped behind him, obscuring every other word.

The line crackled. And then he said something that sounded a bit like *I love you* before my phone died and I got lost wandering the halls of that cavernous house, my fingers trailing along the walls, touching all the things that Martha must have touched, feeling out all the different versions of her.

My throat felt like sandpaper when I woke up the next morning. I needed a drink of water. Badly. There was a body to one side of me but not the other. Clearly I'd never made it to my assigned bedroom, although the latter portions of the night were blurry. I stretched my hand into the space where Martha or Primrose should have been and found it empty. Martha's dressing gown was still hanging, lilac and fluffy, on the back of the door. The matching slippers with her initials on them rested beside the bed. In the ensuite, Natasha was lying in the bath, eyes closed and a feather boa around her shoulders. Her wrist hung prettily over the edge, thin lines of blue interrupting the paleness.

Voices floated through the corridors. Their rounded notes pierced my hungover brain, seabirds diving in for the kill. As I hunted for a drink they grew louder, ricocheting in my ears. In the kitchen, I almost fell over a crumpled heap of a girl lying on the marble slabs. It took a few seconds to recognize the heap as Martha, the greenish light of the new year giving her skin a ghostly sheen.

An older woman stood over Martha's prone body. She'd slipped in around 1am the night before, all cashmere and big hair, back from her own ski trip by way of a friend's party. Her lips had smacked the air next to my cheek with a hard *mwah*. In daylight, her features were more defined, rising to the upturned point of her nose, the knot of her dressing gown tied definitively. A closed loop. Her presence felt like an intrusion, even in her own house.

The camera in my mind whirred into motion as I stood unmoving at the entrance to the kitchen. Martha was the focal point in my vision, her hair pooling out around her like ketchup or blood. All my instincts yelled at me to run to her, but I was helpless under the weight of memories that pinned down my limbs and held me in place.

'Fucking hell, not this again.' Martha's mum's voice was about ten degrees cooler than it had been when I was introduced to her the previous evening.

A tall, milky-skinned man who I didn't recognize tried to put his arm around the mum's shoulders – Victoria, I remembered her name was – but was brushed away. He was good-looking in a kind of facile way, toned muscles visible underneath his checked shirt.

'I don't have the time or energy for this. I'm away for five minutes and as soon as I'm back, this happens.'

'Vicky, please. She's trying,' said the man.

'I'm fine. You can go.' Martha's voice crawled out from under her.

'Go? How can I do that when you're thrashing around

on the floor? What kind of a mother would I be? You're practically begging for a response.'

'Just go.' It grew louder this time, fighting its way through the bracken of her sobs. My body unfroze and before I could think it through, I was next to her, the cold tiled floor calming the heat that raged in my body.

'Yes, leave her alone.' Victoria looked like I'd slapped her and then that she was about to slap me. She took one single step towards me, her face contorted, her hands bunched into tight fists. I'd always been nervous of other people's parents and other authority figures, hating the rare occasions when I was in trouble, but on the first day of that year I found I didn't care at all. Whatever she might try and do to me, I wanted to do anything I could to spare Martha the brunt of it. Then she stopped and threw her head back into a hollow laugh, her curls knocking against her shoulders. Her hair was dyed blonde and had none of the vibrancy of her daughter's, just a few hints of reddish roots along her parting.

'Fine. If that's what you want. Will, let's go out for some brunch. I want this place spotless by the time I get back. And that goes for you, too.' She looked at me like I was litter she couldn't be bothered to pick up. Then she was gone.

I helped Martha right herself, pressing my cheek against hers, our tears intermingling. There were no stirrings in the house, no activity after the door was slammed and the car revved off. Our bodies were unmoving against each other, our heartbeats waves that lapped in time. Martha's boobs were spilling out of her pyjama top. I buttoned it up so she could stay warm, putting my arm around her shoulders to help her sit up.

'I get them sometimes, when I'm stressed.' I wasn't going to press her into sharing something she wasn't ready for but after a minute or so she spoke anyway. Her words were louder but still shaky. 'They're kind of like seizures. But it's not epilepsy. They've checked. It's nothing really.'

'It didn't look like nothing.' I thought about the red-haired man in the gilt-framed photographs holding a tubby baby that was somehow the same person as the willowy girl in front of me. 'Can you speak to your real dad? Get him to help?'

'He's dead, Ivy.' The words were completely flat, with no peak and no trough. The lump in my throat was instant and stopped me from speaking. Martha had never mentioned him apart from the night before. And I had never asked, never made the connection even after she'd said the day before that she only had a few parts of him left. In that moment, I hated myself for my lack of care and attention. I hated myself but my heart was beating faster in my chest, not without excitement at the possibility of finding someone who might understand the emotions that swirled inside of me. I could feel myself leaning even closer towards her.

'Do you think I'm crazy?' Her eyes were glazed as she stared at the wall behind me.

'Of course not. I just didn't realize you were sad. Or not like this anyway. I'm so sorry that I had no idea about your dad. I really should have asked or found out or at least known.'

'You know the first time I saw you, I was in the woods avoiding Mum's calls.' Martha wiped her eyes, her tears reduced to a trickle. 'It's the only place I can get her voice out of my head. By the pond, underneath that enormous tree. The rest of the time I can hear her constantly, like she's narrating my life. But no use crying over spilt milk, that's what she always says.'

I held Martha against my body, feeling the fragility of her bones underneath my soothing strokes. She untensed, sinking into my shoulder, all sharp points and escaping strands of hair. Then the door opened behind us and that version of Martha was gone, snatching herself away from me.

'Oh, good morning. I feel absolutely awful.' Natasha stretched, her belly-button piercing glinting. 'Martha, you made us a promise of pancakes for breakfast at about three last night. Oh, god, this morning. Anyway, Aggie wanted me to remind you and pass on that she's expecting it to be honoured.'

Martha stood up, a smile so convincing that even I almost believed it was genuine already on her face. She pulled a frilly apron out of a drawer and curtsied. 'Don't worry, I haven't forgotten.'

The tears receded from her eyes, the steel from her voice. They walked backwards inside of her as she broke eggs into a mixing bowl. I'd never loved her so much as I did then, icing sugar on her nose and salt on her lashes.

TERM 2

Week 1

Our sister kept her eyes to the ground as we saw a group of men in the woods tonight. It was just the four of us – the blood sisters within a wider sisterhood – and we stood behind the biggest tree in the clearing, hidden behind her branches. They cavorted and cajoled each other, and they did not take seriously the precious sanctity of the woods. We caught our sister smiling as the man she has been seen with looked up to the moon and howled. It seems the men have their own society, but why do they need it when all of society is theirs to begin with?

The first time I saw George that term, he ended up with blood seeping down his perfect face. The final part of Dragons' initiations involved a fight. It was the only part that was visible, public. The only part girls were allowed to know about, other than those of us who had been fortunate enough to be invited to that first dinner. The boys we'd come to think of as ours and the boys from a rival drinking society, the Marmosets, met in a secluded part of town where there was a bend in the river and huge willows provided shelter and secrecy. The location of the fight was passed on through whispers and inherited memory. If you knew you knew and if you didn't you didn't.

'How did the fight originate?' I asked Agatha as we sat on a bench, a safe distance away.

'No one knows. But it's been going on for ever. My dad was a Marmoset and he told me stories about it.'

'A Marmoset, really? But isn't hanging out with the Dragons kind of like a betrayal then?' I asked.

'It's not that deep,' Agatha snorted. 'Boys are boys are boys. I'll take them where I can find them.'

'I'm not sure Sophia and Amina would agree,' I replied. They tolerated the Dragons, even enjoyed their presence in some situations, but it was clear that our primary loyalty was to be to each other. I also got the sense that they felt like the Dragons had lost something in being a semi-open secret. There was something about the Coven's guardedness that felt essential to its very nature and, by extension, our sisterhood.

'I did some reading,' Prim interjected. 'And there's some stuff about how one of the Dragons insulted a Marmoset's sister back in the day or something.'

'Are you sure you're okay with being here?' I turned to Primrose who had already returned to reading her book. 'I know you hate unnecessary displays of violence. And testosterone.'

'Thank you for checking in on me, but I'm fine.' She shrugged. 'I don't really mind when it's men choosing to hurt each other and get hurt.'

Martha was bobbing about in the crowd of boys, like a

flickering flame. She and George waved at me at the same time, and I waved back as they laughed together about something I'd never know. It made me happy to see my best friend and my boyfriend getting on so well. It wasn't something I could have ever had with Cara – partly because no boys were interested in me at school, and partly because we were both wary of forming connections with anyone else. She'd been the one who supported me when Mum was crazy or Grandma was sick. When you're such a tight unit for so long, you can lose the art of being able to let anyone else in. It was always supposed to be just the two of us against the world, until I set us on a different path.

It was an unusually mild winter day, bright light illuminating the faces of boy after boy. While who exactly was a member of the Coven was a matter of whispers and conjecture, the fight meant everyone knew which boys were getting initiated – who had been deemed popular enough, ambitious enough, rich enough to make the cut. Still, it was a select crowd. Everyone in the audience was connected to a society in one way or another, which meant we were also connected by bonds of secrecy and silence.

'If the police ever get called – and they won't – just say you were two groups of guys in a disagreement over a girl,' I overheard Freddie say to George as they got warmed up. Crocuses fighting to break through the ground were pushed back down by heavy feet.

Martha joined us and cracked open another can of pink gin and tonic to pass to me. The Marmosets emerged through the trees, looking like a mirror image of the

Dragons. Girls from other colleges, a few of whom I recognized from lectures, lolled around us, a tingling fizzing in the air as the boys began to square up to each other.

Clouds strung across the sky, like breaks in conversation, as the chatter died down. George turned and gave me a big goofy grin and a quick thumbs up. He looked so much like a happy, lolloping, golden retriever that I couldn't help but smile right back. After the few days I'd had at home after Hogmanay, my body ached to be touched by someone. The atmosphere itself almost felt like a caress, crackling with anticipation and a hint of threat. Girls teetered forward, boys clenched their muscles, breath was held. Until the first punch was swung and everything broke.

'Honestly, at least our initiations meant something,' Natasha yawned. 'What's the point of a fight?'

'The fight is the point,' Agatha responded, not taking her eyes off the unfolding scene.

'Kind of like the blood feud as a way of keeping order in an acephalous society,' I added but no one wanted to talk anthropology, not even Prim.

Freddie was being held in a headlock by a guy I was pretty certain I'd seen him playing tennis with. And then George was by his side, elbowing his way to his president. For one glorious second, he stood above the crowd of roiling male bodies. A beacon. And then a fist collided with the side of his head, making an abstract picture of his beautiful features as he fell to the floor.

A part of me wanted to rush to him as I saw blood spurting from the thin skin above his eyebrow. And another part of me felt a forbidden excitement to have glimpsed this chink of vulnerability, to see that George Svenson really did bleed red. And that, just like the rest of us, he could be hurt.

I was having fun in spite of myself. I should have been worried about the way George kept rubbing the cut above his eyes that had been inexpertly plastered up, threatening to split it open again. I should have been worried that I hadn't yet found time alone with Martha and I had the tiniest suspicion she was trying to avoid it. But I wasn't. Champagne bubbles pitter-pattering on my tongue, I was light and free. It was a feeling I knew well from when I was little and Mum was upstairs in bed and I should have been miserable or at least concerned but Cara and I were so caught up in our imaginary worlds that nothing else mattered.

The college we were visiting was like something straight out of our games of fairies, princesses and witches. All gigantic slabs of stone and fiddly crenellations twirling upwards that disappeared into the low clouds of the evening, a blanket of grey threatening to suffocate the city.

White-collared waiters set the table as we stood sipping drinks proffered to us on silver platters. There was a girl with brown hair scraped back into a bun who I thought I recognized from my lectures on kinship but she looked away as I tried to catch her eye. Sometimes students took on extra work at colleges other than their own, even though we weren't really supposed to do anything that distracted us from study. If George and Martha hadn't paid for most things for me that term, I might well have ended up waiting on raucous dinners too. At the time, I couldn't think of anything worse. There was no part of me that could have seen the ways I might have been better off. No part of me that could think of worse things than mundanity and usefulness.

Once food was served, George kept his hand on my knee whenever he wasn't stabbing a piece of meat with the heavy cutlery. Eddy and Freddie were showing off, ignoring the sumptuous food on their plates as they stood on chairs or arm-wrestled each other on the solid oak table. Freddie barely took his eyes off Eddy, revelling in being the loudest duo present, but each time a waiter came over they paused for a moment to let them do their job.

Martha's voice was audible from the other side of the spacious room, and it stood out to me above all others. She was there as Peter's date, in the loosest sense of the word. 'So, the real reason for the fight is because one of the Marmosets fell in love with one of the Dragons' sisters? I didn't realize it was so romantic.' Her laughter was a butterfly, flitting its way up to the ceiling.

Primrose had chosen to stay at home for several reasons – she didn't want to be any boy's date plus no one had asked her to go with them plus she wanted to focus on her long essay. I missed her presence, her wry jokes and the way she fitted into any event without taking it too seriously. George kept turning his back to me to talk to a junior fellow who was a former Dragon, but he always kept some point of contact between our bodies, forever finding my bare skin again if I shifted in my seat.

Once the main course had been cleared, Freddie hit his knife against his glass to get the attention of the room. One by one, boys and girls fell silent, a soft hush descending as candles flickered. The waiters who were about to serve dessert backed up into the kitchen again as he began to speak, loud enough so everyone could hear without ever resorting to a shout.

'Dearly beloved, we are gathered here today—' he began. Girls tittered. Boys laughed.

'No, but really,' he continued, his voice matching the mellow light of the room. 'I want to thank everyone for being here – Dragons, former Dragons and allies. It really is very special to have you all in one place, with our brand new next generation of initiates.' He raised his glass and nodded towards various boys around the room, including George. 'You know who you are.'

'I don't want to go on and on and keep you from the fun of the night ahead, so I'm merely going to propose a toast. A toast to my brothers. None of us would be who we are without the others.'

'Amen,' Eddy shouted and for a second, the dinner had the atmosphere of a church with mumbled repetitions of *Amen* and the kind of quiet that only a large group of people trying to suppress their noise can create. Then it broke. Backs were slapped, voices were raised again, dessert was brought out and drinks were drunk.

I watched Martha play with her panna cotta, then slip

out of the dining room, and I got up to follow her. It had been hours since we spoke. I wanted to check that she was okay, that we were okay. But in the candlelit corridor, there was no sign of her. I popped into the toilets to continue my search but when I couldn't find her, I came back out and leaned against one of the heavy oak doors that lined the corridor.

For a moment, I enjoyed the relative silence and the wood supporting me, my thoughts drifting to the tree that the door had once been and where it might have come from. But only for a moment. Loud voices snaked out from the crack at the bottom – none of the doors ever fitted in that place, all warped by time – but I couldn't tell whether they were raised in excitement or anger. Despite myself, I stepped closer to the solid wood to see if I could hear anything. As I was inching forward, the door swung open, almost smacking me in the face.

Freddie jumped at the sight of me, letting out a squeal before clasping his hands to his chest. 'God, it's you. You almost killed me.'

'We've got to stop running into each other like this.' My face was red and my breath had quickened but I kept my speech steady.

'You're quite right,' Freddie murmured but kept his gaze towards the floor. Then Eddy stepped out from where Freddie had a minute before, his eyes low, giving me the briefest of smiles.

He slipped past me, just as George appeared, walking towards me with a quizzical look on his face.

'Is everything all right here?' he asked.

'Everything's fine,' I said, although the way Freddie wouldn't meet my eye made me unsure of myself even as I spoke. I wanted everything to be fine – for the evening to unfold fluidly, for Martha to appear again, for George's cut to heal quickly now that I'd seen he could be hurt and for me to close my eyes as we kissed until there wasn't so much as a scar.

'Good. You won't mind if I steal Ivy away then.'

'Of course not,' Freddie said, his body a little more relaxed. Eddy had vanished.

On the way out, the corridor's maroon and white wallpaper danced before my eyes, the pastoral scene of peasant girls with farm animals alive and moving.

'Did you see Martha?' I asked George hopefully.

'Martha? I think she left with one of the guys, I'm surprised you didn't notice.'

'Which one?' I queried but he didn't answer me as he said goodbye to a clot of Dragons waiting in the entrance hall.

'Yours or mine?' he asked, once we were alone in the cobbled street, a light drizzle coating our clothes and hair.

'Mine, I think.' If we went to his, there was no chance of passing Martha on the way home or once we got there.

George put his arm around me and kissed the top of my head. As we walked, it remained just the two of us, no one else around on the windy back streets as we scurried towards the looming turrets in the distance. Over the weeks, I'd grown comfortable in George's presence so that although I was still in awe of his beauty and his confidence theoretically, in practice we could make each other laugh and walk through the quiet roads swinging our intertwined hands.

In my room, he ran his fingers over the doily he'd made, on its place in the windowsill next to the ones I'd brought from home. The penknife Prim and Martha had bought me sat alongside them, as well as Martha's crystal – I'd put George's bloody hanky in the bin after a few weeks – but George's hand didn't make it that far. As he turned to face me, there was a soft smile on his lips that lit up his whole face.

'Do you want another glass of wine?' Something in his gaze made me squirm and want to reach for something external to myself, something tangible, something that we could cling to with our hands that was other than our own bodies. Most of the time, I loved being alone with him but occasionally there was something so penetrating in his gaze that it terrified me, like he could see straight through to all my hidden parts – or if he couldn't already see them, he wanted to.

'Sure.' I slipped out to the cramped shared kitchen to grab the bottle of red that Primrose, Martha and I had half-finished a few evenings before. Rain beat against the windows as the floorboards squeaked on my way back to the room, rumbles of thunder indicating that the weather was only going to get worse. The moment I walked through the door, the air in the room felt different than a few minutes before – colder, like the outside was sneaking in. Years of living with Mum and the volatile weather of her moods had made me an expert in sensing temperature changes immediately.

'What's this?' George was holding up the notebook where I'd written my every observation the term before. It was one I'd stolen from the school stationery cupboard, unable then to imagine the kinds of things I'd end up using it for.

'Why have you been reading that? It's private.' I tried to laugh as I spoke but I knew by the look on George's face that I hadn't succeeded in keeping the bite out of my words.

'You're my girlfriend, Ivy. Is it so wrong that I glance at something lying on your desk?'

'It should have been in a drawer.' I hated my earlier self for my untidiness. For leaving it out after I'd scoured it for any details that I could use in my essay for Harold. The self-loathing made me see my room for what it was; a mess with pants and books and pens and lip balms strewn across every available surface. Truly disorganized with none of the chaotic cuteness Martha's surroundings always possessed.

His eyes narrowed as he stared directly at me. 'Well, it wasn't.'

'It looked like you were doing more than glance at it.'

'I didn't intend to,' George protested, like he couldn't believe I was the one who was annoyed. 'I was just poking about, waiting for you, and I picked it up and when I saw the word "Dragon" – well, I couldn't stop reading.'

I closed my eyes and made my breaths longer, pushing them in and out to avoid showing too much negative emotion, too much of myself, in front of George. I needed to be bright and shiny and unbothered, just like him and Martha. That was how you moved through life like a knife through butter.

'Why shouldn't I write about it?' With a concerted effort, I kept my tone light and questioning.

'It's just if you're interested you could have asked me questions.'

'I did ask you questions about initiations and you wouldn't tell me anything.' He didn't reply, so I kept going to tackle the misshapen silence that was filling the room. 'It's not a big deal, it's only things that I noticed and wanted to note down so I'd remember them. It's my way of thinking about things. I used to make videos, and I changed to this, I guess. I realized I'm more of a writer or at least a behind-the-scenes kind of person.'

'You don't actually believe any of this is real, do you? All this stuff about the Saint Clair sisters. I told you the accepted facts, Iv, and there's really nothing more to it than that.' Before I could answer, he pressed on, leafing through the notebook. 'I should really tell Freddie about this. Eddy, too.' George sighed and rubbed his free hand across his forehead, where I guessed wrinkles would one day develop.

'Why?'

'Because they're the presidents. Why else?'

'Does that mean you have to tell them everything?'

'Everything Dragon-related, yes.'

'I'm not sure it's reciprocated.'

'What's that supposed to mean?' George was pacing the short length of my room. His feet made a racket every time they stepped off the rug. The visible display of emotion was too much – my George was meant to be all smiles, knowing winks and laughter.

'It's not supposed to mean anything.'

'Are you sure?'

'Yes.'

All of a sudden, he stopped pacing and ran his hands through his hair. Even annoyed, he looked gorgeous and dashing, like an exasperated protagonist from a novel. 'I wish you'd just be honest with me.'

'What do you mean?'

'Well, there's this and you know – Christmas.'

'What about Christmas?' I asked, although as soon as I did, I knew exactly what he meant. He turned away from me, shoulders gently rising and falling. Terror flooded my body at the thought that he might cry, at the realization that he even *could* cry. I stepped closer, so that I was right behind him, as if my proximity could prevent any puncture to the bubble we'd created. 'I'm not being dishonest. The notebook is just stuff for me, stuff that I might want to write an essay on, that's all. It would all be very generalized. I know how important it is to keep some things opaque, even secret. And I love being with you. I love the way you make me feel.'

His body softened, his weight leaning back into me, almost knocking me over. I braced my legs so that we could both remain upright. 'Do you really mean that?'

I thought about how everyone always spoke George's name like the very taste of it was sweet. I thought about how he looked first thing in the morning, when the sun brought out the lightest flecks in his hair. I thought about the way people looked at me when we were together. 'Yes,' I replied, surprised to find that my words came out a little choked.

My mouth found his, and there was something both frenzied and distracted in our movements as we fell in a tangle onto the bed. Laughter echoed down the corridor, seeping under my door, and I wondered if it was Martha or Primrose. George kept glancing towards the desk where he'd dropped the notebook, and then back down into my eyes. I turned my head away to catch sight of us in the wardrobe mirror, watching two bodies crash and break against each other in a golden haze.

Week 2

Spring is coming, and so are men. In the lengthening evenings, we bathe in the pond in the woods to purify ourselves of their touches in our daily lives. We wash ourselves clean of their voices, their judgements, their fingers. But packs of them roam the countryside – more than they used to. The king – that man among men – has given them a new lease of life and they've clung to it with both hands. We hear whispers, skittering through the trees, of accusations, violence and plot. But we know we do nothing wrong. We do nothing against our own conscience, and so we dance freely as the buds awaken.

The unseasonably warm weather had gone and it had begun to snow, fat flakes that held the promise of solidity but melted as soon as they touched flesh. As white layered on white, the beauty of the buildings and the grounds was heightened to such a degree that it almost made it impossible, unbearable, to think that I actually lived there. The courtyard was iced as if with fondant, the roof of the chapel a triangle of white, legs splayed wide towards the cold. The whole thing felt like being inside an advent calendar.

My cycle to Harold's office took twice as long as usual but I didn't mind as I got to crunch over patches of untouched snow, my hands frozen to my handlebars, chilled even through the gloves Grandma had knitted me. From the top floor of the tower where he worked, the city appeared in shades of silver, cream and occasional black, whenever a road slashed through the gardens and buildings.

'There's some good work in here, Ivy.' Harold smiled at me as he put the essay plan I'd been working on down on his desk. In the corner of the room, a heater rumbled away but our breath still spooled out in dragon puffs.

'Thank you.' I couldn't help smiling back. Harold's praise meant something to me, even as I tried not to show it. His accent sounded different from my other supervisors', and when he pushed me, it felt like he was doing it to try to get my best from me rather than to catch me out. Thoughts of my essay kept me awake at night, and not in the stressful way that other students complained of. That was something Prim and I shared back then – we had come to university not solely for the nights out, the parties or (in my case) because everyone else in our family had.

'Soon, you can get into the fun part – the actual writing stage. Your plan looks pretty thorough. Although the one thing I'd be keen to see more of is some comparison to the present day. You've got to remember that this isn't a pure history essay. In history of political thought and sociology, we're always looking for something that links to the current, the modern, the now. Plus, as an anthropologist, ethnography should really be your bread and butter.' He paused and I nodded, although a tense feeling crept into my stomach – I knew what he was about to say.

'What I think would make this essay truly flourish is if you added something about these secret societies *now*. You've got some thoughts here about the link to witchcraft and the history of persecution in the university as being the starting point for some of these societies – but how do they function currently? What do they achieve? They started at a time where people still believed in literal witchcraft but they have continued up until the present day. Why? What are they doing now?'

I sat in silence, the scene of George and my notebook flashing across my mind. Parts of my life that were never meant to touch had become intertwined – I saw now that it had been naïve to think that I could be a part of one of the societies and hold them at arm's length academically. I thought about the Coven too – how I was sworn to secrecy, which meant that any academic writing I did would only be about the Dragons, the Marmosets and other male drinking societies.

'Hmm?' Harold prompted me out of my dwam.

'Sorry, I hadn't realized that wasn't a rhetorical question.'

'I want to hear your thoughts. That's what we are here for, after all. I'm not telling you what to think, we're thinking through this together. That's always been my pedagogy. Asking you to reflect.'

'Right. Yes. The modernity aspect is interesting,' I replied, playing for time. 'I can see why you want me to add it in.'

'But what do you think?' Although the conversation made me feel conflicted, I loved that Harold asked that question with genuine interest. At school, my and Cara's side projects had been treated with indulgence at best both by our parents and by teachers. The only person who'd really supported us had been Grandma Olive. I'd wished fervently for a sense of belonging, and perhaps part of that came with taking my own ideas seriously too.

'I think that in the past I've always been more historically focused. The project I told you about before that I did with my, um, friend – that was about witch trials in our hometown, hundreds of years ago. We wanted to make a video commemorating them, looking at the memorial, that kind of thing.'

'But see, even there you're touching upon the modern. The memorial. There's no history without the present, Ivy, just as there's no present without history. As I said, you're going to need to make some intriguing – even exciting – links if you're going to get the first in this coursework that I know you can. I was going to say "deserve", but you'll only deserve it if you work for it. "Can" seems more appropriate as it's definitely within your grasp.'

'You still think I can get a first?' I asked, trying not to let how pleased I was show too much on my face.

'Absolutely.' The wrinkles beginning to form at the edge of Harold's eyes crinkled when he smiled. 'But I'd strongly advise you to think about the mechanisms of control and punishment we still have in the university now. Back in the day, things might have been kept in check by more obviously violent means, but from your notes it seems like these societies still operate on systems of exclusion but also patronage. They seem like they're outside the status quo, but to have all these dinners and former members, a lot of people must be tacitly condoning them – or perhaps not even tacitly. That would be an interesting angle.'

'It seems a bit drastic to compare the current societies to what might have happened in the past, don't you think?'

'There's no need to protect these societies, Ivy,' Harold frowned. 'There's been plenty of cases of their bad behaviour in more recent years too. Harassment, destruction of property, that kind of thing. And we all know the stories that have come out about the past escapades of our most senior politicians.'

'I'm not protecting them.' The words shot out of my mouth so fast I felt my jaw reverberate. I didn't add in anything to defend the Coven and its enclave of sisterhood, because even in defending it – us – I might have somehow betrayed a secret.

'Well then, I'm glad to hear it.' Harold's eyes pierced mine. I'd never noticed how deep they were, a muddy brown like Cara and George's. 'So you'll work on this aspect of the essay?'

'I'll try,' I promised – although after everything that had happened I yearned for simplicity and a clear path ahead, so it wasn't a lie.

'Good.' His body relaxed again, and from the way he uncrossed his legs I could tell the supervision was over.

I raced all the way home, down the spiral staircase,

across the cobbled courtyard, onto my bike and through the mishmash of narrow streets. My thoughts followed me in a pack, but the harder I hit the pedals, the quieter they became. It wasn't until I saw the tower and front arch that I slowed down. By the time I dismounted, my body was hot, although the fingertips of my gloves were dusted with icy crystals.

Across the quad, I could see a huddle of boys crowding round a flash of red hair, as if it were a flame. Martha. The boys were immediately obvious, their voices too low and their laughter too raucous in the feminine landscape, but it was Martha who truly stood out. Peter was to her right, nodding along and smiling as she spoke, and George and Eddy were standing opposite her, bent over at a joke that I wanted to be in on. George's laughter rang the loudest.

Making my way over to them was made more difficult by the snow, my boots punching holes into the untouched ground. I hurried but I didn't want to appear clumsy or graceless. By the time I reached them, my face was flushed and Peter was telling a story about something stupid he'd done when he was drunk.

'We were just leaving actually, Iv. But I'll see you later, maybe?' George said, giving me a peck on the cheek and still chuckling at whatever joke had happened before I arrived. His lips were cool and quick, like a kiss from a snow cloud.

'Of course,' I said, as if that was the plan all along. I watched the boys begin to leave college, throwing the odd snowball as they went, and then turned around to Martha.

I still had a sense that things were off. I couldn't place it or explain exactly why but it was the same feeling I'd got that last day on the beach with Cara. The night before, I'd had a dream where water rushed towards me and I couldn't tell up from down. I'd stupidly ignored it, convincing myself that any messages I imagined the water might send me were entirely of my own making. I wasn't going to make the mistake of ignoring a strange feeling about a friend – or anything else – ever again. But all I got of her was a glimpse of her hair as her back disappeared around the corner, and a trail of fresh footprints, walking in the opposite direction from me.

George was away for the weekend at his grandparents' country house, which meant my room and bed felt colder but at least there were no conflicting priorities and I had more time with Martha and Primrose. I loved it when I didn't have to make a decision between all the tempting, glittering things the town had to offer.

That term, we had the first Coven dinner with a male drinking society other than the Dragons. Amina and Sophia told the boys that we were a social lacrosse team so as not to reveal the identity of the Coven, and no one asked any questions. George had grumbled about me going out with the Marmosets while he was away, but he didn't really mean it, I was sure of it. Any serious rivalry was saved for controlled moments like the fight.

'Be good,' he'd said, brushing his lips across my forehead as he left, making my skin tingle.

Before we left college for the dinner, we'd been asked by Sophia and Amina to gather in the woods. This time, we knew where we were going. There were no hoods, no ties to bind our hands, only voluminous white dresses (slipped on underneath coats, only to be revealed when we were far enough away from prying eyes) and flickering candles so as to give off enough light to see but not enough that the porters would catch us. Primrose and Martha's faces blinked at me between the trees, their features soft and blurry in the gloaming. Every few steps, puddles of snow-drops burst forth from the ground, like patches of mould against the forest floor.

Amina and Sophia stood underneath bare branches, slashes of crimson lipstick across solemn faces. They didn't have to ask us to be quiet; the blanketing silence was auto-matic as we drew close to where they perched on a wide tree stump.

'Beloved sisters,' Amina's voice boomed in the clearing. 'Before the night ahead, we wanted to take a moment to join together in an act of remembrance. Here, in the very place where the Saint Clair girls were drowned, we gather together to honour them.'

'We say thank you to the Saint Clair sisters,' Sophia continued as a shiver at our proximity to water ran down my skin. 'Our inspiration, our reason for existence, our guiding lights. We are so sorry you were the victims of men. But we promise never to forget that fact, or you.'

'Weren't they informed on by their sister?' I whispered to Prim but she shushed me.

'Can I hear you promise that, sisters?' Sophia raised her voice, and I found my lips moving to agree, desperate for easy explanations for awful events.

'Now, for a minute's silence.' The only sounds were the flutters of a dozen girls breathing and the faint hoots of an owl. I'd felt many things since arriving at the university – longing, rightness, love, headiness – but that was the first time I'd felt truly calm. Like I was exactly where I needed to be. Like the balm of the present might even soothe the wounds of the past. The only intrusive thought that interrupted my serenity was the knowledge that Martha hadn't fully been at ease with me since I'd seen her seizure at Hogmanay.

'And now,' Amina's voice cracked through the night air, 'we have the Mistress here to lead us in our final toast. Drink deep from the blood of your sisters and draw strength from them.'

The Mistress stepped forward, sloshing red wine around in her glass before gulping it down. We followed suit, droplets spraying onto our dresses, Natasha choking to my left at the wine, which was far drier than the bottles we usually shared. As the last dregs were swallowed, Amina and Sophia snuffed out the candles and, for a drawn-out second, we were in total darkness. Then a couple of torches were switched on and we made our way back to the Coven's house to get changed before the dinner.

Inside, our white dresses were shrugged off, revealing a rainbow of silk and satin lingerie underneath. Fabrics swirled as we changed out of our uniform, the lines of our individuality becoming clearer once again. Martha's lace bra and pants emphasized the ghostliness of her skin as she tossed her dress onto the sofa. She looked over her shoulder to meet my gaze, and then we both looked away. There was something hard in her eyes that was difficult to stay locked onto.

'Are you excited for tonight?' I asked Prim as she pulled a purple rollneck over her head.

'I should really be studying,' she said, biting her lip.

'You've got to give yourself a break. Otherwise, we'll never see each other.' I worried about the dark circles that were appearing under her eyes – I knew how hard she worked, always the last to leave the library in the evenings and the first to get there as the doors opened in the morning.

'I guess,' she replied, but the indents from her teeth were visible on her mouth as we made our way out into the waiting cars to take us to dinner.

The Marmosets were like the Dragons, only their college was bigger and they lacked George. The dining room was surrounded by stained-glass windows, depicting biblical scenes and famous alumni in turn, and chandeliers bounced a thousand points of light from wall to wall.

Prim had livened up during the dinner, her comforting laugh audible from the other side of the room, but it was Martha's giggles that sounded like a klaxon in my mind. Each time I tried to catch her eye, she turned her focus towards the boys that flanked her. The ones on either side of me were like poor imitations of George, with the floppy hair and the easy laughter but none of his warm charm. They tried to engage me in conversation but I could only bring myself to respond with monosyllabic replies and short bursts of forced laughter. It didn't seem to deter them.

As the plates were cleared and tables pushed back against the walls to make space for dancing, I made straight for Martha. Even as I stalked the room towards her, she shifted and blurred in front of my eyes. Maybe she was slipping away, or maybe it was just the wine. Either way, I wasn't going to lose another friend.

I brushed past Agatha and several guys to get to her, her hair and the sequins on her crop top catching every snatch of light refracted by the chandeliers. She signalled to a waiter to top up her champagne but I spoke anyway, loud enough to be heard over the crush of excitement and hormones.

'I wanted to talk to you about—'

'Talk to me about what, Ivy?' Martha turned the full force of her attention on me for the first time in days, her voice feathery and tight. It still had enough weight to almost knock me over.

'About Christmas. Well, Hogmanay more specifically.'

'It was a beautiful night, wasn't it.'

'Yes, but the next morning – I mean, were you even okay? Natasha came in and then we didn't get a chance to speak after. Or since, really.' My voice trailed off. I'd felt so certain I had to talk to Martha about it, but with every word I spoke I was becoming less sure of myself. Perhaps she and George were the same in that respect – everyone was on safer ground when their golden surfaces were shining brightly enough to deflect attention from any cracks.

'There's nothing to talk about,' she said.

'It's just because you began explaining, you know, about the seizures. I wondered if you wanted to finish that conversation?' I powered on, determined to give Martha space to talk about anything she might need to. Even though I was certain Cara had just had a horrible accident, the worry that she had left anything unsaid still niggled at me.

'I said there's nothing to talk about. Forget about it, Ivy.'

'But you were so upset—'

'I said forget it.'

'Okay,' I murmured at her back as she walked away. Part of me was worried and another less admirable part of me was relieved. Agatha had warned me that Martha couldn't let herself be loved, and perhaps there were elements of her that neither of us was ready for yet. I could already see Martha by the bar, clinking glasses with Sophia and Amina, her head tipped back in amusement as boy after boy stole glances at her. Whatever part of her I'd seen at Hogmanay had crawled back inside. Maybe it was easier that way.

The Coven was getting up onto the dance floor, our presidents leading the charge, calling on the boys to join them in a way that was both mocking and seductive at the same time. The boys didn't need asking twice.

Among the fray of pulsing, homogenous bodies, Martha leaned in close to me, her chest brushing against my arm. My breath escaped me. She looked me straight in the eyes for the first time that evening and whispered, 'Can we make an oath to each other that we won't look back, we'll just keep looking forward?'

It was the first time she had come truly close to me all night. I kissed her cheek and nodded, because back then I believed that my past had only loss and my future only gain. I couldn't have known what I was promising.

Week 3

Yew. Daffodil. Dying snowdrop. We frolic among them all as the blackbird sings her tentative song. The water of the pond is warmer than the air, greeting us as friends, as family. One of our sisters warns us something is coming but what can we do in the meantime but play? Across the land, women are being taken. They are being questioned – and worse – for less, but while we have these mortal bodies, we must live to the extent that we can.

The tree rose up like a mythical sea creature from the ground, tentacle branches swaying in the mid-afternoon breeze. It was bare of any leaves, no fiery red like the day it had coughed Martha up from the ground and she had discovered me right there in the grove. The sun was pale, lacking the kind of crispness I preferred as a backdrop.

I was back behind the camera for the first time since being at college, even if it was only on my phone with its cracked screen. I'd asked Prim and Martha if they wanted to come with me and they'd both had excuses – Martha that she'd promised to speak to her mum and Primrose that her supervisor had asked for a first draft of her long essay by the term's midpoint. The cold snap was freezing us into rigid poses, icing over those aspects of ourselves that had been so free and easy before Christmas.

Filming things had been my childhood, my safety net. My way of squinting at the world without having to meet its gaze head on. And since George had unearthed my notebook, the urge to return to it had been strong. I still hadn't started writing the essay for Harold, and I decided that wandering down to the clearing where the Saint Clair sisters drowned would help me think. In the day, alone, it looked more subdued than when adorned with Coven sisters. It still charmed me, though, with its skittering husks of leaves, musky smell and single entranceway through a narrow path and thickets.

The stump where Amina and Sophia had stood provided me with a seat to survey the near-perfect circle in the woods. But the light was all wrong and the scene looked washed out. It was impossible to capture the majesty of the tree or the hints it gave of safety and possibility all at once. The camera had failed me or I had failed it – and I knew which of those was more likely.

I pressed the stop button, a little too hard, and ended the recording. The branches of the great tree waved overhead, half-encouraging, half-admonishing me for giving up too soon. The surface of the pond caught the light, and I moved so that I was lying next to it. Not caring that my fleece was getting dirty, I started filming again, focusing on the water choked with weeds. This was the last view the sisters would have seen before they died – the least I could do was try to translate it into something palpable. I stayed down there long enough that squirrels and voles started to move around me, my body no longer a warning but a part of the scenery. I only got up because a sharp pain shot up my leg and into my stomach, the cramp making me splutter.

When I replayed the scene, there was a vibrancy that hadn't been apparent to me when filming. Even though I hadn't done any editing and the winter sun acted as a leech, all the colours popped. Everything was a little too bright, a little too glittery, like an enchanted filter had been applied to the world.

Before I left, I circled the tree, running my palms over her rough bark. As I walked around the trunk, I made a wish that no matter what happened the three of us would always come back to this place and to each other. As I completed my rotation, I noticed a small note attached to a bunch of red roses at the base of the trunk, near the tiny pond where we'd submerged our locks of hair. It wasn't the first time I'd seen flowers in the clearing but I'd never seen anyone leaving them, not even members of the Coven. There weren't even any footprints for me to examine. I stooped down to read the water-blotted scrawl written in crimson ink.

Keep your friends close but your sisters closer. Never forget.

'I'm just so sick of Mum phoning me all the time, expecting me to listen to all her tiny problems, without recognizing that I have stuff to do. It's exhausting being an only child.' Martha threw herself down onto the armchair, sniffling delicately. I wanted to commiserate, being well aware of how much harder every tremor within a family hits when it's just you there to absorb the impact, but in the first few weeks of that term, Martha was especially unpredictable. Sometimes, things were almost normal, like when we danced at the dinner with the Marmosets. And then sometimes I had a horrible suspicion that even my presence irked her, as if I was a reminder of something she'd rather forget, a door she'd rather keep wedged tight shut.

On my cycle back from a lecture on constructivism versus social constructivism, I'd picked up lozenges and essential oils for Martha and dropped them off in her room. I had been hoping to catch her alone but she had Natasha and Agatha for company.

'Maybe what you need is a break?' I suggested. Martha had been saying yes to exclusive invite after exclusive invite, always with a boy draped around her shoulders or hanging on to her every word. The snow had melted, and the whole town felt like it was weeping. There was slush everywhere and each time you walked by one of the gabled buildings, you ran the risk of getting soaked with icy water. I loved the sense that spring was coming, but I could see how for someone like Martha the loss of perfection could hurt.

'That's a good idea, Ivy,' Natasha cooed from the bed, where she was trying to tame Agatha's thick hair into French plaits.

'What kind of thing are you thinking?' Agatha didn't raise her eyes to look at me as she spoke.

'Maybe we could take our bikes into the countryside, stay at a hostel or something?' I shrugged, remembering impromptu camping trips with Cara and her mum when I was younger and how exciting setting out together for the unknown had been. 'I haven't really thought through the details.'

'Oh. I thought you meant like an actual holiday,' Agatha snorted.

'You don't have to come. I was suggesting it for Martha,' I said.

Martha smiled at me, in a soft way that I'd never seen before. It looked a little too close to pity. 'Maybe that would be cute in summer term.' She patted my leg briefly, before turning to pick out an outfit from her overflowing cupboard.

'Are you sure you should go out again if you aren't feeling well?' I asked as she discarded a burnt orange silk blouse onto the floor.

'I'm fine, Mum,' she replied, and Nat and Ag giggled like Martha had made the best joke in the world.

'Aren't you coming with us? We're going to that wine bar that's just opened near the marketplace.' Natasha walked over to me, pulling my hair out from the back of my jumper. 'I could do your hair like Aggie's if you like?'

'We said we'd have a movie night with Prim, if you remember, Martha?' I felt rude ignoring Natasha but I needed Martha to understand that the sanctity of our trio had to be protected. I tried with a pointed look to communicate everything I'd learned about the amount of work friendships take to keep them strong.

'Oh, whoops. I totally forgot.' I could only see her eyes reflected in the mirror as she held up a velvet dress to her frame, her pupils small and beady. 'Could we move it to this weekend?'

In the golden glow of Martha's salt lamps and candles, even Agatha and Natasha's bodies bent into inviting shapes, calling me to forget everything and follow them into the night. But Prim, with her heavy rucksack full of books and calendar with its carefully allotted slots of fun, wouldn't leave my mind. I slipped out of the room while the others were taking photos as a trio, snatches of laughter hunting me down the empty corridor. I pulled my curtains tight as soon as I walked through my door, allowing my fingers to brush against the embroidery on the sill.

Prim arrived and eased her bag from her shoulders. 'Shall we wait for Martha?' she asked.

'She's not coming.' I tried to keep my tone light, willing us both to believe that it wasn't a big deal.

Prim nodded, saying nothing. She snuggled into me, snorting with laughter as the woman in the movie tried to show the hapless man that she was interested in him through increasingly ridiculous measures, until some of the hot chocolate we were drinking came right out of her nostrils. It was a struggle to get my giggles under control enough to mop up the patchy stains on the duvet. Prim's hiccups from too much hilarity reverberated around the room, reminders of the here and now as thoughts of the past and the future fled.

Our bodies were as close to each other on my narrow

bed as I'd ever been with George. As we snoozed, her chest shook with little snores – I'd never noticed before that she wasn't a silent sleeper. We were so close and yet we were different people. There were things about each other that we didn't know, maybe could never know. I knew there was danger in the parts of someone that they kept unsaid, that they could grow fangs in the darkness, but I pushed any monsters down that night, to sleep in the glorious present next to one half of my best friends.

George came back just as the weather snapped into coldness again. I'd missed his easy laugh, which always brimmed close to the surface, and the way his hands warmed mine. But things moved fast in college and when I'd gone out with the Marmosets and the Coven, I'd found that just as many people spoke to me when he wasn't there. It was becoming apparent – even to me – that I could garner attention in my own right, not solely because of my proximity to George and Martha. Even in my wildest pre-university dreams, I hadn't foreseen how much I would develop my own shine. Still, as he dismounted his bike at the college gates and tossed his hair from his eyes, George sparkled like a drop of dew on a spring leaf.

'How was seeing your family?' I asked, as I let my lips enjoy the warmth of his cheek. He'd hinted before he left that I could go with him, but he'd never actually asked and I didn't want to bring it up myself, especially not when I wasn't sure whether I'd prefer to stay in college with Prim and Martha.

'Oh, you know, the usual. Mum and Granny were ecstatic to see me and Dad kept asking why my grades weren't as good as my brothers' were. Anyway, how are things here?'

'Same old,' I said, even though there was a whisper in the wind telling me that wasn't true. 'Shall I make some tea to warm us up?'

'I thought we could go for a little walk first.'

'Really? But we haven't seen each other for ages.' Days felt like months back then.

'Is that all I am to you, Ivy Graveson?' George held his hand to his chest, mock hurt. 'A piece of meat?'

'Of course not. But fine, you win. Let's go for a wander before it starts snowing again.' I led us out of the main courtyard, winding away from the more landscaped gardens into the wilder reaches of college.

'Where are we going?' he asked.

'The woods.' We made our way through the trees, the lack of grip on my trainers causing me to hang on to his arm for some of the iciest patches. The last of the snowdrops still fought their way through the hard ground, and holly berries inserted themselves into the monochrome scene every few metres. The walking was slow but George didn't seem to mind, whistling loud enough to make the birds scatter. He placed our entwined hands into his pocket. It felt warm and comfortable, reminding me that I was glad he was back.

Without really intending to, my feet led us through the waterlogged paths to the biggest clearing. Dirty patches of snow still clung to the dark spots beneath the canopy where there was no light. The ends of branches curled in like fingers – it was unclear whether they were beckoning or scolding. It hadn't occurred to me that George might have been the first man in that sacred space for some time.

'What's so special about this tree then?' George nodded upwards at the trunk ascending to the heavens, and wrapped his arms around himself as if for a hug.

'Well, it's where I met Martha for a start. And obviously I didn't know this at the time but that pond there is where the Saint Clair sisters were drowned. But you should know that.'

'Would we really call it a pond? Looks like more of a puddle to me. Anyway, I've only read about it in books, never actually seen the place itself.'

'You never wanted to come and visit it before?'

'Usually when I'm at your college, I prefer to hang out in cosier spots.' He chuckled and twigs rattled. 'I think I remember Freddie saying he came out here for a hook up once though.'

'That's not very respectful.' Leaves swished all around us in disapproval.

'You just said yourself you didn't know about its significance until recently.'

'Yes,' I agreed, absently, distracted by the majesty of the trees.

'Did you learn it from the Coven?' George asked casually. We'd never actually discussed the Coven explicitly – although I imagined he'd garnered some knowledge from Freddie and Eddy – and I wasn't about to start now in our hallowed place.

'I've been coming here almost every day lately,' I offered instead.

'By yourself?' He narrowed his eyes.

'Sometimes.'

Maybe it was the dull light of the new year, the flickering shadows cast by the trees or the clearing's bitter memory of a sister who had long ago taken the side of men, but for once George didn't seem to glow so brightly. As soon as we were in the woods, he looked small – shrunken almost – despite being bundled up in a designer quilted jacket. His hair didn't have its usual golden gleam. There was nothing for him to reflect off, save me.

'Well, if it's special to you, it's special to me.' He reached forward and brushed my hair out of my face. It was on its last day before it needed to be washed but George didn't seem to notice or care. He leaned into me for a kiss. I kept my eyes open as his mouth plunged towards me.

'People died here, George.'

'People have died everywhere. Someone's probably died in every single inch of this college, this city. Is that going to stop us having fun?'

I couldn't argue with that but the warmth that flooded down my body still felt wrong as he hitched my skirt up and pulled my woolly tights down. The bark of the tree pushed sharply into my back – when I checked that night there were angry red marks against my skin which looked almost like angel wings. My hands scratched at his back but he was tender, his whole body radiating heat despite the freezing temperatures.

'I love you, Ivy.' It was barely a whisper, whisked away by the trees but there was no denying it. Not this time. In the glade, something shifted. George let his guard down and spilled the words as he came. I didn't move, my back still against the witching tree like I was an insect speci-men pinned to a display cabinet. Unlike Martha, George was ready to let me love him and part of me was ready for that too. But another part of me was scared – scared of men, scared of what they could do, scared of the magnetic pull I felt towards him and how that magnetism might interfere with the poles that were Prim and Martha. As he buttoned his trousers, the respectable amount of time for me to respond ran away from us, the words sticking in my throat. I could sense that we both knew it, even if neither of us was willing to confront it.

'That was amazing,' I said eventually. A chink of light broke onto us, and once again George was brilliant, beau-tiful, shiny. 'Being with you is amazing.'

'Yeah. Yeah, it was.' He slung his arm around my shoul-ders, squeezing me in tight as we walked back to college in silence. Even through my heavy winter coat, I could detect a slight tremble in his fingers, echoing the fresh flurry of snow that had begun to fall.

Week 4

Our sister is no longer our sister. She has begged and pleaded with us, but we will not let her back in. She will never dance with us again, never read poetry with us again, we shall never caress her and braid her hair. It transpires that she told him about us, about our joys in the woods. About our escape. She told us with tears in her eyes, with sobs wracking her throat. But we do not care. We cannot forgive one part and risk sacrificing our whole. She tells us it was love, that he was interested in her and by extension us, that we do nothing wrong anyway, so there is nothing to keep hidden. Secret. But we saw those men in the woods. We know they have their own societies and we are certain that some part of their sport will be against us, even if we do not yet know in what fashion. She is a fool to think that danger does not often present itself in attractive packages.

Sometimes when an injury happens, the damage that takes place is internal. A person can look completely normal and it is impossible to pinpoint the exact point of rupture, the cause of pain, the reason for their demise. But that doesn't mean it isn't there. I should have known that. It's how Cara died after all.

The Red Dragons were having a dinner to celebrate the halfway point in the academic year at George's college. As we got ready, I tried all the tricks in the book. I made myself interesting, tried on Martha's clothes obediently, did my eyeliner the flicky way that she had complimented before. Wore an orangey lipstick because that was her favourite colour.

'You look cute,' was all I got from her.

'Let's take a photo.' Natasha clapped her hands together, once we were dressed and made up. 'I want to record everything while we're here. I'm trying to make my time more meaningful, so that it doesn't feel like it's slipping away quite so quickly.'

'Please don't tell me you're back on the self-help books.' I could tell without even looking at her that Agatha was rolling her eyes. But she still stepped in for the picture. I stood at the back, peaking out between her and Primrose's heads.

Each of us was wearing black, a theme set by Amina and Sophia after the remembrance ceremony. Even if it wasn't a Coven event, we were still in mourning. Our presidents had reminded us how important it was to celebrate our freedom while remembering our sisters and so we were instructed to wear all-black to any party or event we went to. A month would pass before we were back in our white dresses. When we walked into the private dining room, we were a swarm of bats or something darker. The Dragons turned from where they were crowded around the fireplace to stare at us. Freddie raised a glass of port in our direction, nodded and grinned. George scanned our little crowd from where he leaned against the mantelpiece, and I tried to hook onto his gaze.

Freddie walked over and handed me a glass of champagne. 'You look lovely,' he said. Boys' lips were stained with red as we drank enough bubbles to make us float up to the ceiling.

'Why the black?' he asked, once he and Eddy had checked that everyone had a drink in their possession.

'It's a sign of respect,' I shrugged.

'Respect to whom?'

'Why do you ask?' I'd learned from my supervisions that answering a question with a question could be an excellent way to turn a debate – or a conversation – in the direction you wanted.

'I'm always interested in the Coven.'

'Who says this has anything to do with the Coven?'

'Come on, Ivy. I wasn't born yesterday.'

'So you're allowed to know things about us but we can't ask about the Dragons?'

'You can ask, we just won't tell.' He winked at me, but it had none of the same energy as when George did it.

'Why does everything have to be so secretive? If everything is about us letting loose, bonding, having fun, why can't other people know what's happening?'

'You're the one who was just saying you can't tell me why you're in mourning.'

'That's just because what we shared in the woods was

special. Intimate. Not because there's anything to hide. For us, any secrets are about protection and safety. They're serious,' I sniffed.

'Ah, so it took place in the woods.'

'This isn't a murder mystery, Freddie. Anyway, I heard you've visited our woods yourself before. What could you possibly have been doing there?' I waggled my eyebrows at him, trying to distract from the fact that I might have revealed too much.

'Who told you that?' His reply was sharper than I expected.

'No one.' I injected some of the lightness from the alcohol into my voice, and after a moment we were laughing together, the cloud that had momentarily been above our heads almost forgotten. Almost. I had a queasy feeling – something close to seasickness – that we'd been an inch away from tipping into dangerous waters. I looked down into my glass and saw the liquid distorting my reflection. For a second it almost looked like my face was dissolving into words, as though it was trying to tell me something, send me a message.

Then the gong cut through our titters and everyone scurried to their seats. At dinner, I was seated at the end of the table next to Peter, with Sophia on the other side of him. I kept trying to catch Primrose's eye from where she sat a few seats along but Sophia's voice and Peter's laugh were too loud to let us have a conversation. After a while I gave up, and just watched Martha, George and Eddy taking it in turns to shriek at each other's jokes and refill each other's glasses. Twice, George shot me a small smile but Martha was too engrossed in the boys on either side of her to look at me. I was too busy looking at her to properly return George's attention.

'Would you like another?' Peter mostly spoke to me to check I had enough food and alcohol. Being George's girlfriend made me respectable but not wholly interesting to the other Dragons. It was like I was marked, so that they knew all our interactions had to toe the line between polite and friendly, and overly familiar.

I chucked back the fizz. Then another. And another. Any message my water had been trying to convey was lost. We finished dinner, at least half of the food still untouched, and moved into a smaller room where a fire roared and serpents decorated the walls. Freddie and Sophia, and Amina and Eddy, started off the dancing, whirling round and round in pairs. We all whooped and cheered and – inexplicably – a few of us cried. Then time turned slick and treacherous. A gelatinous mess of hours, minutes, seconds disembowelled and dissected, elongated and cut in half.

I'd caught Primrose sneaking off with one of the girls who'd been working behind the bar. I was happy for her – I knew she wasn't interested in a relationship in case it distracted her from her studies, but I also knew that she needed to let off steam from time to time to keep her focused on said studies. I'd messaged Martha but she hadn't replied. Which left George. I'd lost him in the fray, but I knew that if I found him, he'd want to see me. Maybe I could even say I loved him back. Maybe that would seal the deal on me feeling at home in my new life. I'd been wishing for complete belonging and I'd thought that path lay with my girls. But maybe I'd misunderstood and needed to throw myself completely into George, meld myself to him, imbibe him, drink deep from his lifelong confidence, his angelic glow.

When I got to his room, the door wasn't properly closed. His room was in the oldest part of his college and the door was a heavy hunk of oak that didn't pull to unless you yanked it. I peeked through to see George's body on the bed, reaching all four corners. The light from his bedside lamp caught on the muscles of his torso, making him look geometric and abstract. Like he didn't really exist. Another body lay underneath his, elegant toes emerging from underneath his strong legs. My vision blurred and they weren't two bodies but one. The body writhed, a tangle of flawless flesh. Limbs reached out, grabbed and grasped whatever they could.

My eyes focused again, even though part of me willed them not to. The other part couldn't tear myself away. Couldn't do the right thing and force myself to walk back down the arched corridor and pretend I'd seen nothing, letting me and George carry on exactly as before. Easy, charmed, full of pleasure and devoid of questions.

His weight blocked the other person's body and it could have been anyone for all I knew. Until it wasn't. Until it very much wasn't. Until anyone turned to someone.

A tendril of red hair escaped over his shoulder blade,

like blood on snow. It was all the colours of autumn, distilled to a sharp point. It was my first period, the rusty stains drying into my legs as I desperately tried to clean myself in the school toilet. It was the vibrancy vanishing from a red lollipop as it was sucked, and it was the first and only goldfish I'd ever had getting flushed down the toilet as I sobbed into Grandma Olive's arms. It was Martha. It was her through and through. I knew it in an instant.

It took me longer to act. My limbs wouldn't move when I told them to. The only small mercy – and it was almost invisible to the naked eye – was that they were in his room and not hers. I couldn't have survived if their bodies had met on the bed where I had lain next to her, growing into myself.

I tried to flick the camera in my mind on, view it impassively like this was the kind of nature documentary Prim and I enjoyed watching and they were engaged in an interesting mating ritual. They were birds, I told myself. Just some brightly coloured birds of prey. Talons out.

Normally, it was George that overwhelmed a room with his gorgeous face but this time, he was battling a worthy opponent. And Martha was winning. Their hands twisted together. Even George's abs, glimmering with sweat, couldn't match her radiance. She was the sun and I was a big, wet cloud about to spill.

My mouth made a noise I'd never uttered before, giving birth to every pain that wracked my body. They broke apart like they'd been pulled from a fight, their eyes flushed with confusion, then fear, then horror. Perhaps my face was contorted into a version of me they'd not witnessed before. Perhaps it spoke the truth and they didn't like it.

They fell over themselves trying to get to me, so that they ended up in a crumpled heap on the floor. The life that had been in their bodies seeped away. George struggled to put his chinos on. Martha covered her chest with her hands. I took a moment to look at both of them. Really look. When George and I had sex, I never got the space or the silence to observe every inch of his body. He was too active, always moving. And in all the times Martha had changed in front of me, there hadn't been a moment where all the parts of her were exposed at once. That was what hurt the most, I think. That George had seen her in ways I hadn't.

I walked out of that room as if someone had shoved me hard in the back.

My body ricocheted off the walls of the corridor, swaying from champagne and shock. Footsteps scampered behind me, trying to catch up. Blood beat a storm in my ears so that I couldn't tell who they belonged to.

'Ivy, wait.' The voice was deep but cracked, like the body of a riverbed. It could have been either of them. But I'll never know which one of them came after me because my body kept marching me forward. Propelled towards another future I didn't choose.

For one second, I paused, trying to imagine some explanation. Or some possibility for the three of us. But then I swayed, my tummy rumbled, and the realities and limits of my body kicked in once again. I wasn't one of them. I'd thought that because I was next to them, because

I was having sex with them, because I was friends with them, that I was the same as them. Untouchable and unbreakable. But I wasn't. I shook my head, quickened my pace and fled.

Week 5

We have been named.

Week 6

The man wishes to marry our sister. He thinks we are obstacles in his way. And he is right. We would have whispered in our father's ear, as well as our mother's, and told them this man is not suitable for their beloved daughter. But now we know they deserve each other. Although she knocks on our bedroom doors at night, wailing and begging, she is no longer admitted into our hearts. She tells tales of how she loved him and only wanted to share her joy. But we are clear – she is as much to blame as him.

Week 7

This will be our last time writing in the book. It seems foolish now that we kept our identities hidden when our names will be written across the pages of history. Our mother has wept for us, our father interceded where he could, but the country is swept by danger, and the ground is not solid beneath anyone's feet. We do not welcome what is about to come – make no mistake, we want to live. We want to live and dance and feel the water against our skin and the sun warming our flesh. But if we cannot have that – and it is getting clearer by the hour that this will not be permitted to us – we accept the embrace of the water in the clearing where we have felt our greatest joys and shared our greatest sorrows. Keep your sisters close, and your enemies closer still.

My eyes were still shut tight against the world when the knock sounded against my door.

'Ivy. Come on, I know you're in there. It's me.' Prim's fist pummelled the wood without mercy. 'It's gone ten on a weekday.'

Pulling the pillow over my head didn't fully block

out her voice or the weak light sneaking in through my thin curtains.

'This can't go on for ever.'

'Why not?' I forced the words out, my voice unused to speaking. Somehow, Prim managed to hear the whisper.

'Open up, Ivy.' She banged against the wood again. 'Or I'm going to have to go and tell the porters that you're sick and I'm worried about you so they'll open it for me.' The porters meant potential referral to the forbidding college nurse, potential consequences beyond what I was already dealing with – God help me, potential calls to my parents. Dad had texted me to say that Mum finally seemed to be with a counsellor who was helping and I didn't want to be the thing that upset their delicate domestic balance.

Getting out of bed took almost all the energy I had left, after I'd used most of my reserves on dragging myself to supervisions and churning out mediocre essays to keep on top of my degree. Even at my lowest, academic work had kept me going. It was the same as when Cara died, when I'd buried myself in preparations for university as my guiding light to some kind of future. Theories were complicated but they had a simplicity too – if you studied them enough, you could understand them, master them so that they became applicable and predictable. Prim wrinkled her nose when I creaked open the door – I hadn't changed my pyjamas or my sheets since the incident – but she didn't say anything. As I lay back down again, she began piling up cups and folding a few stray T-shirts to go back in my drawers.

'How are things?'

'How do you think?' I rolled towards the wall, shocked at the venom in my voice. Prim pulled the armchair closer to the bed so that she could sit near me, her hands twisting in her lap.

'What have you been doing, Iv? I haven't seen you in days. I've been really worried.'

'Trying to eat. Going to supervisions. Trying to write my long essay. How about you?'

'Pretty much the same. That and the gym. I've actually got some time for it now.' A small smile flitted across her face. 'I miss you, though. And Martha. She's not the same without you around. None of us are the same without each other.'

'How's your essay going?' I asked, unable to think about 'us'.

'Good, actually.' Her smile widened. 'And yours?'

'I can't concentrate on it.'

'It's been a rubbish few weeks. Give yourself a bit of a break.' Prim reached over and squeezed my hand. Her skin was warm – too warm, after I'd touched nothing but my weighted blanket in so long. 'But not too much of a break. I'm counting on us both seeing our names underneath the firsts list when it gets pinned up at the end of the year.'

'What makes you think that's still possible for me?'

'Everything's possible for you still, Iv. I know you're hurting now but believe me, it gets easier. My first ever girlfriend, Ria, cheated on me so I get it.' I doubted that she got the depth of the double whammy of my hurt but I didn't want to risk pushing away the one person I had left by saying so.

'Harold keeps pressing me to think about whether I'm going to mostly concentrate on historical scholars or have more of a sociological angle in my essay. But I've got more important decisions to make.' Even as I said it, I knew I sounded petulant.

'What makes you so sure that you're the only factor in that choice?' Prim played with the fraying hem of a blanket Grandma Olive had knitted me, unravelling the threads between her thumbs.

'What do you mean?' The edge was back in my voice, pressing into the stillness of the room.

'Nothing really.' She shrugged, frown lines visible on her usually smooth forehead. 'It's just – time hasn't stood still while you've been holed up in here.'

'What's changed?' I demanded.

'Oh, there's been some drama between the Coven and the Dragons. I just mean life goes on, Iv, one way or another.'

'George texted me every day for a week saying he was sorry.' I'd scrutinized each message, even though I hadn't replied. One of my major issues was that there was no way to keep what had happened quiet – colleges were leaky vessels for information so there was no reality where I could just pretend it had never happened. No way to return to the ease of first term. If that had been an option, I might have bargained with my mind to scrub itself clean.

'And now?' Prim asked.

I didn't answer. It hurt when the messages petered out, even though each one had caused my chest to burn and something uncontainable to bubble up in my throat. There was a silence, filled only by laughter coming from down the corridor and what sounded like Sophia's drawl as someone walked past on the phone.

'Do you really want to lose another friend?' Prim's question was almost a whisper.

'What are you talking about?' I snapped, hating myself for being mean to her when she was only trying to help but unable to stop myself from lashing out.

'Come on, Iv.' She rolled her eyes at me. 'I've seen the pictures you've got hidden around the room of you and your friend from home. Cara, was it? That was the name your mum mentioned at Christmas.' Her tone softened as I pulled my knees into my chest. Out of the corner of my eye, I could see the scrunched-up doilies in the corner of the windowsill, including the one George had made. 'I know you don't want to speak about her and I'm not going to push it or ask what happened but I know you must really miss her.'

'Why are you still speaking to Martha?' I changed the topic of conversation to marginally safer ground, hoping Prim might just think Cara and I had fallen out or stopped talking. Perhaps if she believed that, I could trick myself into thinking it too for a while. I'd have done anything for a bit of relief, during those long, lonely weeks.

Prim's sigh was a gust rattling through the orchard. 'She says she was drunk. Like really drunk. I know she hurt you, Iv. I get that, I promise. But it's always been us three, right? We have something really special. Are you seriously going to let a guy like George get in the way of that? We're supposed to be sisters, remember.'

'George and Martha got in the way of each other. I had nothing to do with it.' But Prim's words echoed in my head – it was the lure of boys that had caused me to abandon Cara and go to the pub, after all.

'She's so sorry, Iv. And her lack of capacity's got to count for something, doesn't it? I'm tired of being the go-between but if you'd speak to her, you'd see that she really is. Sorry, I mean.'

'What about his lack of capacity? We'd all been drinking.'

'Maybe neither of them knew what they were doing then. Though he's so much bigger, he probably gets drunk less quickly.'

'Well, if she didn't do this to me, then he did. This pain has to have come from somewhere.' I was desperate to assign it, to apportion blame, to have an obvious answer and an obvious solution – a cure to my suffering, even.

Prim turned away from me so that her face was silhouetted against the blank winter sky. Her features were a mountain range, peaks and troughs that I'd learned so well but that were becoming foreign to me even as I scrambled to get back to my previous position.

'Maybe I don't need either of them,' I declared.

'Do you really believe that?' Her voice was small and shrunken like some morbid medical curiosity.

'Well, I've still got you.' It was meant to be a statement

but it came out inflected at the end, a bit too much like a question.

I wanted to believe it. I truly did. But looking back into her deep brown eyes, I knew that I couldn't survive college without Martha and Prim. And I couldn't have one without the other. Without Martha there, Prim was flickering – stuttering, even. On my own, I couldn't provide enough oxygen to sustain her brilliance. Without Martha, my gloom would snuff her out.

There was still a choice to be made. Everything existed in binaries back then. Good or evil. Boys or girls. George or Martha. Dead or alive. I didn't see how I could stay the latter without picking one of the former.

My fist hovered above the door, like my knuckles were scared of the impact. Inside, there were faint sounds of movement. It was late enough to be pitch black, late enough that I knew the stars would be reflected in the sisters' pond but not late enough for Prim to have stopped working on her essay.

I knocked. Three quick raps before I could change my mind.

She appeared at the door, awake and alert like she'd been waiting for something. I said nothing but she saw my gloves and my muddy old trainers. Frowned, but didn't ask questions as she chucked on a raincoat hanging from a hook. Her footsteps clacked down the corridor as we walked towards Martha's part of college. Up three spiral staircases, and then down one more, arriving at the turret where she rested.

Prim hovered a few paces behind me as I stared at yet another door. The glittery initials *MGB* were stuck on the outside.

Before I'd steeled myself to knock, she opened the door. Wild-eyed and messy-haired, she had a wine glass in one hand and clutched a shawl around her shoulders with the other. The room smelled of sage and something darker – something musty and hard to place.

I squinted into her face. It was like looking into the sun too long, even with mascara smeared round her eyes and knotty tangles in her curls. She could have blinded me, there and then. But that was my moment. I'd made a decision. I was going to act on it. I was going to do something. Be something. For once, Martha wasn't going to outshine me.

'Come on.' I cut her off just as she opened wine-stained lips to speak.

'Ivy—' Her voice floated after me, breathy and high, but I kept marching, the two of them scurrying to catch up. The corridors were empty as we walked towards our destination, weaving our way out of the warren, all of us knowing the unspoken fact of where we were going.

Under the moonlight, a frost glistened on the hard-bitten ground, illuminating each blade of grass so that it sparkled. The air needled into me but I shrugged my jacket off all the same, and let my bare skin soak in the freshness. After going through the motions for so many days, I was too alive to feel the cold.

The moment we stepped from open field into the trees,

the silvery light grew muted but it still slipped through every few metres, bathing patches of the forest floor in metal. Twigs crackled around us as small creatures moved out of our way. An owl hooted somewhere to our left. Brambles caught on me, causing tiny pinpricks of blood to bloom on my arm, but I forged on until we got to the clearing.

The moon and the stars shone brightest there, like we'd emerged out of a storm. I pulled out the penknife from where it was dragging the material of my joggers down, and flicked the blade open. Seeing the light catch on it as I'd lain in bed, unsleeping, was what had got me up and out. Like its point was sharpened to that very moment, an instrument made to guide me there.

'What's that for?' Prim asked and I saw a flash of something fleeting and unguarded in her eyes. Martha gripped her arms against her chest – I hadn't given her time to put anything over her pyjamas other than the shawl – but her mouth was knitted shut.

'A blood oath.' Leaves fluttered as I spoke the words with all the confidence I'd been wishing for since I arrived at college. I didn't even let the possibility that my plan might not work enter into my mind – my own thoughts could be powerful but they could also be treacherous.

'A what?' Prim looked half-aghast, half-tempted.

'We're making a blood oath.' Branches stirred in appreciation. It was something Cara and I joked about when we were small but never actually did – and maybe that was the problem. We thought our lives were intertwined but we had never done anything to secure the loose ends so that our threads couldn't be unpicked.

'Does this mean you forgive me?' Martha's voice trembled.

My throat hurt too much to reply. 'We can use my penknife. The one you got me for Christmas,' I managed to croak. In those weeks, I'd started carrying it wherever I went, my fingers tracing the indents where the engraving was. Sometimes I even fell asleep clutching the knife, praying to the friendship we'd had when it was gifted to me. But until then I hadn't so much as opened it since we'd admired it together at Christmastime. My heart beat out of my chest and I could have sworn I heard theirs too. Prim's, Martha's and those of girls long dead. A rhythmic thudding, at first slow and then quicker and quicker. The three of us stock-still underneath the branches. I closed my eyes, imagining I was the heron flying back to the pond so that I could see our trinity. The perfect shot.

Martha and Primrose lifted their hands to the night sky, even as they exchanged glances. Mine moved without me thinking, first brandishing the blade in the air and then plunging towards them.

Prim flinched as I drew closer, the wind whipping loose curls from her bunches. 'Don't you trust me?' I asked, wounded before I'd even cut into skin.

'Of course, I do.' Her hand relaxed in mine but she still closed her eyes as I dragged the knife across her palm.

I left her, turning to Martha and tripping over a root. 'Shit.' The knife was sticking into the ground, an inch away from my foot. It was covered in dirt but when I wiped it with my sleeve, it looked new again in seconds. Martha put her arm around my shoulders to help me up, and I allowed myself to breathe her in for a moment. The scent of soil mingled with zest and incense and something else sweet that I couldn't identify.

'Careful, we don't want any accidents.' Prim flicked her torch on so that we were illuminated and the details of the clearing retreated into nothingness. I hadn't looked into Martha's eyes since everything had changed. Since she'd fiddled with the fabric of us and ended up yanking it apart. But she was right there in front of me, equal parts softness and high cheekbones, promise and regret. I forced my chin up towards her, her pupils pitch black and dilated despite the artificial light. For half a second, I thought I saw not my reflection but George's staring back at me but then I blinked and it was just us again. Martha tipped her head back, biting her lip, as the knife created a gouge in her perfect skin.

It surprised me how easy it was to slice into their flesh, blood trickling from Prim and spurting from Martha. An ugly part of me took pleasure in the pain that splayed across her face, like I was a child again, grabbing the plait of a girl who'd pulled my ponytail. Then I turned the knife towards me. I felt the cut as a friend, as the sea in my hair, as the rustle of the witching tree, the sound of Martha's laugh.

I gathered her and Prim towards me, placing our hands on top of each other's so that we were a triangle with me at the head. Our blood sang together, snaking down our wrists and onto the dead leaves, as the branches serenaded us with creaks and snaps. I'll never know how long we stayed like that for, bound together in the woods, swaying in time with the trees, Martha's chest rising and falling with breaths that gradually evened out. Something was mended over moments or lifetimes. It was nothing and it was everything.

Prim was the first to break away, stamping her feet to warm herself. The blood was drying on our palms, our bodies intertwined without even touching. I flicked the knife down, slipping it back into my pocket. It was time to go back. Our feet stumbled, our lips slurred. We were headier than if we'd drunk all the Red Dragons in the town. I was almost floating off the fact that we'd needed a glue and I'd been the one to provide it. No matter the cause of the rupture, I was the saviour, the fixer. The heroine.

The heron was on the edge of the shallow pond as Martha slid her hand into mine – something I hadn't asked for but didn't refuse. It didn't move when we walked past it, up on tiptoes so as not to disturb its hunt. The moon had faded and the first hints of morning showed the tall bird standing, fixated on its reflection as it looked for prey among the reeds. It said to me *I see you, Ivy Graveson. I see where you're going.* And I think it told me that where I was going was somewhere good, somewhere I was always meant to be. But I might have misheard that part.

Week 8

We are the survivors. It is impossible to stamp us all out. We are too many. We were the onlookers as they took our sisters to the pond. It took all our might not to cry out, not to fight back with tooth and nail when we saw them trussed up and brutalized, but we had already discussed how some of us must remain. To continue. To be a guiding light for the shunned, the curious, the different across the land. The water did not want to take them. The trees creaked and complained. The birds would not stop shrieking. But eventually man's will finds a way and our sisters stopped their struggles. They are at peace now, but we are not. We shall never know peace again.

Martha chucked in a dash of bitters and some cranberry juice to the martini glass so that the liquid turned a violent pink. 'Here, have a Martha.' She handed me the drink after garnishing it with a cocktail umbrella and a maraschino cherry. 'Me, Ag and Nat created it when you were – when you were away.' Her voice fizzled out.

'You were still having drinks parties when I was hiding in my room?' I asked, not really trying to conceal my indignation. Lying on her orange silk bedcovers it was like nothing had changed, and I didn't want her to remind me that it had.

'Only because I didn't know what else to do. It wasn't the same without you, Iv. I just needed a distraction. Any distraction.' Martha sank down onto the bed with a sigh. She'd been jittery since we started speaking again. One day she wanted to bake cookies in the shared kitchens and the next she wanted to stay out as late as the city would have us. That night, we were doing face masks and painting our nails. Anything to make our façades shine.

'I know we haven't spoken about it but – I really don't remember anything about that night. And I don't think George does either.' Her face was turned away from me, as she rubbed a piece of amethyst between her fingers.

'You've been speaking to him?' My cheeks flushed red-hot at the thought of another potential, secondary betrayal but I was conflicted by my desire for information about George. I hadn't so much as caught a glimpse of him since he'd seduced my best friend despite supposedly being in love with me. Although we had fractured, I still found myself thinking about him. What had happened with Cara had shown me once before how quickly things can unravel and now that I was released from his spell, I saw that I couldn't – shouldn't – have ever built my world around him. And yet I hadn't managed to untether myself fully from his pull.

'What? No. I mean, yes. I have. A bit. But only because he was so worried about you, he kept asking me if you were okay or if I'd heard from you. I think he really wants – or at least hopes – you can still be friends.'

'Friends?' I spat the word out like a curse. 'How can I possibly be friends with both of you?'

Martha gulped and nodded, an animal backed into a corner. Sometimes I wonder whether things would have turned out differently if I'd been able to keep the fury from my voice. 'Yeah. Of course. You're totally right. Screw him.'

Just as she moved towards me on the bed, Prim pushed the door open. 'Jesus, it's freezing out there.' She shook snow off her hair, pulling off a quilted coat that looked like a wearable sleeping bag. 'Sorry I'm late, I was in the—'

'Library.' Martha and I finished her sentence for her at the same time, our giggles warming the room. Something snapped in the air, something that had been holding us apart, and Martha snuggled up to me with renewed ease.

'Here, we've got cucumber for your eyes and we did a homemade toner thing as well with rosewater and tea tree.' I pointed to the desk where everything was laid out in cute dinky bottles but Prim just slipped into bed with us.

'It's so nice to be the three of us again. I don't need any of that stuff,' she said.

'Agreed. But I do feel kind of bad about Ag. Maybe we should have invited her tonight.' Martha chewed on her lips. For the first time, I noticed little flakes of dry skin around her mouth and eyebrows.

'What did I miss with Agatha?' My curiosity won

out over the irritation of the mention of anyone outside that room.

'Oh, of course. You don't know,' Martha said.

'Lucky you,' Prim muttered as Martha gave her a shove with a pillow.

'Her and Freddie broke up,' Martha explained.

'I didn't even realize they were properly together,' I said, thinking back to how little I'd spoken to Agatha in the previous weeks, always arriving to supervisions at the very last minute and then lingering with Harold at the end to avoid her.

'Well, they were. Kind of. Ugh, I don't know, it's complicated. But she seemed really into him and now she's sad.'

'She was really into getting drunk with him. She'll find a new guy soon enough.' Prim pulled the blanket around her. The snow had melted on her hair but her lips still had a blue undertone to them.

'You don't know that,' Martha argued. 'For those of us into boys, it can be hard to meet them when we're just surrounded by girls.'

'Why did they break up?' I chose to ignore the implications of what Martha had said.

'He said he wanted more time to focus on the boys or something,' she shrugged.

'Really?' I began to speak but Primrose cut across me.

'Come on, Iv. You know Freddie's all boys, boys, boys, Dragons till I die,' she snorted. 'There's nothing more to him than that.'

'Are you sure? I agree he's all boys, boys, boys, but there's something about Freddie which doesn't quite add up. The way he apparently hangs out in our woods and always asks questions about the Coven. And him and Eddy. What's that about?' I asked, half to myself.

'They're just friends. This isn't about him, anyway. We don't need to dissect his every move. It's about Aggie,' Martha sighed and I didn't care enough to push my point. I was sick of thinking about boys. 'I wish we could do something nice for her.'

'Not to change the subject but I think I found something in the library earlier. Something even Sophia and Amina don't know.' Prim got up to heave a leather-bound book out of her bag and opened it to point to a page in the middle. 'Apparently the Saint Clair sisters were drowned in the pond in the woods, underneath that tree, because that's literally where they used to practise their "magic".' She waggled her fingers like bunny ears over the last word.

'Like a liminal place?' I said, trying out some of the new vocabulary I'd learned in anthropology lectures.

'Exactly,' Prim grinned at me. 'Supposedly, they felt it was somewhere they could connect with the "other". Water's important to liminality. The body of water there used to be much bigger but it mostly dried up after they were murdered.'

We sat in our own silence for a moment as gusts of wind stroked the windowpane. Even through the thick curtains, we could hear its moans. A flicker of something reminiscent of George reverberated in the room after Prim brought up the Saint Clair sisters, a hint of when he was relaxed enough to show his love for history. Whatever it was, I stomped on it.

'Hey, why don't we go to the tree and make a wish for Aggie there?' I grabbed both their hands, inviting their body heat into me. I wanted to keep our momentum going so that we had no time to look back – unless it was to the golden days of first term – and I knew the tree could help us with that. Even if she hadn't been able to save our sisters before, I had a strange certainty she could save us.

Just like that, Martha shot up, and kissed me on the forehead like it was a reward. 'You're a genius, Ivy Graveson.'

'Didn't you hear me say it was snowing again?' Prim kept her eyes fixed on the book.

'Ooh, but it's so pretty out.' Martha bounced on the bed, so that we all fell towards its centre. Prim turned to me, her eyes a question mark.

'This has got to be the last snow of the year. Might as well make the most of it.' I shrugged, trying to appear casual. 'It can't hurt, Prim. Come on. Look at it this way – you can see it as a historical recreation of the atmosphere of the time. It will help with your long essay if you're sticking to your idea about approaches to female criminals in late medieval times.'

'Fine. You got me.' Prim placed the book gently back into her rucksack. 'As long as I make it clear that I am participating in this expedition only as a research project. Honestly, you two will be the death of me.'

I held her hand all the way down the path into the woods. Our feet crunched into the snow, the first sets of prints to walk through the whiteness. The night was clear and the moon was so full it looked like it was about to burst. A rabbit skittered in front of us just before we reached the clearing and Martha shrieked, a sharp talon in the silence. When we arrived, we were small in the hugeness of the witching tree. All silliness and posturing shaken out of us.

'So, what do we do now?' Prim asked, shivering.

'We need to wish for something that's going to make Aggie's life better,' Martha answered. 'Something that will help her forget about Freddie.'

'Why don't we wish that she always attracts people?' I can't pretend it wasn't my suggestion.

Martha nodded, a smile sneaking across her face. 'Yes. That's exactly what Ag needs. If she just attracts the right kind of people everything will be okay. But how do we do it?'

My palm itched where the cut from the oath had just started to scab over, and it was as if Prim could read my thoughts. 'We can't cut ourselves every time, Iv,' she said. 'We'll have no palms left.'

'I've got another idea.' I pulled out my penknife and spoke over Prim before she could object. 'It's not for another blood oath but because it's valuable. Because you both gave it to me. We need something special to wish with, something that has worth beyond the material object.' I flipped it open so the engraving glittered in the moonlight. All the essays I'd written that year about gifts and reciprocity bubbled up in my mind.

'We – the Coven – keep taking things from this place and we give back a little but I don't think it's enough,' I went on. 'And Prim's right. We can't just go through the motions. If you do the same thing again and again, it gradually becomes tarnished. Duller. The tree needs something from us. Something important.'

After the words sped out of my mouth, I looked to Martha to lead us in the next part. The spell. But she just stared back at me, expectant. I coughed, trying to clear my throat in the chilly air. Something had shifted, the dynamics of who was leading who less clear than they had been.

'We are gathered here today—' I started.

'It's not a funeral,' Prim interjected.

I took a deep breath of the piercing air, the taste of cold and pine and history lingering on my tongue. 'We are here because we are asking you, witching tree, to grant us something.' Prim looked at me sideways, trying to make me laugh or realize that this was all just a stupid game. But the thing is, if you don't believe in what you're saying it will never come true. No matter what it is.

'We are here in your power where the lifeblood of our sisters was spilled.' The tree creaked, cracking its knuckles, and Martha jumped, knocking into my arm. I held firm, providing the steady hand we needed to guide us through whatever might come next. 'I need something from you both as well if we're going to do it properly.'

Martha pulled her crystal pendant out from under her sweatshirt. She'd started to wear a different one depending on what she was trying to manifest, reminding me of the matching pair of mood rings me and Cara used to share. The one Martha wore that night was a smooth stone the colour of blood clotting that would have been ugly on anyone other than her. She undid it with delicate fingers, kissed it quickly and dropped it into my palm, still charged with the warmth of her body.

Martha and I turned to Prim at the same time. 'You both know I'm not the kind of person to carry something precious on me. I care about people, not things,' she said.

'People *are* things.' Martha rubbed her collarbone where the crystal had rested a minute before. 'You could wish on us if you like.'

'That doesn't feel right. You guys are too precious. What if it doesn't work the way we thought?' For a moment, a look I didn't recognize passed over Primrose's smooth skin. 'And I don't want to boost your ego, Martha.'

She reached into her back pocket to retrieve the pristine notebook she always carried with her and pulled something out of its pages. 'What about this?'

'Why is it special?' I asked. The yellow and red leaf in her palm was the colour of first kisses and fights and light fleeing summer's grip. It was dry and flat and perfectly preserved, given an afterlife through her care and attention.

'I pressed it after the nature walk.'

'I was on that walk, too,' I said.

'Yeah, I know you were. That's kind of the point.' Prim gave me a pointed look. 'I kept it ever since.'

I placed the knife, the leaf and the crystal at the bottom

of the tree, where the bark of the trunk was thickest and gnarled. Just next to the pond where we'd let our hair become one with the water. The wind rattled every other tree in the woods but the witching tree stood almost unmoving, reaching out to beckon us in. She was too wide for us to encircle with our arms so instead we each stood with a hand pressed against her roughness.

'We ask you to bless Agatha Love with the gifts of attraction. We ask you to do this so that our friend—'

'Our sister,' Martha corrected me.

'Our sister can be free and happy and have something to keep her occupied. We've given you these tokens as a way to recognize this place, the sisters, and all you've done for us. How you've brought us together again.' I bowed my head to my hands, so that I didn't have to look Prim in the eye.

We were done. We were giddy with the cold, the virgin snow, the threads stitching us back together. And that could have been it. It could have been a half-forgotten memory, hazily remembered over a reunion in twenty years' time where we laughed about our obsession with the small college woods and wondered how we could ever have let our best days slip through our fingers without grasping on to every moment.

We could have had that dismal, wonderful, comforting future. But the wind whipped a single branch forward, almost cutting Prim above the eyebrow. The rest of the tree stood still as the branch curved – it should have snapped but it didn't. A buzzard glided overhead, settling on a stump behind us, unthreatened by our smallness next to the majesty of the historic trees.

I blinked and when I opened my eyes after a fraction of a second, our offerings had been pulled closer to the heart of the tree, gleaming in the fragile March sun.

'Leave them.' Martha's voice matched the breathiness of the breeze around us. 'She has them now.'

We scrambled back along the path just as the snow began to melt, slipping and sliding into each other. By the time we reached the tame, tended college buildings, I was soaked in water, sodden in love.

TERM 3

Week 1

We continue. We see the traitor and the man in the market square but they avert their gaze, although we do not spare them ours. We still see men in the woods sometimes, including him. Their society seems to exist for the sole pursuit of pleasure. They have no respect. Yet we are the ones who have to be careful, keeping ourselves hidden, snatching pockets of time, when they are the ones who should be ashamed.

I hadn't seen a boy in weeks. So, when Agatha stood in the middle of the dance floor surrounded by them, it was like seeing some kind of mythical beast.

The Coven held a party each year to say goodbye to winter and welcome in the spring. It was co-hosted with two other girls' drinking societies – the Sirens and the Green Faes – so that exactly which girls belonged to which society still wasn't entirely clear to the boys in attendance. Like us, the other girls' societies kept their cards close to their chest. We could party together but we didn't ask too many questions, which suited everybody just fine. The occasion was a secret kept well enough that when invitations – scented with floral perfume and decorated with pressed flowers – were dropped into our pigeonholes, even Martha was surprised.

I'd spent the Easter holidays in a hollowed-out version of the college, the building a skeleton lacking the flesh of the girls who made it come alive. Prim had gone to stay in her aunt's spare house in the countryside to focus on her long essay and revision. Martha was skiing with her mum somewhere in France. I'd taken a job calling alumni and asking them to donate to new gyms and an upgraded library. The only other people who'd stayed behind were Masters students and PhDs looking to top up their stipend. They were always friendly to me, and the old ladies who I spoke to were delighted to regale me with tales of their college days. Sometimes, I thought they even got close to mentioning the Coven – they'd talk about the woods with a kind of reverence in their voice before abruptly changing the subject.

But every interaction I had was threaded through with stitches of Martha and Prim. Echoes of them reverberated in the bare corridors. Occasionally, they were intermingled with George – the smell of him, the weight of his body – before I pushed him away. I still hadn't seen him and I didn't know how I'd cope if or, more realistically, when I did.

I'd even found myself missing Natasha's easy giggles and Agatha's acid comments. I'd thought I couldn't survive another day in a home that didn't feel like home. But then Martha and Prim came back a day before everyone else and we drank oat milk hot chocolate and everything was right again, like nothing had ever happened outside of the three of us.

The next day, when Land Rovers pulled up to the front gates to deposit daughters and college was swarmed with girls again, I missed the peace and quiet of the Easter holidays. Prim and Martha alone had been the right level of fullness for me, and the chatter and shrieks as friends were reunited was too much.

'You okay?' Prim linked her arm through mine as we walked to Sophia and Amina's house, our feet snapping twig after twig.

'Yes. It's just that I was pretty much by myself in this place for three weeks over the holidays and now there's so many people again. It's a lot. It's so—'

'Busy?' Prim finished for me. 'Tell me about it. But we should enjoy tonight while we can. Exams will come round soon enough.'

I didn't reply, not wanting to think about revision or anything else that could burst our bubble. Exams were a sharp-edged thing, meaning stress and worry and less free time. I knew that from how Cara and I had fewer and fewer hours to spend together as our school days wound to a close, exacerbated by the wedge of my choice to go to a different, faraway university. I wanted everything to be softness, as I leaned into Prim and breathed in the clean smell of her laundry detergent undercut by the mulchy scent of the surrounding woods.

'Hurry up, you two!' Martha called from further

down the path, where she was laughing with Natasha and Agatha.

As we arrived at the house, the sun began to set, shining red, purple and orange over the orchard. The crooked building was losing its features by the second as the light burned then faded. Prim and I paused for a moment to take in the fire in the sky, then stepped over the threshold and shut out the outside world.

A wall of laughter and incense hit our ears and nostrils as we looked for a free space to hang up our coats. Girls lounged on every piece of furniture, sat on every windowsill, each one of them wearing some kind of white garment. This level of busy didn't bother me as much as the general hubbub of college had. I was back with my people. My girls.

In the corner, there was a dark shape slumped against the wall. It was the only shadow in the space. All the others had been chased away by thick, dripping candles and fairy lights. Except it wasn't a shadow at all. When I squinted, I made out the outlines of a boy.

On his pale skin – the colour of milk on the turn – there were black inky scrawls. Leaning in closer, I could see that there were names signed on his arms, alongside poorly drawn pentagrams and a few smudged lipstick kisses.

'That's Laurence. Or at least we think that's his name.' Sophia made me jump. She was standing so close behind me that I trod on her foot as I stood up, but I hadn't heard her arrive.

'Who is he?' I asked.

'He's Eddy's cousin. Or Freddie's. Not sure which. One of the sisters brought him home after a pub lunch earlier today. He was too drunk to perform so we stuck him here in the living room instead.'

'Shouldn't we help him?'

'That's why he's here, silly.' Her tone was sugary, the kind of voice you would use with a baby or a dog. 'Out in the open. So we can check he hasn't choked on his own sick or something else equally revolting.' She wrinkled her nose and took a tiny step back on her stilettos.

'But he doesn't know what's happening,' I protested.

'Exactly. Like I said. This is the best place for him.'

'Did you get in touch with Eddy or Freddie?' I whispered his name but I was safe; Martha was busy on the velvet sofa, letting Amina plait her hair, and I couldn't see Agatha.

'Do you really think he'd be better off with them?' Sophia looked at me, pityingly. 'Boys don't know how to take care of each other. But we do.'

Her gaze softened and she bent down to ruffle the boy's hair, his curls flecked with gold but not nearly as bright as George's. 'You'll be just fine here, won't you, my angel?' For a second, Sophia in her pure white dress and heels was gone and was replaced with someone much older and more motherly. Then she straightened up, taking my hand in hers, firmly enough to drag me away.

'Let's join the others. There's no problem here, is there, Ivy?' I considered whether I cared enough to protest and George came surging into my mind, unwanted. Laurence

could easily have done something as upsetting, as confusing as George had done to me. Or worse even. In fact, I had
no proof that he hadn't.

'No, you're right. There's not. As long as we're keeping
an eye on him.' Even if he had the potential to be awful,
I still didn't want him to die. I looked down at the boy,
his face calm and his chest rising gently. 'Before we go,
Primrose mentioned that there'd been some drama with
the Coven and the Dragons while I was out of action at the
end of last term? Everything okay?'

'Where did you go at the end of last term?' she asked me.

'I was ill.' It was an excuse I'd seen Mum use time and
again, although I guess for her it was true. Either way, it
functioned in pretty much the same way as bereavement –
neither were things the unafflicted wanted to examine
too closely.

'So that's what we're calling it.' Sophia raised an eyebrow but didn't ask any questions. 'They got one of our
parties cancelled. They wanted the venue we'd already
booked for a boys-only thing that night so they pulled
some strings with the senior tutor – a man, obviously – and
they cancelled our soirée last minute. We were meant to be
going there after a thanksgiving ceremony in the woods.
We don't even know how they found out about it – that's
the worrying part. That we're somehow compromised.'

'But why couldn't the Dragons just go somewhere else?
Or ask you or Amina if it was so important?' I didn't
enquire about how they found out because I was pretty
sure I already knew. After all, Freddie was charming when

he wanted to be and Agatha loved to be in on things and make others aware of that fact. I wouldn't have been surprised at all if she'd let slip something to him when they were still seeing each other.

'Oh, sweet summer child. Because they can. Because they're classic boys, stomping all over everything. The longer you're a sister, the more you'll learn that.'

'Surely there must be more to it?'

'No, sister.' She pressed her finger against my lips so I could practically taste the rose aroma of her hand cream. 'No more questions. Tonight's not about them, it's about us.'

She took my hand and we left the uglier version of George behind and drank glass after glass of Amina's special punch. It tasted of peaches and candied peel and the promise of summer. By the time we were ready to leave the drinks and head to the venue, my body was loose and my cheeks were flushed from dancing. We'd ended up as one big circle, hands linked, skipping round and round in the middle of the huge room. At one point, Prim and Sophia had lifted Laurence into the centre – so everyone could keep an eye on him – and we'd spun around until we collapsed from dizziness. As we left, Prim and I propped him up on a cushion to make sure he was comfortable before we turned out the lights.

The drive to the actual party was a blur of bright stars, brighter street lights and white, white dresses. We tumbled out of the hired cars and up a twisting flight of steps until we emerged in a huge room with a vaulted ceiling and row after row of leather-bound books. Martha gasped and gave my hand a little squeeze before she and Natasha rushed over to examine a table laden with cakes and fruits. A waiter offered me a glass of champagne and I took it without hesitation. The coolness calmed the spot where Martha's skin had warmed mine.

'Do you think it's okay to get drunk in a library?' Prim asked me, examining the spines on the nearest shelf.

'Of course,' I reassured her. 'It's not like anything's going to happen to the books. I think everyone's mind is elsewhere.'

At that moment, the doors at the other end of the room creaked open and a flood of boys poured in. Marmosets, some Dragons, and a few who must have been members of societies too small or secretive for me to know their names. A sea of eau de cologne and suits moved towards us, wave upon wave of guys who looked remarkably similar to each other. A flash of gold appeared in the midst of the crowd and I flinched.

My hand found Prim's and she brushed her fingers across mine. She was right there when I needed her, like she knew I required her comfort at exactly that moment. 'It's all right. He won't be here. Sophia and Amina would have made sure of that.'

'How do they know?' But the question felt naïve as soon as it left my mouth, especially given my previous suspicions. 'Wait, I forgot that even the walls have ears in this place.'

'Yep, no secrets round here. Or none that last, anyway,' Prim said.

'I couldn't see them in the same room again.' My voice came out as a whisper.

'You won't have to,' Prim promised. 'Just keep it in your head that Martha didn't know what she was doing.'

Martha didn't know what she was doing. I repeated the mantra to myself as I watched her from the other side of the room, the only flash of red in the building. A boy I didn't recognize took a glass from one of the waiters and handed it to Martha like he'd procured it himself. Her mouth was open, light shone against the whiteness of her teeth and my eyes couldn't help but stare at her. It was a scene I'd seen a hundred times since I'd met her. Until something shifted.

At first, it was just a murmur, the kind of quiet information that gets passed through a crowd without anyone being aware of how. Then there was jostling. A boy stepped on Amina's foot and she gave him a quick shove in the small of his back when she thought no one was looking. The crowd pressed in, closing the gaps between bodies. I side-stepped to peer through a chink in between heads and shoulders. A glimpse of blonde hair, a sneak of long limbs, the sound of a low-pitched laugh laced with sarcasm. Agatha. She was at the centre of a group of boys who were by then not only peering at her but pressing in, all elbows and self-belief.

'Who is she?' a guy with floppy black hair asked.

'That's Agatha Love,' Peter replied. I hadn't noticed him before but even his eyes were momentarily pulled away from Martha.

'What on earth is going on?' Martha herself was at my shoulder, popping a glacé cherry between her teeth.

'Looks like the charm is working,' I smiled. My life was back on track enough that I could be happy for Aggie, especially when she was otherwise occupied. And if it meant that she might not make as many demands on Martha's time for the rest of the term, that was even better.

'I think you're right.' Martha's mouth was a thin line, and her eyes were somewhere else even as they bored holes into Agatha's back.

'Aren't you pleased?' I was genuinely surprised at the note of jealousy that had snuck into Martha's voice. Even after everything that had happened, it hadn't occurred to me that someone with all the things she possessed could be envious.

'Of course I am. Why would you say that?' She drained the rest of her cocktail and walked onto the dance floor. The library had been adorned with paper chains and other handmade decorations, some vaguely in the shape of bodies. When I squinted, I recognized them as the ones the Coven had made at New Year. I sent a wish upwards into the rafters when I caught sight of the figure I'd created. Mirror balls painted the room with a thousand patches of light. Most of them seemed to land on Aggie, making her hair sparkle and her skin shimmer.

I spun Martha under my arm, the skirt of her dress a full circle as we went faster and faster. But no matter how quickly we went, I couldn't twirl her out of that room. She kept looking over her shoulder at Aggie, at Peter, at the boys, at who was looking at who. Her feet weren't as nimble as usual, either. More than once she tripped, tumbling into my arms, like a planet whose centre of gravity is warped when the orbits around her change. A giant made vulnerable by the slightest of movements.

Like many days in my life that I'd feared, when it actually arrived it almost slipped by without me noticing. When Grandma Olive had finally drifted away from this world, it hadn't even been on one of my visiting days. I'd been eating lentil bolognese with Cara, watching repeats of old David Attenborough documentaries from when he'd been young and kind of hot. And yes, there'd been the dream that I ignored about Cara which I would always blame myself for. But once I'd managed to squash my instincts, I'd enjoyed a lie-in after the flurry of exams and the afternoon pub trip with the popular boys and girls. It was only the call of the sea that drew me away from beer and laughter to make my way down to the beach.

It was the same on the day I saw George again. At the end of that term we had exams that we had to pass to progress to the next year, so Prim and I had created revision schedules together, hers carefully colour-coded and mine with little doodles and stickers to liven it up a bit. My schedule that morning allowed for a slightly later start so I treated myself to some greasy baked beans and hash browns from hall for breakfast rather than my usual cereal bar. I headed back to my room and plaited my hair, using some of the techniques I'd asked Natasha to show me, before I left for the anthropology library. My cycle to the library was pleasant – I passed a small brook close to my destination and I felt its flow increase as I whizzed by. I thought it was just cheerfully gurgling at me, but perhaps it was intended as a warning.

I parked my bike on the edge of the river proper, choosing to walk the last five minutes so that I could pause to look at the swans and ducks along the way. Everyone was already talking about how they were going to fill their summers with holidays and internships, and I found being in nature distracted me from the fact I had precisely zero plans. I couldn't wait for the legendary post-exam balls and garden parties, but I didn't want to so much as contemplate a long summer back in my hometown. Instead, I was thinking about how much I hated it when people ignored the signs and fed the birds despite it being bad for them, when a flash of gold rushed past me.

A wave of nausea rose up deep inside me but I pushed it down. One of the things the school counsellor had taught me was that just because we think something, it doesn't make it true. I wasn't sure I believed that, but I tried to repeat it to myself. *Just because I see George everywhere, doesn't mean it's necessarily him.*

I made it a few paces forward, reiterating this mantra in my head, when someone shouted my name from behind. There was no mistaking that voice, that deadly combination of huskiness sprinkled with sweetness. What would I do, what would I say when he caught up with me? He was on a bike and even though I was a fast walker he'd be at my side in seconds. I'd fantasized about all the things I could say to George to seem variously nonchalant, vengeful or righteous depending on my mood, but confronted with the reality of him I strongly suspected I'd just be a mixture of anger, tears and confusion.

The river was as agitated as I was. Usually so calm, that morning it was in spate, bobbing a gaggle of new ducklings up and down at an alarming pace. It was even lapping onto the path, setting a sloppy trap to soak ankles and skid wheels.

'Ivy,' George shouted again. I scrunched my eyes tight shut so that I saw stars bursting against a deep red. I wished he would just go away. Part of the reason I came to the anthropology library was that it wasn't in the vicinity of his college. He shouldn't have been there. He shouldn't have been anywhere near the new story I was writing for myself. He'd written our ending and then I'd closed that chapter.

As I opened them, I heard wheels shriek. Then a large splash, followed by more, slightly strangled, calls of my name. I started to run, flooding my senses with my hammering footsteps, my clamouring heart, my heavy breathing so that my moving parts would block out his voice. Speeding up, I ducked off the footpath and into the tangle of libraries and other university buildings, all towers and narrow alleyways. I kept going until the painful shortness of my breath stopped me, my lungs feeling like they were about to explode.

Part of me was mortified to have let George see me run

away from him, and part of me was just grateful to have escaped the temptation his very existence presented. I willed myself to focus on the pain in my right hip and the ache in my lower back from where the books in my rucksack had knocked against it – anything other than the thorny knot of emotions in my chest. I'd made my choice. I had to look forward, straight ahead, with no space to contemplate other paths or, God forbid, doubling back on myself.

'It didn't work.' Martha walked into the coffee shop where me and Prim were studying and, already, I could tell that we weren't going to get any more work done. I had already felt distracted since my near-miss with George the day before and I could sense by the way she was twisting her hands that Martha was agitated. Outside, the sky was a soft blush and there was a warmth to the breeze that hinted at spring. Martha's hair was still the brightest thing in the room.

'What didn't work?' I asked, even as I knew the answer. Martha settled in opposite me and ordered a hot chocolate with extra cream. I'd seated myself with my back to the window so that I didn't have to catch a glimpse of the turrets of George's college a few streets away. I'd also steered us to the table in the furthest, shadowiest corner.

'The blessing. For Aggie,' she added as Prim looked blank.

'I don't know, Marth, she seemed to be getting a lot of attention the other night.' I picked at the skin around my nails, not wanting to enter any territory that might put Martha in a huff again.

'You didn't seriously expect that to work, did you?' Prim asked, still trying to read an ethnography about endogamous kinship structures that I'd recommended as reading for her elective anthropology paper.

'It wasn't the right kind of attention.' Martha chose to ignore Prim and turned to face me. 'Those boys – I mean, yes, they were good-looking and relatively polite and everything but we don't want just another Freddie. God, I hate him.'

The waiter came back with Martha's hot chocolate, and her face went from thunder to sunshine in a second as she thanked him. As he walked away, he bumped into another customer's table, spilling their water. The smell of sugar and cinnamon clawed at the back of my throat.

'Do you really hate Freddie?' I asked, sipping the dregs of my camomile tea. It had grown too strong, making my lips pucker.

'Obviously. I hate anyone who hurts my friends,' Martha said.

'You seemed to get on well with him at dinners before,' Prim pointed out, unable to ignore our conversation entirely even as she highlighted passages.

'That was before,' Martha retorted. 'And you know I can get on with anyone if I have to.'

'It always looked like you enjoyed his company,' I shrugged.

'And you didn't?' she asked.

'I suppose I did,' I said, shrugging again, like it was all my shoulders could do. 'He asked me about myself. I think he might have been genuinely interested. And he asked me about the Coven, too. Sometimes it felt a little nosy but nothing to make me hate him. Like I said before, I find him kind of intriguing. I think there's more to him than just being a guy, you know.'

'What did he ask you?' Prim had put her book down, careful not to crack the spine.

'Just what our initiations were like, that kind of thing,' I replied. 'He's been to our woods before so he was intrigued.'

'Sophia mentioned that to me, actually. When she was up late praying to the moon or something else kind of woo-woo, she spotted him and Eddy there one night out of the window. But by the time she made it to the path, they were gone.' Prim chewed the end of her pen absent-mindedly.

'Oh, my god. He's trying to spy on us.' Martha slapped her hands against the table in triumph.

'I'm not sure it's spying,' I said carefully, knowing how Martha could get latched onto things. 'Just being curious. I asked him about the Dragons initiations, too.'

'Come on, Iv.' Martha placed a hand on my shoulder and fixed me with an intense gaze. 'He's been creeping about the woods, asking about the Coven. He's obsessed with us.'

'If you say so.' I tried to be as non-committal as possible. It could be hard to suss out how to manage Martha in moods like this. Sometimes if you indulged her a bit so she could see that she could get what she wanted, she lost interest, like it was only the knowledge that other people would bend to her will that mattered.

'I do. What if he tries to ruin things?' she asked, her voice low and urgent.

'I don't know, Marth. I haven't even seen him in weeks. He's more focused on the Dragons than anything else – you said so yourself.'

'Shh, that's enough,' Prim hushed us. 'Girls, exams are only a few weeks away now. We need to concentrate. Revision is more important than Freddie. Didn't our sisters know that education was the way to power?'

'Let's meet at the tree tonight,' Martha whispered, before Prim's glare made us all return to work.

For the first time in days, I walked to the clearing on my own. During the Easter holidays, I'd visited during the daytime but I'd never been brave enough to come alone at night. The first time I'd gone back after we'd left our offerings, they'd gone – vanished, like they were never there. But in the place where they'd been, a clump of daffodils had sprung up, slender and trumpeting. They were the variety with the whitest petals and the orangest flutes and they were the first. As the holidays wore on the clearing grew full of them, all kinds of daffodils covering the grass, chasing out the last hints of winter.

That evening, as the light vanished from the sky, their brightness was what guided me as I stepped out of the woods. Martha and Primrose were already there, their backs leaning against the bark of the tree. My foot stepped on something at first hard then squishy as I tried to make my way to them. I didn't want to look down but I forced my

eyes to focus on the dim outline of my trainer. It was covered with slime and shards of shell. My stomach lurched.
No, no, no, no.

'Ivy! Finally, you're here.' Martha called me over so I
didn't have time to properly mourn the loss of the snail.
Still, I muttered a quick prayer. It was something my mum
had hated me and Cara doing – picking the snails off wet
pavements to save them from other people. She'd said it
was dirty, that snails could carry diseases which could
cause blindness in humans, but whether that was true or
not I didn't care. I still saved snails whenever I saw them.
More than once, it had made me late to lectures on a wet
day. Each time I failed to save a tiny life, I somehow felt
like I was failing Cara again, too.

I hugged Martha and then Prim when I reached the
tree, taking comfort in their solid, unbroken bodies even
though we'd only been parted for a matter of hours. An owl
hooted sorrowfully somewhere nearby. The dregs of daylight drew out the angles of their faces, so that my friends
became a collection of hard edges and points.

'You arrived just in time.' I could still make out Martha's
smile on her face, though it looked less curved than usual.
Less soft. 'This is a powerful moment. I can feel it.'

Something scurried through the low undergrowth and
Prim jumped. Martha threw her head back and laughed.

'Calm down. It's not that funny.' Prim folded her arms
across her chest. 'This place changes at night.'

'Exactly. It changes,' Martha said. 'It's the perfect place
to use our power. To use it against Freddie.'

'What reason do we have to hate Freddie?' I tried to keep the irritation out of my voice that we were circling back to the Dragons again.

'He's friends with George. Isn't that reason enough?' Martha's eyes challenged me. Invoking George was a low blow but I didn't feel like rising to it. I didn't want to discuss him with her – I wanted to keep the two of them separate for evermore, even if it was just in speech.

'We were all friends with George. I was George's girl-friend. It's not a crime,' I stated.

'That was before,' Martha replied, echoing what she'd said in the coffee shop.

I looked down at the earth, hoping to lose any thought of before in the moist brownness full of beetles and woodlice. The woods whispered to me, stirring the surface of the pond, and I wondered if the others could hear them. One day, I wanted to get to the point where I could remember all the beautiful bits of various 'befores' without tears stinging my eyes but I hadn't found my way there yet.

'This is now, Iv,' Martha continued. 'We can't be sure what the Dragons are up to. You said so yourself. They cancelled our party. They don't want us to have our fun, our time together. What with exams looming, we'll have less parties anyway, less time together. And Freddie's been in these woods. He's been here. This term has to be all about protecting us and our sisters. Every moment we have together is precious.' She stomped her foot on the ground. The branches behind Martha's head shook at this violation, twisting into a shape that looked almost like a crown. She leaned closer to me so that I could see the strands of hair that were stuck to her lip gloss. The woods suited her. I shook my head.

'Let's make this about us. There's no outside world just now. No one else,' I argued. The trees leaned into us again, gossipy and green. 'That's what we should be thinking about. Us. We can agree on that at least.'

'Ivy's right.' Prim's voice was as low as the murmurs from the new leaves. 'We're what's important. Not Freddie.'

'But girls—' Martha said but she had lost the trees. The wind spoke over her, whipping her hair across her face so that she was obscured.

Prim reached for my hand and Martha's so that we formed a tiny circle next to the pond. The gusts died down and for a moment everything was still. The owl stopped hooting, the animals stopped hunting and the leaves stopped rustling. Night had set, fast and hard, but I wasn't afraid. I'd lived in the dark before, and this time I wasn't alone.

'We left the tree our gifts and she answered us.' I was the first to break the silence, just as it felt like it was about to burst. 'Agatha is getting all kinds of attention, just like we asked. That shows she believes in us. We're on the right path. She'll always be here when we need her.'

Week 2

Without our sisters, we keep learning, keep teaching each other. It is the least we can do to remember them. We sit by the pond, a picture of femininity on an early summer's day. They think we do not recall what happened here, that our girlish minds can only hold so many things at once. But we ensure that new sisters are taught their history, alongside everything else we know about letters, about the forest, about life. One day, we have faith that a learned woman will be so quotidian that they shall forget they were right about one thing: there is danger lurking within us.

Agatha was late. As Harold and I waited for her, sunbeams danced across the floorboards of his office. The view from his window was coming alive. Trees that had been bare sticks over winter were now in bud. Even the forlorn cactus that was shoved to the edge of his desk to make room for more papers looked healthier.

'How was your Easter, Ivy?' Harold smiled at me from behind wire-framed glasses.

'It was fine. Nothing too exciting. I stayed in college to do a fundraising job.'

'Ah. I remember that well.'

'Really?'

'I'm not that ancient,' he laughed.

'I didn't think you were. It's not that.'

'Ah. You didn't think I needed the money?'

'I wasn't sure. I thought maybe you did.' I glanced at Harold's polished brogues and his neat chinos – they were convincing but when I was with him and Agatha at the same time, I could tell his body lacked the natural ease hers possessed. He was more like me – a bit tense, a bit nervous, always watching.

'Well, I did. At the time. No shame in having a job during the holidays, Ivy. As long as it doesn't distract you from your studies,' he cautioned.

'How were your holidays this year?' I asked, not wanting to dwell on the fact that I was at risk of being distracted by something else entirely – late nights in the woods with Martha and Primrose.

'Lovely, actually. My fiancée and I were in Italy for a few weeks. Though I think she was a bit sick of looking at archaeological sites by the end.'

The minutes ticked by on the dusty grandfather clock in the far corner of the room. There was still no sign of Agatha.

'Let's just get started, shall we? After all, the countdown to the end of the academic year has begun in earnest.'

'Okay,' I agreed but I couldn't stop glancing at the door.

'So, tell me about how the long essay is going.'

I told him about how when I'd had nothing to do after

my shifts over the holidays, it was the essay that had distracted me from the empty corridors of college. That for
the first time since the start of the first term, the words had
flown easily after I'd transcribed my notes from my journal
to my laptop. That when there'd been no Coven (although
of course I didn't utter our name), no Martha and no Prim,
it was the Saint Clair sisters that had kept me awake at
night, alongside the land and the woods. I listed off the
theorists who'd been opening up new windows in my
mind, Federici and Strathern and others whose thoughts
I was trying to apply to what I wanted to say even if I
wasn't quite sure exactly what that was yet. The only thing
I didn't mention was the writing I'd done on the rituals of
the Dragons and the Coven.

'I've kind of been trying to do some site-specific
research, as well,' I added. 'You know, mix in some modern
stuff like you suggested.'

'What kind?' The skin between Harold's eyebrows
creased slightly.

'Going to the place where the sisters were supposedly
drowned. My friend found that information in a really old
book from the history library. You'd like her. She's brilliant.'

'I'm sure I would. And what do you do when
you're there?'

'It's hard to explain. I feel, mostly. Get a sense of the place.
At different times of day, during different weather. How
they would have lived. How they would have died. That
part is hard to think about but it feels important. Respectful.
Thankfully, the water's not deep enough for anyone to come

to any harm now. Sometimes, I do a bit of filming. Nothing special, just so I can watch it back later.' I was speaking quickly, excited by my project even if it was a solo one. Of course, I missed Cara anytime I so much as thought about filming but her absence also gave me space to figure out the aspects of the process I really liked. Her talent for being in front of the camera had been so obvious that I'd never really paused to think where mine might lie. 'I like imagining what it would have been like during their time – do you know some of the trees date from before the Reformation?'

'I did, actually. That's all fine, you certainly seem very lively when you talk about it, which is always a good thing. As long as you don't lose track of the archival material as well. Eyes on the prize, remember? There's only a little over a month until you'll need to hand the essay in.'

'Eyes on the prize,' I nodded. But I wasn't sure we were referring to the same prize.

'Oh, and Ivy – remember what I said before. Really dig into the modern aspect. See if there's anything you can link to now. Anything concrete. Embodied academia is great and it will be interesting to see your response to a place at the heart of what you're writing about, but any kind of sociological comparison you can make to the current university would flesh out the essay. How have the mechanisms of control changed? Does ritual still have a place here? Are there any kinds of performances that have replaced the witch trial? Where might more contemporary fears and dangers work themselves out? That kind of thing.'

As I cycled back home through the maze of zigzagging streets, a flash of gold caught my eye. I shook my head, trying to dispel the phantom George that I'd seen so many times since the incident, especially since the time he fell in the river trying to get to me. Apart from that one occasion, it was never actually him, just a shadowy likeness. The man would turn his head and I'd see that he lacked George's high cheekbones or his full lips or the mole just below his nose. Except this time – this time, it was George.

The sun came out from behind a cloud and caught his profile. Unlike the week before, I got a proper look at him. He was slipping in and out of a mass of tourists, clutching a handful of books to his chest. He looked more vacant than usual and less cheerful but it was definitely him. Almost no one else could catch the light like that, a beam following him down the crowded pavement like it had been created just for him.

My bike bumped up and down on the cobbled streets as I followed George. He turned left towards the history library, and I swung left too. Then he turned right to cross the river, stopping to look at the new ducklings bobbing on the water. I paused so that I wouldn't be too close behind him. Having him in my sights again propelled me forward, even though I knew he was in all likelihood only going to study. Despite the fact that last time I'd fled from him, I wanted to see him do the mundane, normal things that we had once done together before he tore it all apart. Being the observer rather than the observed gave me the confidence to indulge a ghoulish part of me that yearned for information about him even when it hurt, like the urge to press on a tender bruise.

I pushed my foot into the pedal, inching forward. Leaves skittered across the road, the wind sweeping my hair back off my face. And then nothing. No sound, no sensation. Nothing. Until a sharp pain kicked into my hip and the concerned face of an elderly woman I didn't recognize peered into my eyes.

The handlebars were a tangled mess. George had vanished. A few people paused to see what the commotion was but he had gone, over the bridge and into the scrum of winding side streets. I'd almost died and he hadn't even seen me.

'Are you sure you're okay?' Prim asked me for the hundredth time as I sat on her purple bedsheets, a fleece blanket wrapped round my shoulders.

'Yes, I'm fine. I promise. Just a bit shaken.' I sipped the herbal tea she'd made me. She'd given me the homemade mug with an abstract design painted by her sister that she usually reserved for herself. I hadn't mentioned my first encounter with George, only the one where I'd fallen off my bike. Maybe that was because I couldn't explain the synchronicity of him falling, then me. Or why I'd desperately wanted to be imperceptible, then was hollowed out when he didn't spot me.

'We really should go to Matron,' Prim muttered.

'Like I said, I didn't hit my head.' I put my arm around Prim's shoulder and rubbed the fluffy material of her sweater.

'I should be the one reassuring you, not the other way round,' she said.

'I think this whole incident has been more worrying for you than it has for me.' I tried for a laugh, and my chest only ached slightly.

'You seem remarkably okay.'

'My hip hurts.' I lifted a hand to silence her before she could mention Matron again. 'But mostly I'm just mad.'

'Mad?' Martha appeared in the door, which had been left ajar, just for her. Her eyebrow was raised and the corners of her mouth twisted upwards, like ribbon curled for a present.

'Yes. Mad. Angry. Furious.' I stood up, even though my hip still ached. I knew that it would bruise – I even wanted it. Wanted to see my pain flowering, where I could touch and prod it. I had to translate all the confusing feelings inside of me into something else. Something more manageable.

'What's got you so riled, Ivy?'

'She just had an accident, Martha,' Prim said.

'No. It's not that. Well, it is that. But it's the cause of the accident. I saw George when I was in town. He was walking home, I think. Or maybe going on to the history library,' I explained to Martha to catch her up.

'You saw George?' Her mouth fell open, even though it shouldn't really have surprised any of us.

'Yes. For the first time since—' I said, leaving my sentence unfinished to see if she would pick up the thread. She didn't.

'How was he?' she asked instead.

'He looked the same as ever.' I didn't have to say that he still shone, and that none of that would ever reflect onto me again.

'The same as ever. That's so unfair.' Martha pulled a face, her features twisting, her head tilted to one side.

'It is. So unfair.' I stood up, energy bubbling inside my body. Energy that I'd pent up all term, that had to be released somewhere. Staying still was impossible. I paced back and forth across the creaky floorboards. 'I want to go to the woods.'

'The woods?' Prim's eyes widened even as her voice tried for world-weary. It was pitch black outside and cloudy. No moon or stars to light our way.

'Yes,' I insisted.

'Can't we just stay here tonight?' She gestured at the room with its fairy lights, its neat shelves of books, its mismatched mugs waiting to be filled with vegan hot chocolate.

'Prim, you're the one who talks about justice and witches. Why is it fair that George gets to walk around, just living his life and I'm here and—' My voice seized up, painful and awkward.

Primrose moved towards me as the tears made good on their threats to escape. 'Whatever you need, babe,' she murmured as I leaned against her, my body rocking backwards and forwards.

'I need to go out. I need to go to our place,' I said.

'Okay, okay.' Her words were waves whispering over a pebbly beach.

'So, what are we waiting for?' Martha was still leaning against the doorframe, like she knew we were always about to leave again.

'Nothing.' I rubbed my swollen eyes, not caring that my mascara was making me look like a banshee. 'We just need one thing. Follow me.'

We walked almost the whole length of the college via internal staircases and curving corridors, until we were at my door. Inside, I grabbed the embroidery George had made me from the windowsill and slipped out again.

The way to the woods was muddy, our feet sticking in the ground like it was trying to keep hold of us. But the air was warm and it felt like the world was a sponge, waiting to be wrung out. I walked ahead of the others, marching through a path that I had come to know so well that it didn't matter that there was hardly any light. None of us reached for our phones and no one tripped or stumbled.

In the clearing, what scant light there was shone a little brighter. A couple of lonely stars fought through the clouds to cast a watery glow across Martha and Prim's faces. The shadow of the witching tree was faint but warped, creating pockets of darker darkness.

'Martha, do you have a lighter?' I asked.

She paused a moment before pulling one out of the many pockets of her coat. 'I only carry one in case someone else needs it.'

'We appreciate your foresight.' I gave her a mock curtsy and Prim giggled. Once we were actually in the woods and

I had stopped crying, her jaw unclenched and she let her hands brush against the dewy new leaves.

'What are you planning to do with it?' Martha asked.

'Get rid of everything bad,' I said with conviction. And I really felt that certainty within my body. Although so many awful things had happened, I had power, I had agency, and I could forge my path straight ahead, strong and true. I felt rather than heard a ripple of approval as the pond stirred. That was enough to seal my confidence – I told myself I'd never needed George at all, repeating it again and again in my head. These were my sisters and we'd made a vow together.

'Everything bad?' Prim questioned me again.

'Yes, like this.' I held up the doily that George had crafted with his own hands. It was the closest I'd come to touching him in weeks. A pang rang through me, so physical I almost doubled over, but I pushed any notions of complexity or nuance down where they belonged. 'We gave the clearing something positive – something we loved. Something of us. And now it's time to purge the bad stuff too.'

'I thought you didn't want to involve the boys in this place?' Martha said.

'Like you said, that was then. This is now.' Seeing George again had ignited feelings in me that I'd tried to ice over. It took me a moment to recognize them as the hot side of grief. Everyone thinks of grief as cold, sluggish, deadening. But it can be full of heat, making you jitter and burn.

'It's only been a few days.' Martha raised a perfectly plucked brow in my direction.

'Don't make me admit that you were right.' Anger still fizzed inside of me, and I couldn't tell which direction it might spill out in. *She's my sister*, I told myself again.

'It was just a joke, Iv,' Martha said.

For the first time, I didn't meet her eyes or laugh it off. I just bent down, breathing in the rich scent of the forest floor and getting to work. Because of the previous night's rain, the wood took a while to light, whistling and whimpering as I coaxed a flame. I wracked my brains for everything Cara and I had learned in our campfire badge for Brownies. Eventually, a small tongue of the palest orange took hold, flickering as it brought out the same colours in Martha's hair.

The flames whipped the air and hissed at the night. The heat was so intense that every inch of my body told me to back away. But my brain said no. I needed to feel something uncomfortable – painful, even – that wasn't coming from inside myself. Falling off my bike had been the start, but I wanted to feel *more*. The doily vanished in seconds. As the flames grew, reaching towards the heavens, Martha shrugged her coat off and tossed it in to feed them further.

'What did you do that for? I loved that on you,' Prim cried out but Martha just laughed.

'One of my mum's boyfriends bought it for me. Not the nice one you met, Ivy, but one of the shitty ones. And there will always be another one of them coming along, wanting to buy my favour, if I only wait long enough.'

'Well, in that case.' Prim slid the scrunchie from her hair, letting it fall around her face. 'When I tried to date a shitty guy in high school,' she explained as she dropped it into the flames and the fire licked it clean.

'Was that Olivia Rose's cousin by any chance?' Martha asked.

'How on earth did you know that?' Prim said, her voice rising in surprise.

'I know everything.' Martha tipped her head back and let out a little howl in the direction of the obscured moon. After a second, Prim and I joined her, letting our yelps lose themselves in the velvety night.

Usually, it made the colour in my cheeks rise when they talked about people I didn't know – would never know – but that they had in common. That night, the flames cleansed any fear of missing out on what had already been. I watched as I burned half the life that I'd made at university. The other half – the more important half – was divided into two and stood either side of me. The strange energy burned out of me too, replaced with something still fiery but more comfortable.

Whatever life I hadn't lived before was gone and there was nothing I could do about it. But I'd made a choice about the life I wanted in that town and anything that didn't fit into it was only worthy of being turned to ash.

Once the fire had performed its magic and spent out its own flame, I stamped on the remains to make sure it couldn't spread and harm the woods. Then I reached down and scooped up some of the ash, ignoring the heat.

I walked a few paces and plunged my hands into the cloudy water where three girls had once lost their lives, letting it purify and drain away all the hurt that had come before.

Week 3

We sign the book again. Each generation of us signs. Some of us are growing bolder – we sign our first names, if not our family names. Our first names are the ones that feel most natural to us, as our sisters are our family now. The list grows ever longer. Sometimes the sisterhood is smaller and sometimes it is larger. It expands and it shrinks but it always exists. Even if no one else can see us, we are here. We were always here.

Down two flights of winding stairs, through the heavy oak doors and past the corridor where all the windows were made from stained glass. Then down a smaller non-winding flight of stairs, past the refectory, two lefts then a right. The first time I'd tried to find the common room using the map we'd been given in Freshers Week, I'd ended up walking in circles and had to stop Amina and ask for help. After two terms, the route was ingrained in my mind. I already knew then that that path – and so many others – would never leave it.

Despite the increasingly warm days as the college eased into spring, a fire remained lit in the hearth. Agatha,

Martha and Natasha lounged about in shorts and floaty tops. The odd one out in jeans and a jumper, I was already beginning to sweat.

'Where were you the other day? When you missed the supervision,' I asked Agatha, the first words we'd exchanged since the Easter holidays.

'I overslept.' She giggled, the kind of light, fluffy laugh I associated with Natasha.

'Overslept, huh?' Martha leaned across to tickle Ag's ribs as she spoke and they collapsed into a heap on the sofa. Agatha emerged flushed, her hair tousled and her lips red. Martha winked at me over the top of her head so that Aggie wouldn't see.

'Something like that,' Agatha said. The sleeves of her white shirt fell backwards to reveal a splash of something dark on the skin of her left forearm.

'What's that on your arm?' I asked.

'Ooh, do you want to tell her or should I?' Natasha chipped in.

'Be my guest.' Agatha's smile was lazy as she leaned back on the sofa so that she was horizontal. Her face looked fuller – less angular – than before, and some of the jittery energy that had haunted her previous movements was gone. She'd begun to move like a favourite pet who knows its position will never be usurped.

'We got matching tattoos.' Natasha's grin was so innocent, so full, that I couldn't help but return it.

'Let's see then,' I said.

She rolled up the bell sleeve of her top, exposing a

delicate full moon on her bicep. 'I've got this, and then Agatha's got the sun. I wanted the moon to commemorate our Coven initiations and then Agatha suggested this to show that we're two halves of the same whole. We complement each other.'

'Wasn't it your idea?' Agatha said.

'I'm pretty sure it was yours.'

'Would you ever get one?' I asked Martha as Agatha and Natasha bickered.

'I've thought about getting something to remember my dad by but then I'm not sure I need it. He's already written all over my body,' she replied.

'I understand.' I squeezed her arm, feeling the heat of her flesh through the thin material of her top. 'But I was thinking more about us. It could be nice to have something to bind us together, don't you think? Something literal that we can't remove.' That term, I wanted to wind us all ever closer so that we could never be disentangled again. There weren't many landmarks in the saggy middle of the term – everything was focused around exams and their aftermath – but I was prepared to make our own.

She was about to reply when Prim pushed open the creaking door, and beckoned to Martha and me. She pushed her finger to her lips and nodded at Natasha and Agatha who were still engrossed in conversation by the fire.

'It's so much colder out here.' Martha shivered as we walked along the flag-stoned corridor, but I felt the coolness as a relief.

'Nonsense, it's a beautiful day,' Prim replied. 'And I've got something that's going to make it even more beautiful.'

'And what's that?' I asked.

'I'll tell you when we get to my room,' she said in a hushed voice as we all picked up the pace. When we'd climbed up to her turret, Martha and I sat on the bed facing Primrose.

'Okay, so. I found something in the museum at George's college. I had writer's block and I thought I'd go there to get some new ideas, some inspiration. That kind of thing,' Prim explained.

'Colleges can have their own museums?' I was genuinely surprised, even though I should really have learned by then that the extravagance of that town had no limits.

'Of course they can, Iv. Didn't you two ever go there?' Prim asked, not mentioning George directly.

'No, I didn't even know it existed. But that building is so huge, it's like a palace.' Prim nodded but didn't meet my eyes.

'As I was saying, I found something there,' she went on. 'Something to do with the Saint Clair sisters.'

'And what is it?' Martha practically shouted. 'I'm dying to know.'

Prim pulled out her phone as if she was going to show us but then shoved it back into the pocket of her leggings. 'Actually, no. In person would be better. They deserve that.'

And so, we walked back down the spiral staircase, across the internal courtyard and out of the front arch. Cherry blossoms fell softly on our heads as we made our way out of the grounds and onto the cobbled roads outside. Instead of cycling, we walked to George's college hand in hand, the warm air of the early evening stroking our skin, the light bathing the town in gold.

As we got closer, I glanced down the different alley-ways and back streets but they were all dark and shadowy despite the remnants of the sun. The only way that was lit up was the one straight ahead, towards George. The one route I didn't want to take.

'I'm not sure about this,' I said to Prim, just as we were about to cross the bridge over the river. 'Can't you just show us the picture on your phone?'

'George shouldn't have this kind of power over you.' She turned to me as we stopped on the highest point of the bridge. 'Isn't that what the bonfire was all about?'

I pressed a lock of my hair to my nose and inhaled deeply. It still smelled of woodsmoke, and if I concen-trated, I could feel the soothing sensation of pondwater on my hands. But I wasn't in my place and I began to doubt myself. 'I just don't know. I don't feel the same level of confidence, of power here. And when I saw him the other day – what if we bump into him now?'

The pain came quickly and intensely after I spoke. A flash across my face, deep and fast and then it was gone. For a second, I thought that it derived from somewhere inside of me. The only reason I could be sure Martha had hit me was because of the way Prim was staring at her open-mouthed. My hand flew up to my cheek but it was too late – the bulk of the sensation was already fading.

'You slapped me,' I said to Martha. It wasn't even a question.

'I did.' Her voice sounded the same as ever. She glanced down at a host of ducklings bobbing on the river and then turned to face me. 'You're Ivy Graveson and I won't hear you speak like that. Whatever power we get from the woods, the Coven, or from each other, it doesn't just fade because we are half a mile away. Isn't that an insult, to us, to her, to your sisters, to even imagine that could be so?'

'God, Martha, there are other ways of saying that without slapping Ivy.' Prim examined my cheek to see if any damage had been done but I already knew that there would be no visible impact.

'Someone had to knock the self-doubt out of her. Ivy, I love you. And I promise I will never hurt you again. But I won't let you sell yourself short by thinking that George has this hold over you. He doesn't.'

I took a step towards Martha on the bridge so we were standing almost nose to nose. Cyclists whirred past us and the mother duck started quacking and trying to gather up her babies. I raised my hand but it was slow and there was no power in it as I struck Martha across the face. She stumbled backwards and for a second, I was worried that I'd gone too far and that she might topple. That I'd misjudged everything. The fear and anger that I'd struggled to contain towards water, that I'd made just about manageable so that I could exist in a town with wet veins, rose up again. But then her laughter burst forth and I realized she was mimicking a fall. It was all just pretend. A game.

'You got me. I really thought you were going to fall off the bridge for a second there. Sorry,' I added, realizing that Martha had never said that word to me.

'I'm glad you had it in you to push back,' she grinned. 'See. Harness that fire. George has nothing on you. On us.'

'Well, now that's settled, let's get on with this,' Prim said, her voice lighter than it had been when she was scolding Martha.

Martha linked her arms into ours so that we were a line and she was the centre point. Bikes kept having to swerve to avoid us but no one actually said anything as we took up the path.

The museum that I'd never been in before was at the back of George's college, in a different building from his bedroom. I stopped glancing around to check if he was there, and straightened my posture. Even if I saw him, I knew my façade would stay regal and unconcerned, no matter what might be happening inside of me.

Tucked behind the chapel, the museum's walls were covered in gargoyles pulling grotesque faces with water spouting from their mouths. Prim pushed open the door with her shoulder and we were greeted with the kind of cool air that churches always have, no matter the season.

'We close in fifteen minutes,' an elderly man told us without looking up from his book.

'We'll be quick,' Prim promised. She led us towards the back of the room, the ceiling so high it disappeared into darkness. We passed rows and rows of shelves and exhibits, catching glimpses of faded maps, leering skulls and glittering precious stones.

'What exactly is this a museum of?' I asked Prim, quickening my pace to keep up with her. Everything looked fascinating – I knew I'd have to come back on my own – but I shared Prim's singular focus on that visit. Our interest in the Saint Clair sisters expressed itself in different ways. She was always spending time hunting down various contemporary sources in archives whereas I was more interested in the woods and how powerful they might have felt when they were even bigger hundreds of years ago. But it was something strong and shared, our excitement feeding off each other.

'The college itself. So it's pretty much a history of power. Which means a little bit of anything and everything.'

She raised her arm to stop me and Martha. We stood before a glass case displaying an embossed book that was propped open. Where the story should have been, there were small drawers with brass knobs.

'It's this book – well, not exactly a book – from hundreds of years ago,' Prim explained. 'Women sometimes made their business out of dealing poisons or did it as a hobby and this was a way to keep them secret. Hidden. You know, because poisoning was a feminine art, a woman's way of enacting violence. Power. But the thing about this one . . .' She prodded her finger towards the cabinet, without actually touching the glass, '. . . is who used it. Which women were accused of wrongdoing in this city, hundreds of years ago?'

'The Saint Clair sisters,' I answered.

'Exactly. When I cross-referenced the book in some local histories I've been reading, a few mentioned this was one of the key pieces of so-called evidence that was used to convict the sisters. Evidence that they'd been practising witchcraft.'

'But you said it was to do with poisoning? Surely that's just straight-up run-of-the-mill murder,' I said.

'Well, there's a fine line between healing and hurting. They may have simply been practising herbalism and history has taken the worst interpretation possible. Anyway, that's not really the point. Follow me.' Prim walked around the cabinet so we were staring at the back of the book. Illustrations of mythical creatures – serpents, dragons, a griffin with a golden crown on – danced up to its spine where there was a scrawling of symbols and a few names.

'It's a list. But it's not just names,' I said, keeping my voice low as dust motes swirled in the few sunbeams that managed to penetrate the high windows.

'Correct again,' Prim smiled. 'They said these symbols were the devil's mark and used them to identify witches, although they didn't have any real evidence as to who a mark belonged to. But they drowned so many people anyway, not just the sisters. Peasant women and poorer women. A couple of men too. All less high profile so history's forgotten them. But it's all linked. Don't you see? They thought this list was the coven.'

'Like their actual coven? Who they practised with?' I asked in a whisper.

'Yes.' Prim was struggling to keep her voice to the usual hush she reserved for places of learning.

'The illustrations are beautiful.' Martha traced her fingers over the glass, leaving smudgy prints behind.

'It's not just us.' I spoke too loudly as well and my words echoed around the room.

'It never was.' Prim's braids fell in front of her face but I could tell by her voice that she was grinning. 'When I first came here, I was so excited for things to be different. And then it was a bit too much like school. Nothing felt new, apart from you guys. But I should have been looking back, looking at the continuities. Finding a history.'

'It says on the inscription here that they believe there was also another book with more detail that has been lost to time. An actual *book* book,' I pointed out. 'I'd love to read that.'

'All visitors are asked to vacate the museum in the next five minutes,' an old, official-looking man's voice boomed from behind us.

Escaping out into the sunshine felt like returning to a different country. The city was getting warmer by the day, and we stopped on our way home for ice cream. By the time our college came into view we were full of sugar and sisterhood, sweetness and solidarity.

'Maybe you're on to something, Prim,' I said as we lolled on Martha's bed. She'd fixed us a Martha, her new favourite drink. 'Maybe we need to lean even more into the history of covens. Our history. We could do something crafty again. Use what you showed us as inspiration.'

'Ivy,' she said, her voice wounded. 'I thought you knew how seriously I was taking this.'

'I do. I absolutely do. And I'm taking it seriously too. That's why I suggested this.' I tried to inject something of exactly how serious I was into my voice. Alongside my long essay for Harold, I'd decided that intertwining myself, Prim and Martha into as tight a knot as possible was my project for the term. That, and purging myself of any vestiges of George. 'What better way to honour the sisters and their legacy than to get a real feel for the kind of things they were doing? I've been talking to Harold about material culture and I've been trying to read about, you know, like embodied researched practices. All the things you find out in the library are so important, Prim, but perhaps this is too.'

'I think you're right, Ivy.' Martha leaned against the headboard as she plaited her hair ready for her next social engagement. 'That book – it felt like it had so much energy. What if we create a list of names to direct some of that energy towards people?'

'But that wasn't what the list was for,' Prim protested and I found myself nodding along until Martha shot me a sharp look.

'Exactly. This is experimental. Like Ivy said.' She snatched up an orange leather-bound notebook, her manicured nails making light furrows on its surface. I recognized it as the one Natasha and Agatha had gifted her months before. When she opened it, the pages were fresh and white. Untouched. She grabbed a lipstick from the pile on her shelf where hundreds of pounds' worth of makeup lay haphazardly. I didn't mention my notebook, where I had scrawled every strange, unfamiliar detail about the Coven and the Dragons, or how it had got me into trouble before.

'There. That's a start.' Her arms were covered in goose pimples as she rotated the book towards us. Written in neat yet loopy writing in the truest of reds, the name Freddie Alexander stared back at us. The reasons that Martha's fury had landed on Freddie still felt vague and ill-defined to me but I well understood the feminine urge to project one's anger. Each one of us had been wronged at some point in our life – perhaps especially in ways the others didn't know about – and our sisters had been fatally wronged in the past. That kind of hurt didn't just disappear on its own. It fizzed, it seethed, it was passed on through generations. It needed answers. It needed a target.

When we'd been studying for our final exams at school, Cara and I used to get up early, head to our favourite of the town's two coffee shops and help each other revise. It was easy because we'd chosen exactly the same subjects. Neither of us would mention that I'd diverted from our plan since then, choosing to go to a different university and study something other than film. Our time together outside those revision sessions grew more strained, buckling under the weight of the unsaid, but those scant hours before lessons started were held together by a shared meaning and purpose. I could never have got through exams without her, especially not after Grandma Olive died.

I wanted that kind of drive that term, but I was struggling to get up in the mornings. The days were shorter further south, so I didn't have light streaming through my windows at 4am like I was used to. I stayed up late too, scribbling away in my notebook while staring at the witching tree through my window for inspiration. Sleep haunted my body into the late morning.

But one Wednesday, I managed to get up at six thirty without my limbs feeling heavy and sluggish. I knew there was a café near the market where Prim liked to work from around seven so I decided to go there in the hope our timings would align and we could enjoy revision breaks together.

The day was so beautiful that I decided to walk rather than cycle. I'd still be there in about twenty minutes and I wanted the chance to savour the golden patterns shining through green foliage, and the chirping birdsong. It's funny how little decisions like that can change the course of a life – or at least make you commit to the one you're on.

I was about halfway to the café, walking on a pretty residential side street, when I felt a hand on my shoulder. I'd been wondering if this was where Harold and his fiancée might live, in one of the cutesy semi-detached homes with bright doors and candyfloss hydrangeas, but as soon as I felt the hand touch me my mind went blank. Without turning, I knew it was George. Somehow, I'd internalized the exact weight of his hand, the way his fingers spaced themselves as they clutched my shoulder. It smelled like him too – a mixture of expensive aftershave and something close to burnt sugar. A smell that could only belong to a boy.

'Ivy, please. Can we at least talk?' The birds sang louder as he spoke – not to cover him up but to enhance him.

I turned to face him, made brave by the traces lingering in my body of the woods and the pond and my sisters passed. Still, when I looked at his face I could have drowned in its sticky honeyed beauty. Judging by his dreamy expression, I was having a similar effect on him.

'Five minutes,' I said, breaking whatever spell had befallen us. Five minutes couldn't hurt, I told myself. I was still upset, of course, but I was also curious. At first, I had ignored George's calls and texts because everything was too raw but now my heart had scabbed over a bit, I wanted to hear his explanation.

'Thank you, Ivy. It's more than I deserve,' he said, keeping his voice gracious but not pathetic. I nodded in agreement but didn't say anything.

I led us to a bench a few metres away, which sat underneath a weeping willow. Its green tendrils stroked me soothingly as I settled myself onto the wooden slats that were still slightly damp with dew.

'So, what did you want to say to me?' I prompted.

George dragged his hands down his face, exposing the red underside of his eyelids for a moment. 'What I wanted to say is how sorry I am but I'll only say that once because I don't want to insult you with multiple snivelling apologies.

I just need you to hear me say it one time, and know that I mean it.' There was a gravity to his words and I knew that what he said was true – I just wasn't sure about why he meant it. Was it my hurt that bothered George or was it the damage done to his perception of himself?

'I know I can't provide a proper explanation for what I did – it was almost like I was in a trance and I just wasn't sure you felt the same way about me, and then I was in this, yeah, dreamlike state. But anyway,' he interrupted himself. 'I *can* explain why I want you back.'

'And how is that? You haven't even tried to speak to me apart from chance encounters like this one.'

'You ignored all my calls. I didn't think you wanted anything to do with me. I was trying to do the right thing. To give you space, Ivy.'

'Well, you gave me so much space, I almost forgot that you existed.' It was petty and we both knew it was a lie.

'The shortest explanation is that I miss you,' George continued, choosing to ignore my comment. 'It's selfish, I know, to hurt you and then want you back. But first term – that was beautiful, wasn't it? And you were so different, Iv. You weren't like all the other girls I met before. You didn't know who my family was or ask what school I went to. We just had fun, you and me.' It never occurred to me before then that all the things I was most self-conscious about might be what drew George to me, even as I thought he could plug those gaps.

'Something got lost along the way. I don't know how, like I said it was almost like something came over me. It's a cliché but I really wasn't myself,' he said and I could feel myself teetering dangerously, on the edge of something. 'But we can get past this. I really believe that. It was one fucking stupid lapse and I won't ever let that happen again. I will spend the rest of our time here making it up to you, if you'll let me. If you'd give us another chance, I think there might still be a future for us. Maybe not exactly the future of the path we were on. But something better, even. Something more honest.'

A vision rolled out in front of me. Me and George at parties, as a pair, people looking at us and smiling. A clear future spelled out for us with all the things that make life straightforward – money, good looks, connections, confidence. A beautiful home, a lolloping dog, maybe even children. That future tried to embrace me. It would be so easy, and hadn't I been looking for ease? And perhaps I wouldn't only have ease but devotion. I'd always have an advantage over George, just like Cara would always have been able to guilt-trip me into visiting her after I'd broken our pact to go to the same university.

But then George's final words echoed in my mind. *Honest.* Honesty would mean more of George telling truths about himself, more depth, more complication. The path we had been on before was so golden, no one would have ever questioned it or us, but now wouldn't everyone in our circle know that we had once fractured? During one of her episodes when I was fourteen, Mum had fallen down the stairs and broken her elbow. Even though the doctors described it as a clean break, she said it had never been quite the same since, always causing her a bit of pain. There was no way of things running quite so smoothly after they'd been broken.

And yet – George was there in front of me and everything about him screamed that if only I would pick him, perhaps my life would be all soft corners and no hard edges. Perhaps there would even be love. Love, like a warm bath, a roaring fire, a faithful hound. I knew the Coven would shun me – or worse pity me – for taking back an undeserving boy. They'd made it clear from the very start exactly where our loyalties should lie. But even if that meant I had to give up on them, on my long essay about secret societies, on my girls, I'd be lying if I said it wasn't enticing.

I closed my eyes and focused on the vows I'd made. The first to my sisters, under the midnight sky and the watchful eye of the witching tree. The second to myself to make sure me, Prim and Martha would never come undone again. It would be easier if the temptation George presented could be eliminated, if it simply ceased to exist, but seeing as that wasn't possible, I had to trust my own strength and resolve.

I pushed myself up from the bench. I could feel his pull like a whirlpool but I knew the dangers that lay in making the wrong choice. My hands were trembling. It was now or never.

'You took advantage of Martha, George. And of me and my trust. You should be ashamed of yourself.' I was aiming to hurt him, hoping that if I wounded him it would slow him down, keep him away.

'But, Ivy, that's not what happened at all,' he shouted after me, as I turned towards the city centre. 'Please, let me explain that part at least.'

'Don't follow me,' I spat, not trusting myself around him for too much longer.

He had the decency to respect my instruction, even if there was some small part of me that wished he'd kept chasing me.

I went into the woods alone that night. That whole term, I barely had a moment to myself. Even revising in the library, I was encircled by other girls who were also high-lighting notes or typing violently on laptops. Then George seemed to crop up whenever I thought I might get some time alone. I was forever surrounded, forever part of some-thing bigger than me. It was like living in a hive, even if I wasn't always quite sure of my function.

But that evening, Prim pleaded an early bedtime – though I suspected she would stay up late with her books – and Martha had a reunion dinner with Aggie, Nat and other girls from their school. I could still feel the shape of her hand on my cheek as I walked into the trees, although I'd examined every inch of my face in the mirror and my skin had looked more flawless than it ever had before she slapped me. I didn't mind that neither of them were with me – I didn't want to feel guilty whenever I looked at them and thought about how convincing George had been that morning.

On my way to the clearing, the stars sparkled above

me. Out there, I was just far enough away from the light pollution that they could shine with something like their true potential. I closed my eyes and let myself imagine how bright they would have shone in the Saint Clair sisters' time, feeling my way into the lives of three unnamed girls. I trusted my feet on the path, the twisted roots, the birds chittering in the branches. I knew I wouldn't fall. With each step I took, my cheek smarted more.

In the glade, the heron flew overhead with long lazy flaps of their wings. I half-closed my eyes as I walked towards the witching tree, not wanting to see any blackened marks on the earth. What if I'd got it wrong and the bonfire had been an insult? But when I forced myself to open my eyes, there was no sign of fire at all. Everything looked perfectly normal. No blackened circle or charred undergrowth. It was like we'd never been there.

I stood for a while underneath the protective branches of the tree, her new leaves muttering as they brushed against each other. The longer I stayed, the more my cheek hurt. It was like Martha was still with me, even as she was somewhere else in the city talking and laughing with girls who'd had the privilege of knowing her for years. I stayed as long as I could, until my face felt like it was going to fold in on itself with the pain. A thought crossed my mind that perhaps this was punishment for almost straying from the path of sisterhood. Just before I left, I reached my hand into the water – the pond had become almost a puddle in the warmer months – and slopped some against my cheek. The relief was instant, the invisible wound on my flesh melting away into nothing.

On the way back, I walked past the larger ornamental pond, so different from the scrap of water where girls were once drowned. The heron was there again, tall and elegant among the reeds. I watched it for a minute until I realized just how still it was. Too still.

Once I'd seen that it was just a plastic decoy placed there by the college gardeners, it was impossible to unsee it. I didn't understand how I could have mistaken it for the real thing when it was so obviously not. It was just a fake, a mockery of the sinew and blood of that bird who was the only charm I allowed myself.

'We need a break,' Prim insisted. 'It's still weeks until exams. We can't wait till after.' Sun was pouring in through the long library windows, and the air in the room tasted of concentration and sweat. I was close to a polished draft of my long essay for Harold, but for the previous hour I'd just read the same paragraph on King James VI and I's obsession with witchcraft over and over again, without making any changes.

'If you're insisting on a break, then we really must need one.' Martha closed her laptop. I'd caught a glimpse of her screen and could see a TV show open next to her study notes.

'There's a train leaving in fifty minutes to this place.' Prim showed us pictures of a cute seaside town on her phone. 'We could make it if we move quickly.'

'Primrose Manu being spontaneous. I'm sold,' Martha said.

'Me too, I guess. But I'm not in the mood for actual swimming.' I tried to sound casual, but I could already feel my palms growing clammy. Getting out of the town sounded like a welcome distraction and I was curious to see something of the surrounding area, but being near the sea again was an entirely different matter than being close to the river or the pond. Wilder. Stronger.

'That's fine, I might not be either. The water could still be way too cold,' Prim agreed. 'Let's meet back at the front arch in twenty.'

We scattered to our different corners of college, and in no time at all we were back together again, our hair streaming out behind us as we cycled ten minutes to the station with its two platforms. Prim always liked to be early and we had time to wait but we didn't care. The journey itself only lasted forty-five minutes but it was like we were escaping to a different world. With each chug of the train, my shoulders untensed and the breath in my chest felt at once both lighter and deeper.

As we arrived into a station decorated with tubs of flowers carved to look like steam trains, my coursework vanished from my mind. The town was almost too perfect and we were the youngest people for miles around, apart from a few toddlers being pushed by mums with sleek hair and big pushchairs. Prim already had a café in mind that she wanted to visit so we followed her through a mishmash of streets with cottages painted all the shades of the rainbow.

When Martha and I had vanilla 99s in our hands and

Prim clutched a tub of green apple sorbet, we turned towards the sea, the lifeblood of the town. The seagulls were circling our heads, squawking incessantly to see if we had anything good to eat.

'Are you sure we should go to the beach?' I stopped abruptly enough that Martha and Primrose had to pivot back towards me. For the first few steps, I'd thought I felt okay but even a little further on, I started to feel overwhelmed.

'What are you talking about? That's why we came here.' Prim raised her eyebrows at me. 'I haven't seen the sea in weeks, if not months. Not since we were at yours over Christmas, actually, I think.'

'The seagulls. They might attack us. They can be really vicious, you know.' I fidgeted with my fingers, trying to expel the nervous energy from my body so it wouldn't betray me to Prim and Martha. Even after months together, I was still uncertain of how much of myself I could share with them and still have them want me.

'We saw the sea at Christmas at yours and there were seagulls then too. What's the big deal?' Martha pushed her sunglasses back onto her hair so that I could actually see her eyes, and not just my own reflection.

'That was winter. The beach in summer. It's different.' Summer. Beach. Heat. Weather. Tides. Gone. My mind was playing a word-association game, one that I didn't want to be a part of. The thoughts themselves were like waves – they had enough force to drag me down but each time I tried to grab hold of one of them its substance slipped right through my fingers.

'I just don't want to go,' I said.

'That's fine. You wait here and we'll come and pick you up once we've had a paddle.' Prim's tone was kind but firm. 'There was a bench just back there.'

'No. That's not what I meant.' I rubbed my hands over my face, glad I was wearing sunglasses so no one could see the tears that were starting to form. 'I don't want you to go without me. If you're going to insist on going, I'm coming.'

'It's not insisting. I just want to get some sea on my toes, some wind in my hair. I need this.' Prim hardly ever said that she *needed* anything, other than time to work, sleep and exercise. Sitting on the bench not able to see what they were up to would have been infinitely worse than knowing, even if the knowing was bad. Without my eyes on them, I couldn't control anything. I took a deep breath in, just like the school counsellor had showed me, and forced my feet forward towards the promenade.

We walked to the end of the road and the sea opened out in front of us, vast and terrible in comparison to the tameness of the town. The few kiosks that were selling plastic buckets and spades looked like jokes next to a body of water that could swallow us whole if it chose. Still, a few families dotted the beach and a cluster of older women were swimming out to sea, their bright swim tow floats bobbing like a warning.

Martha took off her wrap dress, her orange swimsuit already on underneath. Prim pulled her swim cap on, tucking her natural curls inside. 'I finally got one that fits my hair,' she smiled at me. 'I wasn't sure I'd want to swim until we got here but the water looks lovely. You want to dip your toes in at least?'

'I'll just wait here,' I said, spreading my legs on Prim's stripy beach towel. I changed into my bikini so that I'd be ready just in case, then tried to read my book but the words swam in front of my eyes. The water was loud as well – speaking to me in slithering, sneaking patterns that I couldn't make out but that lodged themselves in my brain nonetheless. There was no point in trying to concentrate on anything else. I had to keep my gaze trained on the sea. Prim was further out, doing serious lengths, whereas Martha was bobbing about in the shallows. I could see some boys in school uniforms looking at her from near the pier.

I was watching them watching her, and when I turned back, she was gone. Gone. Then an arm. A gasp. A spout of water from the sea. A struggle of limbs and a blaze of red hair.

I ran towards her before I even knew what I was doing, her name on my lips. When my feet hit the sea, the water was cold but not cold like it was back home. Either way, it wouldn't have mattered. I'd have kept on ploughing through the dark blue regardless. My feet slipped and scraped against stones but I didn't stop until I was close enough that I could see her hair floating in the water, a colour somewhere between autumn leaves and blood. I grabbed the first bit of her I could get hold of and yanked, harder than I thought I knew how. She burst through the surface and I saw that I had a hold of her by her forearm.

A gush of water shot onto my face, as salty as tears. 'Are you okay? Martha, can you breathe?' She was spluttering and for a second, I tried to remember all the first aid lessons that I'd obsessively brushed up on and had suddenly disappeared into the recesses of my mind. But then the splutters continued, louder but less urgent and I saw them for what they were. Laughter. The water in my face had been on purpose. This was a game. I'd played my part without even realizing.

I let go of her arm, the pebbles jabbing into me again as I returned to the shore. I tried to look dignified but, in my anger, I stumbled over the rocky shoreline. The gulls circled overhead, screeching and divebombing couples who were trying to enjoy picnics.

'The look on your face,' Martha howled as she reached the spot where we'd laid our things.

My fingers itched to hit her again – to have any kind of contact with her skin, to check it was still warm, that her heart was still beating – but they wouldn't do as I told them to. They were too cold. They couldn't move. Just like that day on the beach with Cara. The day where home stopped being home.

'You still there, Iv? It was just a joke.' She'd calmed down a little and was looking at me with mild concern.

'That's your problem, isn't it? Everything's just a joke to you.' My insides seethed, far more treacherous and volatile than the outgoing tide.

'This isn't a joke.' She took a step closer to me and placed my hand on her chest. 'I mean, us. Look, you can feel I'm still here.' Her heart beat against me, fast at first and then slowing to a steady rhythm.

'You're too cold, you need to warm up.' I dragged myself away and offered her Prim's towel – she was the only one of us who'd had the foresight to bring one. I didn't want to let my emotions get in the way of Martha's safety.

'Is everything okay?' Prim was back by our side after finishing her lengths of front crawl. 'I saw you two splashing around. Well done for getting in the water, Ivy. And thanks for asking if you could borrow my towel, Marth.'

'We were just—' Martha began.

'Everything's fine,' I cut across her. We walked away from the gathering wind and the gulls, the first secret that didn't include Prim blossoming in my heart.

There wasn't a train back for over an hour. My skin was tight with salt. The hammering in my chest hadn't fully died down. And my stomach was beginning to rumble, long, low growls that echoed the turning weather. Prim's lips were slightly blue after her swim and Martha had stayed silent as we made our way into the town centre.

'How about we get some chips?' I suggested. They reminded me of home, and for the first time in a long time, that kind of seemed like a comforting thought.

'Amazing idea,' Prim nodded as she blew on her hands.

Nothing's tasted better since than those chips did on that day. The salt and the heat brought us back into ourselves, reminding us of our spontaneity, of the fact we'd gone somewhere else. We'd done that. We'd got away during a punishing exam term. I let my anger towards Martha fade – because I had never told her, she couldn't know the terror she'd forced me to relive.

'These are so fucking good that I keep burning my tongue. I can't stop.' Martha spoke with her mouth full – something she'd never done before – and her voice had lost all the chill of the sea.

'Do we have to go back?' Prim asked.

'You know you love it really. You couldn't live some-where without a library. You're a true scholar.' I wrapped my arms around her, rubbing the cold skin on her shoulders.

'You're right, I suppose. But still, it would be nice to skip to the part after exams where we get to relax and do Coven things again.' Prim's eyes were wistful but tired. I knew she'd been pulling some all-nighters, and I was worried about how exhausted she was getting. *Burning the candle at both ends*, as Grandma used to say.

'Why don't we get a memento of our time here?' I said. 'To remind us of each other and to keep us going when we need a little extra support.'

'What do you mean?' Martha asked.

'There's a tattoo parlour right around the corner. I saw it when we were walking here.' I shrugged, nonchalant, even though I knew the idea was perfect. I could feel it in my bones. The tattoos would heal in time for post-exam cele-brations, and in the meantime they would be a memento of fun and freedom.

'You mean get a tattoo right now?' Prim's eyes were wide but there was a hint of a smile on her face.

'What else would I mean?' I grinned back.

'I'm in,' Martha said. 'I've been meaning to get one for ages, I just haven't done it yet. We can't let Nat and Aggie have all the fun.'

'Ours will be better than theirs,' I promised as I put the last chip in my mouth.

The inside of the tattoo parlour was dark and smelled of incense. All the light from the outside vanished in a room kitted out in sombre woods and sumptuous velvets. As beautiful as the weather had been earlier in the day, slipping inside felt something like coming home. A woman with long black hair plaited down her back smiled at us from behind a desk.

'How can I help, girls?'

'We're here for tattoos,' I replied, the scents of clove and vanilla and something unrecognisable catching in my throat.

'I gathered that.' Her laugh was light, like spring rain. 'Do you know what you'd like?'

I glanced at Prim and Martha, their faces obscured in the shadowy room. 'Yes,' we all said in unison. We hadn't discussed it but we didn't need to – the more I worked to weave us together, the more seamless our communication became.

'Right this way, then. I'll take you one at a time. You can come first if you're the leader.'

'Oh, I'm not – I just had the idea for this,' I began to

protest but she was already walking down a short corridor into a different room. I followed her, finding that the description of me didn't feel as bad a fit as I thought it might. Somehow, in my time at university, I'd come so far from the quiet girl with only one friend without noticing each step on the journey to get there.

Two hours later, we emerged into the honeyed light of the late afternoon, our intended train long gone. But we couldn't have cared less. There was a new drawing of the outline of a heron on my foot, an autumn leaf on Prim's ribs and a flame on the back of Martha's ankle. They weren't the same tattoo – we didn't need anything as obvious as that – but it was still another line linking us, drawing us closer together.

Week 4

The threats shift. We are no longer hunted in the same way we were when our sisters were drowned. The threats now are trickier, like slipping shadows or drops of dew that fall from leaves when they are taken from their branches. The men have intellectualized their weapons, wrapped their blades in words and fancy speeches. But they are still the same men, still present the same dangers. They gather in their societies – they have proliferated now, are plural. Some are even rivals to each other. But they forget that it is us that they were forged in opposition against, that it is we who claimed the woods first and us to whom the woods are loyal. They may trespass but they will never belong.

For a moment, we were satiated. We didn't see George or Freddie or Eddy. Martha's mum rang her out of the blue and they had a conversation which didn't end in tears. Prim's mum won a case against a European war criminal and sent her a hamper with bottles of cordial and piles of fruit, addressed to all three of us. Lola came to visit from Paris before she moved to the States for a PhD, and Prim actually took a full day off from revision. My mum sent me pictures of the garden she'd planted long ago with Grandma Olive, now flowering under a watery sun. Dad sat next to her with a fleece on and a beer bottle by his side, his milky flesh visible in shorts. Always shorts, as soon as the weather showed even the first sign of give. He sent me messages to say Mum was still getting on with the new counsellor and that her migraines hadn't made an appearance in months. In selfies, they were both smiling, and sometimes I caught a glimpse of youth about their eyes, even with their crow's feet.

The heat in college came so fast, thick and early that it caught me off guard. I got sunburned on my chest when I sat outside trying to read notes on endogamous marriage, the word *ego* becoming meaningless, surrounded by circles and triangles in endless kinship diagrams. One morning when I was cycling to the politics library to return a book, I realized I'd forgotten my water bottle and by the time I arrived my mouth was parched, all the water in my body expelled through sweat.

When Prim and Martha weren't available to me, I stayed up late in my room, poring over revision so that I'd be freer the next time I saw them. The windows sat wide open in an attempt to cool the stuffy air. Outside, the trees were still, and the only sounds were the occasional hoots of the owl and flurries of laughter from girls taking a break from studying.

A week before my first exam, on the anthropology of science and medicine, I closed my books with a thud. That term, my mind seemed to have only become softer and more jelly-like, not harder and cleverer as I had anticipated. I was finding it more and more difficult to concentrate. Harold was noticing – even though he was kind enough not to say anything, I saw him shooting me concerned looks every time I left a supervision.

Standing next to the window, the fresh air calmed my flushed face. The witching tree danced in the distance and, on an impulse, I knelt. On the sill in front of me, the crystal Martha gave me in first term rested alongside the doilies I'd brought from home. Dust had long since covered the circle initially left by George's present.

'Please, make exams go well.' My voice came out as a thin scratch. I hadn't talked to anyone since lunchtime when Prim and I had a quick picnic in the shady orchard.

'Please,' I said again, my words stronger. 'I can't handle resits or anything like that. I have to come back here. Be here next year. With them. I have to enjoy the end of term, after exams. This is my home now. I can't go back. Don't let anything disrupt us again.' The sentences rushed out of my mouth, my breath ragged. I felt like I'd joined Prim on one of her Saturday morning runs, my skin sweaty, my heart pumping. I focused on my words, on willing the future I imagined into existence through my own belief in it. 'Please. I'll do anything.'

As I finished speaking, there was the sound of footsteps. Footsteps right outside my door. They were the noises of someone attempting to be quiet, but straight away I knew that it was the sound of a boy. It was other in a way I couldn't put my finger on – I just knew it was. Countless

girls walked past my door every day on their way to the
refectory, the library, perhaps maybe even the chapel. So
many girls that my mind had filtered out the sound of their
feet. But these noises made me sit up immediately.

'Who's there?' I called out. The only reply was the piercing silence of someone not moving. Heat and fear gripped
my bones as I heaved myself off of the floor. Too slow to
catch whoever had been in the corridor. The muffled noises
started again, then stopped, and by the time I opened my
door, it was deserted. Whoever had been there – and I was
sure there'd been someone – was gone.

I reached down to stroke the heron tattoo on my foot.
Everything was fine. I was due to go for a tarot reading
with Martha the next day, and my exams would be over in
a matter of weeks. Everything was fine and nothing could
stop us from having the time of our lives after revision –
certainly not whatever boy had been in the corridor.

'There you are,' I said as Agatha walked through the door
of the study room. I tried to smile but it was through gritted teeth – I could only book the room for an hour and
she'd arrived fifteen minutes late.

'Let's get started, shall we?' She tucked a stray strand
of hair behind her ear as she sat down, not bothering to
apologize. At least she got down to business straight away.
We both knew that we were only spending time together
one-on-one because it would help us to go over political
thought past papers together. We only had three weeks
until exams started and I was desperate to ensure I did

well enough to glide into next year. It was a crucial part of making sure Prim, Martha and I stayed together, after all. I'd do whatever it took, even if that meant spending more time with Agatha.

As we went through questions from the last few years, the mid-morning sun streamed through the high windows. We were in a small room next to the library with just enough space for two comfy armchairs and a desk. The light lit up stacks of old, leather-bound books and then slid across Agatha's face. Illuminated, her eyes were puffy, creased and purple. She had more spots than usual and she'd lost weight from her cheeks. Every inch of her looked worn out, and by something more than the usual exam stress that we were all facing.

'Are you okay?' I asked.

'I'm fine,' Agatha said, a little startled by the change of subject.

'Are you certain?' I knew I was breaking our unspoken agreement by trying to talk about anything other than work but she'd looked bad enough that I was unsettled.

'Yes, I said I'm fine.' Her voice was adamant. She even gave me a small smile to prove it. The smile surprised me – I'd have guessed that she would have snapped at me. A shadow passed over the sun and whatever I'd seen was diminished. *Everything was fine.* Maybe we all just needed to tell ourselves that to see exams through, and meet whatever sweet release was waiting for us. If we repeated anything enough times, perhaps we could make it true.

Week 5

Sometimes we name a man in our books. We realized the power of naming things beyond just ourselves and so we act accordingly. Occasionally, a sister becomes too fascinated with one of them and we must act. We know our history. We know the threat posed by charming, handsome boys with floppy hair placed just-so. We will not underestimate them. We will ask the woods to work their magic. We must act first.

'Are you sure you're happy to use them for me?' I asked Martha as she splayed the cards across her desk.

'Of course. Why wouldn't I be?'

'At Christmas you said they were your dad's. I didn't even know you'd brought them back to college with you.'

'I didn't want them to be left in my bedroom all alone.' She kept her eyes down as she began to shuffle the deck, flashes of yellow and orange peeking through. 'I was worried about them getting lonely in that big house with only Mum and her string of men for company.'

'If you ever want to talk about him, I'd love to hear—'

'You need to ask a question,' Martha cut across me.

'What? I didn't want to be insensitive – that's why I haven't asked. I know how hard it is when people pry before you're ready to talk about something. Someone.'

'About the cards. That's how they work. You need to engage with them, demand an answer.'

'Oh, okay. Let me think.' It was just the two of us because Prim was in the library. I should have been there too but Martha had wanted to do something and so I'd found myself packing away my books into my rucksack earlier than I'd expected. I'd wanted to get a little more revision on kinship done before I stopped, but I was also touched that she was happy to use her dad's tarot cards for my reading. 'Will I have a good rest of term?'

'Take it seriously, Iv.'

'That *was* me taking it seriously. It's important to me that exams go well – for all of us. And that after that we get to relax and enjoy some well-deserved fun.'

'It's better if you don't ask just a yes or no question. It's more complicated than that.'

'All right. Give me an example.'

'No.' Martha shook her head. 'It has to come from you. Just something more open-ended.'

I could tell I wasn't going to get anything more from her. I hadn't really thought much beyond the parties after exams – Amina and Sophia weren't specific but promised us that all our hard work would be well-rewarded – so it took me a minute or so to come up with another question. We sat cross-legged, me on her bed, her on the swivel chair pulled close towards me. There was a gap of a couple of inches between our bodies. If I'd leaned forward and stretched out my big toe, I could have touched the end of her silky pyjamas.

'All right. What about how can we make sure we don't repeat past mistakes?' I said. Martha let out a long, low whistle of air, her eyes still on me until she shattered our shared look and turned to the cards.

'Pick three,' she instructed, and I pulled them out at random. Martha lay them face down, before flipping them over one by one.

Her gasp was loud and quick. 'Well, would you look at that.'

But I never got to find out what Martha had seen. Before she could speak again, there was a knock at the door. Two timid taps. Martha stood up, walked across her Persian rug and opened the door to a figure who was just about recognisable as Agatha. Her hair was matted in clumps, and mascara ran down her cheeks in watery black lines. Instead of its usual golden colour, her skin was the colour of off milk.

'Aggie, come in.' Martha ushered her into the room with her arms around her shoulders. 'What on earth happened?'

'You look like a banshee,' I said and then clapped my hands over my mouth. The words had come from nowhere and from somewhere deep inside. Either way, I hadn't intended to say them and I was paying for it by being skewered by Martha's gaze.

Agatha didn't talk as she walked over to the bed. I made space for her, then put the kettle on and began making cups of tea without having to be asked. I fetched the oat milk from where it was keeping cool on Martha's window-sill – she could never be bothered to walk the few steps to her shared kitchen – and then stopped before I added it, remembering that it was Natasha who drank her tea weak, Agatha who preferred it black.

'Take this, it will help you feel better.' I added a spoon-ful of sugar despite Agatha's reproachful look. 'You need the sweetness, even if you don't have milk. My Grandma always used to say that it was just the thing after a shock.'

'But what shocked you, Ag? You need to tell us.' Martha worked the tangles in Ag's hair out. We sat like that for what could have been seconds or minutes as Agatha clasped the steaming mug to her body. By the time she spoke, Martha had tamed her hair into something closer to its usual glossiness.

'It's just all too much,' Agatha half-sobbed, half-spoke.

'What is?' Martha asked.

'The boys.' Agatha rubbed her hands over her eyes, smearing her makeup further down her face. 'So many boys. Too many.'

'You're not yourself, Agatha,' I said, looking anywhere but at her stained and crumpled form. If she'd looked bad in the study room, this was a million times worse. I felt guilty for not guessing that her troubles lay with boys. It was the obvious answer. And, much as I didn't want her to intrude on the sanctity of me, Martha and Prim, she was still a sister – *my* sister. You didn't choose your family, but it was still horrible to see her so defeated.

'No, I'm not. You're right.' Her words were directed at me but had none of the subtle bite I'd come to expect. 'This whole term something has felt off in a way I can't properly describe. At first, I liked the attention, but now I'm just exhausted.'

'That still doesn't explain why you look like that.' Martha gestured at Agatha, her lips somewhere between a wobble and a curl. 'If a boy did something to you, I'll kill them. We can't keep letting them get away with stuff like this.'

'I fell in a ditch, okay?' Some of Agatha's old snap was back. 'I was trying to make a quick exit from a date when I realized that Eddy and Peter were in the same bar, plus another guy I went on a different date with last week. I couldn't handle them all being there, so I tried to cut across the meadow, the one with the cows, and I slipped and dropped my purse. Another boy – I recognized him from sociology lectures – appeared from nowhere and offered to walk me home but at that point I was so upset and covered in mud, I practically ran the whole way here.'

'You went on a date with Eddy as well as Freddie?' I asked, struggling to keep up but Agatha just blew her nose.

'It didn't work. Not like we intended,' Martha murmured to me as she patted Agatha's forehead. I was struggling to concentrate – yes, Martha was right that this isn't what we'd envisaged for Aggie. But she was wrong on the other count. It *had* worked. It had really worked.

'What didn't work?' Ag asked, more alert than she'd been since she arrived.

'Nothing,' I replied, a little too quickly. Agatha narrowed her eyes at me but the flash of her old self dissolved with more sobs.

Martha held Agatha to her chest, her pyjama top wet with tears. She spoke in a soothing tone the whole time Agatha cried but her eyes gave her away. While the rest of her body was soft, they were hard. Bright and alive. She caught my gaze and wouldn't let it go. I tried to avert my eyes but I couldn't. Martha had me speared. And then I recognized it – the look that was plastered on her face. It was the same one she'd got when she pulled my cards earlier, the same one she wore whenever there was rice pudding on the menu in hall, whenever she collected a new parcel from the porter's lodge. Martha was excited. And that meant something was going to happen. I wasn't sure what yet. But she was the cause and that meant there had to be an effect.

'We wrote Freddie's name in the book but nothing happened.'

We had the common room to ourselves, and it should have been a break from practice essays, flashcards and past papers. The cool flagstones should have been a relief from the penetrating heat outside, the dry, yellowing grass, the shrinking pond. Prim had brought some homemade lemonade and I'd cut up cucumber slices to rest on our eyes. But Martha couldn't stop pacing.

'Of course nothing happened,' Prim snapped. 'It was just a name in a book.'

'The further we are from the clearing, the easier it is for you to say that,' I pointed out, my voice calmer than Prim's for once. The oppressive temperature was making the whole of college irritable, and I wanted to bring things down a notch. 'When we're in the woods, I can tell you feel differently.'

'It's easy for me to say that because I don't want you both to think we hold more power than we have,' she said.

'And I don't want you to try and convince us that we have less,' Martha replied. 'Things have been happening, haven't they? Since the bonfire, since Ivy purified the ashes, since the book. Since we joined the Coven even. You can feel it. I know you can, no matter how much you try and deny it.'

I poured us more lemonade as Prim and Martha stared at each other, lips pursed. 'Let's do something else. Like a test. That way we can see if it works or not. It's practically scientific,' I suggested.

'What did you have in mind?' Prim asked.

'A curse.' I held up a finger to stop the protests I could see forming on her lips. 'It's something strong and specific. So it allows you to prove or disprove our actions and any consequences. And it lets Martha feel like we're doing something more – and if she's right, it should mean that something bad happens to Freddie pretty fast.'

'It won't prove anything though,' Prim said. 'Freddie could fall off his bike tomorrow and die.'

'I wish,' Martha smiled.

'And if he did, that could just be a coincidence,' Prim

continued, ignoring Martha. '*Would* be a coincidence in fact. Definitively.'

I shivered, thinking about my and George's falls just days apart from one another. I didn't even want us to be linked by a coincidence like that – the fewer ties between us, the better.

'No such thing as coincidence. It's a gorgeous idea, Iv.' Martha clapped her hands.

I slid onto the sofa next to Prim, my thighs sticking to the soft leather in the heat. Martha walked to the other side of the room to throw the windows open. The thick old glass warped the sunshine outside until she removed the barrier and light and air rushed towards us.

'What harm can it do?' I asked Prim, my hand on top of hers in a clammy mess.

'I feel like you're always asking me that question.'

'But it's true. If it works, it works. If it doesn't, it doesn't. And either way it will be fun.' I willed her to agree – every time we went into the woods or did a ritual as a trio, I could sense us winding closer together.

'It doesn't sound like my idea of fun.'

'I promise I'll make it your idea of fun. An intellectual yet accessible curse, how about that?' I punched her gently on the shoulder and was rewarded with a shadow of a smile.

'I don't know why I always let you talk me into things,' Prim sighed. 'But okay. I guess we're on this journey together now and I'm willing to see where it takes us. No one could say I'm not inquisitive.'

'No, they couldn't,' I agreed. 'Martha, fetch your note-book.' Prim and I sipped the lukewarm lemonade as she ran off down the corridor, and in my mind, I followed her up the staircases until she got to her room. Within minutes, she was back again with the book where we'd written Freddie's name tucked under her arm.

'Okay,' I said, gesturing for her to hand it to me. 'We each tear out a page and—'

'You cannot do that,' Prim interrupted.

'Why not?' I asked.

'It's just – bad. It would be like eating all your advent calendar chocolates in one go rather than waiting day by day.' She shuddered. 'Sacrilegious.'

'I always do that with advent calendars,' Martha shrugged.

'What about if we use scissors?' I asked, walking over to the cupboard where art supplies were kept for craft sessions. 'We'll cut carefully and precisely, and you wouldn't even know a page is gone.'

'I still don't love it but I guess if you don't mind, Martha – it is your notebook, after all.'

'I promise I don't,' Martha said.

'It's kind of like a collage, see, Prim? Art.' I cut out three pages as neatly as I could and handed them to the others.

'Now what?' Prim asked.

'Now we let our creativity flow,' I explained. I thought I'd have to make it up as I went along but the instructions came to me naturally. 'We each write our own curse. And then we dispose of it in whatever way we see fit.'

'Right here? You don't think we need to be in our place?' Martha nodded towards the window, at the foliage outside, unmoving without a breath of wind to stir it.

'We've got the three of us. That's all we need. This way we get to do our own thing but also stay together.' I delved back into the cupboard pulling out pens and pencils in all shades of the rainbow. I chose a black fountain pen, Martha an orange fineliner and Prim a dark purple.

We each scribbled on the page, apart but together. My hand put words to paper without me thinking about them. Words I didn't even know I had inside me, about George, about Freddie, about the Dragons, about every single frustration that my body had felt but my mind hadn't known since I'd arrived at university – and some from before. They didn't feel like mine as they rushed out of me. They felt like something that had to be purged.

By the time I wrote my final full stop, the paper was covered in my terrible handwriting and Martha and Prim were both staring at me, hands folded in their lap.

'Sorry. I don't know what came over me. Once I started writing, I couldn't stop. I just wrote about—' I said.

'No, don't tell,' Martha almost shouted. 'It's like when you make a wish. You have to keep it a secret or it won't come true.'

'Okay, if that's what you want.' I was going to ask what she'd written but I couldn't argue with superstition, and the power of one's own mind – either to inadvertently bring about the things it dreaded most or to will its greatest desires into existence.

'It is what I want. As long as it was about Freddie, that's good enough for me,' Martha said slyly, pulling out a lighter and setting the edge of her paper on fire so that it curled up into a grimace. 'There. It's gone.'

'Careful. You'll set off the smoke alarms.' Prim fanned her curse back and forth.

'I'm pretty sure those are just antiques. They don't actually work,' Martha replied, glancing up at the old hunks of off-white plastic that felt like intruders in the oak-panelled room.

'I think you'll find it's a legal requirement—'

Before Prim could go any further, I'd shoved the paper in my mouth. It tasted of glue and Martha's perfume and the satisfaction of stopping an argument before it even starts.

'Did you seriously just eat that to avoid conflict?'

'Not going to answer that,' I smiled at Prim. She flipped her paper towards me to show two words written in perfect handwriting. *The end.*

'I didn't know what else to write. You two were scribbling away and I could barely think of anything. This seemed to sum it up. This term has felt like drawing a line under some things, and beginning others.' She reached over to squeeze my hand.

'What are you going to do with it now?' asked Martha.

'It feels wasteful to destroy a bit of paper,' Prim said.

'It's just one piece,' Martha pointed out.

'It might be good for you to do something without thinking it through, for once. Cathartic?' I suggested.

'I wish you still had your knife, Iv.'

'Don't say that,' I said to Prim, although part of me wished the same thing. Before I'd given it to the tree, I'd always had it on my person, even sleeping with it under my pillow. I felt its absence like a ghost.

'We don't need the knife,' I rallied. 'Get physical. Use your hands. Let some of that exam term stress out.' And so, Prim began to tear the paper with her fingers, her movements jagged and messy with none of their usual grace. Martha's mouth fell open as Primrose created a kind of confetti.

'I'll keep the scraps as evidence in case any of this works,' Prim said. 'Something to tell the grandchildren.'

'I promised it would be fun, didn't I?' Prim collapsed on the sofa and I snuggled up to her, letting her warmth seep into me despite already being too hot.

'You were right.'

The day I discussed the final draft of my coursework with Harold was the only day it rained that term. It was what Dad called a soft day, where the light drizzle seems like hardly anything at all at first, but as the minutes wear on you realize that you've become practically soaked to your skin without even noticing. By the time I reached the door of Harold's office at the top of the stairs, my hair was dripping.

'Oh, dear. Would you like a cup of tea, Ivy? We can't have your teeth chattering while we discuss that fantastic essay of yours.'

I accepted, and he made me one with an ancient travel

kettle tucked into the corner of the room. It had been weeks since I'd felt cold by that point, so that the chilliness after the rain was novel – curious rather than uncomfortable.

'One sugar, please,' I instructed Harold and when he passed me the mug it was hot enough to almost burn my hands. 'You said fantastic?'

'Oh, yes, sorry. I shouldn't keep you waiting. You'll be wanting to know my thoughts, I'm sure.' I nodded and Harold explained how the essay was in good shape, just a few line edits needed – he advised me to read my work out loud to check for flow and any typos. It was something I'd have to do in the privacy of my own room rather than the library. I couldn't help myself from smiling as he pointed out parts he'd especially liked, thankful that all my time spent observing and scribbling had paid off and I'd managed to produce something passable on the history of witchcraft in the university and its effects on the modern day, without revealing details I didn't want to. My personal experience with the Coven felt separate from all the theories and the tens of thousands of words I'd read in books and journals. It was so much more embodied and alive and I never wanted it to bleed into my academic work in a way that could be deciphered by anyone else. After half an hour, Harold began to shuffle his papers, his usual signal that the supervision was coming to an end.

'There was one more thing I wanted to ask,' I said.

'Of course.'

'Way back in first term, you mentioned the drinking societies and acephalous societies, and it sounded like you had more to say about them. Since then, you've been keen for me to include them in my essay – what was the story that you said was for another time back then?'

'Did I say that? I have a bit of a penchant for the dramatic or so my fiancée tells me. I honestly can't remember what I was specifically referring to but it does reflect my general view.'

'General disapproval?' I hazarded.

'Yes, you could say that. I suppose wariness. And maybe a little tinge of jealousy.' He laughed, although not in the booming way he usually did.

'Jealousy?' I prompted, not wanting him to stop.

'Well, I never got into the Dragons, you see. That was my college for my undergraduate degree – I've ended up here of course, home of the Marmosets, but that's not where I started out originally. I was invited but I just wasn't cut out for it. At initiations – well, I won't go into details, but I found it all very debauched and I backed out.'

'Why not go into details? Do you want to protect them?' I leaned forward in my seat.

'Oh, no. No, it's not that. Well, I don't think so anyway. Always good to self-reflect, I suppose. But, no. It's just all a little unpleasant to talk about. But what I will say is this – it involved defiling a tree at a certain college and I wasn't interested in doing that. I've always loved nature, respected it, and I can't bear harm coming to other living creatures.'

'Was this tree – was it at my college?' I gulped, the unsaid filling up the blank space in my brain.

'I think we're done for today, Ivy. Really brilliant work on the essay. You should be very proud of yourself.' Harold shook my hand as he led me out of the door. 'If I don't see you before the end of term, have a drink on me after you're done with exams.'

As I tumbled back out into the light of day, the clouds began to recede, the sunshine punching a way through. The heat was back and it wasn't going anywhere anytime soon.

The skin on the back of my neck had started to peel. Martha had taught me that wearing SPF every day of the year was important for how I would look in later life and I tried my best, but there were parts of my body that I could never seem to remember. That spring the sun was hotter than I expected, hotter than it ever was at home, and my neck was constantly red and flaky. I missed the weather from the start of term, where it had been warm and breezy, and the spring foliage made everything seem new and fresh.

I'd put a hat on that morning before I cycled to the sociology library so that Martha wouldn't scold me if my skin got more burned. I wanted her to fuss around me, applying ointments and reassurance, but without it being painful.

By 10am, the sun was already a huge orb in an other-wise clear sky. I chained my bike up next to the river and walked into the maze of the city centre, with the intention of borrowing a guide to Tocqueville's ideas on the tyranny of the majority that I told myself would help with my politics exam. That term, the only thing that I could concentrate on besides Prim and Martha and the Coven had been my long essay for Harold.

I was procrastinating by window-shopping at a display of faux leather satchels when I saw him. Unmistakable even in a reflection, George was only a few metres away from me. If I moved, I might bump into him. But if I stayed still, he would catch sight of my reflection – a pale, warped image of me. Somehow that was worse.

The skin on the back of my neck itched even more. There was a side street coming up that led to an antiques shop and a quiet café, I was sure of it. I just needed to make it there before he saw me.

'Ivy, is that you?' He turned his head, squinting under the weight of the sun. I'd told him to leave me alone, but I supposed someone like George wasn't used to having to follow other people's instructions. Shielding his eyes, he stepped to the side. It was the first time we'd looked at each other head-on since I'd come dangerously close to faltering. He was close enough that I could see the flecks of amber and gold in his brown eyes but not close enough that I could lose myself in them.

No, it's not me, I wanted to scream. *Not the me I used to be. Not the bits of me you knew.*

I could have caused a scene then. I could have become hysterical, the scorned woman, in the middle of spires and stained-glass windows. I could have been an interesting distraction to the tourists around me, interrupting their sightseeing and gawking at my home. I could have been the fresher who went crazy under exams pressure – the cautionary tale to next year's intake of first years.

But instead, I reached into my pocket and felt the weight of the knife there. It wasn't the one Primrose and Martha had got me, but an almost exact replica that I'd bought myself on a whim the day before. I let the metal warm under my hand as it provided some freshness to my skin. My body and its blade reaching the same temperature. An equilibrium. It reminded me of why I'd made my choice in the first place, why I'd made it anew when George pleaded for me back, and why I'd keep making it time and again.

A group of students cycled in front of me, obscuring my view of George. I didn't wait to see if he was still there once they'd whizzed past. The only thing left to do with the morning was return to my turret, all thoughts of democracy and Tocqueville burned away.

The smell of roses filled my brain for one sweet, simple second. The fragrance chased out any thoughts of upcoming exams and my looming essay deadline as long as I held the bunch close enough to my face. Amina and Sophia had asked us to bring a gift to an impromptu gathering in the clearing that night, not knowing that we'd already given our most precious things weeks ago. So, I'd lost myself in one of the market stalls, surrounded by flowers of every colour, shape and size. It had been two days since I'd seen George near the sociology library and I was still scanning every alleyway and outdoor seating area as I hid among the lilies. I was resolute in my choice, but I also wished that I didn't keep having to have that resolve tested again and again.

'Boo.' The voice came from right behind my ear, so quiet at first that I thought it must be a part of me, one I hadn't met yet.

'Boo.' The second time was louder, a rough scratch, followed by laughter as I swung around, nearly taking a vase of white orchids with me.

'Your face is priceless.' Freddie was in front of me, his arm in a sling. One of his eyes was slightly bruised but otherwise his skin was clear, his teeth white, his smile wide.

'Fucking hell, Freddie. You nearly killed me.' It was the first time we had spoken in weeks and in my shock, I initially forgot that I was mad at him, president of the Dragons.

'Chill out, Ivy. It was just a joke. I was shouting at you from across the marketplace but you didn't hear me so I came over.'

'I can't be seen talking to you.' I picked up a bunch of black roses and started to walk over to the blonde woman who ran the market stall and always smelled of old lady perfume, a bit like Grandma Olive's. The symbolism of the flowers was too obvious, too vulgar for the clearing, but Freddie was robbing me of my time to linger.

'Why not? I know the whole George situation makes it a little awkward but we've always got on fine, haven't we?'

'It's not about George.'

'Really? What is it about then?' His body grew taller,

blocking my path out of the flowers so that I had to side-step him.

'It's Agatha. You ruined everything for her. I don't even think about George.' Yes, I told myself. My anger at Freddie was all for Agatha. I was being a good friend, a good sister. It was righteous – natural, even – to despise men who made your sisters cry. Particularly when they were men who also defiled nature and took pleasure in it.

'Agatha? I just told her that I wasn't as into her as she was into me. That's hardly a crime, is it?'

'You shouldn't have done it, Freddie.'

'Shouldn't have cut things off with Aggie? Between you and me, she was starting to be a bit of a nightmare, to be honest. She was jealous. She wouldn't leave me alone when I just wanted some time with the boys.'

'Shouldn't have messed with us. Is what I meant.' The blonde woman hid a smile under her fist as I handed over cash for the roses.

'Messed with you?' Freddie's laugh was like a cloud that hasn't yet spilled its rain.

'Yes. Well, Martha specifically. She's very protective of Aggie, you know, so she's furious with you.'

'Martha? Martha doesn't frighten me. Not as much as you do, anyway, when you're in a mood like this. Besides, I would have thought she was more of a threat to you.'

'What happened to your arm?' I nodded at the sling as I began to walk across the square, towards where my bike was chained to the railings under an enormous statue of one of the university founders.

'Rugby injury. Dangerous tackle. They got sin-binned.'

'You should be frightened of Martha.'

'Ivy, I don't even know what you're talking about.'

'What we've done is completely justified. Just remember that.' I wasn't certain whether I was trying to scare him or convince myself.

'What do you mean, what you've done?'

'I don't have to explain myself to you.'

'You're the one talking in riddles. I don't understand what you're talking about so I asked a question. That's how conversations work.'

'It's hardly a conversation when one person has all the power.' I fumbled with my lock, my fingers clumsy and hot.

'All the power? Seriously, Ivy, this is just a chat. We're not in a lecture now. This is real life.' The statue's shadow fell across his face so that I couldn't see his expression.

'Is that so? You blocked my way out of the flower stall, you dumped Agatha, you did God knows what in the woods at initiations, now you're making demands on my time.'

'I didn't block your way out – that's not even possible, it's a stall, it doesn't have any walls.' The hand gestures that accompanied his words were getting more and more animated. The lock finally unclicked and I chucked it in my rucksack, before mounting my bike. Freddie stepped in front of me, placing his hands on my front wheel.

'This is what blocking your way looks like.' His smile was still there but it was the coldest thing on that late spring day. 'Who told you about our initiations, anyway? Was it George? I always did think he might be more loyal to you than to us – guess I was proved wrong there, though.'

'Move.'

'And what if I don't?'

'You think you're untouchable, Freddie, but you're not.' I reined in my voice after a group of passing students glanced at us. I didn't want the whole world to know about the Dragons – not because I wanted to protect them, but because it might lead them to the Coven. 'You think you can sniff about gathering information for the Dragons but I see through you.'

'The Dragons?' he repeated, putting on a good show of genuine puzzlement. His hands slackened for a moment on my wheel and I took advantage, putting all my weight against the pedal. The bike lunged forward at Freddie, pushing into his crotch. Men really did have so many weak points. He doubled over, moving backwards, and I was away. Free. My hair flying, my blood coursing.

'Ivy, you've got it all wrong. Come back! Let's just talk.' His voice was choked with pain but it somehow still made its way to me as I dodged tourists and lurched over cobbles. It echoed along the tree-lined streets as I made my way to college. It was only when I saw the tops of the trees and the twisting turrets of home that I was able to block it from my mind.

I placed my black roses in a nook at the base of the tree. Primrose put a hand-picked bunch of wildflowers down next to mine and I cursed myself for not thinking of a more natural gift. Other girls poured bottles of wine into the earth or left handwritten notes or poems nestled in the cracks. Martha drew a love heart with her favourite lipstick on a fallen leaf and then propped it against the trunk.

'This is our thanksgiving,' Sophia said as she walked among us, nodding approvingly. 'Education is important to the Coven so your main job as sisters this term is to ensure that you study and do well in exams. That way, we can make sure that the full sisterhood returns to continue our legacy. But we recognize that we still need to foster our connection with each other, with the tree, with the pond, with this place. And to give back as well. To thank the woods for everything they have done for our sisters over centuries.'

'Thank you,' we all murmured as one. Then a sleepy, comfortable silence descended over us as we rejoiced in doing nothing for once. We just stood there, soaking up the sound of the breeze and the energy of the clearing that had seen our sisters' joy before it had seen their sorrow.

'And now we must part ways momentarily,' Sophia said, breaking our reverie. 'A good night's sleep is important to our mission of academic excellence.'

'Stay focused and then we'll have all the fun in the world. Just a little while longer, sisters,' Amina promised us. And in the clearing, I believed her. I believed that good things were already here, and that even more good things were on their way. Exams might be hard but they were nothing compared to what I'd survived before. And I'd been taking my vows seriously, working to draw myself ever closer to my sisters.

'Thank you,' I whispered again. I pressed my lips against the bark of the tree, knowing that no matter how many times I said the words or however many gifts I gave, it could never be adequate to repay what that place had given me.

Week 6

The first women to have officially been accepted into the university matriculated today, and of course we count them among our sisters. We have our own college with our own Mistress where we must learn and also attend to all the domestic duties like laundry and the cleaning of our own bedrooms – all the duties that men have women to do for them. It is summer and birdsong penetrates into our rooms which smell of fresh paint and new leather. We are excited, we cannot deny it or else we would be liars. To be on this land, so close to the place where women have found their joy in the cracks for centuries and to be a part of that inheritance – for once, words almost fail to describe it. None of us lived during the lifetime of our foremothers, but we are both their children and their sisters regardless. We will make them proud.

The town was getting even hotter. Tops were coming off, cleavages were out, bikinis donned. The real heron was driven away from the lake and forced to seek refuge in the shrivelling Saint Clair pond by knots of girls, brows furrowed as we tried to squint at laptops and notebooks as the sun pushed any understanding away. On the last weekend before exams started, the sky was a vivid blue, almost violent in its clarity. Clouds were afraid to come to the city that month, the sun ruling supreme day after day.

'It's like something's about to break around here,' Natasha yawned as we all tried to fit into a shrinking patch of shade cast by a weeping willow tree.

'It's going to be you if you don't shut up,' Agatha replied. She had been staring at a heavy book with a peeling cover that was nestled in her lap without turning a page for at least ten minutes.

'Ag, be nice.' Martha tossed a pen at her, just missing Agatha's head.

'Ugh, I give up. I've read this paragraph about the male gaze for my history of art elective about a million times by this point.' Agatha untied her hair from its ponytail and shook it out so that the gold captured the sun.

'If you're not all a bit quieter, I'm going to go back to the library.' Prim was only there because I'd begged her, telling her the fresh air would be good for her.

'It's okay, Prim. You and I can go and find a bench in the orchard. We'll be able to concentrate there.' I shot Agatha and Natasha a dirty look but they were too engrossed in each other, already made up. Agatha had been more cheerful in recent weeks, seemingly less mobbed by boys – perhaps they were distracted by revision. We began to pack up our things, mine into a tote bag with faded lettering from the health food store back home, and Prim's into her rucksack with endless pockets.

She took my hand as we made our way through groups of girls, mostly sat in twos and threes. Their chatter blended with the hum of insects from the surrounding flowerbeds. It was a low-level noise punctuated only by the occasional voice that broke through the thrum. Until a splash reverberated like a gunshot.

I grabbed Prim's arm, digging my fingers into her skin without thinking. My head whipped round – fast enough to crack my neck – to see Natasha and Agatha bobbing in the shallow water of the lake. A few seconds later, Martha waded in after them, wearing just her underwear. Sophia and Amina stood among the reeds whooping and clapping as Agatha dunked Natasha and she came up with pond-weed in her hair, like a medusa.

'I should go back.' I strained against Prim but her grip was stronger than mine.

'They'll be fine. They're just blowing off steam,' she reassured me.

'But maybe if I'm watching them I can—' My sentence trailed off.

'Do what, Iv?'

'Protect them. Stop something bad from happening.' I could tell from her face that she thought I was being silly but she was too kind to say so. I knew better though.

'Martha can literally stand in that water. It comes up to her ankles, at most her thighs. You've seen the way the heron can wade across it.'

'I wasn't only thinking about her.'

Prim tugged at my hand, a little more gently, but she

still didn't let go. Although every part of my body wanted to go the other way, I took a deep breath and forced my feet forward. After a minute or two of walking along the paths cut by the college gardeners into the long grasses, the shouts and laughter from the lake faded into silence.

'You're scared of water, aren't you?' Prim said as we sat down on the bench. It was halfway between a statement and a question.

'How do you know?' I cracked my knuckles, still not sure I'd made the right decision to leave Martha in the pond. I consoled myself with the thought that there were so many other girls there, and pretty much any one of them would have done anything to save her.

'It's not like it's a big mystery, Iv. You're not always as enigmatic as you think you are.'

'I'm not trying to hide it,' I said, although it was kind of a lie. 'You've just never asked. And it's not bad to be scared of water. It's sensible.'

'Right. I'm all for sensible. But there's sensible and then there's being terrified Martha might drown in the college pond.'

'I prefer to think of it as a lake. The one in the clearing is a pond, this one's bigger. I'm mostly scared of the sea. With smaller bodies of water, there's more you can control but you can still drown in a bath—'

'I know, I know. You can drown in any amount of water if the circumstances are right. Or wrong, I guess,' Prim said. 'I'm sorry I didn't ask about the water thing before. Truly. I assumed you'd bring it up if you wanted to talk about it.'

'I don't.'

'Are you sure?'

'Yes.' I didn't mind Prim knowing about my fears but her being aware of them was a far cry from me having to explain them.

'You never talk about anything from home. Even when we visited you, we only got to see little snippets.' Prim didn't mean it as a positive, but I was pleased that my curation of my life, of myself, had been at least somewhat successful.

'Have you ever read the dedication on the bench here? I noticed it in first term before we were sisters but I didn't think anything of it.' I nodded towards the small plaque that bore the engraving 'To the Saint Clair Sisters. Gone but never forgotten, taken from us but still here.'

'What about your friends from before, Iv?' Prim persisted.

'Friend.'

'Your friend, then. Are you still in touch?'

'No. I mean, we can't be. I'm not sure if I want to talk about it.' With just a bit of Prim's gentle prodding, my certainty that I wanted to keep everything to myself had dissolved into an 'I don't know'.

'It can be good to talk.' Prim smiled at me and for a moment she morphed into the counsellor in the grey, grey room that Dad had forced me to go to in the days after. 'Did you fall out?'

'No. I mean, yes. We fell out. First. Before.'

'Did something happen to her?' The skin between Prim's

eyebrows knitted together creating wrinkles that looked out of place on her smooth skin.

'I couldn't get there in time.' My words were croaky but once I started, I couldn't stop the flood. 'The water took her. We had a fight. It was so stupid. We were meant to be going to the beach together, as usual, so we could take videos of each other, like we always did. It was our thing. Being documentary film-makers. Or playing at being them. But then she went on her own. She was always a bit reckless with the sea, with everything really. I was the cautious one. She would go out of her depth, not ever worry about rip-tides or anything like that, not check any safety warnings. I had this bad feeling in my stomach but I didn't act on it. I ignored it. And then—' My body interrupted me, my mouth taking huge gasps of air unconsciously. The pain in my chest was stabbing, like someone was squeezing my heart with their bare hands.

'What was the fight about?' Prim leaned closer, closing the gap between our bodies as the swish of the green leaves grew almost unbearably loud.

'It was over a boy. I don't even remember his sur-name now. But these popular girls invited me to the pub and there was this boy there who'd always been in my class and—'

'A boy?'

'Yes. But it was probably about other things too. I don't know. And then – then she went to the sea and I still don't know why she went in other than she was brave and stupid and loved to swim and always ignored all the warnings about the currents. When I got there and I couldn't see her, I knew something was wrong. I went into the water to look for her but I couldn't see her, let alone save her. I couldn't even find her.' The explanation had to be a wave – a crashing, obliterating wave – because I could say it once and only once. The truth was a tsunami ricocheting my body, making my palms sweat and my breath ragged.

'That's not your fault, you know that, right?' Prim cradled my shoulders as I rocked back and forth on the bench, ignoring the splinters that were working their way into my bare thighs. 'It's normal to have fights. The two things aren't linked.'

'Are you joking? She wouldn't have been at the beach alone if it wasn't for me,' I whispered or shouted or maybe didn't say at all. I hadn't even mentioned the dream I'd had the night before Cara died where water encased my body – surely Prim would have found me guilty if she'd known I'd ignored that warning.

'I wondered where you two had snuck off to.' Martha's voice rang out across the orchard as she walked towards us, her wet bra sticking to her white T-shirt. 'What are you chatting about?'

'Nothing. We were talking about nothing,' I repeated before Prim could speak, forcing my words not to waver. 'Did you have a good dip?'

'The best. The water was to die for. So refreshing. Next time you should come in.'

'I'll think about it,' I promised Martha as the sun began

to bleed from the sky, the reds and oranges nothing compared to the last of the light dancing on her hair.

That night, after Prim left me, I lit one candle for Cara and one for Grandma. They were cheap ones that I'd had at the back of my drawer since the start of term but the process of lighting them drew my shoulders away from my ears and stopped the tremble in my hand. My breath had calmed, and my body had drooped. I felt like I'd swum fifty lengths, despite doing no exercise at university apart from cycling.

I don't know how long I sat there, staring at the flickering flames and the long, twisted shadows that my own body cast against the wall. I just know that the candles were both burned almost to the quick by the time I couldn't deny sleep any longer. Grandma's had burned lower, but Cara's was blacker, its edges disintegrating. I blew them out, and pinched the wicks with my fingertips, a little hiss escaping from the dying heat.

My bed felt chilly that evening, despite the warmth of the day. The sheets wrapped around me, as my body exuded a cold sweat. I slept in fits and bursts, until after five minutes or two hours had passed, I descended into a state of deep nothingness. For the first time in a long time, I had no dreams.

I would have slept right through to the morning if there hadn't been a scrabbling sound coming from the far wall. I waited a minute or two and it didn't disappear – instead, it grew louder. Natasha had told me she'd almost fainted in first term when she'd seen a mouse run in front of her fireplace. I wasn't afraid of a mouse, nor would I want to hurt one, but I did want to get back to sleep. There was a packet of earplugs somewhere in the drawer of my bedside table, and I forced myself to sit up to hunt for them. When I couldn't find them, I stood up to walk over to the chest of drawers but I didn't make it the few short steps to the other side of the room.

A hand wrapped around my mouth and I was scream-ing but no sound came out, just a series of shushes that sounded like waves breaking themselves against rocks, again and again. The shushes were outside me, inside me, everywhere all at once. Time slipped past, fleeting and unbearable, until the pressure of the hand released.

'It's me, Iv,' a voice whispered in my ear, close enough to be ticklish. The arms that were holding me let go and I spun around, my heart hammering in my chest, but I already knew exactly who it was. That term, he haunted me like a ghost.

'George. How the hell did you get in?' The question came out more fluttering than I would have liked, like I couldn't catch my own words, like they were a creature that could escape me.

'You shouldn't leave your window open.' He ruffled his hair and flashed me a smile that I would have killed for a few months before.

'Jesus Christ. You really thought it was a good idea to climb in through a third-floor window?' My nails dug into my palms, my flesh bearing the marks of the fear that I was trying to push down. It was just George. Not scary, only stupid. I didn't need to be afraid of the effects he might have on me. I was strong.

'I needed to speak to you.'

'What, again? Are you trying to get yourself killed? That pipe is ancient. I'm surprised it even held your weight.' I tugged the curtains shut, not wanting anyone to see a boy in my room. That way, they'd only see a shadow and really, who could tell that a boy was a boy from just a shadow?

'I know what you're doing, Ivy.' George's brow was creased, his voice solemn, the smile long gone.

'What are you talking about? Are you seriously going to break into my room and start hurling around accusations? Even after I told you to leave me alone?'

'You need to stop,' he continued. He'd positioned his body in between me and the door.

'Stop what?'

'Whatever it is you're doing. I heard – I don't know what I heard but I heard something. Some weird ritual. Something like a prayer, except I know you're not religious. Some game you're probably playing with the others. But you need to stop before someone gets seriously hurt.' There was a wheedling note in his voice that I'd never heard before. Even when he was asking me to get back together with him, it had never sounded like begging.

'So you were creeping around outside my room then too?' I demanded, thinking back to the noises I'd heard in the corridor a few weeks before that were so distinctively that of a boy. With the flurry of exam term and the contentment of being with Martha and Primrose, I hadn't paid it too much thought because – although it disquieted me at the time – the noises hadn't materialized again until that moment. I was partly freaked out, partly a little bit excited that I was worth all this effort on George's part. But no. That wasn't how I should be feeling. That wasn't how I should be feeling at all.

'It's not how it sounds.' He passed his palms over his eyes, which were underlined by uncharacteristic dark circles, visible even in the gloom. 'I came to see you – to try one last time to make things right. But then I got cold feet. I thought that maybe I should put what you wanted first, even if I didn't fully believe you wanted me to leave you alone. I was about to turn back when I heard you whispering some – some incantation to yourself.'

'What's so wrong with that, George?' I asked but I couldn't help myself blushing. 'Lots of people have rituals that make them feel better.'

'I know, I know. It sounds ridiculous when I say it out loud. But something about it felt off. I feel like you've changed – someone in the Coven must have got you onto all that bullshit. That's not like you, Iv.'

'You don't know the first thing about me, George. And you gave up the right to know anything when you got with my best friend. And don't use my nickname either. None of this is for you anymore.' I was deliberately harsh – maybe if I injured him again with my words, I'd deal a fatal blow and he'd stop coming back to me, threatening to divert me from my course.

'I'm doing this because I'm worried about you. I'm trying to help.' His eyes were soft and pleading, catching the scant moonlight wending its way through the window and turning it into a charm.

'No.' Everything was too much and the word came out like a bullet, ricocheting off my walls. 'No,' I said again in a lower voice. 'You don't get to break into my room, scare me half to death and then pretend you want to protect me. And make out like I'm so easily led, such a wallflower, that I couldn't possibly be doing something of my own accord. No. You made a choice. And I made mine. Now you have to live with the consequences.'

'Like you say, I'm not the only one who made a choice.' He scrunched his hands into fists and pressed them against his eyes again but he didn't try to argue with me further. 'Freddie says he tried to talk to you—'

'Ah, I should have known you only care about protecting Freddie. About protecting boys.'

'What?'

'Keep your voice down,' I warned.

'I'm just asking – asking you not to wage a war against the whole world, Ivy. Or to buy into everything the Coven tells you. You don't have to cut yourself off from everything and isolate yourself in this place.'

'I'm not cutting myself off from everything. I'm cutting myself off from you.' Although I knew that cutting myself off from him meant that I needed to shrink my world so that it was small, tight and certain.

'Okay. I know what I'm saying doesn't make much sense

and it's the middle of the night and I sound a bit crazy but I had to say something and to warn you – those girls aren't all sweetness and light.'

'Why should I listen to you and not them? If I'd stuck with my sisters all along, I'd never have gotten hurt by you.'

'Your sisters? Listen to yourself, Ivy.' I'd forgotten he didn't know how deep the Coven's bonds ran.

'Fuck you, George.' I gritted my teeth. I couldn't let him sway me. I knew what happened when a sister sided with a man and I wouldn't let the terrible parts of history repeat themselves. Not again. Not on my watch.

'Fine. We're not getting anywhere.' He held up his hands. 'But I want you to know that I know you're up to something. And let the records show that I tried to do what's best for you. All that stuff with the notes you made on the Dragons. Then the weird ritual. And Agatha – there's something bizarre going on there too, I just can't quite figure it out yet. But I will.'

'Everything you touch turns to shit, you know that, right?'

'That must include you then,' he retorted, sounding nastier than I'd ever heard him.

'Just go.' I stuck my head out of my door to make sure no one was in the corridor. 'And pull your hood up. I can't have you seen here.'

'Why?' His voice had turned taunting and bitter, all the usual sweetness sucked away. 'Because Martha might see?'

My hand shot away from my body, slapping George across his right cheek. The sound of my skin on his was crisp and satisfying. The first physical contact that I'd initiated with him in months, and it only lasted for a second. 'You don't get to say her name. Not ever again.'

I bundled him out into the empty corridor, his face shocked and gaunt under the lights that stayed on all night. My door shut with a snap and I was alone again, in the darkness.

Week 7

The men laugh at us as we enter our exam hall – it has to be separate due to their lack of sophistication and civility, rather than ours. They cannot let us be, and they would be a far greater distraction with their antics during our examinations than we would be for them. They look for our threats in all the wrong places – in our skirts, in our long hair, our femininity, our prettiness. They never look for threats in what we do after dark, in our song, in our dance, in what we teach future generations. For the most important part of our learning is not what we write in our essays, but what we pass on to each other through our bodies and our words. What we pass on through this book. For if you're reading this, we have given you our knowledge going back centuries. Our knowledge of how to survive.

Question 2: What is Freedom?
Ivy Graveson, Practice Essay for
Introduction to Political Thought

For freedom to be substantiated and to have an impact on the lives of the free, it must exist at an individual level. The individual is the bedrock of society in this respect, and not because of a neoliberal definition of the individual entire to themselves. But because we are all interconnected, relational beings and so freedom for all necessitates the freedom of each part of the whole.

Scotland had a much higher incidence of witch trials than England. In my hometown, witch trials lasted two years from 1590 and involved more than seventy people, most of them women. One of these women, Mildred Simpson – also known as the 'Wise Wife of Berrick' – was interrogated by the king himself, illustrating the persistent fear that (clever) women threaten the freedom of men. She was later found 'guilty', and subsequently tortured and murdered.

For a person who was not only flesh and blood but thoughts and ideas and dreams and hope to be referred to as only a 'wife' diminishes their freedom in death as well as in life. And not only theirs but others' too – mine and perhaps yours. Because it renders so many of us as belonging to someone else, as appendages. The freedom of the individual is that of the whole and of its parts.

The Saint Clair witch trials are scandalous and sala-cious, largely because Millicent Saint Clair informed on her three sisters. A tale of a woman denouncing not only other women but her own sisters is so shocking that there's not even a word for it. There is no feminine equivalent to fratricide (although that may have more to do with the fact that our language is masculine, even if it is not gendered in the same way that French, Spanish or Italian are). But archival research has recently suggested that a man in Millicent's circle – who certainly had more social power and capital than any of the women involved – suggested to Millicent that her sisters might be witches.

The greater freedom is surely to be able to exert your own freedom to the exclusion of other people's. But is this the kind of freedom we aspire to? Perhaps the pertinent question is not 'what is freedom' but 'what are freedoms'? Because the kind of freedom we should strive for is not couched in the destruction of someone else's but in the uplifting of it. We will be free when the links to the past and its continuities with modern day persecution are not merely severed but rendered visible.

Ivy, I like this. I feel you are perhaps oversimplifying the involvement of women in this in an attempt to paint Millicent as a straightforward victim, too. Remember that binaries are a useful heuristic but that isn't always how the world actually works. People can be victims and aggressors too. The fascination (and the best marks!) lie in the complication. The tricky, messy parts we often don't want to look at head on.

Also, there is a word that you might want to look up – sororicide. And have you read any theorists? Would be worth mentioning one or two in the actual exam.

And I looked up Mildred Simpson. When they say 'wife of Berrick', I think they are using wife as a stand-in for woman (potentially still problematic but all knowledge is useful) and Berrick was a place not a man.

I love your passion but let's just refine it a little before the big day.

The city was a melting ice cream by the end of May, sticky and cloying wherever you looked, touched or trod. A sweetness clawed at the air, dragged down your tongue. It was three days until my first exam, two till Prim's and one till Martha's. And both of my best friends shared the misfortune of having birthdays right in the middle of the most intense period of the academic year. During school, I'd always thought my birthday being in August was the worst, most forgettable time but I'd been wrong.

'We still have to go to the clearing,' Martha insisted while Prim shook her head. 'It's my exams that start tomorrow. You guys have time to recover. So if I say we're going, then we're going.'

We mixed homemade cocktails that matched the pinks and reds of the sky and then walked down the path into the woods with the drinks sloshing in our water bottles. The warmth of the day clung to the evening like it didn't want to get left behind. Pockets of light penetrated the thickets of undergrowth every few metres, so that I caught flashes of Martha's grin and Prim's slight frown.

That morning, when I was supposed to be returning books to the towering central library, I'd slipped into one of the narrow, cobbled passages off the market. The kind that people probably got stabbed in in medieval times but now were full of independent shops that smelled of incense and money. At the back of one with a pink façade, there was a shelf with stacks of semi-precious stones and crystals. In curly handwriting, with love hearts to dot the Is, piles of stones were listed under each month. Smooth lumps of agate sat underneath May. I couldn't get Prim and Martha anything like the penknife they'd bought me. My mind had drawn a blank when I'd tried to think of something as special as the object whose notches in our palms had drawn us together, but the cool rock felt right in my hands. Their shared birth month made it easy; I was desperate for sameness back then. To mix Martha and Prim together and make their meanings one. Unity was easier than following each of their threads to their own conclusion – it meant less chance of fraying.

On the walk, the stones were in my pocket but they were mocking me. They whispered that Martha probably already had emeralds – her real precious birthstone. They taunted that Prim probably thought they were stupid.

'I bought you guys something.' It took me three drinks to tell them about their presents. 'It's nothing really but I wanted to get you both a little thing.'

'You didn't have to, Iv. That's so sweet of you though,' Prim cooed, as she undid the purple wrapping paper.

'Oh, my god. This is like, so meaningful.' Martha held up the agate to the dying light to get as close a look as possible, then turned and hugged me. 'I have so many crystals but I don't have this one yet.'

'It's beautiful,' Primrose agreed.

'You're so welcome. So, so welcome,' I kept saying, as my body sparkled with heat and alcohol. It got later and later and we got drunker and drunker, our whoops scattering birds into the air until they got used to our presence. Leaves swished and so did Martha's hair, tossed side to side, a red glimpse of autumn on the final day of May.

'Why don't we hop in the pond?' I suggested, thrilled at my own loose spontaneity, and the others nodded. I'd never thought I could feel comfortable in water again but this pond had been breaking down my barriers, singing me songs of its shallowness. The water let out its breath as I clambered in. There was barely enough room for the three of us in the tiny body of water, and our submerged skin fizzed, shedding the heat of the day. Our laughter reached up towards the heavens, the moon beginning to make her way out. The whispers of the woods were loudest in the water and I was the last to heave myself out, soothed by the half-formed sentences that my brain couldn't quite grasp onto.

Prim rested her head in my lap, as we all dried off post-dip. 'Do you guys ever worry about, you know, this?' Prim gestured around the glade.

'This place?' I asked. 'All the time. It feels like a friend that I – we – need to watch over.'

'Yes and no,' she answered. 'Not just the place. Like the things we do. I don't know, maybe it's just the stress of exams. But I've been having these dreams where Freddie, or some other shadowy male figure, kind of gets back at us.'

'What do you mean?'

'I don't know. It's all indistinct and probably silly,' Prim laughed.

'She'll protect us.' Martha nodded up at the tree, whose great branches provided shadow in the day and shelter at night.

'I suppose we ought to get back soon,' I said reluctantly, noticing the goose pimples on Martha's bare arms. As we stood, her birthstone fell off her lap and landed next to a gnarled root. On her way up from bending down to get it she bumped her head, hard enough to make a hollow smacking sound.

'Ow. I swear that branch wasn't there a minute ago.'

'Are you all right?' I fussed.

'Of course I am. I'll always be all right.' Martha slung her arms around me and kissed me on the cheek just like Cara had done two years before. Her body retained the heat of the last dregs of the sun as it pressed against me.

I got to know the cracks in the city's skin through the rooms that I took my exams in. Whether they were in repurposed dining halls or offices folded into forgotten corners of ancient buildings, they all had the same smell. Dust and prestige, mixed with a little sweat and desperation. There were four exams in total, each one more taxing than the last. My brain fell flat every time I struggled to remember a Plato quote or recall the way Harold instructed us to include surprise conclusions in our essays.

Or that had been the way it was when I was revising. When I lined up my carefully selected fine-tip blue and black pens on my rickety desk so that they were organized in the perfect formation, my stomach aching and empty from skipping breakfast, something happened the moment the bearded examiner announced we could start. I touched the knife in my pocket and then the words came snaking out of the pen, chasing each other onto the paper, hungry to bite into the blank page. I wrote about humanism and whether Machiavelli could be seen as part of that movement, and whether Locke was the originator of the secular right to resistance and how Thomas More's daughter Margaret was the living embodiment of his belief in education for all and seemingly a thousand other ideas and theories.

When I dotted the final full stop in my final exam, I knew I'd done it. I knew I'd get a first, weeks before I'd stand outside the results board on the town's main thoroughfare and see a 72 shine back at me. As I squinted at the bright sun after three hours spent in a windowless room, I knew the odds were in my favour. I could taste it on the air. Fresh with a metallic edge, like sucking blood from a paper cut.

My plan was to go home and rest for a few hours alone in my room so that I could be full of energy for Prim's and Martha's last exams the next day – they both started earlier and finished later than me. But a throng of other students was blocking me from making my way to where my bike was chained to a railing. Boys laughed and punched one another on the shoulder in that playful act of faux violence I've never understood. I turned to the side to make myself smaller but I still couldn't get through.

'It's not that funny,' complained a voice I recognized.

'It kind of is though.' Eddy slapped Freddie on the back, his hand creating a squelching sound. Freddie was drenched, his sling gone but his T-shirt and shorts soaked through so that I could see the angular contours of his body. Tiny bits of slimy green pondweed hung to the material of his clothes as he tried to pick them off. We were right next to the river, and the boys' chatter was punctuated by the squabbling of ducks and swans.

'I swear I've cycled down here a million times and this is the only time I've fallen. I can't fathom how it happened. And right before my exam as well,' Freddie said.

'First time for everything,' Eddy replied, taking off his dry jumper and giving it to Freddie.

A gap between bodies opened up and I slipped through, giggling. I might not have got to see George after he fell in the river, but I imagined it through Freddie's moans and discomfort. It was the ideal fate to befall him; pretty much harmless but a reminder that none of us are untouchable. That was the day I truly arrived in the town. It hadn't been when Mum and Dad dropped me off in our scratched old car, but there, seeing Freddie – who had seemed the bastion of confidence and certainty – twist and fret. I'd needed the witching tree to give me roots, but I'd watered them all on my own. There was no getting rid of me.

Week 8

The men cannot despise us openly like they used to. They invite us to dinner dates with them, both individually and as two separate but aligned groups. They visit our college for formal hall and extend return invitations. Everything that was once raw and out in the open has been stitched shut and tucked away. But we know. A scar still remains; the wound cannot be erased. We feel it in our bones. The trees tell us so. Something is coming. Something is always coming. There will be tests and there will be trials. Our job – your job – is to make sure that the sisterhood shall remain.

Martha soaked me with the bottle held between her legs – she'd needed both hands to remove the cork. Huge, tall arcs of liquid spurted out, hitting my mouth. A flood of bubbles rushed across my tongue. The liquid dripped off my hair, into my mouth. It tasted like real champagne – knowing Martha it probably was. I popped off the cork from the bottle of prosecco I'd bought, and sprayed Martha back, soaking her white T-shirt so that it became as see-through as Freddie's had been the day before. All around us, other students were shrieking and jumping up and down as they pretended to avoid the liquid their friends were directing at them.

'You're done. It's all over.' I put one arm around Martha and one around Primrose, not caring how sticky we all were.

'Well, until next year.' Prim dabbed her face dry with the hem of her skirt.

'That's so far away at the moment, it might as well be a different century,' I said.

'Thank you for coming to spray us.' Martha kissed my head with a loud *mwah*.

'Of course, I wouldn't miss it for the world.' And it was true. I'd been binding us closer together all term and being there for them as exams came to a close felt something like a finishing touch.

When we went out that night, my hair still carried the scent of fizz. No amount of concealer could hide the bags under my eyes, the price of doing four exams in as many days, so I matched my moody purple eyeshadow to my dark circles. Martha dressed all in crimson and Prim in maroon. We were done. Free. Finished. Summer stretched out ahead of us, inviting us into its embrace. Except it was one that I found cold and lacking. I pushed the thought of months without Prim and Martha down, tucked them somewhere inside my chest where my white skin had turned a pale red after hours drinking in the southern sun.

There were Dragons in the club and more boys than I could count, but we'd spiked the Marthas we'd drunk with extra vodka and I was high off exhaustion and life. Pretty much everybody had finished exams that day. I'd been lucky that I'd got an extra day to catch up on sleep before the madness ensued. Sophia and Amina were doing tequila shots off a guy's bare torso. I caught a glimpse of Eddy going into the men's bathrooms, and I heard Peter's braying laugh in a pause in the music. Natasha was spinning round in the middle of the room on her own, smiling to herself. I half-expected to see Harold or the Mistress. When I went to order drinks, the mirrors behind the bar showed how the red of the strobe lights flashed against my hair, turning it coppery. For a moment, I didn't look like myself at all.

I turned away from the bar, gin and tonics in my hands, but I couldn't find Martha or Primrose. The music got too much, and I emerged into the smoking area, the fresh air a slap in the face. But they weren't there. There was only a flash of big, blonde hair. Agatha. Agatha's mouth clamped to someone tall with darker hair flecked with gold. A familiar someone. Aggie's lips were on George.

In a second, all thoughts of red hair mixing with brown curls evaporated. They were replaced with a new image, one which made sense, even though it stung in the same momentary way that stubbing a toe did. Agatha was just reaching the logical conclusion of that term, for her. And George had never promised to wait for me for ever. The fact that he had even waited as long as he did astonished me.

'There you are.' Martha pulled me into a hug from behind and led me back inside to the dance floor. She swapped me a G&T for a drink with a tiny umbrella and gestured to Prim to take a photo of us. Then Prim twirled me under her arm and Martha rubbed up against me as she danced. I lost the threads of our bodies – where they ended and I began. In their flesh, the thought of what was happening under the midnight sky didn't matter at all.

Later that night, I added Agatha's name to the book when Primrose and Martha weren't looking.

At garden parties, girls were dropping like flies in the heat. Natasha had told me that her supervision partner had fallen and cracked her head on the side of an oyster truck. Bottles of water were handed out by porters to partygoers to try and prevent fainting, but it was a losing battle.

Except for the Coven. There was something in the air the day of our garden party that ensured our makeup didn't run and our hair didn't flop. Of course, we couldn't really bill it as 'our' garden party. It was styled as the Mistress's party instead, but really it was the Coven who hosted and organized it, pulling strings behind the scenes to make it one of the most exclusive invites of the year.

We were dressed all in white, and the sun reflected off us. We were beacons, drawing people – boys – to the Mistress's garden. It was tradition that she hosted the party, in her sprawling house that backed onto the river and the backs of several of the most ancient colleges. The smell of wild-flowers permeated the air, and bunting fluttered in the light breeze of the afternoon.

Before the guests arrived, the Mistress gathered us all

in a circle and instructed us to hold hands. 'I want to raise a toast to the Coven.'

'To the Coven,' we echoed as one as we broke apart and picked up champagne glasses that we held aloft. It felt good to speak our name in unison before we'd have to keep it off our lips for the rest of the evening.

'You really are the beating heart of the college – don't quote me on that – but I wanted to extend my thanks for your commitment to tradition and heritage. And for your understanding that this college is the people that have been a part of it – now and then – and that, as women in education, we have to look after one another. So, bottoms up.' We all drank deeply.

'Thank you, Mistress, for your continuous support,' Amina smiled as her white dress billowed around her. 'And we'll be deciding who to pass the baton to next as presidents soon. We just have a little more thinking to do. But for now, we want to thank all our newest sisters for their commitment to our family. We can't wait for next year – and to celebrate with you today.'

'Let the games commence.' Sophia threw her arms out wide and – on cue – two men dressed in white tie creaked open the cast-iron gates. A queue of guests had already formed and they each handed their black paper invites over to be checked. Slowly but surely, the leafy garden began to fill up with people laughing and drinking. The bubbles from the champagne went straight to my head and I flitted from group to group, like the butterflies that sunned themselves on the cornflowers.

The only thing marring my day was the presence of George and Freddie. They'd sauntered in about half an hour after the party started, defiling what had been a safe space. Amina had taken me aside a few days earlier to double-check that I was okay with them being invited, but I knew that if I could bear being in their presence, I really needed to say yes. It was easier to have the Dragons onside if at all possible, to get insights into their movements and to check that they were just up to their usual stupid debauchery and nothing more. Keep your friends close and your enemies closer and all that.

But even George and Freddie couldn't blot out the glorious sunshine and the friends around me and the feeling of being a part of both the past and the future. When my glass was empty, I walked to the shady oak tree to get a refill. There were waiters everywhere but I liked the feeling of doing something for myself. Hidden from the main party by the trunk of a great tree, Sophia was pouring a clear liquid from a vial into a dozen cocktail glasses laid out on a table.

'What are you doing?'

'Only the boys have the whisky sours,' she replied without looking at me.

'That's not true. I saw Nat drinking one.'

'Whoops,' she giggled. 'It won't do them any harm. It's just funny.'

'What is it?' I demanded.

'Now that would be telling.'

'You're spiking their drinks. Someone could get hurt.'

'It's a chance to show them that there's steel in among all this beauty. I thought you of all people would be a fan of that.' All traces of tipsiness and fun disappeared from Sophia's voice. 'They'll be fine. They always are.'

'And Natasha?' I called out but she was already walking away. I set out to find Nat and tell her not to drink the sours but there were hundreds of bodies in the way and temptation at every turn. A waiter handed me a glass of prosecco and another offered me a tiny pancake decorated with edible petals, and Natasha slipped further and further from my thoughts.

'Boo!' Martha giggled as I jumped. 'I've been looking for you. Where have you been?'

'I saw Sophia do something to the drinks,' I began to explain.

'What?' Martha cupped her ear with her hand as a jazz band started to play behind us. 'I can't hear you. It doesn't matter anyway. I've got you now. Let's go find Prim and see if we can slip off for a few minutes.'

'She's over there by the helter-skelter, I think,' I said, already losing track in the chaos of what I'd been so bothered about. We wandered over, hand in hand, and pulled her away from a girl with blue and green hair who was laughing at everything she said. The sun had begun to slip away and the whole world looked like it was filtered to show the best, prettiest version of itself. Candyfloss clouds chased each other across the sky and the silhouettes of buildings grew more abstract and less detailed as night fell, soft and slow.

'Girls, guess what?' Martha asked, but gave us no time to reply. 'It's nearly the witching hour. Let's go for a wander.'

A little unsteady on our feet, we tottered through marquees, slipping away from the crowds. I saw Natasha from a distance and she didn't look any more spaced out or dreamy than usual. The evening tasted of dewy grass and buttercups and the cows that grazed along the river during the daytime. The ground was on the verge of becoming mud, churned by too many steps, and my pale pink shoes turned brown.

We emerged from behind a weeping willow onto the banks of the river. I recognized where we were as not all that far from where I had my supervisions with Harold. Then fireworks burst across the sky, and it felt a world away. Splashes of colour exploded, and the crimson of the biggest rockets fought the red in Martha's hair in a bloody war.

'This is perfect for a spell,' Martha grinned.

'It's perfect full stop,' I whispered. For a second, the light caught her cheekbones and she looked just like the day where we found each other in the college woods. Before exams, before George, before anything.

'You're right, Iv. This has been the best day.' Prim couldn't take her eyes off the fireworks. We were all transfixed, oohing and aahing, until Martha broke the magic.

'I want us to make a wish,' she declared. 'Come on, let's hold hands.'

'Okay.' Prim reached for me and her hand slotted into mine like a key into a lock. 'I'm happy to do anything you want today as a send-off before the summer.'

'Don't say that,' I pleaded.

'It's only a summer, Iv,' Prim replied.

'Won't I see you at all?' I asked.

'I'll be in Ghana visiting family, and then doing work experience at that international justice NGO in London. But you can come and visit me then if you'd like?' She squeezed my hand.

'You're ruining the moment by talking about the future,' Martha scolded us. 'This is now.'

We formed a tight circle, just the three of us, underneath the caressing tendrils of the willow. Martha began to chant, her voice rising so that it seemed at one with the breeze, with the rustling of the leaves, the chirping of the birds. Prim and I joined in and without thinking about it, we knew what to say. We were so languid, so relaxed, so in our element. Meditation had never worked for me and I hated the chanting at the end of the yoga classes Mum had got into for a couple of months, but there on the bridge I was transcendental.

'What are you lot up to?' A voice that wasn't our own felt like an affront. Especially when that voice was coming from George. I could see the recognition on Martha's face, too, even though neither of us was facing him.

'Get out of here.' I was the one to break off the chant while Martha and Prim elevated their voices to drown him out. Maybe if I hadn't said anything he'd have got bored or better, scared, and wandered off. But he stayed there, his back resting against the tree trunk, fireworks reflecting in his eyes.

'Oh, wait, don't tell me. Another spell.' For a second, I wondered if Agatha had told on us but then I looked into George's eyes and saw that he *knew* in a way that wasn't the result of gossip but of certainty. Even if neither of us was sure exactly what it was he knew. Liquid slopped out of his martini glass. I noticed his white shirt had several damp patches on it. One looked a bit like a smiley face. His eyes ping-ponged between me and Martha as a cloud slid across the sky. A great, grey, feathery thing. With their lights blotted out, the noise of the fireworks sounded like gunshots.

'You took Ivy away from me for this?' His lip curled. A snatch of the man he would have been in middle age crossed his face. 'For this bullshit, performative, mystical shit. For this, and horoscopes and tarot and a bunch of other stuff that I know none of you is stupid enough to actually believe in. Otherwise, you wouldn't be here.' He waved his hand at the inky sky, the skeletons of colleges piercing the air.

'Would you kindly leave?' Martha's voice was ice on that summer's day. She and Prim had stopped chanting, and the silence was louder than our voices combined.

He laughed in a way that sounded somewhere between a bark and a howl. 'That's a bit much, don't you think? Ordering me around, acting like you own the place?'

Their eyes were glued to each other, their expressions set. George broke first, leaning in towards me, his palm resting against my bare shoulder. 'Let's go. You don't belong here with them. That's what I was trying to tell you the other night. What I've been trying to tell you for weeks now.'

'The other night?' Martha spat the words out.

'It was nothing.' I shook off his hand. 'He broke into my room.'

'He broke into your room?' Prim's mouth hung open. 'Why didn't you tell us? That's so – so non-consensual. We have to tell the porters.'

'I'm trying to help her,' George said. He was angrier than I'd ever seen him. Every other time I'd seen George, including the times after he betrayed me, there'd been something pulling me to him, something hard to resist. It was a bit like a riptide – the more you fought it, the more it trapped you. But for the first time ever, there was nothing drawing me to him. Without meaning to, George had finally freed me. Perhaps I'd stayed still for long enough, so that I exited his current and found myself swimming all on my own.

'I don't want your help.' I couldn't keep my voice low any longer. I was shouting, screaming, not caring who heard me. 'I'm not just some girl in distress who's waiting for you to rescue me, George. I have agency. I do things. Things you couldn't even dream of. And I've made my choice. And I'd make it again in a heartbeat.'

'Ivy, I've been watching you this whole time. From the day we met. I know you do things. Martha doesn't think that. She just sees you as a disciple. They don't see you. I'm the only one who does.'

'She asked you to leave.' Prim stepped in between me and George. 'What part of that don't you understand?'

But he didn't stop. He just kept coming towards me, arms outstretched. Prim moved aside, and the three of us were pushed back to the edge of the bank. Martha threw out her arms to create a barrier.

'She said she chose me, George,' Martha snapped. 'Us.'

'Maybe this magic stuff actually is working if you can convince her that's the right decision. Just like you convinced her that I was the one that made a move on you.' He was close enough for me to feel the warm sweetness of his breath.

'George, leave it. Let's just all go back to the party and enjoy the rest of our night. You can meet some pretty girl and forget all about me.' I'd hated that he'd called me a disciple but I just wanted him gone, and I'd learned that getting what you desire isn't always the same as having the final word. I grabbed the others' hands and turned us around so we no longer had the water at our backs.

'No.' George's mouth formed the word he wasn't used to hearing from others. The word that had been nestled in everything I'd said. 'I'm not leaving you here with them, Ivy. I promise you'll thank me later. Something doesn't feel right here.'

'How many times does she have to say no?' Prim demanded.

'We said get away.' Martha's voice was a snarl, but George ignored it. He stepped towards me in a fluid motion, mirroring the ripples of the river. Time slowed down and for an instant I thought he was going to try and kiss me. A shadow passed across the moon. The darkness got darker. I stuck out my hand to protect myself. My open palm caught George off guard, and he stumbled, his balance unsteady from too much alcohol and sunshine. His hands reached forward as he walked backwards, still searching for me. There was a threat implied in those fingers. The threat of a future – with him.

I stepped to the side but I still saw the shock on his face as he lost his balance. As he tumbled. At the exact same moment, there was a whoop from the trees behind the willow. People. Boys. Boys nearby. Making their way towards us. Our necks snapped round at the same time, so that I didn't see exactly what happened to George and I didn't turn to look. Even with all ties between us severed, I couldn't face those eyes of his again, was scared I'd lose something of myself in them.

The noises of men grew louder, obscuring all others. Peals of laughter floated down through the trees, and there was the sound of footsteps a while off but coming closer.

'Ivy, we have to go.' Martha tugged at my hand. 'We might antagonize the Dragons if they find us here, and George in the water. We don't want them to think that this is the Coven's doing and inadvertently reignite some old rivalry.'

'Shouldn't we check that he's okay?' I asked but we were already running, stooping to swerve under branches.

'Of course he's okay,' Prim insisted in a whisper. 'He just fell over. He'll be picking himself out of the water now. But with any luck, he'll be too embarrassed to tell the other boys.'

'Iv, seriously. That water is like two inches deep.'

'Martha's right.' Prim grabbed my other hand. 'It's George. He's always fine, Iv. That's like his MO. But we might not be if it's our word against his.'

'But there's three of us and only one of him,' I protested but my words were obscured by voices in the nearby bushes.

'We have to keep going. Now,' Martha hissed, and before I knew it, we were scrambling through the undergrowth again. Pain like knives dug into my stomach. I wanted to stop and be sick but I kept going, kept following Prim, as branches whipped at my face. She was the sensible one – if she said George would be fine, she must be right. And then wham. I hit a body like a wall.

Freddie was in front of me, his eyes red and his lips swollen like they'd been stung by a bee. His collar was ruffled and his bow tie lopsided. There was a shadowy shape next to him. My eyes adjusted to the gloom enough to see a boy doing up the buttons on his shirt.

'Eddy?' The name sprung from my mouth before my brain could tell it that the point of all this running was to disentangle myself from George, erase the three of us from the map.

'Ivy? Is that you?' he asked, his hands groping forward but Prim and Martha had vanished and, although I had questions, I had to get out of there too. I sped off, turning my face away from them. We all had secrets from that day and I chose to put my faith in the fact that would be enough to protect me. Us.

I slipped between the gap of two white tents and slotted myself in at the open bar. No one glanced at me as I struggled to regain control of my breath. I ordered the first drink I could think of – an old fashioned. A shoulder hit against my arm, sloshing icy liquid onto my wrist. I licked it off but all I could taste was salt and metal.

'Sorry. Had one too many,' Peter apologized. 'Oh, Ivy, it's you. I haven't seen you for ages.'

'No. Funny that.'

'You look glowing if I may say so. Do you fancy a ride on the dodgems? Getting bashed about a bit is good for the soul, don't you think?'

I assembled the constituent parts of my face together into one big happy army. 'Sure. Sounds fun.'

'Great. Just checking, you and George have broken up now, right?'

'Right.' I shot him my best grin. The only weapon I had left to me.

SUMMER

Sometimes, just sometimes, a man gets what's coming to him. Sometimes something bad happens, something that appears to be an accident, a coincidence even — but we all know there's no such thing as coincidence. Sometimes one stands in for the whole, and we take comfort in the fact that the others may be reminded that they're not untouchable. That their bodies are mortal too. These incidents, few and far between that they are, are not enough to atone for the horrors our sisters faced. But they are something.

It took three days for them to notice George was missing. Three days in which I packed up my little room and all the treasures I'd collected over my first year in my new home. Three days in which Dad drove the long journey down to pick me up, leaving Mum behind due to her travel anxiety. Three days in which I allowed myself to breathe, and to accept that although I wouldn't see much of Martha or Primrose over the summer, I would always find my way back to them. On the third day, the day I left in Dad's juddering car, someone raised the alarm. Soon after that, they found the body.

I hadn't expected to hear from George, had no reason to, so I never knew that he was missing until I saw the headlines, his gorgeous face rendered tragic and beyond reproach. It wasn't the water that got him – it was the fact that he'd hit his head on a rock as he fell. The last days of term were such a rush that I barely had time to think of him. I'd assumed he'd just slunk off in a sulk after the finality of losing me was driven home. That we wouldn't see each other again until some awkward encounter after the summer. It was the boys who let him down in the end. Any anger or sorrow I had twisted into a sharp point facing in their direction. It had almost a physical presence in my mind – a raft I could cling onto whenever my feelings threatened to overwhelm me, to upset the balance of the life I'd created. Why did they not notice that their brother was missing for three whole days? If I misplaced Prim or Martha for even a minute I would know. I would think of them and I would make their safety so.

George only had the boys to blame.

TERM 1

Week 1

'We've decided to make an exception,' Amina declared, a flaming torch held aloft above her head, casting strange, dancing shadows in the dregs of the day.

'Usually, we only pick two presidents,' Sophia continued. 'But for the past year we've been looking and watching, observing even when you think we haven't been. And we feel that there's only one natural path forward.'

'This year, three sisters will be president.' Amina looked satisfied as we all gasped, the trees snickering in response. Agatha straightened up as Natasha's eyes widened. Primrose bit her lip and I twisted my hands in my lap. Only Martha was still, her body unmoving and certain in the dappled evening sunlight. There was a bite to the air that night – the first nibbles of winter – but it was still warm enough that we were wearing white dresses and no tights.

'These girls have impressed us with their commitment to the Coven and to each other. When push has come to shove, they've chosen sisterhood again and again. We trust them to pick out the next generation of sisters and feel confident that we are leaving the Coven in safe hands.' Amina's face was dimly lit under the branches of the great tree, her leaves turning to gold and curling in readiness to fall.

'Martha, step forward,' Sophia called. There was a murmur of appreciation and recognition, rather than surprise. I held my breath as Martha stood and walked towards the very spot where we first met. For a second, an image of George intruded into my brain – the tree, my back, his hands, his mouth, our bodies, together. Then his body again, but, this time, lifeless yet still beautiful. I scrunched up my eyes to blot it out. I had to live in the here and now. The only way forward was to not look back.

'Primrose.' Amina's voice broke through my thoughts, and this time the intake of breath at the announcement was audible.

'Me?' Prim mouthed as she used her hands to get up from the forest floor. Natasha was clapping but Agatha's face was thunder as Primrose took her place next to Martha. They were both beautiful, their skin glowing, their hair shining, but they didn't look right next to the pond when it was just the two of them. There was something missing. And that something was me.

'Ivy.' Sophia smiled at me, genuine and welcoming. Her hand was outstretched. It was both an invitation and my last chance at refusal. I could have walked away then, probably unscathed, and spent the rest of my degree in a boring yet comfortable routine of essays, supervisions and formal halls. I could have mourned George appropriately, found myself a new boyfriend after a respectable amount of time, made some bland, uninteresting friends, and made myself dull enough that even my ghosts tired of haunting me.

Prim and Martha waited for me, alongside Sophia and Amina. The torch was burning low and stuttering. George rushed into my head again, a sickening thud that I never actually heard filling my ears. But there was nothing I could do for him now. I had to protect the people I could protect. I stepped forward. As I did so, I thought I saw a shadow of a familiar face in the woods. Something in the shape of Cara nodded at my decision. Then the heron burst out from the trees. The moment was gone but I could still feel her around me. I'd learned my lesson. Never choose a boy over a sister.

Amina plunged the torch into the pondwater so that the only light was what managed to break through the thick canopy. Then she dipped her fingers into the water to brush its wetness over our foreheads, as Sophia reached her hand into a hole in the tree I'd never noticed before to reveal an enormous tome.

'Sisters, this contains all the knowledge of those who have gone before us, those who have looked after the Coven right from the very start,' she explained, flipping the book open with a creak and a puff of dust. 'Only the presidents are allowed to read it and once your term is up it must be passed on. All other sisters are dismissed for this evening. Your new presidents will be in touch again in due course.' With some grumbling, the other girls stood up to go, spectres in white moving away from us among the trees.

'It's the book that was lost,' I whispered to Prim. 'The one mentioned in that museum.'

'You're right. God, I can't wait to read it in full. Just think about the stories that might be in there,' she replied.

'So, presidents, add yourselves to the book,' Sophia instructed. 'But it's traditional to pick out a symbol for yourself, rather than your given name. Even now, we have to guard ourselves. It's your job now to keep your sisters safe and preserve the Coven for future generations.'

Martha drew a flame, then Prim stepped forward to add an autumn leaf to the book. I lingered at the back, not from shyness or uncertainty but because I knew that my position was assured. I didn't have to rush to or from anything. I was exactly where I was supposed to be. Martha and Primrose flanked me as I drew a heron on the ancient paper, taking time to make sure this mark that would last centuries was just right.

Below our symbolic signatures, which for ever drew us together, there was an inscription written in faded ink. *A sisterhood is never extricable – once entwined together, our bond lasts for life.*

Week 5

A few weeks into term, the leaves turned the colour of Martha's hair, then started to drop off the trees entirely, leaving twiggy skeletons behind. The last leaf fell from the witching tree on the day the investigation into George's death was concluded. I was somewhat familiar with the process because there'd been a brief inquest into why Cara died – it was ruled an accident – but I chose not to go along to hear the final verdict. Prim went instead. In many ways, she was the most certain of all of us – she detested what had happened but insisted that, rationally, the likelihood of what had befallen George was incredibly slim. We mustn't blame ourselves.

Still, I hated the idea of meeting his parents and brothers in circumstances such as those, so far from the way I once imagined. So, I stayed home and leafed through the notes I'd begun making about the new intake of fresher girls. I'd done well enough last year that I felt confident that I could dedicate time to the Coven and still flourish academically, especially as I'd chosen to focus more on politics and all its machinations. I'd been scribbling details on who seemed loyal, who seemed too boy crazy, who seemed to possess an inner strength, who was a little too gossipy. I didn't want to rely fully on first impressions, so I wrote things down over days and weeks, noticing patterns of behaviour and always leaving room for someone to change, to show us the best side of themselves.

I was so engrossed that when the knock came, it made my hand jerk and scrawl ink across the page.

'You should know by now that you don't need to knock,' I said, as I opened the door to Prim. We'd moved into the Coven's house so we could be closer to each other and the woods.

'I didn't want to startle you on a day like today.' She leaned in and kissed my cheek. 'They decided it was an accident. No one could have saved him, just like I said. He was out as soon as he hit that rock, Ivy. He wouldn't even have felt any pain.'

I nodded, but for a moment I was too choked up to speak. I sat down at my dressing-table stool, my head pounding, blood rushing in my ears. We'd never been called as witnesses, so we were never seriously worried, but it was still a relief to hear the news. Sickening, but a relief. Even if we had been called, we had a totally reasonable excuse – George had tried to push me. He wouldn't take no for an answer. He had broken into my room a few weeks before, for Christ's sake. There was a pattern of behaviour. Prim and Martha had reassured me that I was very lucky nothing worse had happened. Who knew what he was capable of? Whoever knows what a boy is capable of?

Martha walked in without knocking as I was nursing my head in my hands. She helped me to my feet and pulled me onto the bed, where we all sat side by side, backs against the wall. 'It's okay, Iv,' she soothed. 'It's all over now. And we're all in one piece.'

She was right. We were in one piece, the boundaries between us blurry and marginal. The threads in our tapestry had only been yanked tighter by the fact that we had shared something unspeakable, something that we knew we could never fully discuss outside of our closed trinity. Secrets can tear you apart, but they can also bind you together.

'Shall we do something to mark the correct decision being delivered today?' Prim suggested.

'We need to be in the clearing as soon as the sun goes down,' I said. 'I saw Nat after breakfast and she said she and Aggie will bring the wine.'

'We will be, don't worry. We've got plenty of time.' Martha laced her fingers through mine. I breathed in deeply and let myself enjoy the moment. There really was nothing to worry about – I'd spent an uneventful summer with Mum as her treatment continued to progress, even enjoying the occasional walk on the beach together, the voice of the sea a soothing whisper in my ear rather than the treacherous song it used to be. Dad kept me up to date; she was still on an upwards trajectory, thanks to the now not-so-new counsellor. And the Dragons hadn't bothered us, distracted as they were by their mourning. We'd even sent them a bouquet of black roses to express our sympathies.

'Yes, you're right. I've been meaning to discuss with you who we should pick as initiates for the Coven. Let's get down to business,' I said, readying my list of who I thought were the best candidates for the next generation of sisters. 'Whatever decisions we make will change these girls' lives.'

Acknowledgements

A book is never, ever a one-person feat. *These Mortal Bodies* only exists because so many people have given their time, energy, encouragement and love to the story you hold in your hands. I am especially grateful to my agent, Caro Clarke, who believed in me and *These Mortal Bodies* when it was still in its early draft stages, and has provided so much reassurance and insight throughout this process.

An enormous thank you to my immensely talented, patient and kind editor, Judith Long, who I felt understood *These Mortal Bodies* and my writing from the very first time we spoke. There are so many people at Simon & Schuster who have worked on this novel behind the scenes and I am only sorry I can't thank each of them here. I am so grateful for all the hard work of Sarah Jeffcoate, Laurie McShea, Karin Seifried, India Minter, Susan Opie, Gillian Hamnett, Maddie Allen, Heather Hogan and Naomi Burt.

I have been very lucky to have support from other writers and literary organizations throughout my journey to publication. My thanks to Rachel, Anna, Lucy, Julie and everyone at Spread the Word. I'm also grateful for the mentoring I've received from Jamie Hale, Stephen Lightbown, Emma Glass and Francesca Beard, which all significantly helped improve my craft. Special thanks to Kirsty Logan who mentored me in the early stages of this novel.

These Mortal Bodies was finished in Catalan sunshine. Thank you to Lluís and Philippa for giving me the time and space I so sorely needed to finish this book.

To my non-writing friends, you have given me all the love, laughter and support to help me believe I could do this. Gregory Puffin you've believed in me since day one and your unwavering friendship has been a wonderful constant in my life. D and Ginny, you have given me all the snacks, cups of tea, tech support and cosy moments prerequisite to keeping writing. And to Laura, happy birthday, my love.

I feel extremely fortunate to have grown up with parents who believed in art and believed in me. Frequently, these beliefs coincided in a way which I feel is (sadly) rare and special. My dad once tried to make me promise him I'd write a novel when I grew up! Without the unerring support of my parents, I would never have had the confidence or perseverance required to keep going and get my novel published. So, thank you, Mum and Dad: I'm so lucky to be your daughter.